DEATH'S EXECUTIONER

THE MALYKANT MYSTERIES

VOLUME 3

CHARLOTTE E. ENGLISH

CONTENTS

THE ZOLIN CONSPIRACY

1

'Seven,' said Nanda, laying a brightly-inked card upon Konrad's parlour table. She held four more in her hands, close to her face; these she surveyed with a roguish half-smile, and cast a sideways glance at Konrad.

He was not fooled. Nanda's strategy for card games was to appear as though she was on the point of winning, always, but never to let on how.

'Hats,' said Alexander Nuritov, police inspector by day and… well, frequently by night as well, when he wasn't playing cards at Bakar House. The deep darkness of full night beat against the parlour windows, but inside all was warmth and cheer. A bright fire crackled in the grate, two of Konrad's favourite people sat around his table, and all of them were rosy on apple brandy.

Konrad himself might be termed somewhat more than rosy, though not quite inebriated enough to fumble the game. Hopefully.

'Incorrect,' said Nanda, with triumph.

Alexander scowled, and drew a card.

'Chalices,' said Konrad, in his turn.

Nanda rolled her eyes at him. 'Your snakies told on me.'

'They did not.'

'They did. I can practically feel them slinking about somewhere.' She cast her eyes around the parlour, her gaze lingering upon the shadows in the corners, and shivered.

'Are you calling me a cheat?' Konrad demanded.

'Yes.'

He narrowed his eyes at her. 'Chalices,' he repeated.

'*Correct.*'

'I want a three, or a five.'

Nanda gave him a card elaborately inked with a scrolling numeral five. The smug look was back on her slightly too-pale face. She would never own to losing.

I heard that, hissed Eetapi, a sudden jangle at the back of his mind. He shuddered as an icy chill rippled down his spine: she was displeased.

The cheek! he agreed.

Now I shall cheat, just to punish her.

You may not.

Eetapi grumbled. *Why not?*

Because I would rather lose than cheat, as you very well know.

You never did have any sense, muttered Eetapi.

Konrad ignored that. Play continued, delivering Alexander a pair of nines and Konrad a useless two. He was losing, alas. He had no head for cards, unlike the inspector, who won at least two games out of every three. Nanda and Konrad both had more sense than to play for money, if Alexander was present.

'Crowns!' announced Alexander, beaming, and spreading cards before him. He'd won again, curse him. 'Three, seven, nine, and—'

'Konrad!' A youthful, cheery voice hailed him from the parlour door, and Tasha came barrelling in. Fourteen winters old, at least in appearance, and an endless fountain of energy (or so it seemed), she brought a cold wind swirling into the room with her, and had left the door wide open behind.

'That is Mr. Savast, to you,' said Konrad, without much hope.

This she waved off. 'I won't call you anything so priggish, and you'd hate it if I did.'

'Priggish?'

'Only prigs insist on formality. Isn't that right, Mr. Nuritov?'

Alexander just looked at her, and took a sip of brandy.

'Cool head,' said Tasha. 'I like that.' She leaned Nanda's way, and said confidingly, 'He's much more fun.' Her pointing finger indicated Konrad.

'He does take the bait so nicely,' Nanda agreed.

Konrad let this pass. 'Alexander wins,' he said, and smiled at his friend. 'Again. I bow to your superior skill.'

'Many long winters with little else to do,' Alexander remarked, though he looked pleased.

Konrad was going to enquire why Alexander had found himself so short of entertainments, but Tasha interrupted. 'Don't you want to know why I am here?'

'Do you need a reason, besides the unending desire to disturb our peace?'

'It is a favourite hobby of mine,' she allowed. 'But I did, as it happens, have another reason.'

Konrad sighed. 'All right. Why are you here?'

Tasha drew herself up importantly. It did not help much. She was an undersized child, and if the *lamaeni* were capable of physical growth, Konrad had never witnessed any evidence of it. 'Well—' she began.

'Your hat is torn,' said Konrad, frowning. She wore a black cap and dark coat as a matter of course, indoors and out; in fact, both of them were ripped.

'I've been brawling,' said Tasha indifferently. 'Anyway—'

'Brawling?' Konrad exchanged a look with Alexander. 'Is that any way for a police ward to behave?'

'It is if they are named *Tasha.*'

'Let it go,' murmured Alexander. 'You will never prevail with her.'

Konrad grinned. 'I don't expect to. I am just enjoying forestalling the news she is dying to tell us.'

'It is *important,*' snapped Tasha.

'How important?'

'To you? Supremely. In fact—'

'I had better let you get on with it, then, had I not?'

Tasha gave him a flat stare of pure hatred. 'Don't think I won't drain the life out of you, just because you're the Malykant.'

'You cannot,' said Nanda serenely. 'Konrad isn't allowed to die anymore, remember?'

'Then he had better behave himself, hadn't he?'

'Fine,' said Konrad, and sat back, letting his cards fall to the table. 'Tell us your news.'

'There is a dead body,' said Tasha, slowly and distinctly, 'in the alley behind this house.'

'There is no alley behind this house.'

'All right, it isn't *directly* behind— oh, hold your tongue.'

Konrad permitted himself a brief smirk. He did not often get the best of Tasha. 'Is there truly a dead body, or are you just entertaining yourself at our expense?'

'As often as the latter is true, no. There is a body, and it's headless, and you should maybe think about looking into it.'

Headless! trilled Eetapi with glee.

She is right, Master, said Ootapi, wafting into the parlour by way of the wall. *I have observed it myself.*

No doubt you took the greatest pleasure in it, Konrad said sourly.

Ootapi said nothing, only radiated blissful satisfaction.

'Ugh. Well. If you will excuse me.' Konrad rose from his elegant chair, pausing for an instant before he made for the door; if he was drunk enough to suffer a swimming head, he had better discover that fact *before* he fell over his own feet.

Alexander rose, too, and followed him to the door.

So did Nanda.

'Nan,' he murmured. 'There can be no occasion for you to be dragged into the snow on such a night, and for such a reason.'

'Can't there?'

'No.'

'Are you going to try to stop me from going with you?'

'I would prefer it if you remained here where it is warm.'

'And safe?'

'And also safe.'

'It is good of you to share your perspective.' Nanda went out into the hall, plainly in search of her coat.

Konrad sighed. Since Nanda had become, in some mysterious way, ill, she had if anything grown more prickly about being (as she saw it) coddled. Even the smallest solicitude, or the most sensible precaution, tended to irritate.

He had watched her for signs of deterioration, trying to do so without seeming to. On the latter point, he'd failed; Nan always knew, somehow. But to his relief, his vigilance had so far proved unnecessary. She was her usual self, if a little wan at times.

Corpses, Konrad reminded himself, withdrawing his attention from Nanda with an effort. He could worry about his best friend later. First, he had to be the Malykant for a while.

Tasha led them to the site of the murder, walking like a tiny military general, her head held high.

'You shouldn't be quite *so* pleased with yourself for stumbling over corpses,' said Konrad, raising his voice to carry over the freezing wind.

'It is a skill any self-respecting Malykant's assistant ought to have in her arsenal,' she retorted.

'*Hush*,' growled Konrad. 'Do you want everyone to hear?' His identity as the Malykant was — *had* to be — a deep, dark secret, or he'd have half the city on his doorstep, all of them wanting something. His death, perhaps, or someone else's.

'Everyone who?' said Tasha, and made a show of looking around at the deserted street.

'You never know who might be listening,' he chided, though she was right enough. The night was unusually forbidding, even for Ekamet. The coldest he could remember for some years; even the alcohol singing in his blood could not blunt its effects. Bundled though he was in thick layers, the high, shrieking wind pierced him to his bones. Most of the city's residents had sense enough to remain indoors.

At least it was not snowing, now, though several days' worth of accumulated snowfall lay piled against the dark brick walls of the houses, pale and glinting in the moonlight.

He should be thankful, perhaps, that Tasha's reported corpse had fallen close to home. No carriage would brave the snow-clogged streets on a night like this, and he did not relish the prospect of having to trudge very far though a few feet of snow.

'Here we are,' said Tasha brightly, pausing some twelve feet into the entrance of a narrow alley. Konrad's house, handsome and expensive, was built in the most salubrious quarter of the city. Alleys it had, but the clean kind; they were even swept, occasionally, though not when choked with snow.

Someone had cleared a thin path through the snowfall, just wide enough for one person to venture down. The path ended abruptly in a wall of snow four feet high, obscuring access to the rest of the alley.

Just below it lay the body.

'Good work, assistant,' Konrad said, crouching down for a nearer view.

Tasha said nothing, but he felt her puff up just a bit with pride. Old beyond her years she may be, but she was still young enough to

5

seek approval — even if she would deny it to her last breath.

The body was that of a man, though nothing of his age and little of his appearance could be determined. Not only was the body headless, but the head was missing.

Konrad wasted little time searching for it. If it had rolled away, its trail would be clearly visible in the snow. If it was not *with* the body, then whoever had removed it had also taken it.

'What do you think, Alexander?' murmured Konrad.

Nuritov joined him, and spent a moment observing the body in silent thought. 'Could be anything at all,' he decided.

He was right. Konrad could draw conclusions from the man's clothing, if he wanted: the attire was both fashionable and expensive, indicative of wealth and status. But anybody could wear a gentleman's clothes. By themselves, the garments meant nothing.

'Why does he have no coat?' said Nanda, peeping over Konrad's shoulder.

'That is a point of interest,' Konrad agreed, perhaps the only obvious one. The man wore the dark suit and pale waistcoat of formal, evening attire, but he had neither coat nor cloak, and there was no sign of a hat. Konrad did not imagine the killer had bothered to cart the hat away with him; more likely, the man had not been wearing one at all.

Had he been attending a ball, somewhere in the vicinity? But what might have brought him charging out into so unforgiving a night, without even pausing to retrieve a coat? And what had he been doing, forcing his way down a snow-choked alley in the dark?

'Soaked,' Alexander observed. 'Everything, including his sleeves. He must have been tunnelling his way down, using his hands like shovels.'

'He badly wanted to get somewhere,' Konrad agreed. 'One of the houses on this street?' He glanced down the length of the alley, as far as he could see. The rear entrances of several city mansions could be so accessed.

'He cannot have known himself pursued,' Nanda said. 'Or he would not have chosen so difficult a route, surely.'

'I think you are right, Nan,' said Konrad. 'But then what was so urgent as to bring him out here at all?'

'And where,' said Tasha with relish, 'is the head?'

Without the head, it would be virtually impossible to identify the man. Konrad went through the motions of searching the man's evening coat and waistcoat for identification, but without much hope. Nobody carried anything with them to a ball. Any identifying objects the man might have possessed were doubtless still in his overcoat, or cloak, or whatever he had worn to the party.

His fingers encountered nothing — no, there was something. A slight bulge in the tiny pocket of the man's waistcoat yielded up a ring. He held it up, straining to discern much about it even in the strong light of an almost full moon. Smooth, the band, and unadorned; his fingers told him that not a single jewel graced the ring.

'Plain, for an apparently wealthy man,' he said.

'Could be anybody,' Nuritov reminded him.

'Clothes do not make the man? My tailor will be disappointed to hear it.'

Nuritov smiled, and gave his own modest garments a deprecating glance. 'I hope they don't.'

'In your case, no,' said Nanda. 'You ought to be dressed like a prince, Alexander.'

Konrad privately agreed, but did not choose to say so aloud, for the inspector shuffled from foot to foot in an obvious mixture of pleasure and discomfort. He was probably blushing.

'Very well,' Konrad said. 'You will please to turn your backs for a moment, while I perform the repulsive part of my duties.' He had to take a bone from the hapless murdered man, even if he did not yet know who it was.

'And then what?' demanded Tasha.

'Then, we find out who's been holding evening entertainments in these parts tonight; who might be missing someone from their guest list; and we *definitely* need to find out what's become of the head.'

'That last part should be quite easy,' Tasha said, dripping sarcasm.

'Actually,' said Konrad, 'it might.'

2

Walking off with severed heads, Konrad knew, tended to be a bid to attract attention.

The fact that he possessed a wealth of such macabre trivia occasionally depressed his spirits; such knowledge was ill-gotten and reviled; but setting that aside, it could also prove useful.

In this instance, for example. No one first decapitated somebody, then availed themselves of the head, only to throw the latter away, or dispose of it separately. What would be the point? If a killer went out of their way to walk off with their victim's head, there was something they intended to do with it. Most of the time, the head was taken as a kind of trophy, probably destined for display. Konrad had once dispatched a killer who had no less than three such trophies kept in pride of place in his own house, which gave him a poor opinion of the man's intelligence as much as of his morals.

If this killer had displayed his prize somewhere, word of it may yet reach the police. Nuritov, installed in his office at the police headquarters, undertook to send him instant word should that prove to be the case. He had also promised to scour any recent or incoming missing persons reports in case of a clue.

That left Konrad to follow up the question of the man's identity via other means. And since the victim's last known act — besides tunnelling through four feet of snow in a back alley — had been to attend a party, if the evidence of his clothes could be relied upon, well, he had an idea about that.

'Nan,' he ventured the following morning, over their shared

breakfast table. 'Do you still collect the gossip papers?'

'Still?' she echoed, blinking haughtily, poised in the act of spreading butter upon fresh toast.

Hers was a dangerous look.

Konrad was not deterred.

'You certainly collect all the ones that mention me,' he said.

'I don't—'

'It cannot be denied! You admitted to it yourself.'

'—do that anymore,' she finished, and returned to buttering her toast.

Konrad watched her narrowly. 'You are blushing,' he pointed out.

'I am not.'

'Then something else is turning your cheeks pink.'

Nanda sighed, and set down her knife with a clatter. 'Very well, I am the kind of forlorn soul who lives a vicarious life of pleasure by way of tabloid report. I admit to it freely, and without shame. Why do you ask?'

'I want to find out who in these parts was holding entertainments last night.'

'It probably wasn't a grand ball. Nobody could be fool enough to hold a big party on such a night.'

Konrad just looked at her.

'What? You mean you *do*?'

'Me personally? No, but I hold parties as infrequently as I can get away with. Other people of my approximate social level? Absolutely.'

'Impossible. Nobody could be so foolish as to expect half of Ekamet society to drag themselves across the city in the dead of winter.'

'You clearly haven't met many members of Ekamet high society.'

'Clearly not.'

'That's what money means, Nan. There is no degree of foolhardiness that cannot be committed upon the smallest whim. Welcome to the blind insouciance that comes of spectacular wealth.'

'Why would anybody bother to attend?'

'Surely you aren't suggesting that mere weather should get in the way of making an appearance at a highly select social event. Not when everybody who is *anybody* will be there.'

'You weren't,' said Nanda shrewdly.

'Let us assume that my having been born, approximately, in the

9

gutter renders me immune to some of the worst excesses of the rich.'

'But not all of them.' The twinkle was back in her eye.

'Not quite all. A man has to have *some* fun.'

'Do you though?'

'What? Have fun?'

'Mm.'

'Naturally.'

'Like? When was the last time?'

Konrad didn't even have to think about it. 'Last night, in the parlour with you.'

'That isn't what I meant.'

'I know.'

She grinned, rueful. 'Touché. Very well, supposing somebody was idiot enough to plan a ball for last night, perhaps the papers made mention of it. Unfortunately, they are at my house, and we are not.'

'Perhaps it is more likely to appear in today's paper, no?'

'True.' Nanda got up from the breakfast table, abandoning a stray crust of toast, and gulped the last of her coffee in one swallow. 'If you will excuse me, I shall stage an emergency shopping trip.'

'Many a woman has dreamed of being able to say something like that with a straight face.'

'Many a man, has, too, in his secret heart. I shall return.' Nanda did not wait for him to accompany her. She whirled out into the hallway, and moments later Konrad heard the front door open and close.

He cast an unhappy glance out of the window. The snow had come in again with the dawn, and the sky was a white blur. Poor conditions for a walk.

Do not worry for her, Master, said Eetapi. *She is stronger than you.*

'I know. But people don't worry for their friends because they doubt their strength. We worry because we know that it isn't always enough.'

Eetapi dismissed this with a sniff. *I would like to see the blizzard that can carry off Irinanda.*

'I wouldn't.'

He did not waste time wondering whether the papers would appear at all in such inclement conditions. He knew better. Assevan was a harsh country year-round, and its winters were always brutal; no newspaper worth its salt could afford to be deterred by bad weather. And that went double for the tabloids. Relentless, those, like packs of wolves. He had never chosen to ask Nanda what they said about him; doubtless he would be devastated, if he knew. Or far too pleased.

An idea occurred to him — too late, alas, to call Nanda back — and he sat up. He rang the bell, and when the maid appeared — new girl, he had forgotten her name — he asked for his butler.

Gorev appeared promptly. 'Yes, sir?'

'Gorev. It is true, is it not, that invitations and such occasionally come through the door?'

'Yes, sir.'

'Excellent. And what becomes of them?'

'You ordered that they should be burned, sir.'

Konrad blinked. 'Burned? Did I indeed?'

'Yes, sir.'

'That seems unreasonable of me.'

'I believe it was on one of your... bad days, sir.'

'My bad days.'

'When you were in... poor spirits, sir.'

'You mean when I was being a tiresome, self-pitying idiot.'

Gorev's lips twitched. 'I cannot be expected to agree with that, sir.'

'Nor shall you, at least out loud. Well, but you did not say they *have* been burned, did you? Only that I gave instructions to that effect.'

'I took the liberty of making other arrangements for them.'

'In other words, you blatantly ignored my orders. Why might you do that, my good Gorev?'

'I thought you might think better of it, sir.'

'And I cannot be displeased with you, for you appear to have been right. Could you by chance produce any such invitations that might have arrived in, say, the past month?'

'Instantly, sir.' Gorev bowed and withdrew, returning mere minutes later with a stack of white envelopes in his hands. These he set before Konrad.

'You are a prince among butlers, Gorev. Thank you.'

'I know, sir.' Gorev left Konrad to his perusal of the promising stack.

Konrad steeled himself. He needed a stronger stomach than he possessed, to tackle such a pile. The majority of these kinds of missives fell into two categories: those that flattered and fawned over Konrad in hopes of coaxing him to attend, and those who invited him with the lofty air of those condescending from a great height. The former were bedazzled by Mr. Savast's purportedly enormous wealth, together with his reputation as something of a hermit; he did not often attend evening engagements, and had become therefore an exclusive prize to adorn some ambitious hostess's drawing-room. The latter like to consider themselves superior to a mere Mr. Savast. Perhaps because he was only a commoner, however wealthy; perhaps because his gypsy blood, and the swarthy countenance that went with it, was difficult for a few particularly elitist hosts to accept.

All of them turned his stomach. Leafing through these, he found the usual mixture of the two, and soon remembered why he might, in a black mood, have ordered that they all go into the fire.

The pile rose higher than Nanda would readily believe; many a courageous hostess had flatly refused to wait for better weather. He discovered no fewer than three invitations to events on the previous evening, one of which he discarded for being too far distant.

Two remained. There had been *two* events last night, held in houses just about close enough to the fatal alley to qualify. Neither house backed onto the alley itself, however, to Konrad's disappointment. The mystery man must have crossed a street or two after he had left the party.

Supposing, of course, that he'd been at a party at all. Konrad reminded himself that the clothes might mean nothing. He could have been wearing them as some kind of costume, or as a disguise.

Still, he had a way to proceed. One invitation was to a "select" soirée at the house of Lady Lysak, a bowing acquaintance. He tried, and failed, to recall her face. The other announced a glittering ball to be held at Kravets House, its host a Mrs. Petrova. He did not so much as remember her name.

He had permitted himself to drift farther from city society than he ought, of course. He had been installed at Bakar House not merely to secure his comfort, though the luxury was perhaps one of the compensations of his job. He had also been given the means to command a place among the city's highest echelon, because rich people committed crimes, too. He had to be able to wander the houses of the wealthy at need, and here he was losing his grip.

If only sparkling social events were not such a *bore*. He would far rather be playing cards with Nan, and Alexander.

Thousands would kill to attend either one of those parties, hissed Eetapi, interrupting his reverie. *You must realise that.*

I hope they would not literally kill for it. But if you mean that I am being ungrateful, perhaps that's true.

Take Irinanda with you, next time, said Eetapi with a snicker. *That might cheer you up.*

Konrad was about to object that Nanda would never agree, but then he remembered all the times she had jumped at the chance to rig herself out in finery. And there was the matter of the gossip papers, too. For all her protestations, she was as drawn to luxury as she pretended to be repelled by it.

He put the idea away for future consideration. For all he knew, she might be delighted at the prospect.

Nanda returned nearly two hours later. Konrad had long since taken to standing at the window, glaring at the driving snow as he watched for her approach. Just as he was on the point of sending Eetapi out in search of her, he spotted her. Her usual brisk, purposeful walk must be impossible in such conditions; she trudged her way up the street, head bent, one hand clutching the brim of her hat against the wind's attempts to snatch it off her head.

When the doorbell rang a few moments later, Konrad was waiting to answer it himself.

'That took a long time,' he said, holding the door wide open for Nanda as she bustled inside.

'I apologise for keeping you waiting,' she said dryly, shrugging off her snow-covered coat. A pool of water quickly formed under her feet as the snow melted off her.

'I just meant—'

'I know. I am only being difficult. Here.' She withdrew a folded newspaper, slightly crinkled, from within the folds of her coat, handing the latter to Gorev, who waited with silent solicitude to assist.

'I shall ask Mrs. Aristova to send in something warming to the parlour,' said Gorev.

'Perfect,' said Konrad absently, shepherding Nanda in the direction of said parlour, and the blazing fire that waited there. 'I am not fussing,' he said, when she opened her mouth to — most likely — object.

Nanda rolled her eyes, but permitted herself to be ushered to the comfiest chair before Konrad opened up the paper.

'Page seventeen,' said Nanda, sagging into the chair's soft velvets with obvious gratitude. She gave a final shiver, and closed her eyes, a slight smile on her lips.

Konrad turned his attention to page seventeen. 'I don't know how they find so much to say about us,' he murmured, having turned through multiple pages of society reports before he arrived at the relevant one.

'You are endlessly interesting, I assure you. When there are so many rules governing behaviour and etiquette, there are naturally a thousand ways to break them, so there's always another scandal. And if there is nothing dramatic to be reported, enquiring minds will always want to know about Lady X's daring new fashions, or Lord X's rumoured indiscretion with his sister-in-law.'

'You make it all sound so sordid.'

'If it were not sordid, I'm afraid no one would be interested at all.'

Konrad grunted, and fell silent as a maid appeared with a tray, compliments of his wonderful cook. Nanda applied herself to a pot of some steaming beverage. Konrad ignored the lot.

'Here,' he said. 'Lady Lysak's soirée. Has to be this one.'

'Oh?'

Konrad read aloud. 'Fracas at Surnin Place. Lady Lysak's Select Soirée — capital S — suffered a moment of tension when the evening's illustrious hostess fell into conflict with one of her guests. The nature of the dispute is not known to this writer, but the affair ended with the abrupt departure of her co-disputant Mr. Bogdan Zolin, a shining light in Ekamet society. Such a fracas comes as an embarrassment to her ladyship, whose record, previously without blemish, etc etc.'

'Are you sure that's the right one?' said Nanda, pouring out something in a soft cloud of steam.

Konrad discovered that a cup of whatever it was had materialised before him. 'It fits,' he said, and set Lady Lysak's invitation before her. 'Surnin Place is only two streets away. It isn't adjacent to the alley, but it's close enough. Mr. Zolin could easily have walked that far.'

'That does narrow it down.'

Konrad put Mrs. Petrova's invitation down beside the first. 'This house is also close enough, and ought to be investigated, but this argument seems significant. We had better find out if Mr. Bogdan Zolin ever made it home last night.'

Nanda nodded. 'I will bet you one cake that he did not.'

'No bet. Too easy.'

'All right, two cakes.'

'That's not how this works.'

The parlour door, closed against the draughty hallway, flew open. 'Report from Inspector Nuritov,' announced Tasha, removing her cap and vigorously shaking the snow from it.

'Hey,' said Konrad, as freezing water splattered over his arm. 'Customarily one removes outer garments first, *then* charges into a private parlour without invitation or announcement.'

'I'm here to do a job,' Tasha said, subjecting her dark coat to the same treatment. 'Nobody ever said anything about manners.'

'Evidently.'

'So do you want the report?'

'Go ahead.'

'The head,' said Tasha, and paused dramatically.

'Yes?'

'Has been found.'

'Oh!'

'Or at least, *a* severed head has been found, and it's a man's head, and Nuritov says he can't imagine there are two bodiless men's heads floating around people's drawing-rooms this week, so it is probably the one we want.'

'People's drawing-rooms?' Konrad repeated.

'Right. It was discovered this morning by a housemaid. She went in to clean the grate and passed out from the shock.' The words dripped with scorn. Tasha did not approve of fainting females.

Nanda sat up a bit. 'Just where exactly was the head?'

'Set on the mantelpiece. Like it was some kind of ornament.'

'Which house?' Konrad pressed.

Tasha took in the litter of invitations and newsprint scattered among Mrs. Aristova's delicacies. 'You look like you already know.'

'Surnin Place?' Konrad guessed.

'I bow before your awe-inspiring detecting skills.' Tasha literally bowed.

'If I thought you meant a word of it, I might be flattered.' Konrad got up. 'Nuritov's already on his way there, I imagine?'

'Yes. He said to join him. Can I finish this cake?'

'You're… asking permission?'

'Oh. You're right.' Tasha picked up the remains of a cake already decimated by Nanda, and shoved half of it in her mouth.

'I don't know why you eat cake at all,' said Konrad. 'It's not like you gain any benefit from it.'

'I gain pleasure from it,' said Tasha thickly. 'Isn't that enough?'

'Justified,' said Nanda, rising from her own seat. 'Are you coming with us?'

'I'll follow.' Tasha applied herself to her plate, and Konrad made for the door.

3

When Konrad and Nanda arrived at Surnin Place some twenty minutes later, they were not immediately granted admittance.

'I am sorry, sir,' said an ashen-faced butler, clutching the red-painted front door as though his knees might otherwise melt from under him. 'There can be no guests admitted today.'

'We are not guests,' said Konrad firmly. 'We are here at Inspector Nuritov's insistence. Go and ask him, if you please.'

'I have strict orders, sir—'

'Go and ask him.'

'Konrad?' came Alexander's voice, and the door swung wider, revealing the inspector himself. 'Come in, come in. Haven't moved the head yet; thought you might like a look at it before we do.'

Konrad moved past the butler, receiving a goggle-eyed look of horror as he did so. What did the fool man think, that Konrad was some manner of eccentric with macabre tastes, for some reason pandered to by the police? Nobody derived *pleasure,* as Tasha put it, from viewing severed heads. Nobody sane, anyway. 'How long has it been there?' he asked of Alexander, ignoring the butler. 'Can you tell?'

'There's little blood. Likely that the thing was outside for some time before it was brought in. Half frozen, you know.'

Konrad thought of the red-stained snow around the fallen man's head. 'Perhaps it was let lie a while, before being taken.'

Alexander nodded. 'Killer might even have left it where it fell, for a while, and gone back for it later.'

'Or,' said Nanda, 'somebody else found the body before we did, and took the head.'

'Good point,' said Konrad.

'Thank you.'

The inspector led them through the house as they talked, through several rooms and up a flight of stairs devoid of servants or other inhabitants. 'Here we go,' he said as they entered a handsome drawing-room. He gestured in the direction of the fireplace.

Konrad spent only a moment in contemplation of the macabre display. The fire had been permitted to die down; the housemaid, he supposed, had not had courage enough to tend to it after her shocking discovery. The mantel above was of pale marble, set with a pair of tall golden candlesticks and twin porcelain ornaments. In the centre, where there might more rightly stand a clock, was the head. If it was Bogdan Zolin, he'd had dark blonde hair, dark brown eyes, and the smooth complexion of a young man — not yet thirty, Konrad judged. His dead eyes stared uncomprehendingly at Konrad.

Serpents? Konrad called.

Ootapi answered. *Yes, Master.*

Is there perchance any trace of his spirit, hereabouts? Konrad held only a small hope for a positive response, but he thought it worth the asking. When the head was severed from the rest of the body, which part of its erstwhile physical form might the ghost attach itself to?

None, Master, said Ootapi. *He is too long dead.*

There was also that. Too many hours had passed since death.

Konrad turned his attention to the rest of the room. Everything in Lady Lysak's drawing-room spoke of money and taste, not much to his surprise. Marble and fine oak, velvet and silk, a little gilding but not much. The room lacked personality. Elegant, beautiful as it was, it could have graced any of the city's finer houses. Konrad could have replicated it at Bakar House, and it would not have looked out of place. Nothing in here so much as hinted at the personality of its owner.

'Have you yet interviewed Lady Lysak?' Konrad asked.

'She is not here.'

Konrad's brows went up at that. 'Not? Where could she possibly have gone?'

'The servants say she went out early, in some kind of hurry. They didn't know whether she had seen the head or not. The first housemaid thought not, or she'd have heard her ladyship walking about up here — she was in the next room, cleaning, for nearly half an hour before she heard the front door open and shut.'

'Might be true, might not be,' Konrad mused.

'Quite.'

'Has news of the death reached the media yet?'

'No. Your people removed the body well before dawn, and we won't be releasing a police report until this afternoon.'

'So she might not yet know.'

Alexander looked his enquiry.

Konrad filled him in on the contents of Nanda's gossip paper. 'If it is Bogdan Zolin, she had a blazing row with him last night, in full view of a houseful of guests. There were some kind of strong feelings between those two, and she might not yet know that he's dead.'

'We need someone to identify the head—' said Alexander.

'Oh yes, sir, that's Mr. Zolin,' said a male voice.

Konrad turned. Nanda, he found, had quietly gone out and summoned the butler, anticipating this requirement. The poor man turned whiter than ever upon beholding Bogdan Zolin's head and his hopeless, dead stare.

'You are certain?' said Alexander.

'Yes, sir. It's my duty to admit the guests when they arrive, and everybody knows Mr. Zolin.'

The paper had termed him a "shining light" of Ekamet society, which probably meant that he turned up everywhere. 'Have you admitted him to this house before last night?' Konrad asked.

'Once or twice, sir. He has attended gatherings here before.'

'Thank you.'

Alexander permitted the poor man to leave. He did so at a half-run, probably heading for the nearest conveniences.

'It seems unlikely,' said Konrad, 'that Lady Lysak would put Zolin's head on her own mantelpiece, and then leave it to be found by the servants.'

'It would be a foolhardy thing to do,' agreed Alexander.

'She might have killed him, though,' said Nanda. 'And someone else saw, or knew somehow. That person might have put the head here, to torment her. And to lead the police to her.'

'It's plausible,' Konrad allowed. 'But it takes great strength to cut a man's head from his neck, especially in one, clean blow. And I think it was, because look — the neck is cleanly cut. No ragged edges that might suggest several attempts were made.'

'And women are too weak?' said Nanda.

Konrad realised he trod upon dangerous ground. 'When it comes to a question of musculature, women are usually less developed—'

'Pish posh.'

'It's true.'

'All right, perhaps it is. But that doesn't necessarily mean that she couldn't possibly have done it, with the right weapon.'

'True enough. And that is another pertinent question. We found no weapon of any kind with the body, least of all one that could have performed such a feat. Where is it?'

'And what is it?' said Alexander. 'A sword?'

'Or an axe. I have difficulty imagining a society hostess hacking her guests' heads off with an axe, however.'

'Or a sword, either,' said Alexander.

Nanda snorted. 'Remember what I said about scandals? They *are* people, you know, same as the rest of us.'

Konrad let that pass. 'Whoever put the head here wanted Lady Lysak to see it,' he surmised. 'If it had been designed purely to attract attention, putting it in one of the front windows might have done a better job.'

'Perhaps so,' said Alexander. 'Either way, I want to find out who Bogdan Zolin was to her, and why they were arguing last night.'

'What I would like to know,' said Konrad, 'is where her ladyship was going at the crack of dawn, and why she has yet to return.'

'I will have the house watched,' Alexander promised. 'As soon as she comes home, we'll know.'

But the day wore away without news of Lady Lysak's return, and Konrad began to wonder. Various possibilities occurred to his mind. She might have seen the severed head after all, and run away in a fright. She might have heard of Zolin's death by some other source, with the same result. Or she might have departed on some other errand entirely — either connected, or not — and was still in ignorance of the night's developments.

Until she returned, or until her whereabouts was discovered, that line of investigation was fruitless to pursue. Instead, he turned himself to the many questions surrounding Mr. Bogdan Zolin.

Nanda returned to her home from Surnin Place, there to raid her collection of newspapers for any mention of Zolin. Konrad questioned his personal acquaintances, with the same aim.

But without success, for while everyone knew of the socially talented Mr. Zolin, nobody knew anything more about him than that he was everyone's idea of the perfect guest. He was invited everywhere, and he usually accepted; but he never gave parties himself. He was a punctilious morning caller, paying visits all over the city, but no one had ever had occasion to visit him in his own home. No one even knew where his home *was*. Konrad received multiple different reports as to the probable street in which he lived, or the possible name of his house, none of which agreed.

He also did not appear to have any family.

Cannot discover that there is any next of kin for Zolin, ran a note from Alexander late that day. *Nothing turning up in our reports, and no one has contacted us about his death. Mysterious?*

Konrad enquired of the Order, too; Zolin's body now lay in the morgue beneath The Malykt's Temple, and if Zolin had grieving family in the city he would have expected someone to have claimed his remains by now. No one had.

'Nan,' said Konrad when Nanda finally returned, just in time for dinner. 'Tell me you dredged up *something* about Zolin.'

Nanda dropped an armful of papers onto a side-table in Konrad's hallway, melting snow dripping down the sheaf. 'No,' she sighed. 'Not really. He's mentioned somewhere almost every week, but it's always the same things. He was among the guests at this or that ball, he was seen shopping at this or that exclusive establishment, etc. There's no personal information at all.'

'No family ever mentioned?'

'None.'

'No romantic entanglements? Hints at dark secrets?'

'No. And before you ask, his name and Lady Lysak's have never been coupled before, either. He appears to have been the perfect man. No mud to throw at him whatsoever.'

Konrad thought. 'How far back do these reports go?'

Nanda frowned. 'You mean, when was he first mentioned? Good question. We can check over dinner, but I don't recall reading anything about him much older than a year or so.'

'So Bogdan Zolin arrives on the Ekamet social scene a scant year ago, takes the city's elite by storm, and dies alone in a snowy alley after the first and only scandalous occurrence of his career. Hm.'

'Strange story, isn't it?' Nanda agreed. 'Lady Lysak has not reappeared, I suppose?'

'Not yet, no. But it can only be a matter of time.'

4

What puzzled and interested Konrad about Zolin was the *how* of his remarkable social success. He himself was widely accepted by the elite, but that was no accident. The Order knew very well what needed to be done. Konrad had the right address (Bakar House, in the most expensive and exclusive part of town); the right income (less than it was rumoured to be, but more than handsome enough); the right clothes (purchased from the best tailor in the city); and the right manners (drilled into him with merciless precision before he ever set foot in his handsome house). He entertained at Bakar House once or twice a year, just to keep his credentials in order; the society matrons of Ekamet needed to be reminded, once in a while, of his impeccable claim to a place among them.

Mr. Zolin had somehow managed without at least half of that. He had no address at all, that anybody seemed to know of; so much for the right house. His income might be judged to be large, considering the way he presented himself. The papers were complimentary about his taste in fashions, and Konrad had seen for himself that his tailoring was beyond reproach. But if he was rich, no one talked of it, or had any information about it.

How, then, had he achieved his introduction into society? By what means had he catapulted himself into the enviable (perhaps) position of society darling?

Had he really done it with little more than a smile, and a good coat?

Enquiries on this subject came up as short as the rest, to his frustration. Nobody remembered quite how it was that they had first come to be introduced to him; they rather thought he was the acquaintance of such-and-such a friend, or that he was the cousin of someone-or-other — stay, no, that could not be right, it was the *other* gentleman who was someone-or-other's cousin. They could not say one way or the other about Mr. Zolin.

When Konrad's connections among his supposed peers were exhausted without result, he changed tack.

If all else failed, he would visit Kavara Halim.

'Mr. Savast,' said that lady, welcoming him into her drawing-room at eleven o'clock on the second day following Zolin's death. The snow had ceased to fall overnight, and some unenvied soul had succeeded in clearing the larger streets around Konrad's house; he had been able to take his own carriage to Mrs. Halim's residence.

He bowed with genuine respect. 'I trust you are well, ma'am.'

Kavara Halim smiled, and gestured him to a seat, returning to her own silk-upholstered armchair. Konrad always enjoyed whiling away a quarter of an hour in her house, for she possessed an original style; the bright colours and exotic silks and jewels of her drawing-room ran contrary to all accepted notions of good taste, and Konrad admired her for it. This chamber could hardly be more different from Lady Lysak's elegant but characterless arrangements.

'I had a notion that I might be receiving a visit from you,' said Mrs. Halim. 'I expected you yesterday, however.'

'Oh?' said Konrad, with a polite smile. 'And why was that?' He did not settle too comfortably into his own silk damask chair. Much as he enjoyed Mrs. Halim's company, she also made him nervous — never more so than when she made one of her penetrating observations, as she was doubtless about to do. He would not linger over this visit.

'It would not be the first time you have appeared in my drawing-room, following the violent death of some unfortunate.'

'That I cannot deny,' he allowed, wary. He knew he ran some risks, in consulting her. She paid attention, she asked questions, and she saw a great deal.

'An amateur detective, I suppose?' she said, with that faint, amused smile. She wore an emerald-green gown today, and the colour brought out the olive tones of her skin, and made her greying hair almost white in contrast. The effect was majestic, especially when coupled with her proud posture and penetrating gaze.

Konrad tried not to squirm under her scrutiny. 'Something along those lines,' he said calmly.

'One with the collaboration of the police, I understand. Inspector Nuritov is said to speak highly of you.'

'He is a dear friend.'

'How obliging of him.'

Konrad permitted himself a smile of his own. 'Perhaps he finds my assistance helpful.'

'Perhaps he does. One concludes, then, that you are a detecting enthusiast of some skill. And now you are here to coax clues from me.'

'I thought to consult your superior knowledge of the city's doings, ma'am, if you should not dislike it.'

Kavara Halim pinned him with a piercing stare, the one that always did unwelcome things to Konrad's insides.

Then she relaxed, and gave him a graceful nod of approval. 'I should not torment you. I know you to be responsible for the dispatch of a severe threat to the city, not long ago; one to which most were oblivious. I have gratitude enough, for that.'

Konrad thought back. She must refer to the matter of the Kayesiri nightwolf, the *ilu-vakatim* who had infiltrated Ekamet society with a view to turning many of the city's residents into his own, cursed kind — starting at the very top. It was Mrs. Halim whose knowledge of obscure folklore had helped him to solve that case. That she had taken some personal interest in the matter had not been clear at the time, but it was evident now. He filed that thought away.

'It is...' he paused, having been going to say *It is my duty*. He could hardly say such a thing to her, not without explaining why. 'It is to my great satisfaction that I was able to do so,' he said instead.

That smile again, the one that suggested she had fathomed his secret long ago. 'Very well. You would like to know about Mr. Bogdan Zolin, I imagine? And perhaps Lady Lysak, too.'

'Anything you may have heard about either, I shall be glad to hear.'

She waved a hand at that, dismissing the comment. 'I shall not tell you everything. Most gossip is at best, exaggerated, and at worst an entire fabrication, as you must know. I listen only to that which comes with some form of corroboration. Or the persistent kind, which comes from a perhaps unexpected source.'

'Is there much of either, regarding the two in question?'

Mrs. Halim did not precisely answer. 'Mr. Zolin has long interested me, more because of the *lack* of news about him than because of the usual excesses. Doubtless you have already learned as much.'

'It is why I came to you,' he allowed.

She nodded. 'He is much talked of, but he has shielded his true self with such skill that nothing of any substance is ever discussed. I always wonder about those who are secretive. There is always, *must be*, something to hide.' Did Konrad imagine it, or did her gaze become particularly penetrating when she said that? His own entry into Ekamet society had been as sudden as Zolin's, and with as little information regarding his past.

He sat still, and said nothing.

'So I enquired,' she continued. 'You are a customer of Zratil's, of course?'

'Of course.' Zratil was a sartorial genius; everybody who could afford it bought their coats from him.

'The first report I have ever heard of Zolin's presence in the city was his appearance at Zratil's. He arrived bearing a huge sum of money, and requested Mr. Zratil to outfit him entirely. So insistent was he upon the very best, and upon the greatest haste, that he paid rather more than Mr. Zratil's usual fee.'

Konrad raised his brows at that. Mr. Zratil's usual fees were already handsome.

'And,' she continued, 'he was not admirably dressed himself, at the time. His garments were those of a gentleman of fashion, but Mr. Zratil saw at a glance that they fit him poorly, and that they were not of the highest quality.'

'Most interesting,' Konrad murmured. 'So Bogdan Zolin was not, perhaps, born to the gentleman's life.'

'That, or he was some country pauper of birth but no money. I have not heard where he may have lived before he arrived in Ekamet, however, nor how he may have come into his apparent fortune.'

Had the money even been his, Konrad wondered. He may have stolen it, or won it. Or someone may have given it to him, though Konrad could not yet imagine why.

'And Lady Lysak?' he said, when Mrs. Halim did not appear to have more to add about Zolin.

'Oh, of her there is little said. Nothing out of place in her life, her manner or her past, nothing unexpected in her behaviour.'

Thinking of her too-perfect drawing-room, Konrad was not surprised.

'But,' said Mrs Halim slowly.

'Yes?'

'There is but one peculiarity that has ever reached my ears. It may mean nothing.'

'Perhaps it may. But pray share it regardless.'

'I have more than once heard of her ladyship's absence from home, on a day when her acquaintance knew of no reason to expect it. It has not occurred every week, but often enough to intrigue me.'

Konrad sat up, alert. 'That coincides with… you do not know where she goes?'

'I have never heard anything to that effect. Certainly it does not appear to be any of the places one might expect a bored aristocrat to go.'

'She has done it again,' said Konrad. 'Yesterday morning, quite early, she left her home — alone, as far as anybody knows — and she has not yet returned.'

'I have never yet heard of these absences extending beyond a single day.'

'It may be unconnected with her earlier behaviour,' Konrad allowed. 'Then again, it may not. I'm grateful for the information.'

Mrs. Halim inclined her head. 'And what shall I hear in return?'

Konrad suppressed a small smile. The lady did not come to be so well-informed by accident. 'Some details about the case?' He had nothing to share that would not be common knowledge soon enough, but the lady liked to be the first to hear these things.

'I believe that will be acceptable,' said Mrs. Halim.

Konrad accepted a second cup of tea, and settled in for another ten minutes' discourse.

'Serpents,' Konrad said, sometime later, when he had made his way home. 'You cannot find Lady Lysak, I suppose?'

No, Master, said Eetapi and Ootapi in unison.

He had asked before. They had failed. That fact interested him. Did it mean her ladyship had gone far enough from home as to be beyond the range of their perceptions, or had she some way of concealing herself from such spies as they?

The latter was far-fetched, he acknowledged. Not only would she have to be aware, somehow, that she might be subject to such surveillance — and he did not see how — but also she must possess some means of hiding from them.

The more likely explanation was that she was no longer in the city.

He returned to Surnin Place that afternoon.

To his surprise, he found Tasha loitering about the entrance.

'Are you the watch Alexander mentioned?' he asked, pausing in the street.

'Yessir.' Tasha saluted.

'You aren't being very subtle about it.'

'Nobody said anything about subtle.'

'I am sure it was implied—'

Tasha rolled her eyes. 'You are so gullible.'

'Am I?'

'I don't need to be subtle,' she informed him. 'Who would look twice at a street urchin like me?'

'Someone who distrusted your plausibly light fingers.'

She grinned. 'I *am* a good pickpocket. But that's fine, too. If someone's worrying about their valuables, they don't think too clearly about anything else I might be doing.'

'Like watching their every move.'

'Yes. Also, you're wrong to assume anyone will notice me at all. You did, because you know me. Aristos usually look straight past me.'

'It's useful being poor and unimportant.'

'Not really, no.'

Konrad let this pass without objection. He hadn't forgotten his own, impecunious youth. 'I take it there's no sign of her ladyship?'

'None.'

'Have you had chance to snoop at all?'

'You mean does anybody know where she went? Not that I can find out. Also, I poked about upstairs a bit. Quite a lot, actually. Any idea how useful it is being a ghost?'

'I hated it, the one time I was obliged to try.'

'That was different.'

'Doubtless. But I do find my serpents convenient to have around.

What did you discover?'

'Nothing that interesting. I don't think she was planning to leave, though. All her things are still in there. No sign that she packed anything up, or took much with her.'

After two days' absence and the serpents' failure to locate her, Konrad had been wondering whether she had left the city for good. She might still have, of course, if she fled in a panic, but the lack of preparation for a long absence suggested otherwise.

'That doesn't look good,' he said, frowning.

'If she was dead, you'd probably know by now.'

'Not necessarily. It would depend where she died. If she got far enough away from the city first, the news could be slow to reach me.'

Tasha shrugged. 'So we wait.'

'My favourite activity,' said Konrad with a sigh.

5

Konrad did not waste any time interviewing Lady Lysak's friends. According to Kavara Halim, she was not known to have had any particularly close associates, only a large acquaintance. Anything that was merely common knowledge about her, Mrs. Halim would already have heard.

That left him with no real idea how to proceed. He delivered Mrs. Halim's information about Zolin and Lysak to Alexander, who promised to chase down anything more that he could. Konrad held some faint hope that there might be a record somewhere of Zolin's original arrival in Ekamet, though perhaps there would not; if he wished to conceal his origins he might have travelled under an assumed name. Or, perhaps he'd been born in the city, and had simply invented the persona of Bogdan Zolin a year ago.

As for Lady Lysak, without some kind of clue as to her possible destination, he wasn't optimistic about tracking her down. 'Somewhere outside the city?' he said, brows raised. 'That could be anywhere.'

Konrad had been able to say nothing more useful than, 'I know.'

He'd found Alexander in his office, apparently in danger of drowning in paperwork.

'What's all this?' Konrad asked, pausing on the threshold in surprise. Alexander's office was always a little disordered, but his shabby old desk was disappearing under bits of paper. Some of them were newsprint, but the nature of the rest was a mystery.

Alexander waved him to the hard oak chair that sat before, and a little to one side, of his desk. Heavy grey clouds had gathered in the skies outside, choking what little wan winter sunlight might otherwise penetrate the gloom of Alexander's office. A single oil-lamp fought bravely against the darkness, but without great success. The inspector wore a weary air and a deep frown as he battled through his piles of documents. 'They should at least let you have a better lamp,' said Konrad.

'A better office in general would be nice. But I have everything I truly need.'

'Except more light. What's all this?' he said again.

Alexander dropped a sheet of paper into the stack before him, and rubbed at his eyes. 'We've run out of leads.'

'I noticed that, too.'

'I've got a lot of things here. Guest list for her ladyship's ball, provided by her housekeeper. Witness statements from some of those who saw the fight between Lysak and Zolin; nobody remembers seeing anyone else leave the party early, and certainly no one seems to have followed Zolin out. At least, if they did, no one saw. Your Mrs. Halim seems to have been quite right about Zolin, besides: everybody came to know him as the friend of a friend, or some such. Nobody knows where he sprang from in the first place, or who secured his first introductions into society. I've had people pull every newspaper on file that might mention Zolin — or Lysak — and several do, but it's just the usual banalities.'

'Have you got anything at all? Even something small—'

'I know, Savast. The smallest detail can be enough to crack a case, yes. I don't think we have that detail. I can't even find out what the fight was about, because they weren't rowing in front of the guests. They had gone off by themselves — nobody noticed when, or has any idea why — and while their raised voices were audible enough after a while, nobody clearly heard anything that was said. At the time, Miss Maximovna was obliging the company with an air upon the pianoforte.'

'Delightful. But then, who saw Zolin leave?'

'It seems he flung back in to the drawing-room after the fight, but immediately left again. Lady Lysak returned soon afterwards, and informed the company that Zolin had been called away, and offered his regrets, etc.'

'Nobody took that at face value, I imagine.'

'No. That the two had fought, and that Zolin was in a towering rage, was evident to everyone.'

'And Lysak? Was she in a rage?'

'Seemed composed. That appears to have been a universal impression.'

Konrad gave a sigh, and stared out of the window. The clouds' dark promise was on the point of being fulfilled, judging from the scatter of snowflakes drifting down. 'I badly want to talk to that woman.'

'Yes, so do we. Perhaps she anticipated that.'

'You mean that may be why she ran?'

'If she'd heard of Zolin's death by then. Consider, in her shoes: what might you think? The man you were known to have quarrelled with is discovered violently killed very soon afterwards. There may have been something relating to that fight that would cast clear suspicion upon her, if it were known. And if she had seen the head upon her mantelpiece, too, she must know that the police would soon arrive with some very hard questions to ask.'

'You speak on the assumption that she's innocent.'

'So far, I have no reason to believe otherwise. I admit that the limited evidence we have looks bad, but I still can't see her hacking off Zolin's head like that. Apparently her ladyship is a slim woman, and not tall. That she could have the body strength seems unlikely. Plus, numerous of her guests have asserted that she did not again leave the drawing-room, and the party went on until very late. Zolin may well have been dead by the time she had any opportunity to follow him, and how could she have known where he had gone?'

Konrad nodded, finding nothing to disagree with. The inspector's clear logic could rarely be faulted.

'The most likely explanation is that someone followed him the moment he left Surnin Place,' said Konrad. 'Whether it was one of the guests slipping away without being noticed, or whether somebody was waiting outside the house for him, I don't know.'

'Could be,' said Alexander.

Konrad continued, 'Though, we're stepping over the question of where he was trying to go. He was very determined to get *somewhere* down that specific alley, despite the extreme difficulty of doing so. Somebody else may have been able to anticipate that.'

'Including her ladyship, I suppose,' said Alexander with a sigh.

'Certainly including her ladyship. If she knew him well enough to fight with him, well, that seems to put her ahead of every other member of his acquaintance.'

'There's someone else involved,' said Alexander. 'There has to be.'

Though less inclined than the inspector to doubt the culpability of wealthy, refined ladies — he had gone through far too many difficult cases to imagine them all fragile innocents, anymore — he could not picture the scenario where Lady Lysak had killed Zolin, either. 'She could have sent someone else to kill him,' said Konrad.

'So she could.'

'A manservant, or a friend.'

'It isn't that easy to find the kind of friend — or servant — who'd kill for you,' said Nuritov. 'But we've interviewed all the servants, of course. No reason to suspect any of them, at the moment.'

The day closed in similarly unsatisfactory state, and since Nanda had pleaded duty and returned home, Konrad spent his evening alone in his study — well, alone save the ever-present glass of brandy at his elbow — turning over the facts of the case in his mind.

He had rarely encountered a case with so little to show for days of investigation. The victim seemed to have appeared out of nowhere, and without apparent source; the only suspect had disappeared into *somewhere*, apparently without trace. And nobody knew anything.

How many people were involved, really? There could be as many as four, by Konrad's reckoning. Besides Zolin himself, and some probable connection pertaining to Lady Lysak, the killer might well prove to be a third, as yet unidentified person.

If that were so, the identity or identities of the killer and drawing-room decorator remained so utterly obscured, Konrad could not see how it would ever be possible to catch them.

If only more might be learned about the victim, at least. His identity was known, but nothing else about him.

Frustrated with inactivity, Konrad downed the remains of his glass and rose from his warm retreat by the fire. The clock struck one o'clock as he crossed the hall, startling him; how had it grown so late?

No matter. The Malykt's Temple was open to him at all hours, and he had business there. A walk through the piercing cold might clear his head, or give rise to some new idea. If not, perhaps Zolin's corpse might have something to offer.

Konrad frequently found an excuse to walk in the late hours of the night. The deserted streets offered an eerie kind of peace, which soothed his often ruffled temper. And though he walked abroad, he need not trouble to maintain his façade, nor recall what was expected of Mr. Savast of Bakar House. He need talk to nobody at that hour; there was no one to talk to. He paced slowly on his way to the temple, walking in near silence, thick snowfall muffling his steps. His serpents, ever loyal, followed in his train: Eetapi drifting behind, Ootapi soaring high above his head.

There were, he decided, two sets of questions that most urgently required answers.

One, just who *was* Zolin? Was it some aspect of his present life that had led to his death, or had something followed him out of his mysterious past?

Two, what was Lady Lysak's involvement in the case? And why had she run away? Konrad would give a great deal to know what those two had been fighting about. He could not shake the feeling that something in that argument held the key to the mystery, even if the quarrel itself had not led directly to Zolin's death.

He *must* learn more about Zolin, then, and he *must* find Lady Lysak.

A side-door afforded Konrad entrance into the temple, to which he held a key. He locked it carefully behind him, and proceeded to the morgue.

To his immense surprise, someone else was there before him. Shadowed though the halls of the morgue might be, he'd know that silhouette anywhere.

'Nanda?' he said, softly, hoping not to startle her.

She jumped anyway, and stood up, turning to face him. She'd been perched on the edge of a vacant table, staring at something before her. 'I wasn't doing anything,' she said quickly.

'No, indeed,' he agreed. 'A visit of idle pleasure, no doubt.'

She sighed and turned her back to him again, regaining her seat upon the table's edge. Konrad joined her. 'I was thinking,' she said, and waved an expressive hand at the tableau before her.

She had apparently been thinking along similar lines as Konrad, for she had found Zolin's corpse and brought him out for perusal. A small lamp cast a dulcet glow over his dead flesh, scarcely enough by which to discern more than minimal detail.

'Me, too,' said Konrad. 'What were you looking for?'

'I hardly know. Only… if he was not born to the gentry-life, perhaps there is some trace of his true character to be found in his remains.'

'And is there?'

'I hardly know,' said Nanda again, frowning. She hopped down from her table, and began to pace around Zolin's corpse. Konrad found the vision peculiarly disturbing. 'He looks the part, does he not? But I suppose that is not so hard to do, if you know how.'

Konrad took a long look. The two parts of Zolin's sundered corpse had been reunited, though his head lolled to one side. Nothing in that face had given him the smallest clue before, and nothing did now. It was a face that could have been anyone at all.

Konrad picked up Zolin's left hand, frowning at it in the low lamplight. 'Some calluses,' he reported, discovering this more by feel than by eye. 'More than one would expect of a gentleman, perhaps, though nothing severe.'

'Possibly just faded,' said Nanda, performing her own examination of Zolin's other hand. She traced a finger slowly across his palm, and nodded. 'No gentleman should have calluses on the palm of the hand, surely?'

'There can be no occasion for developing any,' he agreed.

'Not that this helps us. We had already surmised that he was not born to grand privilege. He may have been some kind of labourer, at one time.'

'Possibly.' Konrad let the hand fall. 'The Order sent me a report,' he said, shaking his head. 'Their examination and autopsy revealed nothing of particular note, either. But I can't help but think…'

'What?' said Nanda.

'We must be missing something. And it may well prove to be something very obvious.'

Nanda accompanied Konrad back to Bakar House, upon his mild insistence. 'It is much nearer,' he said, hoping to sweep aside all possible objections as efficiently as possible.

'Lie,' said Nanda promptly. 'My house is quite a bit closer.'

'I have no idea what you mean.'

'Yours is a peculiar way of reckoning distance.'

'My house is warmer?'

'That I can hardly disagree with.'

'Then it's decided.'

Such a statement would normally ignite all of Nan's quarrelsome side, but today she let it pass, and fell into step beside Konrad without complaint. Perhaps she valued the company, on so cold and silent a night. 'How did you get in?' Konrad said.

'To the temple? I broke in.'

He blinked. 'How?'

'Only a fool would make a present of such a secret to one of the Order's highest officials.'

'Considering that one of said officials happens to be a close acquaintance of yours, you couldn't have simply asked me to go with you?'

'I wanted some quiet thinking time.'

'Ah. How fortunate that it was so productive.'

'I reserve the right to investigate independently at will.'

'What right is that? You aren't a detective, Nan.'

'I can be anything I want to be.'

'And you want to be a murder detective? Macabre choice.'

'Setting aside the utter hypocrisy of that statement, coming as it does from *you,* you're forgetting that I was a poison's trader to begin with.'

'True. You're as bad as I am.'

Nanda shook her head, and slipped her arm through Konrad's. 'Poor Konrad. *No one* is even half as bad as you.'

6

Konrad awoke with a start.

A thin, grey light filtered through the gap in his green velvet curtains, informing him that the hour was some way advanced.

He was also conscious of a headache, and a leaden feeling of weariness. He had not yet slept long enough to refresh himself, then, which begged the question: what had awakened him?

Master! howled Eetapi in his ear, answering the question with depressing promptitude. *The inspector is here.*

The serpents had refused to refer to Nuritov by any other name; Konrad surmised that they enjoyed saying the word. 'Here, as in, here?' he said, yawning. 'In this building?'

Downstairs. He seems excited.

'He does?' That got Konrad's attention. 'I shall be down directly,' he said, throwing off his blankets, and hurling himself out of bed.

He is in the breakfast-room, said Eetapi. *Breakfasting.*

He was indeed, as Konrad discovered a mere ten minutes later. That alone spoke of his comfort, and sense of welcome, in Konrad's house. A few weeks ago, the inspector would have sat stiffly in some receiving-room, or more likely hovered in the hallway, until invited to do otherwise. Now, he guessed, his staff — most likely Gorev — had offered Alexander an unusually hearty refreshment, and Alexander had actually accepted it.

'I hope you don't mind—' he began as Konrad entered the room.

'Not in the least. How could I possibly? Pray carry on.' Konrad selected a plate, and began to help himself from the covered silver dishes arrayed upon the side buffet. A trace of nausea threatened to damage his appetite, but he loaded his plate anyway. He would need the sustenance. 'What brings you here so early?'

'Well,' said Alexander brightly, tucking in to a pile of smoked fish and eggs. 'There's been a break.'

'There has!' Konrad turned, his breakfast forgotten.

'A small one,' Alexander warned. 'Sit. I'll tell you about it.'

Konrad hastily completed his selections, and took a seat opposite his friend. 'All right. Tell me.'

'Well. So. I arrived at the office very early this morning—'

'Arrived early, or stayed late?' said Konrad with suspicion.

Alexander gave a slight cough, and declined to answer. 'One of my men — Belikov, you may remember him — brought me something interesting. Came in three or four days ago, he said, though nobody spotted its significance for a while.'

'Something about Zolin?'

'Maybe. It was a report of a missing object, made by a Valeria Leonova. A piece of jewellery, not of any very great worth, but with sentimental value—'

'The ring,' Konrad said promptly. 'The gold one in Zolin's pocket. It *was* gold?'

Alexander nodded. 'Plain gold, but with an indentation where a jewel used to be. The thing belonged to an ancestor, apparently, and the gem was long since gone. Leonova appears to have kept it as it is, perhaps as some kind of talisman or luck charm — who knows, with ladies. At any rate, she claims that she could never have been so careless as to lose it, and attests that it must have been stolen.'

'Zolin's a thief.' Konrad thought fast, applying that fact to everything they knew about the man. It did not resolve anything, yet... but it cast an interesting light upon the case.

'Possibly,' cautioned Alexander. 'I've yet to absolutely verify the ring as Leonova's property, though it matches her description exactly. And Zolin may not have stolen it, if it is hers. She might have dropped it, for all her certainty otherwise, and he picked it up.'

'Were they acquainted?'

'I can't find out that they were, and she was not among the guests at Lady Lysak's party.'

'Bogdan Zolin, formerly of some other name,' Konrad mused. 'A poor man, performing some form of manual labour for his bread — the docks, perhaps, there is always such work to be had there. A sometime pickpocket, to make ends meet. A habit he retained?'

'Plausible.'

'Perhaps that is how he came by the means to embark upon such a masquerade.'

'Yes, and perhaps it's also *why*. He seems to have gone for a small target this time, with this ring — if he did steal it — but what if he was really after much bigger prizes? What easier way to steal a fortune than to get yourself invited into all the wealthiest homes in the city?'

'He couldn't get away with it for long,' Konrad cautioned. 'If something valuable went missing every time he attended a party, someone would soon start to notice.'

'Well, he seems to have chosen a mix of targets. Valeria Leonova is no wealthy aristocrat. Tradesman's daughter. Prosperous enough, but not rich.'

'One wonders if anything very valuable went missing from any of those aristocratic houses in recent months.'

'One wonders that, indeed. I've put some men on it.'

'In particular, Lady Lysak's house?' Konrad guessed. 'That would be reason enough for a quarrel.'

'He stole something from her, and she caught him at it? Perhaps. But wouldn't that be productive of something more than just a verbal altercation? Surely she'd have had him thrown out, or arrested.'

'We really need to talk to her,' Konrad said, frustrated anew.

'We are also trying to discover whether there was any pattern to the gatherings Zolin attended. You're quite right, he couldn't possibly keep up his pretence forever, not if he was stealing from his hosts. Or planning to.'

'Planning to,' echoed Konrad. 'Yes. He may have had specific thefts in mind — lucrative ones — after which he would disappear again.'

Alexander downed the last morsel upon his plate, and set aside his cutlery. 'Speculation, of course, to a degree. It's not yet certain that he palmed that ring of Leonova's.'

'It fits, though.' Konrad applied himself to the demolition of his own meal, his thoughts busy. 'Is Tasha still haunting Surnin Place?'

'Ought to be.'

'I'm going to need her. If Zolin had a past as a thief, she might be able to trace his former life through her street acquaintances.'

'All right. I can assign someone else to watch Lysak's house.'

'Holding council without me?' said Nanda, striding into the room.

'Just because we are awake bright and early, doesn't mean you have to be.' Konrad smiled up at her. She was looking pale, again, and drawn, but that might just be due to their shared nocturnal ramblings.

'No reasonable person characterises ten o'clock in the morning as "bright and early", Konrad.'

'Most of my aristocratic peers won't surface for at least another two hours.'

'You'll recall that I spoke of reasonable people. Good morning, Alexander. Did you come bearing news?'

Konrad sat quietly as Nanda partook of her own repast, and listened to Alexander's recounting of his and Konrad's new theory. She interpolated few remarks, contenting herself with silent thought.

When the inspector had finished, she sat frowning for some moments.

'Nan?' said Konrad. 'You've a thought?'

'I seem to recall...' She sipped coffee, ruminating. 'There was something about a theft, perhaps two months ago. It was mentioned in one of those gossipy articles we went through, Konrad. A necklace, family heirloom, oceans of diamonds — you know the sort of thing. Taken from somebody-or-other's grand town house, I forget which family. Her ladyship-of-something chose to downplay the incident, and implied that some hapless servant had been to blame. But I'm sure I also read that there'd been a ball held around the time the necklace went missing. I wonder if Zolin was among the guests?'

'Zolin appears always to have been among the guests,' Konrad said. 'You could be right to draw a connection, Nan. Though, if he had already stolen something so valuable, and got away with it, what was he doing thieving trinkets from the likes of Valeria Leonova?'

'Habit, maybe?' said Nan. 'Once a pickpocket...'

'You mean he couldn't help himself? That could well be true. Some thieves are that way.'

'Or debt,' said the inspector succinctly.

Konrad raised an enquiring brow.

'Just because he staged a successful theft, that doesn't mean he got to keep the profit.'

Alexander's words sparked off a vague idea in Konrad's mind, and he rose to his feet. 'I need Tasha.'

'What for?' said Nanda.

'We urgently need to unmask Zolin, and I think she may be able to help.'

Nanda accompanied Konrad to Surnin Place. They made the journey on foot, once again, for heavy snowfall made the use of his carriage problematic. Or so Konrad told himself. If he was also finding companionable walks with Nanda rather pleasant, nobody need suspect him of it.

The house loomed, imposing and solemn, its brick façade dark against the snow-pale sky. Konrad received the fanciful impression that it mourned or something; its windows seemed vacant and staring, and it bore a hushed air of desertion.

'Nonsense,' he scolded himself, and turned away his eyes.

'No, I see it too,' said Nanda. 'It seems... lachrymose.'

'Something like that.'

'Perhaps it is not good for either of us to be wandering the morgue in the small hours. One receives ideas.'

'I propose to spend the next such period of time asleep in bed.' Konrad, failing to spot Tasha anywhere, walked around the side of the house to the rear. Nobody and nothing stirred. 'You don't—'

'Here,' said Nanda.

Konrad joined her. She'd wandered over to a set of stone steps leading down to a low door leading into the property's cellar kitchens. Tucked into a nook near the door, hidden from view from the street, was a small black-clad corpse. Her ever-present dark cap shaded her eyes, but he did not need to see their vacant stare to know that no one was home. 'Tash?' he called.

No answer came.

Serpents, find Tasha please. Doubtless the girl was snooping in spirit-form; Konrad permitted himself the faint hope that she had caught some trace of Lady Lysak.

Yes, Master. A mere few minutes later, Ootapi added, *She is inside.*

Alone?

No. There are workers here.

Servants. Have I reason to take an interest in them?

I think not, Master. They are sweeping things, and stirring pots.
And what is Tasha doing?
She is coming down.

The corpse at Konrad's feet stirred, and took a breath. The small face lifted, and Tasha adjusted the brim of her hat. 'Caught me napping,' she said.

'In a manner of speaking. Did you find something of interest up there?'

'No.' Tasha clambered stiffly to her feet, wincing. 'Bloody cold does get into your bones when you're dead.'

'Language, please. We're in the presence of a lady.'

'So we are.' Tasha made Nanda a brief salute. 'I was just looking in case I'd missed anything,' she explained.

'Like what?'

'I don't know. Anything. *Something.*'

'Bored?' Konrad guessed.

'I've been stationed here for days, and nothing's stirred but a bunch of servants. What do you think?'

'You will be delighted to learn that we came here with a new assignment for you.'

'The inspector won't let me abandon my post.'

'He will. He's sending someone else.'

Tasha brightened. 'Right then, what's on the cards?'

Konrad outlined their latest ideas as to Zolin's possible past. 'There are two parts to this task,' he said. 'One, I'd like you to make some enquiries down at the docks. If Zolin's calluses hadn't faded after a year of living soft, he must have worked hard in his time, and docks work makes sense. See if you can find word of anyone answering his description who suddenly stopped showing up for work about a year ago.'

'Drinking houses,' said Tasha promptly. 'I know a couple down that way, popular with dock workers. If Zolin was one of them, he'd have been a regular. They all are.'

'Good thinking. The other thing might be trickier.'

'I'll be the judge of that.'

'All right. If Zolin was a thief, he may have been part of a gang.'

'Likely,' said Tasha with a nod. 'Few street thieves manage to work alone for long.'

'That's what I thought. What are your connections like with the

Ekamet underworld?'

'Sufficient.' Tasha grinned. 'There are two main gangs with ties to the dockyard. Some of them like to intercept valuable shipments when they come in, and pilfer stuff off the top. If they're clever, they can pinch a lot without being detected — smallish amounts from here and from there, if you follow me. Too little to attract much notice. He could well have been involved with one of them.'

Thinking of Valeria Leonova's ring, Konrad nodded. The style seemed to fit Zolin's possible pattern. He might well have imagined that a ring of such modest value might simply be written off as lost. 'See what you can dig up,' he said. 'Let us know as soon as possible.'

Tasha dashed up the steps and vanished into the swirling snow.

'Useful girl to have around,' Nanda commented.

'Extremely.'

'And what do we do now?'

Konrad thought. 'Well, since we now have Tasha and Alexander on Zolin's trail, that leaves us Lady Lysak. I believe I am tired of waiting for her to return home.'

'You have some idea of where to find her?'

'No. Do you?'

'Not as such, but—'

Master, hissed Eetapi. *Someone approaches. It is a person.*

It is a public street, Eetapi. What makes you think this person is significant?

Because he is looking at the house, as though he wants to know if there is anyone at home.

Right. Back or front?

He is on the handsome side of the street.

The front, then. Konrad lightly touched Nanda's arm. 'We may have a lead,' he murmured, and set off back around the side of the house.

He paused on the point of entering the street, searching for some sign of Eetapi's "person". But the snow had thickened as he had stood talking with Tasha, and a flurry of white obscured everything more than a few feet away.

Where is this person? Konrad asked.

No answer came, but a moment later a ghost-light lit up some short way ahead of him, floating high. Eetapi. *Follow, Master.*

Konrad followed, Nanda close beside him. Eetapi's eerie, flickering glow was white like the snow, probably not discernible to anyone but him. Nonetheless, he moved with caution, unwilling to scare away whoever advanced upon the house.

He reached the carriage-way some few feet beyond the house's front steps, listening for approaching vehicles. Nothing. But there—a faint footfall, to his left.

He veered that way — and, abruptly, a dark figure loomed out of the whirl of white. Tall; taller than Konrad, and broad at the shoulder. So bundled was he in great-coat and hat, Konrad could determine nothing else about him. His posture, though, declared him surprised and wary. He stopped.

Konrad stopped.

The stranger tipped his hat to Konrad, and hesitated, as though he might speak.

But he thought better of it, and began to move away — towards Lady Lysak's house.

'Excuse me,' Konrad said softly. 'Are you calling upon Lady Lysak?'

The man hesitated before he answered, so long that Konrad wondered if he would speak at all. At length he said, 'I had— not— why would you ask that of me?'

'She is not home,' said Konrad.

The man glanced once towards the house. Konrad detected a flicker of dismay, but not of surprise. Had he known of her disappearance, but perhaps hoped to find her returned?

'Are you much acquainted with her ladyship?' said Konrad.

That, for some reason, put the stranger very much on his guard. He looked at Konrad in silence, and then backed away. 'I will call upon her when she returns,' he said hurriedly, and walked off, at some speed.

'Interesting,' said Nanda, already in pursuit.

Konrad lengthened his stride. Two, three impossibly long steps, and he caught up with the stranger. A fourth put him in front, cutting off the visitor's retreat. He stood, permitting just a shade of his Malykant's aura to show. Not enough to frighten; just enough to encourage the mystery visitor to co-operate. 'Do you know where Lady Lysak is?' he said.

'Would I be looking for her here, if I did?' said the stranger, backing away — only to collide with Nanda, who stood directly behind him.

'It is inclement weather for visiting,' she observed. 'What was so important that it couldn't wait?'

'Who are you?' demanded the stranger. 'If you mean her ladyship harm—'

'Not the smallest,' said Nanda briskly. 'But her absence is proving inconvenient.'

'We just need to talk to her,' said Konrad.

'If you imagine she killed that man—'

'We imagine no such thing.'

The man seemed to settle, for some of the tension went out of him. He gave a sigh. 'I, too, would like very much to know where she is. I had hoped to find her returned by now.'

'So had we,' said Nanda. 'She is a friend of yours?'

'Of sorts. She was to meet us at— we were to meet, the day before yesterday, and she did not arrive. I begin to fear for her safety.'

'Where were you meeting her?' said Konrad quickly, remembering Mrs. Halim's tales of Lady Lysak's odd absences.

The wariness returned. 'She would not like me to reveal her habits to strangers.'

'We're acquaintances,' said Nanda. 'Or, he is.'

'Not close enough, or you would already know.'

Konrad, losing patience, reviewed his options. Nanda could attempt to Read the man, but getting through his — and her — layers of coat and gloves might not be feasible, out here in the street. He could summon the serpents, order them to bind his spirit for a time; by such means, he could be forced to talk.

Or Konrad could shed the cloak of normality that hid his true nature, and let this obstructive fellow see just how dangerous it could be to inconvenience the Malykant—

'May we introduce ourselves?' said Nanda, shooting Konrad a warning look. What? How could she possibly guess what he had been contemplating? 'I am Irinanda Falenia,' she continued, making the stranger a slight curtsey. 'And the dark, impatient fellow is Mr. Konrad Savast.'

Nanda, in defiance of all social convention, held out her hand for the stranger to shake. If she had been wearing gloves, she had left them in her pocket.

'Viktor Kirsanov,' said the stranger, with perhaps a trace of reluctance. He moved to take Nanda's hand — perhaps instinctively, for after a moment he thought better of it, and made to withdraw his hand again.

Nanda was too quick for him. She caught his gloved hand in her own, and with a deft movement half stripped off the glove. 'Oh, forgive me,' she said, smiling. 'Such clumsiness.'

Her show of ease did not much soothe Viktor Kirsanov. In fact, Konrad might have said her behaviour actively alarmed him, for he immediately withdrew his hand and took a step back. 'I must...' he said, and trailed off, staring at Nanda. Konrad received his first clear view of Kirsanov's face: pale as Nanda's, and his widened eyes were every bit as blue as hers, too. Marjan? His name did not suggest it, but his colouring was unmistakeable.

Then he turned and fled.

'Let him go,' said Nanda calmly as Konrad made to follow.

'Yes? Did you learn something?'

'Maybe,' she said slowly. 'He... Konrad, that man is a spirit witch.'

'You mean, like you?'

'Yes.'

'Did he Read you, too?'

'I cannot tell. We aren't all Readers. It is no common ability.'

'Very well. And Lysak?'

Here Nanda hesitated. 'I received no clear impression about her,' she said. 'But unless I am much mistaken... whatever his business with Lady Lysak, it is closely related to his nature. As was the meeting she failed to attend.'

'So,' said Konrad, thinking furiously. 'So...?'

'So it is possible Lady Lysak is a spirit witch, too. And if she is... I think I may know where she's gone.'

7

Ice splintered under Nanda's feet, the sound attended by the slush and *squelch* of soft earth drowned in snow, and half frozen. The Bones was perilous territory at any time, but in the depths of the winter, only the foolish ventured to leave the roads, and plunge into the wildernesses that lay in between.

The foolish, or the spirit-sighted. Nanda walked with her eyes half-closed, relying on other, superior senses to warn her where to set her feet, and where lay obstacles to avoid. Here a hillock, scrubby with withered grass and hidden beneath drifting snow; there a sudden dip in the earth, deep enough to break an ankle in, lying meek and deadly beneath an ostensibly solid surface of ice and snow. Even she, sensitive though she was, did not venture lightly into the Bones at such a time.

She only hoped her business might be completed in time for a return before sunset. The darkness threatened to overwhelm even her enhanced sight. The darkness, too, had an unsavoury effect on other things, other torments; she would do her best to return home in time.

'I am going alone,' she had said to Konrad perhaps an hour earlier, as she had rushed to don her deep-winter garments, and the stout boots that would carry her safely through the mire.

'You cannot,' he'd said, typical of him, as though he did not frequently disappear off on some venture without her, or anybody else either.

'They will never let you in, and we do not have the time to waste in attempting to persuade them.' She'd said this as she drew on her thick, wax-coated cloak and raised the hood, Konrad having trailed after her all the way to her home. 'I need not be long. I only have to verify whether she's there, and if so, speak with her.'

'I want to speak with her, too!' said Konrad, glowering under his dark brows.

Nanda ignored the complaint. 'I will try to persuade her to return home,' she'd said indifferently as she marched out of the door, permitting it to close in Konrad's face. '*If* I find her at all. Please lock up behind you.'

She knew there was no escaping from Konrad if he was truly determined to follow her. He had those pesky Malykant's abilities, like the one where he need only stretch out his legs and somehow the ground sailed away beneath his feet, allowing him to travel far too fast for a mortal man. Nanda could not match it. If he had chosen to employ that enviable art, she could in no wise outrun him.

To her secret gratification, he had not. It wasn't that she did not appreciate his company (usually), or that his solicitude for her safety did not sometimes warm her heart. She was not blessed with an overabundance of people who cared deeply for her well-being, after all. But she must be permitted the use of her own judgement, and the freedom to exercise it as she chose. Anything else would be less kindness and more oppression.

She was grateful, then, that he had let her be, and taken himself off about his own business. He could not seriously imagine that she did not know, just as well as he did, how to traverse the Bones safely.

If he imagined her unaware of the stealthy presence of Eetapi, however, whose dulcet spirit-shape drifted along the winds some small way behind her, he was a greater fool than she had thought.

'Keep up, snakie,' she called after some half-hour's journey, delighting in the start of surprise she sensed from that sneaking creature.

You observed me, came the ghost-snake's slithering tones in her mind, laced with reproach.

'I am not quite without perception.' Or assistance, she privately added. If her own senses had not marked out Eetapi, other things wreathed about her that would.

Eetapi digested that in silence, though she consented to stream up as far as Nanda's elbow, and proceed in something that resembled companionship. *Where do we go?* said she after a time.

'There is a settlement, somewhere out here,' answered Nanda, her voice pitched low. Not that she was afraid of being overheard, or intercepted; they could expect to encounter no one, out here. But the soft hush of the snow-drenched forest pleased her; the way the thick blanket of white muffled sounds; the stillness. She did not wish to shatter it.

No one could live out here, objected Eetapi. *Save you and the Master.*

Eetapi referred to Konrad's hut, raised on tall stilts to keep it out of the dreck and muck of the Bone Forest. Nanda had her own, meagre dwelling at some distance from Konrad's, though she had ceased to make much use of it. Hers was a subterranean space sunk deep into the earth, tangled with thick, bone-white roots and smelling of mud. Privately, she admired Konrad's solution a bit more.

'No ordinary folk could live out here,' Nanda said. 'But these are…'

Strange folk, offered Eetapi.

'If you account the likes of me as strange.'

I do, said the snake. *And the Master likewise.*

'On the latter point I can have no argument. I have never known anyone stranger.'

Eetapi seemed pleased with this reflection, her sickly ghost-glow brightening.

Nanda fell silent, the better to concentrate on navigating the terrain. She knew that those who dwelt in the Bone Forest's sole village deliberately complicated the approach, knowing that only those with spirit-sight like their own would be able to cross it. Nanda traversed every obstacle with gritted teeth, ducking beneath twisted, low-hanging boughs; jumping over pits dug into the earth and covered over with brittle sticks; envying all the while her uninvited companion's easy passage, hovering as Eetapi did some way above the ground.

'Who?' came a harsh voice, splitting the silence.

Nanda came to an immediate halt. She scanned the forest with eyes and other senses alike, but failed to detect signs that she had come upon her goal. Their camouflage improved. 'My name is Irinanda Falenia,' she said calmly. 'I am of the spirit-folk. I come in search of a… friend.'

Silence followed, but she felt the scrutiny to which she was subjected. Her skin crawled under it, but she held her ground, her chin high. She had every right to venture here, though she had never been a true member of their community.

'Your name is not familiar to me,' said the speaker. The voice was male, and accented; Nanda thought she detected the lilting tones of one of her own countrymen, speaking the language of Assevan as she did herself.

'I am not surprised,' she said shortly. 'It is some years since I last paid a visit.'

'And why do you do so now?'

'I have told you. Someone I need to see is here. I think.'

'You bring a bound soul with you.' The words were dark with disapproval.

I am not bound, hissed Eetapi in high indignation. *I accompany this strange one of my own will.*

'Sort of,' muttered Nanda. 'Konrad made you come with me, did he not?'

The Master does not make *me do anything,* the serpent sniffed. *Though he tries, of course.*

Nanda hid a smile. Doubtless Konrad was under an alternative impression.

'A soul-pact?' said the invisible speaker, sharply.

Silently, Nanda blessed Eetapi's diverting presence. 'A friend,' said Nanda dryly. 'If you remember such a concept.'

'Of course I—' The speaker broke off with a sound of annoyance.

Then the soft creak of an opening door caught Nanda's ears, a dry sound as of aged boughs stiffly moving. And a way opened up before her: two hoary old trees were slowly leaning away from one another, the tangle of their knotty branches unwinding, leaving a gap between.

'You may enter,' said the hidden one, curtly.

'Thank you,' said Nanda, gracious in victory, and proceeded on. A few careful steps carried her through the gate between the trees, which immediately began to creak and sway itself closed behind her.

Immediately before her stood, she supposed, her grumpy interlocutor. Huge, taller than Konrad and broad, his bulk obscured her view of the spirit-witches' settlement. Her surmise had been correct, judging from his colouring, for he was as ice-blonde as she herself, with the same snow-pale complexion. His eyes, though, were the clear grey of a winter sky. Their expression was... disgruntled.

Nanda offered a curtsey, though only a small one. 'Thank you for permitting me entry.'

'Your business will not take long, I hope.'

'Why? Am I interrupting something?'

The man merely grunted. 'Whom do you seek?'

'Her name is… well, come to think of it I do not know her full name. She is addressed as Lady Lysak. She is an aristocrat of the city, but I believe her to be spirit-gifted. She has run away, and may be hiding here.'

'If she has run away from something,' said her unfriendly companion, 'how am I to know it is not *you* she had fled from?'

'You cannot, I suppose,' said Nanda. 'But perhaps you are familiar with Viktor Kirsanov also? It is on account of him that I am here.'

'I know Viktor,' said the man grudgingly. 'He told you where to find your "friend"?'

'In a manner of speaking. Look, I am aware you cannot trust me and I have no way of proving my sincerity. Only let me speak to Lady Lysak, if she is here. I need not get near her.'

She is here, reported Eetapi. *She listens.*

Nanda extended her other senses, intrigued. She received an impression of much crowded into a small space; thickly clustered trees grown far too close to one another, their woven boughs supporting huts made of living branches. These rude houses flowed along, tree to tree, scant withy-walls dividing one from the other. No ladders or steps ran down to the ground, though most of the dwellings were situated some way over her head.

If her quarry was hidden in one such space, Nanda could not sense her. But she trusted Eetapi.

'Lady Lysak?' Nanda called. 'Do not fear me. I am not here to harm you. But I must speak with you.'

Silence. Nobody answered her, but the big man before her made no move to quiet her, either.

'It is about Zolin,' she continued. 'No one suspects you of any involvement, if that is what you fear. But you may have vital information about him. I come to entreat you to share it with me.'

'Why?' came the question then, but it was the man who spoke, not Lysak.

'Because the man known as Zolin has died, and someone is responsible for it. Some of those I care for are charged with uncovering the truth.'

'You are much blessed with "friends",' retorted the man.

'Yes. May I know your name? I find relations always proceed much more sensibly when the courtesies are observed.'

'It is all right, Niklas,' came another voice, female, from somewhere above. Then a slim, dark shape came tumbling down in a rush, landing on her feet. She turned to Nanda, and appraised her fellow spirit-witch with a keen gaze.

Nanda returned the stare. This woman was an aristocrat, she reminded herself; far above Nanda in the social scale, a woman of wealth and importance. A woman of far greater worth than a mere apothecary, in the scheme of things. But she did not resemble such a woman now. She might be near Nanda's own age, judging from the smoothness of her pale skin: a few years younger, perhaps. Her hair, bound down against the tearing winds, was dark, though not as black as Konrad's; her eyes, cool in expression and dark blue, held a hint of something at odds with her composure. Fear? Wariness? She wore plain garb, wool and leather, drab in colour: nothing befitting a noblewoman. But, Nanda realised, she had spent a great deal of time out in the Bones. Probably these people had trained her spirit-gifts.

'Viktor told you where to find me?' said Lady Lysak.

'In a manner of speaking,' said Nanda again.

Her ladyship's mouth quirked. A smile, suppressed? Or a twitch of annoyance? But then she held out her hand — gloveless — and smiled. 'You may call me Rita,' she said.

Nanda grasped the outstretched hand firmly. 'You may call me Nanda,' she said, and a flood of impressions swamped her mind, temporarily obscuring everything that was Irinanda beneath them: for a few seconds, she was Rita Lysak, spirit-witch and noble.

The human mind is a mess of tangled thoughts, facts, memories, dreams and ideas. Rarely is a person so obliging as to hold in their mind a complete and clear set of information about themselves, with which to answer every question Nanda may be desirous of learning the answer to. Rita was no different. Nanda caught glimpses of Zolin, smiling and at his ease, wearing the clothes he'd died in: Lady Lysak's evening party. A snatch of anger, voices raised; lancing fear; then, confusingly, Niklas, the same man that stood before her, only a softer version of himself, his manner welcoming, loving, his features wreathed in smiles. A snug bed in a tree-bough aerie. Driving snow, alarmed passage through a cold grey morning—

The hand was withdrawn.

'You should tell him,' said Lady Lysak.

Nanda blinked, befuddled, her thoughts still focused upon what she had seen and sensed. 'I beg your pardon?'

'The dark man who wanders through your thoughts. You should tell him.'

'Tell him... who? What?'

'He has a right to know, perhaps.'

Nanda gathered her wits with an effort. 'You refer to—'

'Konrad? That is his name?'

'You are a Reader.'

Lady Lysak — Rita — smiled. 'Unusual to meet such another, isn't it?'

'But why did I not sense that—'

'I do not often think of it. You take greater pride and pleasure in the ability than I, perhaps.'

Perhaps she did. It had so often proved of use to Konrad and the inspector in their work; was it wrong to be proud of that?

But... but Lady Lysak had *Read* her. She knew things that Nanda had not chosen to reveal to a living soul, not even those she loved best. And she had taken those things without thought, without permission...

Nanda bristled. Yes, she had done the same to others, many times, but never just for the sake of it. Only if she had reason to believe they possessed information vital to the solving of a dark case; only if they withheld important information, and capriciously. So she told herself. It *was* different, was it not? And it was Lady Lysak who had held out her hand, Rita who had initiated the contact. Nanda would have contented herself with asking questions the polite way — unless her ladyship had proved stubborn.

'It's all right,' said Rita. 'I shall not betray your secrets.'

'You already have,' said Nanda, her eye turning upon Niklas.

He stared impassively back at her.

'Niklas cares nothing for your secrets,' said Rita with a smile. 'In a good way. Well, shall you tell him? It is as wrong to hide important truths from those you love as it is to take them without their leave. You must know that.'

'It is none of your business,' Nanda snapped. 'And I did not come here to be interrogated.'

'No, you came here to interrogate. Very well, then. How may I help you? If you are minded to avenge Zolin, you are wasting your time. He did not deserve it.'

'Everyone deserves justice.'

'Perhaps. He was no shining light, however, whatever the papers might say. Do you imagine I know why he died? I do not.'

'So you did know that he was dead.'

'Yes.'

'How? Your servants said you left your house very early on the morning after his death. It had been nowhere reported, yet.'

'But someone had ensured that I would know of it, by planting his head upon my mantel.'

'So you saw that.'

'Not with my own eyes. I have a… companion or two, like your friend there.' Rita indicated a spot near Nanda's elbow, occupied by nothing… visible. 'They told me of it.'

Nanda felt a flicker of excitement. 'Then perhaps they also saw who placed it there?'

'They did. It was no one known to me, but I can provide you with a description if you would like.'

'I would be obliged to you. And if you will also tell me why you and Zolin were overheard in a blazing argument the night before, I shall be very grateful.'

'He was a thief,' said Lady Lysak bluntly. 'We fought because I found him out, and confronted him about it.'

'How did you find out?'

Her ladyship scowled. 'I paid attention. As did my spirit companions. He accepted almost every invitation that was ever extended to him — provided they came from wealthy enough families. Those of mere modest wealth he scorned, even if by way of title or connection they were of greater status. Well, I was often a guest at those same gatherings, and I noticed two things. One, that Zolin frequently absented himself from the other guests for a short time, usually without being noticed by anyone but myself. He was clever about it. And two, the incidents of "losses" among the social elite have increased enormously in the past year. And what do you imagine I realised? That whenever lady-something-or-other had "lost" grandmama's pearls, or great-uncle-Tomas's jewel-encrusted pocket watch, Zolin had been one of the party. It was not so difficult to put those facts together.'

Nanda frowned. 'So many missing valuables? I heard of only one such theft, in the papers—'

'Women of my station do not like their private affairs to be bandied about among the press,' said Lady Lysak coldly. 'I don't suppose anyone ever does, but these women have the influence to suppress such reports — usually. And you can imagine why, I am sure. Who wants to advertise that their houses are not so inviolate as they are generally supposed to be? It is an open invitation to a daring thief.'

Nanda nodded. 'Very well, Zolin was stealing from his hosts. And what happened during the fight?'

'I told him I had fathomed his secrets. I had not understood them all just yet; only that he stole. But he grew angry, and when I implied that others must be aware of his doings — indeed, his secrets — he grew agitated. I think, frightened. So I Read him. His head was full of things no aristocrat should know anything about. Rough-spoken people, paupers. The dockyards. Some menace he felt was chasing him, connected with those things.'

'He wasn't an aristocrat,' said Nanda. 'All a masquerade.'

'That makes sense.' Lady Lysak smiled faintly, a mirthless expression. 'He wanted to know *who* I had told, who knew, where did I get my information. I did not answer these questions, of course.'

'Then what happened?'

'Nothing. He stormed away. I returned to my guests, smoothed over the incident as best I could, and went on playing hostess. I heard nothing more of Zolin until the following morning, when his nasty head turned up in my drawing-room.'

'And you fled the house directly.'

'Of course I did. I knew our fight had been an audible one; all my guests must have known that we had argued. The man is then slain overnight, and his head appears in *my* house? What would you have done?'

'Stood my ground and faced down every idiot who imagined I must have killed the man. But I am stubborn to a fault.'

Lady Lysak turned that wry smile upon Nanda. 'I have gathered as much. So,' she said in an abrupt subject change, 'this man in your thoughts is the same one who investigates this crime? The dark one.'

'He is not that dark,' muttered Nanda. 'Swarthy, perhaps, but—'

'I don't refer to his colouring.'

'Oh.' Nanda consulted her own mental impression of Konrad, and conceded that he came attended by a certain… shadowiness. His Malykant side, messing with her mind. 'It is he. And I must shortly convey this information to him, with both of our thanks, so unless there is anything else you can tell me…?'

'Nothing more, I believe,' said Lady Lysak, her face thoughtful. 'Though: perhaps it would be of service to you to know which houses Zolin stole from.'

Nanda stiffened. 'Yes — how can I not have thought of it? Did any of them back onto the alley between Rusev and Tytovar Street?'

'Yes, two of them,' said Lysak.

Nanda's heart began to pound. If she was not much mistaken, the solution to the mystery neared. 'Thank you. I will be glad of a list.'

Lady Lysak thought, and produced a halting list of recollections for Nanda's benefit. It was seven items long; seven houses robbed, seven prominent families offended, seven items of great value purloined. Nanda wondered at Zolin's daring. He cannot have intended to maintain the charade for much longer. If Lady Lysak had found him out, others must soon have cottoned on. Had he been going for one last heist, perhaps in her ladyship's own house?

Lysak's description of the head-bearer meant nothing to her either, but she committed the details to memory for Konrad's information. Perhaps he could make sense of it.

'Stay awhile longer,' said her ladyship, as Nanda prepared to leave. 'It is not often one meets with a fellow Reader. I would like to know you.'

'I cannot,' said Nanda, with some regret. 'This information cannot wait.'

'Then, return. You will be most welcome. And I think perhaps… you are in need of help.'

Nanda cast a sidelong look at Niklas, whose welcome had been so far from warm.

'Do not mind him. He is extra vigilant lately, on my account. Smile, Niklas.'

Niklas did not smile, but he did uncross his arms.

'Thank you,' said Nanda. 'When I have leisure to return, I shall.'

8

Ordinarily, Konrad detested paying morning calls.

The duty held little appeal. One made one's reluctant way to somebody-or-other's sumptuous house, made one's bow, accepted one's refreshments, offered the very smallest of polite small-talk for the allotted, say, quarter of an hour that etiquette dictated, and then took one's leave. Only to repeat the procedure all over again at someone else's house. Konrad knew he ought to be more dedicated a caller; the routine, drab as it was, at least served to maintain the web of connection, acquaintance and influence that some thought necessary. Some might think it especially necessary in his case, for times like these: when a nearer understanding of the doings of his social peers might have proved useful. He might already know who had been a target of Zolin's predations, and would not be obliged to trail from house to house upon Alexander's list, panning (so to speak) for nuggets of information.

At least the ritual of social calls was not so tiresome, this way. He could view it as a contest of wits, a challenge: could he extract what he wanted to know, while leaving his conversationalists unaware that he possessed any special interest?

The hour struck two o'clock, and he sat with Mrs. Sechenova, a matron of sixty years with a benign countenance and, if her attire was anything to go by, a taste for the colour crimson. Her personal parlour, too, for he sat in a crimson-upholstered chair with his feet resting on a rug of that same piercing hue, and the porcelain cup from which he drank tea (thankfully not blood-coloured) bore scarlet tracery.

'My Nessia will be so sorry to have missed you,' bubbled Mrs. Sechenova, part of a flow of ceaseless inanities which Konrad had permitted to wash over him without interruption. 'She is paying a call upon Mrs. Tasseva, you know.'

Konrad was not so far detached from society as to be unable to recognise Mrs. Tasseva's name. Her family was on his visiting list, in fact, for if Zolin had been frequenting the houses of the wealthy then he must have jumped at any opportunity to visit hers. Her husband was purported to be wealthier even than Konrad was said to be, and Mrs. Tasseva never missed an opportunity to display her family's riches. She never appeared in public without a complement of expensive jewels.

Konrad was curious indeed to know whether she had lately lost any.

Which gave him an idea. 'Oh?' he said politely, sipping tea. 'How delightful for her. And she will be such a comfort to poor Mrs. Tasseva.'

Mrs. Sechenova opened her twinkling little eyes at Konrad. 'Why, but what is amiss with the poor lady?'

'Had you not heard?' said Konrad, affecting surprise. 'But perhaps, then, I ought not speak further. She may not wish for such a disgrace to be shared abroad. I had better have said nothing at all.'

The dratted woman's eyes brightened, as expected. The elite courted each other's favour assiduously, yet took great delight in each other's downfall. After all, there was room for only so many social leaders at a time. The decline of one left space for the rise of another. 'She will not mind your telling *me*,' said Mrs. Sechenova coaxingly. 'We are the oldest friends! And so attached to one another. She would have told me already, doubtless, were it not that I have been recently indisposed.'

'I trust you are recovered,' said Konrad.

'Oh, quite!'

'Well.' Konrad set aside his tea, and leaned forward in a confidential manner. 'It seems there has been a theft of some sort, and she has lost some of her most precious jewellery. A pity, is it not, with her excellent taste? They are saying some servant is responsible, but I have also heard...' he paused, watching his hostess's face. 'I have heard it *said* that it might not have been a servant at all. That there is someone of rank, going from house to house, and taking—'

'Jewels! Yes!' breathed Mrs. Sechenova. 'I would not be surprised, for dear Lady Konnikova has lost her mother's emerald brooch, you know. She says it is only mislaid, and will soon be found, but to see how careworn she looks—'

'There are too many such tales,' Konrad agreed. 'They cannot all have been mislaid, can they? Not so many as there have been, one after another.'

'No indeed! But who can it have been, Mr. Savast? It is shocking — quite shocking! — to think that one of *our* number could be capable of such an affront to society!'

Konrad felt a moment's amusement at her manner of characterising the incident. Not a *crime,* but an "affront to society". It was not breaking the law to steal jewellery; it was to insult one's hosts, and to shatter the rules of etiquette around which this fragile little world revolved.

Despite her mild manner of talking, he doubted not that she and her ilk would tear such a person limb from limb, had she discovered the thief's identity. Not literally, of course — though in a sense, someone had.

'You have not heard anything as to who it might have been?' Konrad enquired.

'No! And only think! I held a ball only last week — a vast success, Mr. Savast, you *ought* to have come! Such a crowd! I could not have been more pleased. But I might have hosted the thief then and there! It is remarkable that I did not lose anything of value myself!'

She had, in fact, welcomed Zolin to her house at that very ball; that was why Konrad had paid her a visit. He was disappointed to hear that she had not been a target of his; that seemed to limit her usefulness.

But he had learned a new name, one that was not on the list of Zolin's hosts that Alexander had given him: Lady Konnikova, who had lost emerald jewellery.

'It is no exhaustive list,' the inspector had warned him. 'I am working with incomplete information, and you know how reliable hearsay is.'

Very well, but Alexander's list had brought him here, and now he had a new name to add. He took his leave of Mrs. Sechenova soon afterwards, responding to her simpering invitations with only an enigmatic smile. No doubt she would be boasting of his morning-call for weeks, and flattering herself with all manner of bright reflections as to what importance or success of hers had prompted his visit.

Konrad supposed he should not be amused by such inanity, but he could not help it. A smile, sardonic and cynical, curled his lips as he accepted his hat and coat from the footman, and strode back out into the crisp winter air.

He did not proceed very far beyond Mrs. Sechenova's door before Tasha found him.

'Been chasing you,' she said, a little breathless. 'Inspector said where you'd gone.'

'And? I trust you've discovered something.' The sparkle in her eye seemed to suggest it, and her air of energy.

'I should say so!' she enthused. 'Come with me.'

She did not give Konrad any time to argue, for she took to her black-booted heels, and darted away.

Konrad followed.

Tasha quickly led him to the shabby side of Ekamet, farther and farther away from the clean streets and handsome houses of his own part of town. The ways grew narrower, the dwellings meaner, the pavements dirtier. Even the light seemed to fade as Konrad entered the slums, as though the sun itself had turned its face against the poor. Still, he knew these streets very well. They were not far from the dockyard.

Tasha hardly paused. She shot straight through the tangle of winding, dingy streets, trusting to Konrad to keep up, which he did — though not, to his shame, without some difficulty. He was not quite as young as he once was, after all. When at last Tasha stopped, he was marginally out of puff; a dash across half the city (or so it felt like) was not among his favourite activities.

An old woman sat huddled in a doorway not far away, her clothes a mess of filthy rags. She eyed Konrad from within a knotted mess of grey hair covering half her face. Her fingers moved ceaselessly, but Konrad could not see what she employed herself with. One eye was visible, fixed upon him with a mixture of avarice and suspicion.

Gentry-folk dressed like him did not often wander around in the slums, of course. She mistrusted his purpose in doing so, while at the same time hoping vaguely for some largesse. This he dispensed, before turning his back on her and fixing Tasha with a gimlet eye. 'Well?' he said.

'That's Mother Derenva,' she said. 'And I'm glad you were nice to her, for she has been very helpful.'

Konrad cast a startled glance at the ragged old woman, who grinned rather nastily at him. 'Has she? How?'

'She keeps an eye on things,' said Tasha, saluting Mother Derenva. 'When a light-fingered young man called Boryan Shults disappeared off the streets without warning, and didn't come back, she took note of it. Didn't you, Mother?'

'Them as disappears never does come back,' said Mother Derenva pessimistically.

'Well, this one certainly won't. Mother asked around, but nobody could say that he had either died, or ended up in gaol — the most likely fate. No one knew what had become of him at all, in fact, until today. Thanks to me.' Tasha beamed.

Konrad considered pointing out that it was he who had dispatched Tasha to make her enquiries, but thought better of it. Let her revel in the achievement. 'I take it this Boryan and our Bogdan are the same person?'

'Most likely. Bogdan Zolin is clean-shaven, which Boryan was not, and Boryan's hair was a few shades paler. Otherwise their descriptions match.'

'Hair dye and a shave; easy enough to arrange,' said Konrad.

'Quite. Well, Boryan Shults was associated with the Yudashin crime gang. It seems he had a way of holding out on his debts, and failing to cough up a cut of his profits when he was supposed to. Plus, he had a habit of stealing from his own gang members, if given half a chance. He wasn't popular.'

Konrad rolled his eyes. 'His intelligence does not seem to have been profound.'

'He doesn't seem to have been stupid. I've asked around about him. They say he was wily enough, only too greedy by half, and he couldn't seem to help stealing. He did it all the time, even if the objects he took had no value.'

'All right. So it was to his benefit to disappear, and we'd best consider the possibility that one of these disgruntled gang members killed him. When did he disappear?'

Tasha nodded at Mother Derenva. 'More'n a year past,' she said.

'Much more.'

'Which seems like too long,' said Tasha. 'But—'

'It isn't. It fits.' Konrad, like Zolin — or Shults, if that was his name — had been born far beneath the gentry himself. In order to take up his own masquerade, he'd had to endure months of teaching. How to speak like the gentry did; how to dress, how to walk, how to conduct himself in every circumstance. Etiquette. Literature and art. The myriad things that went into the general concept of "good taste". How to manipulate the social world at need. If Zolin had been such a success, he must have undergone much the same things.

Which begged a question. Such training required a sponsor. Who had taught him? No amount of money could help a man if he did not have the right teachers. Someone who knew every intricacy of the convoluted world of the social elite.

'Did you find out where he went in between?' Konrad asked. 'After he vanished off the streets, and before he first turned up as Zolin?'

Tasha shook her head, frowning. 'Does it matter?'

'Greatly. One doesn't go from street rat to gentleman overnight, however good an actor.'

'I see what you mean. I have something else, though.' Tasha jerked her head.

'If you are trying to draw my attention to something, you may have to be more specific.'

'The *house*,' Tasha said, exasperated. 'That one.' She pointed.

The house in front of which she had stopped — and opposite which Mother Derenva was stationed — was a dark, grubby property, listing unpromisingly against its neighbour. One of its windows was broken. 'This place?' said Konrad, puzzled. 'What of it?'

'This is where our headless gent lived.'

'Back when he was a dockworker-thief?'

'No. Later. After he'd become Zolin.'

That explained why no one had seemed to know where Mr. Zolin lived. He'd never admit to such an address. 'Why here?' said Konrad, baffled. 'Why go to such lengths to infiltrate a better grade of society only to go on living in the stews?'

'It's cheap,' said Tasha bluntly.

'And he was stealing a fortune.'

'Maybe he was saving it for something important, and didn't want to waste it on a mere dwelling. And it's nice enough inside. Want to see?'

Tasha had more to share; the look of suppressed glee on her small face was proof enough of it. Konrad let her have her moment, following her through the creaking front door and up the narrow stairs with a passable air of obliviousness.

The place consisted of two rooms only, one facing the street and one backing onto the alley behind. The latter contained a bed, simple enough but strewn with good, brand-new blankets. A wall closet held a selection of clothing, all gentlemen's attire: far too good for the type of man who usually inhabited such a house.

The room at the front held a simple couch, a mismatched chair, a few shelves containing cheap knick-knacks, and a low, plain oak table upon which an inexpensive oil-lamp stood. Nothing about the place suggested a man of means lived there, but it was far from squalor either.

'He wasn't worried about his clothes being stolen?' Konrad asked.

'Someone'd have to know to look for them,' said Tasha. 'You wouldn't think to find a cache like that in a place like this, would you?'

'No,' said Konrad slowly. 'And perhaps that's why he chose to stay here. Thieves target grand houses. Nobody goes looking for valuables in the slums.'

'Exactly.' Tasha's grin broadened.

'There's more, isn't there?' he said. 'Besides the clothes.'

'Much more. Look.' Tasha paced the length of the room, and paused before the dingy window. The panes were so begrimed, Konrad could see little of the street outside. Which meant, he supposed, no one outside could see much of what lay within, either.

Tasha bent, and devoted herself to some mysterious activity beneath the window. Konrad heard the creak of wood. 'Tada,' said Tasha proudly.

Konrad leaned over her shoulder. She had prised up a floorboard, revealing a narrow cavity beneath. Something palely gleamed within.

'Grandmama's pearls,' said Konrad.

'What?'

'Never mind. One of Zolin's prizes, doubtless.'

'There are more.' Tasha busied herself about the place for several minutes, poking her face and her fingers into myriad nooks and hiding places. By the time she was finished, fully half a dozen treasures lay exposed to the oil-lamp's wan light. Though none of them, Konrad noted with interest, looked to be Lady Konnikova's emerald brooch.

'Lucky his gang-mates didn't know about this place,' said Konrad.

'He showed up wrapped to the eyeballs in a dark cloak. The mangy kind, wouldn't attract a second glance down here. His gang would have given up on finding him by now.'

Perhaps they had, rather more than a year after his disappearance. Presumed him dead, most likely, or fled the city. But what if someone had known better? What if that person had been more interested in revenge than jewels? Might that person have tracked Zolin back to his new life, waited for him outside of Lady Lysak's house, and followed him into the snow?

Plausible enough. Thieves could have a complicated code of honour, sometimes, and would not treat gently with one who stole from their own comrades. But to go so far as to hack off his head? Was it too far-fetched?

'Do we know anything about Shults's particular associates, before he disappeared?' Konrad asked. 'Anybody he was close to, or often worked with?'

'Actually, we do. Want to go meet them?'

'Them? Who are they?'

'The Yudashin. Shults was one of a group of four, thieves all. They used to pickpocket together, way back, and then took up burgling houses later on. One of the others is dead now, but two of them are still knocking around down here.'

'Have you spoken to them?'

Tasha shook her head. 'Just spied on them a bit. Ugly customers, that's for sure.'

'You've been busy.'

'Isn't what you know, it's who you know.' Tasha grinned.

'Remind me to draw on your underworld connections more often.'

Tasha scoffed, but Konrad could tell she was pleased.

'Were you a thief, too?' Konrad said abruptly.

'What?'

'Before you became, somehow, a police ward.'

'I resent the suggestion.'

'I'm sure you do. But is it true? When I sent you to look up Zolin's thieving background, I didn't expect quite this degree of success. And you've exhibited a talent for getting into places before.'

Tasha looked Konrad over, her small, pale face a vision of disdain. 'If you've finished being rude, we'd best be going. People to meet, murderers to catch.'

Konrad smirked. 'Do lead on.'

Tasha took him to a drinking house, or so it appeared at first glance. The exterior proclaimed its calling as a public carousing establishment, from the sour mix of aromas emanating from the ill-fitted windows and the none-too-clean approach (stale beer blended with the sharp tinge of vomit), to the grubby sign swinging gently in the wind over the front door (announcing in lurid letters the name The Drunken Deer, or so Konrad thought; some part of the sign was too filthy to be easily deciphered).

A solid kick from Tasha sent the door sailing open, and in she strode, hailing the publican with a jaunty wave. The place was even dirtier inside, though the thin, sickly light cast by a dismal array of lamps somewhat softened the effect, if only because the worst of it lay in shadow. The stench of old beer hit Konrad's nose with an almost physical blow, attended by the sour aroma of old sweat. He tried not to breathe too deeply, wondering in some distant part of his mind when he had become so fine a gent as to object to such ordinary things — nay, to notice them at all. Time was, he'd been used to such places.

Never mind that now. He was receiving some scrutiny from the drinkers, being as he was far too well-dressed for such a place. It struck Konrad that the looks of narrow-eyed suspicion he was receiving were too keen, too interested, and too uniform; were these ordinary drinkers?

When the worn and wary publican permitted Tasha to lead Konrad straight through the taproom and up a creaking set of stairs at the back, he could answer his own questions on one or two points. No, this was not quite an ordinary drinking-house; probably it was owned by the gang Tasha had spoken of, the ones who had employed the man Bogdan Zolin had once been. And no, Tasha was no stranger to this grimy little world either. Whether she was a thief still, or whether this was a particularly sordid part of her past, Konrad could not be sure. But he made a resolution to speak with Alexander about it at his earliest opportunity. Was she a true police ward now, or was she — horrible thought — planted there by this very gang, many of whose members had doubtless been snatched up by Tasha's new employers at one time or another?

He thought not, or she would not have brought him here, where he could so easily guess at some part of her connections. But the idea, once begun, would not so easily slink away again.

The stairs, creaking alarmingly as he rested his weight upon each step, went up one floor, then doubled back on themselves and ascended a second in the opposite direction. Konrad followed Tasha up both flights, keeping a wary eye out for hidden dangers or complications; it was a comfort to know that Ootapi skulked somewhere in the shadows, vigilant on Konrad's behalf. He did not truly think that Tasha would lead him into difficulty, certainly not deliberately. But he *was* on the trail of a vicious murderer, and here he'd walked straight into a den of cutthroats and thieves.

'Twelve?' said Tasha, pausing before a door that stood slightly ajar. The stairs ended abruptly here, in a landing so narrow there was not room for him to stand abreast of Tasha.

'Who is it?' grunted a wheezing voice.

'We spoke earlier. I've brought someone to talk to you.'

The door swung slowly open — without, Konrad noted, visible means — and Tasha went in.

The man Twelve, if that was his name, sat at a kind of counting desk near the sole window. Piles of coin sat in rows before him, though the desk's surface was otherwise bare save for a grimy lamp. A cheerless room, with its stripped floorboards, peeling paint, and detritus littering the corners. But the inhabitants were not disposed to care for such, Konrad knew. Besides Twelve, three others occupied the room: two men lounging in rickety old chairs before that desk, and a woman, who had perched herself upon the narrow window-sill.

Four pairs of eyes fixed upon Konrad with the same suspicion he had encountered below, only more intense. They had the look of ready violence about them, and Konrad experienced an unaccustomed flicker of fear. If they decided to turn nasty, four of them might be enough to overpower him — and Tasha, assuming she was inclined to assist. And if they killed him, well, this time he would probably die. Permanently.

Peace, Malykant, he told himself. *Remember that you are also a dangerous man.* And he looked it, he knew, despite his fashionable garments and gentleman's speech. Something of The Malykt clung to him, always, granting him a sense of menace.

He permitted that part to strengthen, just a little. Let them think twice before they approached him.

'This the nob you talked of?' said Twelve to Tasha. He was a big man, running to fat as age encroached upon him, but still muscled. Bald, grey-bearded, steel-eyed and missing more than one tooth, he presented the appearance of a man few would lightly cross. Konrad wondered again about Zolin, or Shults as he'd then been. What had possessed him to play fast and loose with such people as these?

'He ain't so bad as most nobs,' said Tasha by way of answer. Konrad was intrigued to note that her grammar had slipped, as rarely happened in his presence now. She had also exaggerated what was usually only a hint of lilting street-cant in her speech. Wily little sneak.

'All nobs are bad news,' said Twelve gruffly. 'Ask yer questions, and be gone.' This last was directed at Konrad.

And Konrad wondered why Twelve had permitted Tasha to bring him here at all. Perhaps his being so obviously a "nob" or noble operated in his favour, in a sense, for no one of his station ever worked for the police. Did they?

'I am grateful for an audience—' Konrad began, for it never hurt to be polite.

'Get on with it,' growled Twelve.

'I am interested in a man named Boryan Shults.'

'*Shults?*' spat Twelve. 'That street-stain still breathing?'

'I believe not,' said Konrad.

'Then he got what he deserved. What of him?'

'Was he... known to you?'

'Aye. Knew him since he was a snivelling tyke picking pockets for tuppence a go. Gave 'im better, didn't we? But did that stop him from biting the hand as fed him? No. Got some big ideas in his head and wouldn't listen to reason. Didn't play fair. Made off with more'n his share and we never saw him again.'

'Big ideas?' said Konrad. 'What kind of ideas?'

Twelve waved a hand. 'Sommat to do with nobs. Like *you*. Said what was we doing, grubbing for pennies when half the streets of the city's paved in gold? Nobody'd go with him. We told him, you get mixed up with that lot — *your* lot—' Twelve paused to give Konrad a disgusted stare '—and you'll be sorry. Ain't worth the risks.'

Konrad doubted that this roomful of hard-eyed men and women were so cautious as all that. No doubt they had thieved from a "nob" or two in their time, and with impunity. But they'd been right, in essence, about Shults. To launch so brazen an assault on the very heart of the richest quarter was asking for trouble. And trouble had easily found Shults.

'He hasn't ever been back, I take it?' said Konrad.

'Never,' said Twelve.

'Once,' said one of the other men. 'Just once.'

Twelve looked as surprised as Konrad. 'What did he want?' Konrad asked.

'He paid me back.' The corner of the man's mouth turned up in a sardonic smile. 'He'd made off wi' some of *my* cash, back when he left. Showed up one night, said he was sorry for it, and paid me twice what he owed.'

'And you forgave him?'

'I got my money.'

'Did he say anything else?'

'That he'd be back wi' more sometime. Planned t' pay back every one of us, so he said.'

Konrad blinked.

'Fat chance of that now,' growled Twelve.

'Did any of you know what he was doing to get that money?' Konrad asked. 'Where he'd gone?'

'Not as such,' said Twelve. 'What did it matter? We had our own business to take care of. Let him get himself hanged if he wanted.'

Konrad studied the man's face, but saw nothing that might indicate a lie.

Not that this signified, necessarily. The man might be a brilliant liar.

Still, he was disinclined to think so. For all Shults's shady dealings with these people, there wasn't much real anger in this room. Whatever his transgressions had been, they were not considered profound by Twelve and his men. Even if they lied about being unaware of his recent doings, had one of them been so enraged with their former comrade as to separate his head from his body, more than a year after his disappearance? It did not seem likely.

Though he could, of course, be dealing with a whole room full of convincing liars.

'I hardly know what to make of that,' Konrad said to Tasha a short time later, when they had regained the street. 'Were they sincere or not?'

'About what?' Tasha hunched her thin shoulders against the biting wind, and tightened her collar about her throat.

'Everything. But especially about Shults. His scheme was very successful, after all, for quite some time. Surely it would appeal to a man like Twelve.'

'A man like Twelve?' Tasha echoed, grinning. 'What kind of a man is that? He's a respectable businessman. Owns a public house, you know.'

'You know what I mean.'

'He isn't that stupid,' said Tasha. 'Look where Shults ended.'

'But was it Shults's scheme that got him killed or some arrangement gone wrong with his old gang?'

'I don't think they killed him.'

'I am not deeply attached to the theory either, but I do not know why. They could easily have done so.'

'Could, and might. But for one thing, to kill Shults would be a waste of a talented man. Whatever his flaws, he was a brilliant thief. And for another, beheading's not their style. A knife through the ribs would be more like it.'

'I cannot disagree,' said Konrad thoughtfully. 'There is one other thing that's bothering me, and that is: where did Shults get the money to transform himself into Zolin? To hear Twelve talk, he certainly made off with some money he was not entitled to, but if he'd fleeced them of the kinds of sums he would need for his masquerade, they would have been livid about it. And they weren't.'

'So he got some money from somewhere else,' Tasha mused. 'Like where?'

'I don't know. Another gang? You said there were two.'

'Yes, but you can't be in both, Konrad. You pick a side. Anybody messing around with a rival gang is likely to get a knife between the ribs sooner rather than later.'

'All right. Then where? Where else might a street-thief get that kind of money?'

'You ask me as if I might know.'
'I think maybe you might.'
Tasha shrugged this off. 'If I did, I'd be rich myself.'

9

Once Konrad had made his way out of the stews, he proceeded immediately to Alexander's office at the police headquarters, confident of finding the inspector still labouring over his papers.

Which he was — with Nanda's help.

'Konrad!' she said, jumping up at his entrance. 'I went home but you were not there.'

Home? Did she mean Bakar House? *His* home? He felt a moment's glow at the idea, and then wondered at himself. 'I was on a goose chase,' he said. 'With Tasha. We spoke to Zolin's old street gang, but... I don't know. They do not strike either of us as likely candidates.' In a way, Konrad supposed, it was simply too easy to pin the crime on a pack of known thieves. Too obvious. And nothing about this murder had been straightforward.

'I found Lady Lysak,' said Nanda.

Alexander, however, was not listening. 'When you say Zolin's old street gang...'

'Man called Twelve. And some cronies.'

Alexander sat up. 'Twelve? You met Twelve?'

'That's what he called himself.'

'I know. I know *of* Twelve, but no one actually sets eyes on the man, let alone *talks*— you did say you talked to him?'

'Tasha's doing,' said Konrad, bemused.

Alexander fixed Tasha with a gimlet gaze. 'And just how did that come about?'

Tasha, for once in her life, looked vaguely uncomfortable.

Without fully meeting the inspector's gaze, she said stoutly: 'He owed me a favour.'

'*Owed you a*—'

'I,' said Nanda more loudly, 'found Lady Lysak.'

Alexander took his eyes off Tasha, but with obvious reluctance. The lamaeni would have some awkward questions to answer later on, Konrad judged.

Not really his business, however, and not the pressing concern at present. 'You are a wonder, Nan,' he said warmly. 'Did she know anything?'

'She gave me a list of other houses that have been robbed in the past few months.'

Alexander promptly produced a hand-drawn map sketched over a sheet of paper. Glancing at it, Konrad recognised the general layout of Ekamet's wealthiest quarter, including his own street, and Surnin Place. 'Shall we add them?' he invited.

'What are these marks?' Konrad asked, tracing a finger over some asterisks firmly marked in red ink.

'Thefts among the elite, at houses Zolin was known to have attended as a guest.'

'We found a stash,' Tasha volunteered. 'At Zolin's house. Also his real name is Shults.'

'You may want to have someone check the pawn shops around there,' Konrad added. 'He may have sold a few articles, as well.'

Alexander produced a blank sheet of paper, which he pushed at Tasha. 'Draw it for me,' he ordered, and Tasha bent to the task of sketching out the cramped, narrow streets of the stews in which Shults's house stood. 'Also,' added the inspector, 'draw what you can remember of the items you found at the house. I'll send some men over shortly but I need this information quickly.'

'She also,' said Nanda, 'gave me a description of the person who left Zolin's— Shults's— head in her house. Tall man, pale and dark-haired. She could not say much as to his clothes, for he wore a long, dark coat over all.'

'So she *did* see it,' said Konrad. The description itself was no case-breaker; many men in Assevan were pale and dark-haired, and he could not even make a guess as to this man's station, without some further detail as to his mode of dress. But it helped.

'Not exactly. She has spirit-companions, of a sort, who witnessed it.'

'Spirit— then she's a ghostspeaker?'

'Not… exactly. No, I don't think she is. Spirit witches have… other ways.'

Konrad would have enquired further, but Nanda went on, relating a slew of details gleaned from Lady Lysak. Listening to Nanda, and watching as she and Alexander added more coloured marks to his map, Konrad began to feel a picture emerging.

'Some pertinent questions,' he said. 'I want to know how Shults paid for his training, or found a suitable tutor either. Also, how did he choose these targets? How did he know which houses had the finest jewels? It is not always a simple case of the largest house, or the most ostensibly wealthy family.'

'Another thing,' said Alexander, still energetically working on his map, 'why are most of his gains lying in a house in the stews? Why hasn't he already sold them?'

'He couldn't move such articles as those at pawn shops,' said Konrad. 'Items of lesser value, like the gold ring, he could pawn, but not heirloom diamond necklaces. It must be obvious that they were stolen goods.'

'And a lifelong thief like him would know that,' said Nanda. 'So, why this scheme? What was he planning to do with them?'

'Twelve's gang might be the answer to all of this,' said Alexander. 'They might know which houses to target, and how to sell such pieces.'

'So their supposed feud with Shults was a fabrication?' Konrad said. 'That could be so, but how could they have arranged for him to so convincingly ape the elite? That's something nobody could do merely by watching from the outside. Too many obscure rules, too many ways to go wrong. He would have needed… someone who was born into it.'

'A former lordling, turned bad?' suggested Alexander.

'Possible,' Konrad said.

'It wasn't them,' said Tasha.

'And how do you know that?' said her employer.

She shrugged. 'Konrad's right. The theory doesn't hold water.'

Konrad felt there was more to her opposition than that, but let it pass. 'Have we talked to the families whose jewels were stolen, yet?'

'Next up,' said Alexander. 'I'll be interested to know if anybody else besides Lady Lysak came to suspect Zolin.'

'My thoughts exactly,' said Konrad. 'If one person saw through him, perhaps others did too.'

'Lady Lysak is a Reader,' Nanda said. 'But she seems to have used that ability only to confirm her suspicions. It was Zolin's own behaviour that put her on the alert.'

'A Reader?' said Konrad. 'Interesting.' Something about Nanda's utter calm when she spoke seemed a trifle forced, and were those signs of strain in her face?

He wondered if her ladyship had Read Nanda, but the words died in his mouth before he could utter them. Not his business either.

'May I leave you that task?' said Alexander, looking at Konrad. 'You can talk to these people as an equal. They tend to close ranks against the police, and most of them have not reported any thefts.'

'I will don my smiling charm and sally forth,' Konrad promised.

'And me?' said Nanda.

Konrad smiled at her. 'How do you feel about a bit of dressing-up?'

An answering smile appeared, faint but discernible. 'Shall I be your cousin again? I did rather enjoy that.'

'You were tremendous at it.'

'I cannot now remember what name I used, however.'

'I can,' said Konrad.

The inspector pushed his map towards Konrad, indicating one section of it with a pointing finger. 'Start here,' he said.

Konrad examined Alexander's hasty scrawls. 'That's the alley we found Zolin's body in?'

'Yes. Look. There are two houses backing onto that alley — I've highlighted them — which we know Zolin, or Shults, to have visited more than once. He paid several visits to this house, here. Could be where he was trying to go when he died?'

'Who lives in these two?' Konrad said, having tried and failed to dredge that information out of his own memory.

'Mr. Lyomin and family, and the Konnikovs,' said Alexander, indicating first one house and then the other.

Konrad paused. Konnikov? He had heard that name recently. Yes: from Mrs. Sechenova. An emerald brooch "mislaid". He had been on his way to visit Lady Konnikova when Tasha had intercepted him.

What else had she said? Some offhand comment; it had not much struck him at the time, but now he came to think closely on the subject…

It was gone. No matter. 'I think we will begin with the Konnikovs,' said Konrad. 'And quickly.' Whatever it had been, perhaps it would return to his mind along the way.

Konrad bade himself keep an open mind, as he and Nanda approached the house of Lord Konnikov. After all, he had no confirmation that anything had even been stolen; it was unlikely, but still possible, that her ladyship was telling the truth when she said it had been mislaid. More probable was that the family had sold it themselves, but hesitated to publically admit to having done so. Such things happened.

Still, the fact that the family's name kept coming up could not but engage his interest. He had learned to pay attention to strings of seeming coincidences.

He gave Nanda a sidelong glance as he rapped upon the grand, white-painted front door of the Konnikov house. How perfectly she fit in his world, when she chose to. She wore her handsome, indigo gown with a decided air, and the appearance of perfect ease. In fact, she managed her acres of skirt with such grace, he suspected her of having got in some practice. A heavy, black-trimmed cloak shrouded her figure, its wide hood framing her face. She was a vision of frills and lace, every inch the wealthy lady of fashion, and he felt obscurely proud of her.

That, he chided himself, was absurd. Nanda as he knew her — pragmatic, independent, absolutely not hampered with miles of silk and frippery — was already a woman so estimable he scarcely deserved her friendship.

Still, he could not help privately thinking that the elaborately arranged hair, rich colours and sumptuous fabrics suited her very well.

The door creaked open at last, not at all promptly, to reveal a rather harried-looking butler. Not that any part of his appearance was out of place; he was scrupulously neat and perfectly turned out, as befitted a chief servant in so elegant an establishment. But he possessed an air of unusual haste, besides having taken half an age to open the door.

Konrad handed over his visiting card — to Nanda's amusement.

He could almost feel her suppressing a smirk. 'Is her ladyship at home?' he enquired.

The butler took his card with a bow. 'If you will be so good as to wait in the parlour?' he said, admitting them into an airy hall, too light on ornament for Konrad's taste. It may have been tiled and papered in the first style of elegance, but it was stark, and his footsteps echoed hollowly as he followed in the butler's wake.

Once left alone with Nanda in a plush enough parlour, equipped with silk-upholstered chairs and a magnificent mahogany table, he began to say: 'You can let me do most of the talking—'

But before he had got through two syllables of this, Nanda said, 'You never gave *me* a visiting card.'

'Do you accept morning callers? I shouldn't have thought you were typically At Home.'

'Working women aren't, as a rule. That doesn't mean I can't have a visiting card.'

Konrad silently retrieved one, and pressed it into her hand. 'There. You may show that around among all your acquaintance — leave it casually displayed upon a side-table in your front hall, perhaps — and bask in the reflected glory.'

Nanda gave him a narrow-eyed look. 'Are you meant to have visiting cards?'

'I beg your pardon?'

'I mean, shouldn't you have a wife to do all that sort of thing for you? *She* pays the morning visits, while you relax at your ease at your club.'

'How do you know about my club?'

'You have a club!'

'I— of course I do, but—' He gave up as Nanda dissolved into laughter. 'I don't want a wife,' he muttered, to which sally Nanda had no opportunity to respond, for the door opened and Lady Konnikova came into the room. Her face and form were familiar to Konrad, a little; he must have seen her at some ball or other engagement, here and there. Perhaps even at the yearly events he gave at his own house.

She was some ten or fifteen years older than he, he supposed, and tried to remember whether the Konnikovs had any children. Majestic, proud in her posture, and self-possessed, everything about her indicated her aristocratic status.

But one or two things were at odds with the rest of the picture. Her gown, for example, was not new; not by a long shot. She wore no lace and no ornaments — except, to his extreme surprise, a glittering emerald brooch pinned to her bodice. It could only be the same brooch she was spoken of having "mislaid", for the stone was both enormous and perfect; an heirloom.

And that was the other thing, he thought as he returned her quiet greeting. Mrs. Sechenova had said she was looking *careworn*, presumably because of the loss of her family's prized jewellery. And she was. Her skin had the pallor of incipient ill-health, and something in her features spoke of strain; the line of her jaw, perhaps, the product of gritted teeth; an abrupt increase of the fine lines around her mouth and eyes.

But if she had recovered, or found, her precious brooch, why would she be so careworn? Mrs. Sechenova might perhaps have been mistaken on a few points, but Konrad did not wish to dismiss her ideas so easily. Gossip was often wildly inaccurate, but just as often bore a kernel or two of truth somewhere within.

'What a beautiful piece!' said Nanda, as soon as she had been introduced, and Konrad silently applauded her initiative. 'I have always *adored* emeralds.'

'Thank you,' said Lady Konnikova, gesturing both of them to a seat, and taking a chair herself. 'It is a family piece, and as you may suppose, of great personal value to me.'

'How fortunate it is that you have not lost it, as poor Mrs. Rayt did her sapphires! And some one or two others, indeed it seems that everyone has been *so* unlucky with their jewels of late. One hears of it everywhere, does one not, Konrad?'

'I have heard some few reports of mislaid heirlooms,' Konrad agreed, watching Lady Konnikova's face closely. He did not imagine it, he was certain: a tightening about the mouth, a decided increase in her already heightened tension. But why? She had not, after all, lost her brooch.

'Carelessness,' she said shortly. 'Such jewels ought to be kept under better management.'

'Only think,' Nanda continued, as if she had not heard. 'After all the care and expense of hosting a fashionable entertainment, to find afterwards that one's most valuable possessions were gone! Quite vanished! But, I suppose, if one *will* choose to wear the family rubies one takes the risk that they may be lost—'

Lady Konnikova rose abruptly to her feet, and appeared on the point of dismissing them. But she recollected herself in time, and sat down again. 'Forgive me,' she murmured. 'I imagined I heard my name called.'

'Is his lordship at home?' said Konrad, on an idle speculation. 'I should like to consult him upon one or two points, if he can spare me the time.'

Lady Konnikova looked sharply at him, and for a split second he saw something new in her eyes. Alarm. But it was gone a moment later, and she was restored to her former self-possession. 'My husband is not at home this morning,' she said with unruffled calm.

'Perhaps I may call upon him another day.'

'He is— gone out of town,' she said quickly. 'He is not expected to return for some few days.' Now she did rise, without her earlier haste, but this time she remained on her feet. 'I am afraid I am engaged elsewhere,' she said, and waited. 'It has been kind of you to call on me, Mr. Savast, Miss Ejan.'

Konrad knew an eviction when he heard it. He and Nanda both rose, and found themselves ushered out of the house again with a promptitude that bordered upon rudeness.

Outside on the street, they exchanged a look of mutual disquiet.

'Zolin has been in this house many times,' said Nanda slowly. 'More than any other, Alexander believes.'

'Then he must be on close terms with either the lord or the lady,' said Konrad. 'I wish I had thought to mention his name; perhaps she is grieving.'

'She could be,' said Nanda dubiously. 'But her ladyship was not wearing mourning. Either because they were *not* friends, so she has no cause, or because she does not like to acknowledge the connection.'

'I also think the Konnikovs are hard up,' said Konrad.

Nanda blinked at him. 'No. How can they be? That *house*, Konrad.'

'The house is inherited. It is looking a trifle bare, though, is it not? And her ladyship does not quite present the appearance of a woman of great wealth.'

'Except for that *enormous* emerald.'

'Yes. And that interests me. Either Mrs. Sechenova was mistaken about that brooch, despite her certainty, or… something else is behind its reappearance. For if they are as hard-up as I believe, it ought to have been sold. And it is hardly a suitable ornament for morning wear, besides. Why is Lady Konnikova wearing it on a day dress?'

'To quash rumours?' Nanda suggested. 'Perhaps she realises that word of its supposed loss has been circulating.'

'Quite likely. But why should that trouble her so much that she would contravene etiquette in order to demonstrate its return?'

'It is genuine, I suppose?'

Konrad shrugged. 'I am no jeweller, but it does not look like a fake. I would like to have that confirmed, if only it were possible, but…'

'I wonder if his lordship really is from home,' Nanda mused.

'Good point.' Konrad reached out for his serpents, and found them airily aloft, and dozing. *Eetapi. Ootapi. Wake. Is Lady Konnikova's husband in the house?*

The answer came back quickly. *No, Master. He is not.*

Konrad thought. 'I believe we will go on with our visits,' he decided. 'But while we're at it, we will begin asking a few questions about the Konnikovs.'

10

Late that night — very late, well past three in the morning at least — Konrad sat in shadow in a corner of Boryan Shults's meagre house, silent and alert. He had chosen a spot from where he could see the majority of both rooms. Not with his natural eyes; the darkness was too complete for that. Nobody troubled to maintain working street lamps in so poor a part of town. But his spirit-vision, half veiling his sight, afforded him a stark but clear enough view of the shabby chambers. That and his serpents, coiled in an ethereal knot near the ceiling. When somebody arrived, Konrad would know at once.

And he fully expected that somebody would. He and Nanda had spent a long afternoon wearing out their welcome among Konrad's social peers, collecting every scrap of gossip about the Konnikovs that might be circulating. The task had been much to Nanda's taste, for she had been in high glee all day.

By the end of it, a picture had emerged, murky but clear enough. Then had come further discoveries of the inspector's and Tasha's, and Konrad had arrived at as much certainty as he required to proceed.

Almost.

'Can you perhaps refrain from clearing the Shults house just yet?' he had asked of the inspector.

'Those jewels have to be recovered, before somebody else makes off with them.' Alexander had shaken his head, strongly disapproving.

'Someone will,' Konrad agreed. 'Very soon now. I am counting on it.'

'Ah.' Alexander had given Konrad one long, measuring look. 'Do you want company?'

'Better not, for this part.'

The inspector had given way with good grace, not much to Konrad's surprise. Probably he had seen enough of the Malykant's grim work to last him a lifetime.

Even Nanda had agreed to let him alone, which was less usual for her. But she, too, had seen her fill of his grisly duties, and preferred to sleep. Konrad did not blame her. He would rather be asleep in his own bed himself, than sitting in a cramped corner in the bitterest cold of the deep night, ears straining for the sounds of the door's lock turning softly back, of someone's near-silent tread upon the stairs.

He could not be certain that tonight would be productive of much, though he felt it likely. No one would leave so magnificent a hoard unclaimed for long.

Master, came the soft hiss of Eetapi's voice in his mind. *He is here.*

A moment later, Konrad heard it himself: the sound of a key scraping softly in the lock. A faint creak as the street door swung open.

Booted feet stole up the narrow stairs.

Konrad held himself perfectly still, barely even breathing, as the as-yet-unknown intruder entered the room in which he sat, adjacent to the window overlooking the alley below. A man, garbed in a dark coat or cloak, etched in harsh, brittle shadows in his spirit sight. Dark hair.

Konrad waited.

The man paused on the threshold. If he chose to light a lamp right away, Konrad would be revealed; he tensed, ready to spring at once.

But the man did nothing of the kind. He moved with the sure step of someone who is more familiar with his surroundings than any gentleman ought to be in such a house. When he moved, he went at once to the window, pausing only a few feet away from Konrad. The wan moonlight filtering into the room appeared more than enough; his fingers found the loose place in the boards, and drew out a string of glittering jewels.

Well then.

'I suppose,' said Konrad conversationally, 'it is no crime to visit a house one legally owns, at any time of the day or night.'

A clatter came, as a fortune in gems fell from the man's startled grip and spilled over the bare boards of the floor. 'Who is there?' he barked.

Konrad stood up, not quickly. He drew himself up to his full height, permitting the shadows and the moonlight a moment's eerie play around his darkened form. 'You *do* own this property, yes? Otherwise I shall have to add breaking and entering to my already lengthy list of your transgressions.'

The man did not reply. He was fumbling with something, drawing something out of a pocket.

A match flared, quickly held high.

Konrad smiled in the sudden glow.

'I— I know you,' said Lord Konnikov, stumbling back. 'Do I not?'

'In a way,' said Konrad.

The match flickered and died, but Konnikov had found Shults's lamp. A new light spilled over the tiny room, and Konrad received a clear look at his quarry's face.

He was not careworn like his wife, precisely, but this was not a man easy in his mind either. A touch dishevelled, as though he had donned his clothes in a hurry — or perhaps worn them for far too long. He had the dark hair, pale skin and dark coat described by Lady Lysak, and a pair of frigid grey eyes that fixed upon Konrad with an expression of flat hatred. 'What are you doing here?' he said harshly.

'Waiting for you, my lord.'

Konnikov's gaze strayed to the necklace of clear diamonds lying at his feet.

'The point that interests me the most,' said Konrad, 'is the matter of Shults. How did you come to meet such a man in the first place?'

'I do not know who you mean,' said Lord Konnikov, backing away a step.

'Or Mr. Bogdan Zolin, as he was more recently known. Did you come up with the name, or did he?'

Konnikov's gaze began to wander. Looking, perhaps, for accomplices. Looking for an escape. He would bolt, in perhaps another minute.

Or he would try.

'Hard up, were you not?' Konrad continued. 'Anybody could have told you not to frequent certain gaming houses; a poor choice on your part. And it is hard to hold up your head in society without money. Perhaps you were down here to pawn some few of your possessions — somewhere you would not be known, or so you hoped — and Shults picked your pocket. Is that more or less the shape of it?'

Lord Konnikov said nothing, but stared at Konrad, devoid of speech.

Konrad took that for assent.

'You were running out of things to sell; some few pieces of art left, perhaps, and your wife's precious brooch. It does not belong to your family, does it? It came to her from her mother. At all costs, you did not want to divest her of that piece. Truly, Konnikov, for all your grievous faults, you *do* appear to care for her ladyship.'

Lord Konnikov moved. A dash for the stairs, half tripping over his own coat in his haste to escape. The thunder of the stairs beneath his feet as he fled down them; no attempt now at silence, only a desperate scramble to get away from the fate he had glimpsed in Konrad's face.

Then the fruitless *thud* as he collided with the street door, silently closed and locked behind him by Tasha.

When Konrad caught up with him, he had the key in shaking hands and was summarily failing to fit it into the lock. He trembled too much.

Konrad easily plucked it from his grasp.

'You hired Shults,' Konrad continued. 'Tested him. He stole two or three jewels for you, and you sold them. A jeweller has already testified to the police — shady fellow, the inspector was not greatly surprised to find him involved. He described *you* minutely enough, though he did not know your name.

'With the money from these early thefts, you transformed Boryan Shults into Bogdan Zolin. He and his clever fingers could be the solution to all your problems, no? And you would gain your revenge at the same time. They sneered at your wife, those bejewelled aristocrats. Found fault with the shabby gowns *you* left her to make do with, having gambled away her fortune as well as your own. What could be more fitting than to make them pay for it? Literally?

'It *was* a brilliant scheme, I grant you. Launch "Zolin" on society for some months; let him divest half your detested peers of their greatest treasures; then you would both vanish. Your lady wife, it seems, has mentioned your family's imminent departure from the city to one or two of her friends. You were to collect the jewels tonight, leave in the morning; how were you going to sell them, by the by? Over the border in Marja? Kayesir? Somewhere they would not be recognised, at any rate. And with Shults out of the way, you would not even have to share the proceeds. Perfect.'

Lord Konnikov made no attempt to interrupt Konrad's narrative. He appeared half dazed, slumped against the begrimed wall in an attitude of stunned despair. Some of these fellows had gumption enough for only half the job, Konrad knew: they could carry out a ruthless scheme in cold enough blood, but went all to pieces when caught.

'That was not quite why you killed him, though, was it?' Konrad said. He would prefer it if the man would talk, admit to something. There could be little doubt of his guilt, but Konrad wanted to hear it from his own mouth.

'He stole too much, did he not?' said Konrad. 'He could not help himself. He stole everything he saw, everything of any value whatsoever. People began to suspect him — Lady Lysak was not the only one. He drew too much attention to your scheme, to himself. It might not be long, you thought, until someone began to suspect *you*.

'And then the final insult: he stole from *your* family, too. He stole your wife's treasured brooch, the one thing you would never have consented to lose. Probably he couldn't resist the temptation to take it, but he knew he'd gone too far. He was trying to return it when you found him. You killed him — I saw a fine old sword, in excellent condition, hanging up in your house this afternoon, was that the weapon you used? — and, as a happy afterthought, deposited his head in Lady Lysak's house. No harm in throwing suspicion onto someone else, no? Perhaps it would grant you just time enough to complete your preparations, and depart. Which, to give you due credit, it nearly did.'

Lord Konnikov came abruptly to life, and hurled himself futilely at the unyielding door. He pounded on it with both fists, kicked it, and finally slumped against it with a groan of despair. Tasha waited on the other side, Konrad knew; if he somehow succeeded in breaking past it, she would make short work of him.

But he did not. 'That worthless *rat*,' Konnikov snarled, hoarse with anger and fear. 'He said he did not trust me, that I would betray him. That I would keep all the money for myself. I am a man of *honour*. I would have kept my word! How *dare* he doubt me. *Me!*'

'Most offensive,' Konrad murmured, quietly retrieving Boryan Shults's cleaned and sharpened rib bone from a pocket in his coat.

'And to steal from Vela,' grated Konnikov. 'After everything she has borne!'

'Absolutely deserved to lose his head,' Konrad said, with a mirthless smile.

'You see that, don't you?' Lord Konnikov pleaded. 'He should not have crossed me.'

'Your wife knows,' said Konrad softly. 'Doesn't she?'

Lord Konnikov went still. 'She... cannot.'

'She can. She does. I do not know how; perhaps Shults told her some part of your scheme. Perhaps she heard enough, stumbled over enough, to work it out for herself. But she *knows*, my lord. And she strongly suspects that *you* are the reason he is dead. You had her introduce him to society, did you not? Did they become, in some degree, friends?'

Another snarl. 'It was unsuitable for her to befriend such a man. She could not have known — I do not blame her — but it was not to be borne.'

Konrad began to tire of the man's justifications. 'So,' he said in a colder tone. 'Having squandered two fortunes and instigated a string of thefts from your peers, you murdered your partner in this charming scheme, tried to pin the blame upon yet another noble, and proposed to disappear into the night with a sackful of jewels, and a long-suffering wife you somehow imagine might forgive you. Have I covered everything?'

Lord Konnikov said nothing. But he saw the white gleam of the bone in Konrad's hand, and panic took hold of him.

Scorning any further attempts upon the unyielding door, he launched himself instead at Konrad.

Folly. He knew it, too, for he gave a despairing cry, grappling uselessly with a foe he must know he had no chance of prevailing against. Konrad was taller, stronger, even without his Malykant graces.

It did not take Konrad long to overpower him.

'Do you know who I am?' he spat, pinning his prey against the wall of the stairwell, the sharpened point of Shults's rib bone just piercing the tremulous skin of Konnikov's throat.

Konnikov swallowed, and the makeshift knife pierced, drawing forth a trickle of blood. 'The— the Malykt's servant,' he gasped, wild-eyed.

'Then you will know,' said Konrad, shifting his grip. 'This is justice.' A lightning movement drew the bone away from the murderer's throat; in another second it skewered his heart, punching easily through garments, through skin and flesh.

Blood spilled in a hot gush over Konrad's hand; Konnikov gave a strangled gasp. The life died out of his face, and his body hung in Konrad's grip, a dead weight.

Konrad let it fall to the floor. He stared at it in silence for some few moments, wondering. What possessed people to murder with such impunity, knowing as they did what fate awaited them when they were caught? Was it arrogance? Did they think they would be the one to elude the Malykant?

What a waste. That Lord Konnikov, given every possible advantage at birth, should end thus—

'Konrad?' came Tasha's voice, together with a rapid knocking upon the door. 'Are you finished?'

He steeled himself, ignoring the flutter of doubt that rose up as he stretched out his hand to the lock. He touched it; the metal froze under his fingers, and the lock released.

Success. This time.

'I am,' he said as Tasha yanked open the door.

They stood in joint silence for an instant, looking down at Lord Konnikov's slumped remains.

'Better get rid of that,' she said at length. 'I'll get the inspector down here for the jewels.'

Konrad sent his serpents winging away to Diana Valentina, she who wielded as much power over The Malykt's Order as he did. Actually, more. She would see that the remains were removed and burned — *without* the rites — and that the scene was cleaned. Lord Konnikov, dispatched into The Malykt's unforgiving care, would suffer as he deserved to; the shade of the man he had slain would see to that, as would the Master.

Konrad's work was finished. He could go home, and sleep. Go

back to being Mr. Konrad Savast for a little while, just an ordinary gentleman of Ekamet in his luxurious home. Even socialise a little with his peers. With Nanda.

Until the next time. Always, always, there was a next time.

11

Konrad found a welcome party awaiting him when he returned home. Not in his study, to where he would normally retreat on such an occasion (there to indulge in a glass of something, or perhaps two or three, before he attempted any repose). Nanda sat in comfort in her favourite of his two parlours. She had a fine fire ablaze, despite the hour being little short of five o'clock in the morning; the best chair sat empty and ready for him, the one with the extra stuffing in its pillows; and in addition to the advantages of comfort, warmth and Nanda's presence she had also arranged for a small repast to be got ready for him. Not even the delicate pastries and such that she preferred, but something that smelled meatier.

He paused in the doorway to admire this vision of welcome, and Nanda looked up. 'Hello, Konrad,' she said composedly, though not without a trace of relief in her eyes.

He smiled in response. 'I was in no danger from Konnikov. You need not have worried.'

'I was not worried.'

'Of course not.'

She prepared a plate for him. 'Not at all. Though it sometimes happens that a desperate man can be more dangerous than he might appear.'

'Not in this case.' Konrad took the seat she had prepared for him, and accepted the plate. It crossed his mind that he had spent many hours thus occupied, in recent months: ensconced in comfort somewhere warm, being fed some manner of delectable by Nanda.

Often, these days, with the inspector, too.

These thoughts warmed him almost as much as the fire.

'It is good of you to wait up for me,' he told her, trying to devour a venison tartlet with something approaching grace. He had not thought to eat, experiencing some of the nausea that often attended the completion of a case, but once he bit into the savoury thing he discovered himself to be ravenous.

'I… had a reason,' said Nanda.

'I am still alive, as you see. Not a mark on me.'

'That wasn't it.'

'Oh?' He paused in eating to look at her.

Nanda hesitated. 'There is something I must tell you.'

He set down the tartlet, his appetite vanished. Something in her tone heralded something serious. 'Go on.'

'I ought to have told you before, only…' Nanda sighed, and shook her head in a gesture of frustration. 'It is hard to know when a given piece of information will help, or merely complicate.'

Konrad endeavoured to decipher that. 'Is… is this about your illness?' he said, in some doubt, for nothing she'd said seemed to relate to such.

'No. It is about yours.'

'Mine? Am I ill?'

'In some fashion. I refer to your Malykant powers.'

'Do you think them… infected? Diseased? What could achieve such a feat?'

'It is not like an ordinary disease. Indeed, it is no disease at all; I should not have characterised it as such. But an infection — that might not be so inaccurate a term.'

'Nan, please just tell me. All this speculation as to terms is heightening the suspense intolerably.'

A brief smile at that. 'Do you remember some months ago? The case involving Danil?'

Danil Dubin, Nanda's fellow herb-and-poison trader of a friend. Or he had been. Their friendship had, perhaps, cooled.

The timid little man had become involved in a strange case involving a pair of rogue lamaeni. In the course of concluding the more violent of the negotiations, Konrad had somehow come to be stabbed. He did not remember how. 'I was in bed for a fortnight,' he said. 'A stab wound, nearly fatal.'

Nanda bit her lip. 'It was fatal.'

'What?'

'You died, Konrad. Diana killed you.'

'*What?*'

'What happened to you at Divoro… that was not quite the first time some hostile soul possessed you. You laid yourself open to it, that time with the *lamaeni,* Konrad. You thought you could handle them. You were an idiot. Diana stabbed you, and you died.'

Konrad couldn't breathe. 'Spirits above. Is *that* why Diana wants to retire me? Is that part of the reason? I've been a danger. Twice.'

'I don't know, but *that* isn't what I wanted to tell you.'

'There's more?'

'Yes. And you aren't going to like it.'

Konrad swallowed bile, and tried to breathe. 'All right. Tell me.'

Nanda took a slow breath. 'The Malykt did not resurrect you. I don't know why. Perhaps He was busy, or…'

'Displeased,' Konrad said.

Nanda shrugged. 'I cannot say. Perhaps He would have come soon enough, if I had only given it a minute or two more. But I— perhaps I panicked. You were stone dead, bleeding everywhere, cold as winter, and *nobody would help you.*'

'You helped me.' Konrad stared at her white, white face, taking in the tinge of fear in her blue eyes. 'Is that it?'

'My mistress. The Shandrigal. I called upon *Her,* and she… revived you.'

'The *Shandrigal*— why would She— what are you saying, exactly?'

'Something about you changed, the first time The Malykt brought you back from the dead. You know it. It's been hinted at, times enough. You became, then, even more His servant than you were before, because some of *His* power kept the life in your limbs, the blood flowing through you. Well, and now you… now you owe some part of that life to The Shandrigal, too.'

Konrad needed no further assistance to follow her train of thought. If The Malykt's interference had changed him, left him with some further traces of His power in Konrad's veins, what then might The Shandrigal's interference have done?

Had it… weakened his connection to The Malykt? Obscured some part of his Master's power with a new influence?

Was that truly why his Malykant's powers had lost their reliability?

They did not always respond as Konrad wished because Konrad was… not quite the Malykant, anymore. Or not *only* that.

'It's possible,' said Nanda, breaking a heavy silence, 'that you are a little diminished, as the Malykant. But you may also be a little… enhanced, in other ways.'

'You mean I am part Shandral, now. Like you.'

'It is possible. Have you noticed anything else different in yourself? Anything you can do that was not possible before?'

'I—' Konrad, about to deny it, stopped.

One thing was different. Nanda's very presence in his house at five in the morning declared it such. His friendship with Alexander Nuritov told the same story.

He couldn't say it. How absurd, to suggest that a frozen heart might revive under The Shandrigal's touch. How humiliating, that he might have needed such an influence to become capable of simple friendship.

Had he fallen so far from such basic humanity, in The Malykt's service?

Yes. Every Malykant did. Diana knew it; that was why she wanted to replace him.

But she didn't know about The Shandrigal's interference. Konrad did not need to ask Nanda to be sure of that.

'I am sorry,' said Nanda, appalled, perhaps, at his continued silence. 'If I have erred — if I have made trouble for you. I didn't know what else to do, and I couldn't…' She trailed off.

Couldn't leave me to die in the snow, Konrad thought. And she apologised for it.

He took hold of her hand, and on some fleeting impulse, carried it to his lips. 'Thank you,' he said. 'The Shandrigal truly blessed me when She sent me you.'

Whatever Nanda might have planned next to say went unspoken, as the guilt died out of her eyes. 'You're *sure?*' she said. 'I appear to have made a mess of you.'

'No. You've… saved me. From everything. And now I hope you will save me from another ignominious death, for if I attempt to consume all this food myself I will surely burst.' He resorted to a joke, hoping to ease the tightness in his throat, and the prickling behind his eyes. Honestly. That was one aspect of The Shandrigal's touch he would gladly dispense with; this embarrassing tendency to start leaking from his eyes. He did not remember that being a problem before, either.

Nanda squeezed his fingers, and accepted half the contents of the plate she had so carefully piled up for him. She did not eat a great deal herself, he'd noticed. The food seemed intended for him. To please him.

So he ate, and so did she, and the conversation passed on to lighter matters. She didn't ask him about Konnikov, and he didn't share. Time enough to be the Malykant and the Shandral again tomorrow.

For tonight, he'd be Konrad and she'd be Nanda, and that was enough. More than enough.

THE
TARASOV
DESPITE

1

Being the Malykant, most ruthless servant of the All-Master of Death, Konrad had been summoned to deal with many a corpse in his time.

It was not often, however, that he stumbled over one in the street, while minding his own business.

There came a chill morning in late winter, spring a faint, tantalising glimpse on an occasional horizon but the air, the aether, and the atmosphere still cold as death, when Konrad ventured out into these wearisome conditions in pursuit of an hour or two at his club. He might, he thought, even find Inspector Nuritov there; his friend, addressed these days by the more familiar title of Alexander, not infrequently took refuge there himself. They sat in adjacent chairs, read large newspapers, sipped identical glasses of brandy (or more likely at this time of day, coffee), and exchanged salient remarks upon the contents of their respective periodicals. Many an intriguing case (not always of the murderous kind) had been discussed on such mornings. It had become a treasured part of Konrad's daily life.

Today though it was not to be, for a mere, soul-destroying two hundred feet from warmth, safety and repose, Konrad stumbled — literally — over the prone and splayed remains of… somebody.

Motionless. Grey eyes staring at a grey sky. No visible wounds, Konrad's professional instincts informed him. The fallen one was female, neither old nor young, neither rich nor poor; bordering upon nondescript, with her brown hair tied up in an unremarkable arrangement and a featureless brown coat hiding whatever else she wore.

Konrad bent, and went through the requisite motions, as he must. No pulse. No reaction.

Dead.

'Well,' he said aloud, and finding himself with no other remark to make, fell silent.

A swift look around followed. The street was still quiet at so relatively early an hour, and in this part of town. Not many passers-by. Still, if she had been here for long, someone else ought to have noticed her by now. Recently deceased, then. A woman passed at that moment, expensively hatted, chin high. Upon beholding the sad, still form and Konrad's tall figure looming over her, she averted her gaze and scurried on, as though afraid that the slaying hand (his, apparently) might fall upon her next.

Konrad permitted himself a small sigh. He was not *so* intimidating a presence, surely? Tall, yes, and broad enough in the shoulder. Dressed, by habit, in a certain darkness of hue. But he was hatted himself, like a gentleman, and with nothing else about him that ought to alarm a female. At least, not when he wasn't trying, like now. He could muster a sinister enough air when it was of use.

Serpents? he called, setting the matter aside. *I do not suppose you might mend my fractured hopes for this morning, and find that this good woman has died of some natural cause?*

He felt a flurry of cold air, separate from the drifting breezes that wafted along the street. A twin gust followed, prompting a shiver. Theirs was a special level of chill, something supernatural about it that cut to his bones.

Then, Eetapi answered. *I do not see how she could have.* The words had a resentful air, as though Konrad offended merely by asking the question.

Her brother Ootapi added, *There is sickness in her. But there is also taint.*

Unclean, added Eetapi, gleeful now, all *her* happy hopes answered in the prospect of a fresh murder. *She has died by the hand of another, Master!*

Terrific. He wondered sometimes how they could tell, these abominable assistants of his. Could they smell it on the corpse, some odour of corruption? Was it a sense? Did wilful murder leave so clear a trace, if one had the means to detect it? He had never chosen to put these questions to the serpents themselves, and again avoided the opportunity. Some things, he might be better not knowing.

Anyway. To swallow his dismay, and go to work. *Is there a shade? Quickly, please, before someone else should happen along.*

The twin presences of his serpents faded from his perception, and shortly afterwards the corpse shuddered convulsively, and — this was unusual — coughed. His hopes leapt. Perhaps, somehow, they had all been wrong, and she was *not* dead—

No. Those were the glassy eyes of someone who no longer had the power to see. Her lips moved, though, thanks to his serpents, but only to utter a low groan of agony. And she gasped.

'What is your name?' Konrad said quickly, keeping a weather eye upon the as-yet silent street. The portico of Zima's beckoned up a ways to his left, tantalising. Before him rose some handsome structure of grey stone and pilasters, a merchant's establishment perhaps. Behind him, some other building much the same. He was not familiar with who else occupied this street, his attention being all for his club.

'I am Verinka,' she choked.

'Verinka...? The rest is?'

'Tarasovna.'

'Who killed you?' Konrad spoke rapidly, moved as much by the knowledge that her ghost would soon flee this macabre scene as by the probability of an intruder happening upon them. They never did last long, the murdered ones, though some of them tried.

Verinka Tarasovna spoke, though, with growing composure, and ceased to choke. 'I am dead,' she said, oddly dispassionate, but with a note of enquiry. The head turned. He did not imagine she profited much by the movement. Could her dead eyes see?

'You are in—' he paused to remember '—Polik Street. Do you know how you came to be here? Do you remember how you died?'

Ignoring these questions, Verinka flashed back to the preceding one. 'My brother,' she said, flatly. 'He did not like Kristov, but I did not know that he disliked him so much as to— as to— I *know* it was Tsevar—'

She was fading. 'Who is Kristov?' Konrad said rapidly.

But the question was not answered. Verinka Tarasovna began, again, to choke, and the borrowed ghost-light vanished from her glassy eyes.

The corpse collapsed back into its former inanimate state.

Talkative, commented Eetapi, returning to Konrad's side.

Very, for a deadwoman, but had she said anything of much use? Having her name helped, yes; it may take a little time, but Konrad could (with the inspector's help, most likely) trace her to her place of abode. Her brother might then be discovered, and the mysterious Kristov perhaps?

But flimsy it all was, and vague. While the opportunity of interviewing a corpse was often of use, Konrad had to handle anything they said with caution. Especially when they named their supposed killers. Especially if they were surprised to find themselves dead, and could not remember how it had come about.

In this case, the question of *how* Verinka had died was an important one. She had no wounds, no injuries, which suggested someone had taken a more subtle approach. And that usually meant poison, secreted in something she had unknowingly imbibed.

A murderer who took pains to conceal not only their identity but the crime itself? Those were the slippery ones. No doubt Verinka's killer was hoping her death might be conveniently ascribed to causes natural — frozen to death in the street, perhaps, or succumbed to a sudden illness — and thus allow him to escape the notice of police and Malykant both. It might be Verinka's brother. It might be someone else entirely, someone she had no notion to suspect.

Konrad would have to take care.

'Good morning,' said Konrad brightly a few minutes later, striding into the reading room at Zima's. A familiar figure sat enjoying his day off (or so he thought) in a deep, leather-upholstered armchair by the fire, his face almost entirely obscured by the pages of his newspaper.

Inspector Nuritov looked up — and, upon seeing Konrad, brightened. 'Ah! I was hoping you would show. Look.' He sat up, and brandished his paper in Konrad's general direction. 'Interesting case in Vand. Do you know it? Small town, not far from here. Someone—'

'I would love to hear all about it,' Konrad said with total sincerity. 'Only, we have a spot of work to do.'

'Work.' Alexander blinked. 'Oh. *Work.* You mean—?'

Konrad pointed. 'About two hundred feet that way.'

Dismay flickered across the inspector's pleasant, slightly weathered face, followed by resignation. He set aside his paper with only a faint sigh, ran a neatening hand through his slightly overlong sandy hair, and hauled himself out of his chair. 'You have no respect for my leisure time,' he said to Konrad, his lips curving in the faintest of smiles.

'*I* do,' Konrad assured him. 'Killers don't.'

'I imagine you know all about that.'

'Don't I though.' Konrad thought briefly back over the many times his obliging serpents had dragged him out of bed at obnoxious hours of the morning. 'Still, there is always the hope that this will be a simple case, and soon resolved.'

Alexander gave a noncommittal grunt, and ventured to peer tentatively out of the nearest window. 'Two hundred feet…?'

'Approximately.'

'Still there?'

'Was five minutes ago.'

'Right, well, down we'd better go.'

Konrad produced a mirthless smile of his own. 'Quickly, quickly, before someone… makes off with the corpse?'

'Stranger things have happened,' said Alexander. As he walked to the door, the mild-mannered, easy fellow Konrad had befriended became the coolly competent, unflappable Inspector Nuritov.

'That… I also know,' Konrad conceded.

'Truly,' said Alexander shortly afterwards. 'I could almost believe someone had left this poor lady here on purpose. Right under our very noses, Konrad.'

'A shocking insult,' Konrad agreed. 'What do you make of it?'

Alexander studied the woman in silence for some time. Konrad said nothing, and did not move. The inspector sometimes made shrewd observations which had eluded Konrad himself, if given time to consider.

'Her posture,' Alexander said at length. 'Look at the way she has fallen.'

Konrad took a fresh look. She lay on her side, her face averted from the street. 'What of it?'

'I am trying to decide. Did she fall here, or was she dropped? With no wounds, there is no blood flow, no spatter. I cannot tell whether she died where she fell, or whether she was killed somewhere else, and brought here.'

'I see.' And if his own surmise proved correct, and the woman had been poisoned, the inspector's question would prove pertinent. If she had fallen in the process of walking down the street, then whichever poison she had ingested must have been a relatively slow-acting one, and probably administered somewhere nearby. If someone had dumped her body here, then it could have been anything at all.

'Why would somebody leave her corpse just here, though?' he said, unable to decide from her pose which of the two was more likely.

'Good question. Could prove very relevant.'

A swift study of the snow availed him little. Much of it was old, fallen some time ago, and packed down by the passage of many feet. No obvious marks hinted at what had happened here.

'What do we know about her so far?' said Alexander, a delicate allusion to Konrad's odd ghostspeaker abilities if ever he'd heard one.

'Verinka Tarasovna. Possible connection with a brother, and someone of the name of Kristov.'

'That's it?'

'That's it.'

'Well. A name isn't bad. I'll have someone on it shortly.' The inspector crouched in the snow, and gently prised apart the fingers of Verinka's right hand. She was clutching something, an object which proved to be a pipe.

Alexander held it up to show Konrad. 'Finer than mine,' he said with some truth, for the piece was crafted from mahogany, polished to a shine, and engraved with a scrolling symbol Konrad could not make out. A band of metal around the bowl — brass, probably — bore an intricate filigree pattern.

'Not cheap,' Konrad agreed. 'I wonder if it was hers. Was she a smoker?'

I was not, came a distant voice.

'What?' Konrad looked first, stupidly, at Alexander, as though such words — and in a female voice — might have come from him.

But he *was* the only other person present.

Eetapi? Was that you?

It was her, came the serpent's reply.

Her who?

The dead person.

It cannot have been. Did not her spirit depart?

It broke, said Eetapi thoughtfully. *But it is not all gone.*

Not all gone? What do you mean?

I mean that bits of her are still here.

Bits? Bits of a murdered woman's spirit? Konrad, speechless, attempted to work out the implications of that, and failed. He had never heard of it before.

She is tenacious, he finally said.

A strong one, Eetapi agreed. Then added, whimsically, *I wonder which bits of her they are?*

Konrad pictured a drifting, incorporeal hand, and perhaps an eyeball, and shuddered. Unhelpful imagery.

Well, but. If *bits* of Verinka Tarasovna remained, however fractured, perhaps that would be a good thing. Perhaps she could help.

'Verinka?' said Konrad aloud.

Alexander was staring at him. 'Who are you talking to?'

'She's, um… possibly not quite gone.'

'Oh.' This unnerved the inspector, judging from the daunted look he cast about himself. Perhaps he expected to see a severed head floating upon the air, ghostly and ghastly in equal measure.

Perhaps he would, at that. How was Konrad to know?

No ghostly body-parts emerged to discompose either Alexander or Konrad, however. Nor did Verinka speak again. 'She said she was not a smoker,' Konrad said. 'At least, she seemed to be saying it in answer to my question. If that's the truth, this was not her own pipe.'

'That is something we will be able to verify, once we find out where she lived,' said the inspector. 'Someone who was close to her will know. She did not happen to mention whose pipe it was, if not hers?'

'That's all she's said. So far.'

'If she speaks again…'

'I'll let you know.' Meanwhile…

Keep an eye on her, please, he said to his serpents. *If she lingers, there must be a reason. And she may provide us with a clue.*

Yes, Master, said the serpents in chorus.

Ootapi added, *Perhaps we shall keep her.*

Keep her? Konrad spoke sharply. *No.*

But my collection—
No.
Ootapi gave a shivery sigh, and drifted off.

2

A scant few hours later, the body of Verinka Tarasovna lay in the morgue beneath The Malykt's temple. The police had studied her as much as they pleased, though without uncovering any very startling information. She was estimated to be in her mid-forties, with signs of no particular vices. She'd had a little money with her, and a moderately handsome timepiece, but no jewellery, nor any sign that she'd ever been wearing any. Probably not a robbery, Nuritov had decided. Nothing had come up that might hint at what she'd been doing in a street far from either shops or any house such a woman might have lived in.

The Order had moved fast. The moment the police released Verinka's remains, they had whisked her to the morgue and proceeded with their own examination. The kind that involved a certain amount of cutting and internal study. Konrad hesitated to acknowledge how much he hated that part. He ought not to be squeamish about such things; nor was he, strictly speaking. But there was something so coldly clinical about cutting into a dead body, as though she were naught but a slab of meat. He liked to encourage his warmer, more human side, these days, and gladly left this task to others of the Order.

The verdict came back speedily enough. She had died of a slow poison. They could not identify which, but that scarcely mattered. A wasting poison acted very slowly. It had to be administered repeatedly, in small enough doses to escape the victim's notice. Its effects were cumulative, killing the victim over a matter of weeks —

perhaps even months. In all likelihood, then, the poor woman had been growing steadily sicker for some time, and had at last keeled over in the street. That did make more sense than that someone had disposed of her body there; if they were going to go to such lengths as that, why take such a long time to kill her?

Still, there remained the question of why Verinka Tarasovna had been on that street in the first place.

These things, too, he hoped the inspector's men might soon be able to shed some light upon.

'The brother, then, is looking more likely,' said Alexander somewhat later, upon his return to his own, cluttered office at the police headquarters. 'It has to be someone known to the poor woman.'

'Someone who had regular opportunity to administer poison,' Konrad agreed. 'Unless it was an accident.' Such things happened. Something became contaminated — water, a food the victim ate regularly, that kind of thing. She might have been felled by misfortune.

'But was it?' said the inspector.

Konrad remembered what his serpents had said. *Taint. Unclean.* 'No,' he said regretfully. 'My snakes do not think it.'

'They tend to know their business, there.' Alexander had Verinka's pipe laid on the table before him, and his own in his hand. The latter was lit, expelling a vaguely sweet-smelling smoke into the air. Taking a puff, Alexander added, 'This pipe is an unusual piece. I may be able to find out where it came from.'

'You think it of recent craftsmanship?'

'That or immaculately well-kept. But it is not so expensive a piece as to deserve such care, one would think.'

Konrad gladly ceded that task to the inspector, he being the pipe enthusiast among them. And the contrast between Verinka's pipe and his own was illustrative by itself. The one, plain and well-loved to the point of being rather battered. The other gleaming, elaborate and pristine.

'If she *was* a smoker,' said Alexander. 'I don't suppose...?'

'Was that how she was poisoned?' Konrad thought. 'My knowledge of poisons is not as extensive as Nanda's — we'll ask her, presently — but I think it could be done. Not easily. The poison must be odourless, or else combined with a tobacco strong-smelling enough to mask its scent. And also ingestible via inhalation, but without causing any immediate reaction — coughing, etc — that might alert the victim to trouble. My main problem with the idea, though, is that we have testimony to the contrary, of sorts, and this pipe clearly has not been subjected to weeks or months of use.'

Alexander had liked the idea, for he seemed disappointed at having to relinquish it. 'Something mundane, then. Poisoned tea. Something in the butter.'

'Dull,' Konrad agreed, which provoked a sheepish grin from the inspector.

'I *should* have more respect,' he said.

'Occupational hazard.'

'It is, rather. Ah.' He looked up as a knock came at his door. 'Enter.'

A youngish police constable came in, stocky and fresh-faced, pale-haired and wreathed in an almost palpable air of deference. Surprised, Konrad soon concluded that the young man's manner was derived more from admiration than intimidation, for he looked upon Inspector Nuritov with a shade of awe. 'Sir,' he said. 'We've found the house.'

'Good,' said the inspector crisply. 'Has anyone been there yet?'

'We thought you might like to be on the scene immediately yourself, sir.'

'And I shall!' said the inspector, rising from his chair with alacrity.

Konrad took a shrewd guess that officers of Nuritov's level were not always so eager to do the legwork. Perhaps that was one of the qualities that won him respect.

'Have you finished with your other assignments, Karyavin?'

'Of course, sir.'

'Then you'll come with us.'

Karyavin looked quietly but profoundly gratified.

But then the word *us* registered, and his gaze travelled to Konrad. Bemusement.

'An associate,' said the inspector. 'Mr. Savast has an Eye.'

'Yes, sir.'

'For detail, you understand.'

'Yes, sir.'

Amused, Konrad fleetingly regretted that he would never have an admiring trainee of his own. But only briefly. Young men were rash

— he'd been one himself not so long ago, after all — and he had as many responsibilities as he could fairly manage already.

Still, as he made his greetings to young Karyavin and graciously permitted him to follow first in Alexander's train, he could not help feeling a moment's attraction to the idea.

Hold, though. Did Tasha count?

Spirits *above,* no. Tasha wouldn't know deference if she drowned in it.

Smothering a laugh, Konrad stepped into Alexander's sturdy and serviceable police cab, resisting an unusual temptation to have Eetapi tweak the young constable's ear.

Verinka Tarasovna's place of residence answered most of Konrad's expectations. Years of observation stood him in good stead when it came to such judgements. He could usually assess a person's place in society and approximate degree of wealth to a nicety, by studying such clues as the way they dressed, the style of their hair or beard, and the ornaments (if any) they wore.

Not always, of course. Some were deceptive. Some were deliberately misleading, like Konrad's own gentry-gear. Anybody would take him for a gentleman born and bred, which he wasn't.

Anyway. Verinka had lived on the edge of the city of Ekamet, nowhere salubrious but nowhere meagre either. House-proud, she: front door and window-frames freshly painted, her garden ordered and well-tended. Two storeys only, but the house was wide enough, and long: she had several rooms.

Konrad took note of the house's location, that being nowhere near Polik Street. Had it been her first visit to that locale, or had it been a regular habit of hers?

In either case, why?

The inspector led the way inside. The door was unlocked, and the rooms beyond — furnished with neatness, propriety and a spectacular lack of imagination — were occupied by more of his men.

'Anything, much?' said he cheerfully.

'Not yet, sir,' answered a subordinate, older than Karyavin, and stout. He, too, cast a curious glance Konrad's way, but Alexander did not trouble himself to explain or introduce his "associate" again, and the man (perhaps wisely) chose not to question it.

Surveying Verinka's space, Konrad felt a mild depression of the spirits. *Cold,* and unnecessarily so, for nothing suggested she was too poor to afford heating. But the embedded chill suggested no fire had been lit in that house in weeks, if ever. The place was spotless, as though someone sought to eradicate every sign of human habitation. And then there were the colours of it, or lack thereof. Dull white. Insipid grey. Beige. Joyless.

Not a happy woman, perhaps? Or merely unimaginative.

'No smoking paraphernalia, I suppose?' said Konrad, with perhaps a trace of diffidence. Alexander had never before taken him along on official police business; he was more in the habit of conducting such investigations himself, and relaying the news to Konrad later. Was it presumptuous of Konrad to question his men?

The inspector reacted not at all, however, seeming absorbed in a survey of Verinka's scant collection of books, arranged in a sorry little stack upon a pine shelf constructed with an almost brutal precision. After a moment's hesitation, the stout police officer replied, 'Tobacco, and the like? No, we haven't found anything like that.'

Alexander, absently, nodded.

Nice to have confirmation.

'Karyavin,' said Alexander. 'Anyone talked to the neighbours yet?'

'Not yet, sir.'

'Off you go then, please. I want to know about her habits. Whether she was close to anybody. Anything about her personal life we can get. And whether she had reason to go anywhere near Polik Street.'

'Sir.' Karyavin touched his hat, almost a salute, and took himself off.

'He's good,' Alexander said to Konrad. 'Natural talent. Knows just the right questions to ask, and good at putting people at their ease.'

Long before Karyavin might reasonably be expected to return, there came a knock at the door, an impatient *rat-tat* suggestive of someone in no way doubtful of their right of entry. And in a hurry, besides.

'Allow me,' murmured the inspector, and with his pipe clamped between his teeth he yanked open the door, interrupting the visitor mid-knock.

'Oh,' said the visitor, blinking in befuddlement at the array of strangers before him. Enlightenment was not long in dawning, and he stepped back, his face falling into a mask of dismay. 'Police?'

'I'm afraid so,' said Alexander.

'Verinka is…?'

'I'm afraid so,' said Alexander again.

Konrad watched the new arrival's expressions carefully, for unless he missed his guess, this must be the brother. The same one Verinka had accused? His features bore a more than passing similarity to his sister's, though he was larger of frame — rather fat, even. He had the same brown hair, and was dressed at a similar level of affluence. He had none of his sister's neatness, though, for his dark brown coat was rumpled and stained, and his boots filthy.

He *did* appear genuinely upset at the news, though not much surprised. And judging from the tears welling, he had jumped — accurately enough — to the conclusion of her demise. A police presence in her house might denote a number of things besides that.

Alexander, though, had the situation well in hand.

'Inspector Nuritov,' said he, stepping back to usher the man inside. He removed the pipe from his mouth at last and stood holding it, watching the stranger keenly. 'You are a relative, I take it?'

'I am her brother,' answered the man.

'Tsevar Tarasovich—'

'—Manin. Yes. Forgive me.' Tsevar dragged a dirty handkerchief from a pocket, and mopped at his eyes. 'We were close,' he sobbed.

'I am sorry for your loss,' said Alexander, and managed to sound as though he meant it. Probably he did. 'You knew she was ill?'

A guess on the inspector's part, but a correct one, for Tsevar nodded. 'For months, she had been complaining of tiredness and aches, sickness. She *would* go out, regardless, though I begged her to use the carriage…she said that walking was good for her. I did not think so. Day by day, she grew weaker, and the doctors could do nothing. No one knew what ailed her.'

'So you came to check on her,' said Alexander with gentle sympathy. 'What a terrible shock for you.'

'Yes.' A few ideas seemed at last to filter through to Tsevar, for he looked hard at the inspector through reddened eyes, and his gaze then travelled to the other police officer occupied some way down the passage, and at last to Konrad. 'But what could bring the police here? And… who are you, sir?'

The latter question being inevitably directed at Konrad, he bowed. 'I work with the police,' he said, without troubling to give his name.

Tsevar's eyes narrowed. '*You?*' He took in the vision of gentility Konrad made in his tall hat and fashionable coat, clearly disbelieving.

'He is quite useful,' Alexander said mildly. 'And it was he, in fact, who discovered what had become of your sister.'

This distraction gambit paid off, for the bereaved brother fell to questioning the inspector as to his sister's fate. While Alexander explained the circumstances, Konrad quietly withdrew to the kitchen. If Verinka had been poisoned over a period of months, she may well have been imbibing the stuff in her own house. And in that case, there could be traces of it in her kitchen.

Verinka's scrupulous, almost obsessive neatness helped him greatly, for he encountered a space with nothing out of place, and no clutter. Everything here had its designated purpose. He examined the jars of dried herbs and one or two spices lined up upon a humble shelf over the plain pine sideboard, and saw nothing untoward. The inspector's men had already been through them, he guessed, for they were a little knocked about. Nonetheless he went through them himself, removing the glass stoppers and taking a slow inhalation of the contents. Diverse odours filled his nose, but nothing that seemed out of place. He returned them, knowing that Alexander's people had doubtless taken samples and would see that they were tested.

He did not think the poison was secreted in the jars, though. He had a nose for such things (as well as an Eye, in Alexander's opinion. Perhaps he was a useful person to have about, at that).

A simple tin tea caddy sat in a corner, but this, too, apparently contained nothing but dried tea leaves. Verinka did not keep much food in her house, by all appearances; the place was too small to have a dedicated larder, and the shelved, walk-in recess that served the purpose instead was rather bare.

He returned to the front room, disappointed of discovery. It was still possible that Verinka had somehow been buying and consuming tainted produce of some sort or another, but if so, whatever it might be was not presently in the house.

Alexander would set his men to enquiring where Verinka bought her food, and from whom, and how it was procured. They would do the dull work of investigating these suppliers in search of something out of place. Konrad was more interested in who might conceivably be behind such an organised plan; the police might uncover a name in the course of these enquiries, but they may also come up dry.

For Verinka might never have encountered the poison in her own home. It was just as likely that the stuff had been administered somewhere else, by someone that she met regularly. And there Konrad would focus his own efforts.

Beginning with the brother, whose grief might have been copious but might, for all of that, have been feigned.

'I hope you will forgive me for asking, sir,' Alexander was saying as Konrad re-entered the room. 'But the processes must be gone through, you understand.'

'Of course,' said Tsevar. His eyes were dry again.

'Well,' and the inspector's tone became rather apologetic, 'One or two of your sister's neighbours have remembered that— well, that she did not quite appear to trust you. You *did* say the two of you were close?'

'What?' said Tsevar, assuming a creditable expression of outrage. 'Of course she trusted me. We saw each other every week. I was her *brother*. She knew how I cared for her.'

'You see, sir, she seems to have thought you might even have been inclined to harm her,' said Alexander, more apologetic than ever. 'Perhaps her illness made her unreasonably suspicious, but—'

'That is absurd,' said Tsevar, his mottled face turning redder. 'She cannot possibly have said any such thing. Whoever made such an accusation is a liar.'

Konrad gave his friend full credit for finding a way of asking about Verinka's belief in a way that might seem plausible to Tsevar, but he could hardly explain that it was *she* and not a neighbour who had accused him — after her death. He was obliged to abandon the line of questioning, but before he could embark upon some other direction of enquiry, Konrad quietly intruded.

'You met every week?' he said. 'That is dedicated care indeed.'

'More often, since she became ill,' said Tsevar, the angry flush not yet faded from his features. 'We have met once a week at a luncheon-club for years, and in recent months I have also been here very often to support her in her illness. I took her to the doctors. I did *everything* I could.'

Which probably explained what she'd been doing in Polik Street,

Konrad thought, for a pre-eminent physician had premises there. A cab had brought her, but she had fallen before she'd reached the doctor's door. 'Which luncheon-club was that?' said Konrad.

'It is held at the Larch eating-house. You may ask anybody there that you like. They will have seen us, every week. Why should I have done that if I did not care for her? And why could I possibly have wanted to harm her, even if capable of it?'

Konrad privately agreed with him on that score; as yet, they had no idea of a motive.

Except for one possible thing.

'Were you aware of anybody in your sister's life of the name of Kristov?' he said.

Tsevar's face darkened still further. 'That miscreant. If anybody harmed her, you should take a close look at *him*.'

'Ah, we will certainly consider it,' said Konrad. 'And who is he?'

'He has been courting her these past six months and more. Verinka always said she did not wish to marry, and she never did, but lately I began to think he had persuaded her to change her mind.'

'And you didn't approve?'

'No. Who could? He is beneath her. A mere grubby, upstart— he has *charm,* that I will allow, but nothing else. I do not know what Verinka saw in him.'

'Do you know what he saw in Verinka?' Konrad suggested. He meant no insult, only she was of middle-age and no particular beauty, and nothing he had seen suggested that she was in possession of an especially sparkling personality. Or of any great wealth, either. None of the usual things, in short, that might encourage a man to court a woman comfortable with her spinsterhood with so much assiduity.

'They met in the *street,* would you believe, on one of Verinka's dashed walks,' said Tsevar, without precisely answering the question. 'Nothing could be more improper.

'You do not happen to know which street?' Konrad said quickly, but Tsevar shook his head.

'What can that possibly matter?' he said impatiently. 'She is dead, and it is *his* doing. I would lay my life on it.'

Kristov. Soft words, echoing somewhere inside Konrad's head. *My Kristov. Poor Kristov.*

Verinka? Said Konrad. *Tell me about Kristov.*

But she did not answer.

Konrad was left to secure the rest of Kristov's name from her indignant brother, and the despised suitor's place of residence. Tsevar took his leave soon afterwards, destined, he said, for the morgue. Someone was wanted to confirm Verinka's identity, for the official procedures must be gone through; Alexander could not write in his report that the victim had confirmed her own identity through direct speech with a ghostspeaker.

Karyavin returned with tidings which might have interested Konrad a little sooner, but now could achieve little but confirming some of the things Tsevar had said. Her weekly appointment with her brother had been a known thing among her neighbours, as had Kristov's pursuit of her. Konrad was interested to hear that her neighbours had not liked the look of the man, either, though none had met him directly.

'She wasn't much for socialising with any of them, sir,' said Karyavin. 'None of 'em had much speech with her, it seems. But they watched who came to the door, and who she went off with. Mostly this brother, and the one who has to be this Kristov fellow. Black hair and beard, they said. Dressed like a merchant or something.'

'You mean prosperous?' said Alexander.

'In a manner of speaking, sir. Didn't look so fancy as to look out of place in these parts, but they thought he must be in business of some sort. So I take it he isn't poor.'

Konrad wondered, then, why Tsevar had called him a grubby upstart. 'What do we know about the family?' he asked of no one in particular. 'Tsevar has some airs, but there's nothing here to suggest Verinka was so superior to a reasonably well-off man of business. Were they wealthier, once?'

'A good question,' Alexander said. 'One we'll look into.'

'Might be why the lady scorned to spend time with her neighbours,' Karyavin offered. 'They did talk like she was a bit aloof. Not that they disliked her, exactly. Said she was always civil, if they happened to encounter one another on the street. But distant. One or two said she was a snob.'

'Conceivable,' murmured Alexander, and noted something in his ever-present pocket book. 'Right, lots to look into. Savast, has Nanda been consulted?'

'Not yet. Shortly to be so.' The inspector was after what manner of poison might have done for Verinka, and that was an important

112

question. Poisons were sold in the city, but they were under strict regulation; purchasing enough of something to kill a woman over a period of months was no easy task. Konrad doubted anyone had been careless enough to buy from the same shops, over and over again. People in Nanda's trade tended to report such purchases to the police, if they were not known to the trader, for while small amounts of some poisons could be beneficial in some cases, large amounts never were.

But he wanted her expertise. What might produce the symptoms experienced by Verinka? How hard was it to get hold of? And how might it be administered without either her or (supposing him to be innocent) her protective brother detecting it?

He never minded an excuse to see Nanda (not that he really needed an excuse, these days). He did quietly hope, though, that he would not also have to pay a visit to Danil Dubin, her closest friend in the trade. Try though he might, he had never managed to overcome his irrational dislike of the timid young man.

'Karyavin,' said Alexander. 'That leaves you and me to track down this Kristov. And perhaps to look into this luncheon-club.'

Karyavin glowed. 'Yes, sir.'

Alexander paused to consider. 'And I think we will set Tasha on the question of illegal poison trades.'

The inspector's undead police ward did seem to have an unhealthy talent for — and questionable degree of experience with — the various underworld activities of the city, that was true. Shady little creature, Tasha. She intrigued Konrad immensely.

Konrad excused himself, and took himself off to Nanda's shop.

3

Upon entering Nanda's fragrant shop, redolent with the aromas of the dried plants she stored and sold, he was greeted not by Nanda herself but by Weveroth. He sat — no, no, *she,* this was officially a lady monkey now — in the centre of Nan's scrupulously clean counter, her long golden tail wrapped around her feet. She sat tall, like a little sentinel, and gave Konrad what he would swear was the evil eye as he walked in.

'Wevey,' Konrad greeted, and held out a few fingers for her to reacquaint herself with.

Weveroth high-tailed it through the rear door into Nanda's workroom, without a second glance at Konrad.

'Oh!' said Nanda a moment later, quite as though the monkey had told her who had come to call. She came straight through, drying her hands on a strip of towel, and beamed at Konrad in a manner he found more than sufficient to make up for Weveroth's lack of interest. 'I thought you'd be at your club today.'

'And I *almost* made it there.' Konrad leaned casually upon the counter, trying not to too obviously scan the sealed pots and jars arrayed upon shelves all around the room. 'Something came up.'

'Something distasteful, and more closely involving a dead body than either of us would prefer?'

'Right. We have a dead lady, almost certainly poisoned.'

'And here I thought you stopped by just to see me.' Nanda's smile faded.

'I would have,' Konrad said. 'Later. I'm just earlier than planned.'

'You only love me for my esoteric know-how.'

'Creepy know-how, too. Don't forget creepy.'

'Knowing how to kill people with plants is creepy? Pot, meet kettle.'

'Yes, but we knew *I* was creepy. Comes with the job.'

'Upon that point I cannot disagree. Let me have the details, then.' The humour faded from Nanda's face as she transformed into the capable apothecary, poison-mistress and shopkeeper Konrad had first known.

He related everything the Order had concluded during their examination, together with the few clues he had gleaned from the appearance of Verinka's corpse, and the scant facts they had thus far uncovered about her life. Nanda listened without interruption.

'Well,' she said when he had drawn his narration to a close. 'I do have a possible answer for you, but you aren't going to like it.'

Konrad sighed. 'All right. I can take it.'

'There is a poison I know of that fits your requirements. It's known as widow weed in the trade.'

'That's... an unusual name.'

'Bear with me. It used to be a staple of the trade some years ago, because in small doses it is said to be effective for those kinds of stomach ailments ladies tend to suffer from about once a month.'

'Nicely put.'

'Yes. But it fell out of favour. It happened that quite a lot of women began dropping dead after some kind of unidentifiable sickness. It was thought to be a dangerous infectious disease, because it sometimes happened among whole groups of friends. It eventually emerged that they'd all been using this remedy. Recommending it to each other, you know.'

'Um. That's horrific.'

'Rather. What happened after *that* was fun, too, because a few put-upon married ladies began using it to solve quite a different problem.'

'Hence widow weed.'

'Quite. The trade and use of it's now banned in Assevan, and Marja, and probably beyond. Which is the part I think you aren't going to like. It's many years since it was last possible to buy widow weed anywhere. So how did your poisoner get hold of it?'

'You're sure it has to be that one? It couldn't be something else?'

'It's not impossible, of course, but I would say with reasonable certainty that it's widow weed. There are other poisons that might be relevant, but no others that produce quite those symptoms, or which take weeks or months to kill the victim. So undetectably, too. Blacklung might do it, but it causes horrific coughing, hence the name—'

'It's all right,' Konrad interrupted. 'I trust your judgement. Different question. Where might a person get hold of widow weed, if not from a trader? Is it a black-market thing?'

'I can't say for sure that you couldn't get it illegally,' Nan replied. 'I... don't know. It is a native to Assevan, but it's not a plant that ever grew in any abundance, to my knowledge, despite being called a weed. It takes some effort to find, and harvest, and I doubt anyone's gone to the trouble much since it was banned.'

'Banning something often makes it more desirable,' Konrad pointed out.

'Yes, but it used to be popular as a remedy, not a poison. Once people stopped using it to treat stomach cramps — because it was incredibly unsafe — demand for it virtually died out. And I doubt there are enough unhappy wives with a murderous streak to make it worth anyone's time in securing a supply for a black market venture.'

'I see your point. Or disapproving brothers.'

Nanda shook her head. 'It can't have been him. Or at least, not for the reason she claimed.'

'You're sure of that how?'

'The logic doesn't fit. Think about it. Whether he and his sister were genuinely close or not, if Tsevar hated this Kristov enough to kill someone over it, he'd have killed Kristov. Why kill Verinka? How could that ever make sense?'

The same thought had crossed Konrad's mind, but remembering the certainty with which Verinka had named both her supposed murderer and his motive, he hadn't been willing to dismiss the idea out of hand. But Nanda was right. No part of it held any water.

'Let me hear the symptoms again,' Nanda said. 'Just to be sure. No coughing?'

'I haven't specifically asked whether she was coughing, but no one mentioned it. Her brother said she'd been experiencing unwonted lethargy, complained of aches and pains in her head and limbs. Nothing to cause all that much alarm; no one seems to have thought she was in any real danger of her life.'

Nanda considered, but shook her head. 'I still can't think of an alternative that fits. I think widow weed is your poison. It produces just the effects you describe, prompting a few extra visits to the doctor in its victims, but no great alarm for his or her life — and then, after some weeks or months of regular doses, fatal heart failure occurs. But I can't imagine how anybody got hold of it, especially at this time of year. I'm afraid I cannot help you with that problem.'

Konrad, on an impulse, kissed her cheek. 'You've helped a great deal already. Thank you.'

Nanda rewarded him with a quizzical look. 'What next, then?'

'One more question. Is widow weed ingested or inhaled?'

'Ingested. Women used to make tea out of it, but you could also put it in food easily enough.'

That absolutely dismissed Alexander's admittedly intriguing idea about the pipe. 'Thanks, Nan. Coming for dinner?'

'Will you be home for dinner? You don't time-keep too well when you're on a case.'

'If I fail to make it home in time, you can have Mrs. Aristova's delectables all to yourself.'

That brought the smile back to Nanda's face. 'They're nowhere near as much fun if I can't press too many of them on you.'

'Life is suffering.' Konrad tipped his hat, and made his retreat. 'I'll be... somewhere.'

'Be careful,' Nanda called.

This being unlike her, Konrad paused. 'I'm always careful.'

'No, you aren't,' Nanda retorted. 'You are reckless and foolish and heedless. But you can't afford to be that way anymore.'

'I'll be careful,' Konrad promised, faithfully enough.

'Either that or you'll be dead. For always. I don't know about you, but I know which of the two *I* would prefer.'

'Am I reckless?' Konrad said an hour later, having found his way to the Larch eating-house. Alexander was still there, with Karyavin, though the rest of his retinue had apparently busied themselves elsewhere. He found the inspector stationed in the front hall, unlit pipe in hand. The ever-eager Karyavin was just visible disappearing through a door into what was probably the dining parlour.

'Reckless?' said Alexander, emerging from a reverie. 'Somewhat.'

'I was hoping for a no.'

'Nanda say something?' said Alexander shrewdly. 'She does have a talent for getting straight to the heart of things.'

Konrad clutched at his chest. '*Straight* to the heart, with a perfect rapier-strike.'

'She is an extraordinary woman.'

'Quite. She says it's most likely widow weed, but cannot say where it was procured.'

Alexander listened quietly as Konrad relayed Nanda's opinion, and ended by putting the stem of his pipe back in his mouth. He inhaled. Konrad wondered whether he noticed that no smoke came pouring out. 'I was hoping for a clearer answer,' he conceded.

'Me too. It may be that our poisoner's of a certain age, though. Might have to be, to remember widow weed.'

'Could be. Nanda knew of it, of course, and she isn't elderly.'

'No, but it's her profession.'

Alexander conceded the point with a nod. 'As to how it was got hold of, well, it might be something as simple as an old jar forgotten at the back of somebody's store cupboard. Such things deteriorate with time, of course, but might still be potent enough to have the desired effect.'

'That, or someone who knows what they are doing planned this back in the growing season, and managed to find enough wild widow weed to lay in a supply.'

'It could also be that.'

'How did you get on here?' Konrad took his first real look at the Larch eating-house, and found it contrary to his half-formed expectations. The place was no passable eatery for purse-poor social climbers, as he had (perhaps snobbishly) assumed. The house may be of modest proportions but it was sumptuously decorated. Expensive figured wallpaper met fine oak wainscoting halfway down the walls; crystal sconces and chandeliers cast a tasteful, clear light around the room; oil paintings hung in ornate frames, echoing the carvings gracing the not-too-comfortable furniture. Either the club had ambitions, or it was already patronised by a wealthier and more superior class of customer than Konrad had considered. In which case, what had Verinka and her brother been doing here every single week?

'I have mortally offended the cook and the entire kitchen staff,' Alexander answered.

'That was fast work.'

'Yes, well. Police inspector I may be, but to so much as imply that they might have been serving contaminated food to any customer whatsoever was a mortal insult, I'm afraid. I've sent Karyavin in to try again. He's good at this sort of thing.'

Alexander was himself good at "this sort of thing", Konrad knew, being mild-mannered and sympathetic enough to stay on most people's good side. The chef of this handsome establishment must be an artiste of fine sensibilities. Or just a grouch. 'While we're hiding out here,' Konrad began—

'I am not hiding,' Alexander interrupted. 'I have paused here to think.'

'Whenever you've finished thinking,' Konrad continued smoothly. 'I've a notion it might be a good idea to consult the visitor register, if they have such a thing. Or the membership lists.'

Never slow to catch on, Alexander said: 'Ah. You think the mysterious Kristov might have been a member, too?'

'If he was making it his business to stick to Verinka, it seems possible. And the neighbours suggested she went out regularly, more than once a week. Yes, she was an inveterate walker, it seems, but she was also increasingly ill. Perhaps she had a strong reason to be going out.'

'Like meeting the suitor she seems to have favoured.' Alexander, energised, set off in search of the club's manager, with Konrad close behind.

They found the man in the dining-parlour, engaged in some manner of dispute with a waiter. The club would soon open, Konrad judged, the luncheon-hour nearing. He could not imagine what the manager could possibly find fault with; the place was gleaming, spotless and sumptuous. He looked up as they approached, his gaze travelling straight past the inspector with a total lack of interest.

It settled upon Konrad, and his eyes brightened.

Definitely a place with ambitions, Konrad thought.

Alexander went through his usual courtesies, introduced himself and his errand, and politely requested a look at the club's membership records, but the man gave this speech scant attention. 'My members?' he said when the inspector had finished. 'Goodness, no. That information cannot be made public. Our members' privacy is of paramount importance to the Larch Club.'

'And one of your members has been killed,' said Alexander, losing some of his politeness. 'In suspicious circumstances which, I am afraid to say, may relate to your club. It is of paramount importance to *me* to ascertain who else regularly dined here.'

That got the manager's attention, but in no helpful way. He drew himself up to his admittedly superior height, dark brows winging down over a thunderous forehead, and stared down the inspector as though he were some manner of social inferior begging for a table. 'You must be mistaken, sir,' said he with withering scorn. 'It cannot possibly have had anything to do with my club.'

'I wonder,' Konrad mildly interrupted, 'whether you might remember the lady in question? Verinka Tarasovna.'

The manager transferred his frown to Konrad, who summoned his most supercilious air in response. The frown altered. Less offended, more… disapproving. His mouth made a moue of disdain.

Or was it disdain? For he said immediately: 'Madam Tarasovna is dead?'

'She passed away this morning.'

'That is a great pity,' said the manager.

'A long-standing member, was she?'

'She had been coming to us for the past year. Perhaps a little more. She was always very welcome.'

'She ate here weekly with her brother, I understand?'

'They were so good as to honour us with their regular custom.'

'Did she ever meet anybody else here?'

'She had the honour of sometimes dining here with—' The manager, becoming aware, perhaps, that he was being obliging, broke off, and the frown returned. 'Are you perhaps thinking of becoming a member, sir?'

'I might,' said Konrad, with a faint smile. 'If I am sufficiently pleased.'

The moue returned. 'I do not make a habit of indiscretion, sir.'

'But you are helping a police investigation pertaining to one of your beloved members, so I am sure you can make an exception today.'

The manager gave a barely perceptible sigh, and fractionally unbent. 'She was occasionally seen in company with Mr. Balandin.' The manager uttered this name with a special kind of reverence, and by the look of him only barely restrained himself from offering a bow to the mere idea of the man.

'Would that be Mr. *Kristov* Balandin?' said Alexander.

'Among our most esteemed members.'

'Well-dressed?' Konrad said, with some scepticism.

'He is a man of excellent taste.'

'Free with money, then.' It had to be either the appearance he presented in the lunch-club's dining parlour, or his readiness to throw enormous sums at his meals. If he had been a person of great social consequence in Ekamet, Konrad would have heard of him.

The manager gave a cough. 'He likes to dine well.'

Yes, then. 'Is Mr. Balandin likely to be dining here again soon?'

'Would you be wanting to meet him here, sir?' The manager's disapproval had gone, vanished in place of something more like cunning.

Konrad resigned himself to the inevitable. 'I am greatly desirous of doing so,' he said, not without some truth.

'We shall be delighted to have you as a member, sir.'

'No doubt.'

'Mr. Balandin frequently joins us on Fridays.'

'Then I shall be here on Friday.'

Karyavin returned half an hour later, munching upon something sweet-smelling, and joined Konrad and Alexander in the dining-parlour.

'I see you've been getting on better with the cook than I did,' said the inspector, peering at his subordinate over his menu.

Karyavin gave a sheepish grin. 'Reminds me of my aunt.'

'Very well. What did you find out?'

'They do run a tight ship down there, sir. Hard to see how anyone could have consistently tainted Miss Tarasovna's food. It *might* have been one of the kitchen staff, but I think it more likely to be a waiter. If anybody.'

Alexander nodded. 'More precision that way. Have you talked to the waiters?'

'Yes. Nobody stood out as a suspect.'

'All right. Ask around about the mighty Mr. Balandin, would you? He seems to be properly lionised around here.'

'Certainly, sir.' Karyavin gazed with some curiosity at the spectacle of his police inspector settling in for a comfortable lunch with the picture of a fine gentleman Konrad presented, and wisely said nothing.

His face, however, said enough.

'It's not about the food,' Alexander said after a moment. 'We're here to observe the guests.'

'And the waiters,' Konrad added.

'Certainly, sir.' Karyavin excused himself and went off upon the inspector's errands.

For some moments there was silence.

Then, 'I can't decide whether you are wonderful or terrible for my credibility,' said the inspector.

'Some of both. Come, we *do* have to eat, and I do want an opportunity to get the measure of the waiters. And to see whether either Tsevar or Kristov shows up. Don't you?'

'Since it seems our Mr. Kristov Balandin also made himself regular opportunities to feed Verinka, yes.'

'Quite so. If she wasn't poisoned at home, then the likelihood is that one of her two lunch-companions did it. Possibly with the assistance of a hard-up waiter.'

The Larch, said Verinka suddenly. *I will have the salmon.*

Verinka? Konrad said sharply.

And a glass of wine.

'She liked to order the salmon,' Konrad reported. 'And she seems to have been a tippler.'

'Ah!' The inspector's face cleared. 'It *was* a good idea to dine here.'

Konrad ordered the salmon. As the waiter retreated, he allowed his spirit-sight to fade in, just enough to detect any unusual presences. He did not see Verinka; not enough of her spirit remained for so much coherence, it seemed.

Alexander emerged from a cloud of thought. 'I wonder if you could hide widow weed in a glass of wine?'

Remembering what Nan had said, Konrad replied: 'I haven't a doubt of it.'

4

The inspector soon dispatched one of his men to take another look at Verinka's house. His instructions were to look for signs of regular drinking, and in particular for any bottles of wine, opened or unopened, that might linger in the home.

There were none. She did not even own wine-glasses, the man reported. She drank only at the luncheon-club, it seemed.

Konrad hoped Alexander's investigations into the waiters would be productive of something. If the widow weed had been administered in her wine, someone had availed themselves of a weekly opportunity to dose her with it, and how better to do so than by bribing a waiter? Any old story might be employed to explain it. Stubborn woman refusing to take her medication. Concerned brother/friend. That was how Konrad would have done it, anyway.

He himself was growing ever more intrigued by the hazy picture emerging of the mysterious Kristov. None of the facts about him made sense with one another. Verinka, supposedly a contented spinster, had nonetheless encouraged Kristov Balandin as a suitor, and had been doing so, apparently, for some time. But they had not been engaged. She'd known her brother disapproved, so strongly as to suspect him of murdering her over it; but that hadn't discouraged her from meeting him.

Meanwhile, Tsevar had described the man as an upstart. But if the manager was to be believed, Kristov Balandin was very well-heeled. Why, then, did Tsevar consider him an upstart? And on what grounds did he disapprove of the man's courtship of his sister? Few brothers would object to a man of means and influence proposing to marry into the family.

If he *had* intended to marry her. There was the lack of engagement to consider. Had he been shy of asking her? Had she refused? Had either of them had marriage in mind at all?

Perhaps Tsevar disapproved because their relationship had been less... formal. But if that were the case, he'd likely have said something to that effect.

Friday was two days away. Konrad intended to be ensconced at the Larch Club promptly at noon, awaiting the arrival of this much-feted man.

In the meantime, he had thoughts of pursuing Tsevar Tarasovich Manin and squeezing him for further information. But before he could embark upon this project, Tasha barrelled in to Alexander's office like a tiny, dark whirlwind, finding the inspector engaged in scrawling hasty notes, and Konrad leafing through a stack of vaguely relevant reports delivered by Alexander's men.

'It's widow weed,' she said breathlessly, whipping off her black cap and collapsing heavily into a vacant chair.

'Nanda thought so, too,' said Konrad.

Tasha deflated a little. 'How repulsive you are sometimes, Konrad.'

'I'm afraid I was born that way. Did you find out anything else? We are still in the dark as to how anybody got hold of any.'

Upon these words, Tasha brightened again, and sat up. 'No easy task, is it? I asked around. Nobody's heard of it in years. No one seemed interested — I was pretending to be in the market for some, you understand. Couldn't find out that anyone else has been trying to buy any in years, either. It's a dead trade.'

'We sort of assumed as much,' said Konrad.

'*But.*' Tasha glowered.

Konrad meekly fell silent.

'But. When I switched to the role of a seller... well, nothing much was different to be honest, nobody wants to buy that rubbish either, it's worthless. Hardly surprising. Who wants a medicine that can kill you? Who wants a poison that takes weeks to work? Most people are in a lot more of a hurry. After all, if you've decided to kill someone you sort of want it out of the way, don't you? Over and done with, quick-*crunch,* so you can get on with enjoying the rewards and pretending it never happened. So anyway—'

'Tasha.' Alexander looked up from his notes, and directed a quelling look at his ward.

'Just enjoying the spotlight a bit, sir. It's easy to be overlooked when you're this short.'

'Nonetheless, could you perhaps move it along a bit?'

Tasha gave a salute. 'I gave up on the traders, but decided on a hunch to try the, er, women's facilities—'

'The what?' Konrad interrupted.

Tasha's brows went up. 'What exactly is the question?'

'What are women's facilities?'

She rolled her eyes, and gave an exaggerated sigh. 'Picture this. You're a lady of questionable repute wanting to not get pregnant. Or you're a respectable female who *is* pregnant under conditions where you'd rather not be. Or you're simply so destroyed with pain every time your cycle comes to its inevitable close that you'd genuinely risk death in order to make it go away. Do you think your above-board, prim-and-proper apothecaries cater to those kinds of problems?'

'So there's an underworld for, er, women's troubles too?'

'Konrad, sometimes your naivety astounds me.'

Konrad shifted in his seat under Tasha's skewering stare, and found himself with nothing to say.

The only thing that could somewhat lessen his discomfort was the realisation that Alexander, too, was trying his best to hide a betraying flush behind a sheaf of notes.

'So *anyway*,' Tasha continued. 'If anybody in the city might be harbouring an illegal supply of widow weed it's probably one of those. No?'

'Yes,' said Konrad, sitting up. 'I'd never have thought of that.'

'Obviously.'

Konrad blushed. 'So, er, did any of them have…?'

'A huge jar of widow weed stashed in a dark room somewhere? Why, yes. Yes they did.'

'And has anybody lately bought any?'

'A few people. All of them female.'

Konrad blinked. 'So not Tsevar or Kristov?'

'Not unless they sent someone else to do the purchasing for them, which they might have. Those places don't deal much with men.'

'Did you get any names?'

'Kind of. People aren't in a hurry to give out their real name when they're procuring illegal medicine, for some reason.'

'Tasha—'

'I have a description. Will that do? All the women who've bought widow weed in the past year were known to the seller. They showed up regularly, took the herb under close supervision, no mysteries there. Except one. About six months ago, a lady procured a large supply of the stuff in one go, supposedly for medicinal use, but she refused any further assistance. They never saw her again after that.'

'It didn't occur to them that she intended to cause harm with it?'

Tasha grinned. 'They described her as middle-aged, nicely dressed, polite. Kindly. Can you picture anyone less likely to be pegged as a murderer?'

Perfect choice of emissary, then, and very clever. 'That's good, Tasha,' Konrad said. 'Thank you. Did they remember any physical characteristics?'

'Hair colour, brown. Pale skin. Medium height. Nothing very helpful.'

'That could almost be a description of Verinka herself,' Alexander mused.

'You mean maybe she was self-medicating, and her death was an accident?' Konrad frowned. 'I have to trust the serpents on this.'

'Probably you're right to,' Alexander said. 'But it's fair to bear the possibility in mind. Not everyone has supernatural assistants; we have to rely on our own wits.'

'I'm not sure how reliable their "wits" are,' Konrad muttered. 'Their senses, though, I am not in the habit of questioning.'

Master, we are aware, said Ootapi snippily.

I know, the snakes are always listening. I owed you that one.

Konrad chose to take Ootapi's silence as either victory or assent.

'Of course,' said Alexander, 'it's not guaranteed that this woman is a person of interest here, or that the weed she purchased was the same stuff used to kill Verinka. But it looks like a likely fit. You've done well, Tasha.'

Tasha gave an ironic little half-bow from her seated position. 'Anytime, Inspector.'

Konrad stood up. 'Hopefully we'll have the means to trace this woman at some point. For now, I want to talk more to Tsevar. I have a feeling there's more he could have said about all this.'

But before he could get out of the room, a knock came upon the door and Karyavin came in.

'See that?' Konrad murmured to Tasha. 'That is how you're supposed to enter a room.'

Tasha ignored him.

Karyavin, Konrad was interested to note, held Verinka's odd filigree pipe in his hands. 'The dealers found one or two interesting things to say about this, sir.'

'Aha. The antiques fellows? What did they say?'

'There's one on the corner of the Verender that's an expert in pipes, sir. He had a good look at it. Said it's a fake.'

'A fake? A fake what?'

'Fake antique. It's been made after a traditional style, used to be popular maybe seventy, eighty years ago. Only it's of recent make. And he said there's something different about the style, but couldn't say why. See the thickness around the bowl? And there is some kind of opaque lacquer there that isn't needed.'

Alexander frowned fiercely at the pipe, as though doing so might cause it to surrender its secrets. 'He did not say what these alterations might be about?'

'He couldn't say, sir. Not without breaking it apart.'

'Right.' Alexander got up, taking the pipe off Karyavin. 'On the corner of Verender, you said?'

'Yes, sir.'

'Coming, Konrad? We're going to have a chat with this knowledgeable shopkeeper.'

'And have him smash valuable evidence to bits?'

'Something like that, yes. We need something definite, and if this is a freshly-made fake, I doubt anyone out there is going to miss it.'

The antiques expert turned out to be a diminutive man, slight of frame, with a quantity of flyaway grey hair and a hunched posture. But his eyes were bright and keen, and he appeared full of energy, greeting his visitors with apparent delight.

So engaging were the man's manners, Konrad felt faintly guilty for the nature of their errand. He was not about to gratify the man's evident hopes with a large purchase.

Then again, maybe he could. Later. A glance around revealed that he had a good eye for fine, unusual pieces.

'You spoke to one of my men a little while ago,' said the inspector, showing the pipe. 'About this. I understand you believe the design to have been changed?'

'Oh, yes. It's unmistakeable. If you'll excuse me for a moment...' The man spoke with a faint accent, Kayesiri perhaps. He wandered away into his shop, and came back after a few minutes with another pipe in his hands. A similar piece, though clearly old, streaked with the patina of ages. Rather more than seventy years old, Konrad guessed. The elegantly curved shape was the same, and it bore the same distinctive bowl, with a flaring rim. The filigree ornamentation, too, was an exact match for the pattern, near enough, but Konrad saw at once what Karyavin had meant. Verinka's pipe bore an extra ornament: a little circular nub at the base of the bowl, inexplicably gilded, and not in especially good taste. The lacquer thickly coated the filigree. Unnecessarily, even to Konrad's inexperienced eyes. The dealer pointed out all of these discrepancies with his quick, deft gestures. 'I do not understand why it has been done,' he concluded. 'Somebody wished to pretend that this is an old piece, clearly, but in that case why these changes?'

'I would like you to look more closely,' said the inspector.

'That will involve causing damage to the pipe.'

'So be it. I need to know what this pipe is for. We, er, received it from a lady who does not smoke, and had no possible use for such a piece.'

Tools were fetched, and the obliging dealer went to work. He scraped first at the lacquer, and examined the peelings under a magnifying lense. 'It is not a standard lacquer,' he mused. 'Something in it... it should not shine like that.'

'What of this bit, here?' Alexander pointed out the gilded section with a finger. Not a large space, in truth: perhaps a quarter of an inch across at most. But its presence in the pattern was anomalous, and it stood out.

'May I have your permission to break it open?' said the dealer.

'Please do.'

This procedure took a minute or two, for despite its lowly status as a fake the dealer treated it with exquisite care. He inserted a sharp implement into the base in two or three places, and prised.

The surface cracked and came away, and something fell out — something minuscule, but which nonetheless sparkled with a strange intensity.

Konrad drew in a breath.

'A diamond?' said the dealer, in puzzlement. 'That is...
unthinkable. To adorn a pipe with precious stones is not unheard of,
of course, but it is a wasteful practice and highly unusual. To inset a
diamond and then *conceal* it — ah! And that is the peculiarity with the
lacquer! It has a little dust in it, perhaps.'

'Dust?' said Konrad. 'You mean, derived from diamonds?'

'Yes, sir. It is not easy to produce, but by a determined man it may
be done. I do not, however, see why it would be in this instance. Of
what possible use is it? The dust is so sparse, scarcely any extra glitter
is imparted. It resembles ordinary lacquer, except by close
examination.'

Carefully, Konrad picked up the fallen diamond. It did not
deserve the designation of a stone, fairly, for it was too small, and a
mere jagged shard; not cut or worked. But why would it be, when its
purpose was not decorative?

The dealer may not know of any reason why a diamond might be
secreted in such an object, but Konrad could think of one. He let his
spirit-sight fade in, just for a moment, which was long enough to
confirm his suspicion.

The shard shone with a faint but distinct glow, pale as the moon,
and oddly flickering.

Serpents. What do you make of this?

He felt them draw nearer, felt it in the way his neck prickled and
goosebumps rose on his arms. *We have seen something of this sort before,*
said Ootapi.

Indeed we have, Konrad replied. *Is there much remaining here?*

Little, said Eetapi. *Now that the jewel is released, she will not linger long.*

The shard served as a trap, the dust as a net closing around it.
Konrad felt a flicker of anger, together with a powerful curiosity. A
clever scheme, bordering upon the diabolical. Just who had been
responsible for this?

He had to ignore Alexander's enquiring looks while they remained
in the shop. Only once they regained the street did he explain.

'It is a manner of soul-trap. Diamonds, you see, are receptive to
spirit energies; I don't believe anybody knows why, but spirits torn
asunder are terribly attracted to them. Sometimes. If they are
prepared for such.' By a ghostspeaker, typically, though some few

others occasionally displayed a similar knack with the mesmerising jewels. Konrad had encountered the scheme before, when an ambitious ghostspeaker had used an unusually enormous diamond to entrap a number of souls, both human and otherwise.

Which was a point of interest. The size of the diamond did matter; the human soul was complex, and in order to swallow an entire... *person*... a diamond of some magnitude was needed.

This tiny sliver of a gem could never manage it. But it could catch, and preserve, a few *shreds*, as his serpents put it.

'This is why Verinka has been still floating about,' Konrad continued. 'Or, bits of her. She was carrying the thing around. Doing so must have somewhat attuned it to her, if it wasn't especially handed to her for this very purpose, which is possible. Either way, when she died, some severed bits and pieces of her spirit were absorbed.'

'Clever,' Alexander agreed. 'But why? What purpose does that serve?'

'I don't know. Was this an isolated piece? Did someone make it especially on Verinka's account, perhaps the person who spent weeks arranging for her death? But in that case, why didn't he or she reclaim the pipe afterwards?'

'Perhaps they might have, if we hadn't taken it. You did arrive on the scene very promptly, did you not?'

'Perhaps. But. What if it wasn't like that at all? What if there are more?'

'More spirit-sucking pipes?'

Konrad grimaced at the turn of phrase. 'Something like that. Not necessarily pipes, either. Fake antiques with a hidden purpose.'

'Again, why?'

'I don't know. But I do badly need to ask Tsevar Manin a few questions. I wonder if he was the one who gave Verinka the pipe?'

5

By Konrad's request, the obliging antiques dealer patched up the damaged pipe as best he could. At a glance, it would pass for pristine, and a glance was all Konrad expected to need.

The hour growing advanced, however, he remembered his invitation to Nanda, and hesitated. Should he pursue Tsevar immediately, or visit with Nanda first? Professionalism demanded the former. Everything else required the latter.

Konrad went home.

Candles were burning in his dining-parlour as he approached, suitably dressed for dinner — he'd dashed upstairs to attend to that part right away, though if asked, he could not have said why. Nan might be amused by costumes, but she did not care for the elaborate rules of etiquette that governed dress among the gentry. She'd be more likely to laugh at his turn-out than to be impressed by it (not that he was trying to impress her; a man might dress for dinner in his own house without needing a special motive, surely?)

With such thoughts tumbling through his mind, Konrad stepped smartly through the door — only to find the room decked out elegantly for dinner, with no one in residence. His staff had gone to some trouble in dressing the table, and laying out dishes. Someone — his housekeeper, most likely — had even contrived to rig up something resembling a fresh flower bouquet in the centre of the table; impossible at this time of year, but the thing looked convincing enough.

No Nanda.

He performed a quick tour of the ground floor, all those rooms in which Nanda was occasionally to be found: their favourite parlour, the other parlour, the morning room, the library. Even his study. Not a trace of her did he find, and when he enquired of his butler, Gorev, whether Miss Falenia had been admitted to the house at all that afternoon he received an immediate negative.

'No communications from her have been received either?'

'Not to my knowledge, sir.'

Konrad paused, uncertain what to do. Doubtless she had been detained by some manner of business; she did, after all, have plenty of her own duties and obligations to tend to. Or, she had simply changed her mind. He had left the question of his own attendance at dinner somewhat doubtful. Small wonder if she did not fancy sitting in that large, echoing dining-room all by herself.

Still, she would normally have sent a note or some such to that effect.

Since the faint stirrings of anxiety would not go away under the influence of such steadying logic, Konrad abandoned all prospect of dinner. A whirlwind dash up to his dressing-room reversed the careful dressing of twenty minutes before; attired once again in street-appropriate clothes, and wrapped in his layers of black coat and hat and boots against the chill of the night, he left the house with little more than: 'My compliments upon the dining-room, Gorev. Pity that it has not been put to use.'

'No matter, sir. It will keep,' said his staunch butler, and Konrad was away.

No lights burned in the windows of Nanda's house when he arrived there, perhaps a half-hour later. She lived above her shop, in the midst of a moderately prosperous tradesman's quarter; a safe enough area, Konrad would have said, with a doughty crew of watchmen keeping the peace at night, and a reasonable complement of street-lamps to deter thieves. He did not know why he was so disturbed by Nanda's failure to appear, for he had no good reason. Some instinct, though, refused to give him any peace.

He did not have to break in, nor to test the enfeebled powers of his Malykant's fingers upon the lock. Either would have been a violation of Nanda's privacy which he would have been loath to commit. Happily, she had at last presented him with a key.

'Only to be used in emergency, Konrad, or by arrangement,' she'd said sternly, as she pressed the cool slip of metal into his palm. 'I don't want to come home to find you hobnobbing with Weveroth and eating my larder bare.'

'I wouldn't dream of either,' he'd said, tucking the key away safely in an inside pocket of his coat. The same pocket that had too often housed harvested rib-bones from the slain people he'd avenged, but this realisation came a little too late.

'You absolutely would,' she'd said, and that had been true, but still this was the first time he had set that bright, new key into the lock on the rear door, and let himself in.

Nothing stirred within, not even the faintest current of warmth. No fires had been lit in the house all day, if he was any judge, and still he saw not a scrap of light anywhere.

'Nanda?' he called.

Nothing. He waited, hoping for the scurry of small feet and the indignant appearance of Weveroth, ready to scold him for his intrusion. But there was no sign of the little monkey, either.

Konrad passed through the darkened workroom and paused at the foot of the narrow staircase leading up into Nanda's living space. He stood, listening, for some time, and then called again, with the same results.

Nanda had been home early that morning. What could possibly have happened since?

He wanted to go up, but hesitated, perhaps absurdly, at the foot of the stairs, unwilling to barge his way up there. What if Nanda was home after all, peacefully asleep, and in her nightgown? Thinking herself alone, and safe, and abruptly awakening to find someone unexpected in the room? He'd scare her senseless. And then she would beat him to a pulp.

Serpents, he called. *A search, please. Is Nanda here? Anybody else?*

Eetapi and Ootapi, it seemed, were well ahead of him, for both answered at once with a decided negative upon both points.

Konrad set his foot to the bottom-most step, and ventured up.

He found a gas lamp upon a small side-table in the cramped upstairs landing, and lit it. Its flaring glow sent long shadows streaking up the walls, which shuddered and leapt as he picked it up and carried it through the nearest door. He found a sitting-room, empty; very Nanda, though, with a matched set of sofa and chairs upholstered in a tasteful blue, a fireplace which had obviously seen much use, a collection of well-loved books upon a humble carved-pine shelf, and an enormous rug covering almost the entire floor, hand-worked in shades of lavender.

He turned his back on the room with some reluctance, for it was a welcoming, peaceful space, seeming somehow to proffer safety.

He found Nanda's bedchamber next, and *there* he could not have said the same. Not at all. The door creaked softly as he opened it, and something — some sense, some instinct — had him recoiling, hovering upon the threshold with a strange reluctance to enter.

The smell might have had something to do with it. For the first time since learning of Nanda's supposed illness, he felt it to be the stark, horrible truth, for the acrid scent of sickness assailed his nostrils. Someone had lain here in a sweat, hour after hour. What had Nan suffered? Spirits above, but the woman was the queen of dissembling. To see and speak to her, he would have sworn that she seemed almost her usual self. But here was the evidence to the contrary, her bed with its rumpled and sweat-stained bedclothes telling a very different story.

Konrad felt a swift stab of fear for her, followed by remorse. He'd waltzed into her most private of spaces and wrested secrets from it, secrets she had clearly wanted to keep from him. Had he the right? Was this an emergency?

He hoped, prayed, that it was not; that Nanda had been called away unexpectedly, that she was even now comfortably asleep in someone else's house, or working the night through somewhere. That she'd be back in the morning, smiling as usual, with airy explanations and apologies to make for missing dinner.

But Konrad could not rest until she did. Nor could he return to the luxury of his own, empty house and simply wait for news. So he returned to her serene sitting-room, arrayed himself upon her blue couch, and finding it deliciously soft, there he remained.

He woke abruptly, some hours later. He had not meant to sleep, but slumber had eventually claimed him, in spite of his disquiet. The lamp had burned out, but a wan dawn light crept in through the window, casting the room in a pallid, dismal grey.

The events of the previous night came back to him in a rush, dispersing drowsiness; he sat up, heart pounding. She had not come back.

'Konrad? Konrad! Honestly.'

Nanda's voice. He looked round. She stood in the doorway, neat as a pin, looking in no wise like a woman who'd spent all night out somewhere unspecified. Or like the woman who had tossed and turned in that crumpled bed, suffering unnamed trials.

The relief was so intense, for a minute he could not breathe.

'You're all right,' he managed to say.

'Of course I am. Is this because I missed dinner? I am sorry. If I'd known you would panic like this I would have sent word.'

Konrad flushed, feeling himself rebuked. Not that he minded, quite. If Nanda was well, he'd take any number of scoldings for his uninvited appearance in her house. 'I was just... concerned,' he said. 'I didn't mean to sleep here, though. That couch accosted me, and refused to let me go.'

'It is rather delicious, isn't it?' she said, with a satisfied smile. 'One of my favourite things in this house. Shall you need breakfast?'

'Please.' He followed her downstairs, aware that she had not offered any explanation for her absence. Aware that he had not questioned her about the state either of her bedroom, or of her failing health. So many secrets between them still, however close they became. He did not know how to ask those questions, which words to use, how to approach her in such a way as to win a confidence. He knew he ought not to push for one; that was not how friendships worked. But did friends conceal things from each other like this?

He did not know. How could he? He was badly out of practice, when it came to friends.

He satisfied himself with saying, as Nanda pushed a cup of steaming coffee at him and a slab of bread, 'Are you sure you are well, Nan?'

That won him her long, cool look, the one that said she knew exactly what he was really saying, and had not yet decided whether to humour him.

'No,' she said, rather to his surprise. 'Did you look around?'

'A bit. I only went into two rooms...' He devoted himself to his coffee and his food, so he did not have to admit to avoiding her eye.

A sigh came, soft and low, and she sagged into a seat at her kitchen-table. 'You're right, of course,' she said. 'I ought to have told you about it by now.'

'You don't have to,' he said, hastily swallowing a chunk of bread.

'I know.'

'All right.'

'It's... complicated. And I haven't wanted to... admit to...'

Konrad waited, but she had run out of words. 'You don't have to tell me anything,' he repeated, though the words he longed to say were more the opposite. *Please tell me. Please put me out of this suspense.*

'I can't,' Nanda said, and his heart sank. 'Right now,' she added, and he looked up.

'Oh?'

'When this case is finished,' she said slowly. 'When your time is your own again for a little while, and you are not distracted, we will talk. But not here, and not at Bakar House. Meet me in the Bones. At your chicken-legged hut, if you like. There are things I ought to... show you.'

This was not at all what Konrad had expected to hear, and he struggled to make sense of it. Why...? What could she possibly...? But however befuddling the words, they boded well; whatever she proposed to tell him, it would be, must be, better than her long, long silence.

'Anytime you care to name,' he said, and promised himself to work doubly hard on the case of Verinka Tarasovna; the sooner he won justice for the murdered woman, the sooner he could devote himself to the task of helping Nanda.

Were he truthful, *that* was all he cared about these days.

Nan smiled at him, touched his hand once in a gesture he interpreted as gratitude, and then briskly changed the subject. 'So, then, what progress on the case?'

'Some few interesting things,' he said, setting aside his empty coffee cup. 'Particularly regarding this pipe...'

6

When Tsevar Tarasovich Manin described himself to the inspector, rather curtly, as "in business", he had allowed the police to picture some modest endeavour; an impression aided by the relative simplicity of his mode of dress, and lack of ostentatious adornment.

This proved to have been inaccurate.

Konrad arrived at the police headquarters soon after dawn, but despite the early hour Inspector Nuritov was already on his way out. Konrad had not got much beyond the first stairwell up before he encountered Alexander on his way down.

'Ah, Savast. Just in time. We've had some information about our man Tsevar.'

'Oh?' Konrad turned about and headed down again, his cane swinging jauntily. Somehow, his time with Nanda had buoyed his spirits. Whether it was still the simple effects of relief, or the prospect of no longer being kept in the dark, he felt more cheerful than he had in some time.

He tried to remember that he was in the middle of a tricky murder case; that he would soon have to kill somebody; that Nanda's news could not possibly be pleasant or easy to hear; and incidentally that he stood in danger of permanent death on the not-too-distant horizon; but nothing dimmed his inexplicable sunshine. Perhaps it was the way Nanda had smiled at him. That image would keep returning to his mind; the faint crease at the corner of her mouth that always appeared, almost but not quite a dimple. The warmth and laughter in her eyes—

'Savast?'

Konrad received the impression that Alexander had repeated his name more than once. 'Sorry,' he said. 'I was—'

'Daydreaming? You had a dreamy look.'

'That can't possibly have been the case.'

The inspector grinned. Konrad had by this time trailed him all the way out into the street, and they were on the point of stepping into a police cab. Not even the bite of the wind eating through his clothes had been able to rouse him from reverie.

Master, Eetapi admonished. *You must pay attention.*

He must, indeed. He took his seat opposite Alexander in chastened silence, and applied himself to the topic at hand.

'Tsevar,' Alexander said patiently. 'In business, yes. You did not happen to catch the nature of his business, I suppose?'

'I'm... afraid not.'

'He trades in antiques.'

Konrad sat up. 'Oh.'

'And in artworks of more recent date.'

'You mean he passes them off as antiques?'

'Not as far as I've been able to find out. He does seem to be keeping the two lines separate. He is very successful, though. He imports from all over the world and supplies several shops in the city. Also sells directly to collectors. He must be wealthy.'

'That explains the Larch Luncheon Club, then. Verinka could never have been paying for that.'

'Most likely. Which suggests that he was the instigator of those weekly luncheon dates, and probably it was his choice of venue, too.'

'It's of a piece with what we know. He does seem to have been more interested in pursuing a close acquaintance with his sister than she was.'

'Yes, though if she believed him to be both inclined to kill her and capable of it, I can't think how or why she kept accepting those invitations.'

'She probably did not believe that, while she was still alive. It was me who put the idea into her head, that someone wanted to harm her — after she was dead. Still, they must have quarrelled at least, if her thoughts flew straight to him.'

'Which centres around Kristov, and I have men looking into his interests this morning. For now, though, we are on our way to

Tsevar's offices.'

'I've an idea,' said Konrad. 'Do we still have that pipe?'

Alexander removed it from a pocket, and handed it across to Konrad.

The thing still looked passable. The diamond was no longer embedded beneath the filigree; Konrad had turned that over to the Order already, together with a report for Diana. They would deal with the problem of Verinka's partial captivity. Konrad also held out some hopes that someone in the Order might know more about the thing. If he was right in thinking there might be more such objects, word of it might have reached Diana's ears.

In the meantime, Verinka's murder was his priority, and the question of how the pipe came to be in her possession at all was of paramount importance. And everything presently pointed either to Tsevar or Kristov — but especially to Tsevar.

'When we get there,' said Konrad, 'Let me go in first. Give me maybe quarter of an hour before we go for Tsevar.'

'Are we sneaking and stealthing?'

'We aren't. I am.'

Alexander grinned. 'All right. Quarter of an hour.'

Finding Tsevar's private office was no difficult task, once they arrived at the site of his various holdings. He had a few buildings clustered together, one or two of them sizeable; Alexander was right in thinking his business was very substantial. Konrad headed for the most salubrious of the bunch, a construct of moderate size but of recent build, judging from the gleaming white paint, clear windows and pristine arches. A brief enquiry of the first person he encountered within — a clerk of some kind, dress and demeanour nondescript, but with an air of efficiency and haste — soon procured him the directions to Tsevar's own office. Up those wide, carpeted stairs, and the door straight ahead.

'Oh, but, sir, he is yet arrived,' said the brisk young man.

'I will wait,' Konrad assured him.

'Do you need me to show you the way?'

'I believe I can find it.'

The clerk bowed, and permitted Konrad to make his way unattended.

Which Konrad did with due haste, for his quarter of an hour was rapidly expiring. The serpents crept ahead, and carolled that the coast was clear. Konrad slipped inside.

The office bore all the luxury and splendour that Tsevar's personal appearance belied. The desk alone was a monument to ego: enormous, it took up fully half of the width of the room. Its polished, darkwood surface bore an array of small statues, ornate candlesticks and jewelled boxes bearing mute testimony to Tsevar's taste and eye for quality. Konrad would have gladly hosted most of them in his own house.

He whipped the pipe out of his pocket, placed it carefully on the desk half-hidden behind some one or two other things, and quickly withdrew.

The man himself arrived less than half an hour later. By that time, Konrad was installed in the front hall with Alexander, biding his time. The inspector had engaged the clerk in conversation; the young man kept shooting concerned glances Konrad's way, as though he felt he might have personally failed to please him in some way. Konrad supposed he did give off the impression of a promising private collector, ready to spend a great deal of money in Tsevar's warehouses.

All conversations came to an abrupt halt when the front door swung open, and Tsevar himself strode in. His entire demeanour had altered, since last time Konrad had met him. At Verinka's house, just receiving the news of her death, he had seemed rather short and unassuming. Walking into his own offices, however, surrounded by his business and his goods and his employees, he had… one might even call it a swagger. His brow contracted when he saw Konrad and the inspector, and a little of the assurance went out of him.

He covered it with bluster.

'Surely there can be no reason to trouble me at my work?' he snapped.

'Our apologies for interrupting you here, sir,' said Alexander mildly. 'We had one or two more questions to ask you about your sister.'

Tsevar schooled his features into a more composed expression, tinged with sadness. 'Poor Verinka. Yes, yes. I cannot spare a great deal of time, mind.'

'It shouldn't take more than a few minutes,' Alexander assured him.

Tsevar waited expectantly.

'Ah,' said Konrad. 'Perhaps it would be better to speak privately? Your office, say?'

Tsevar darted a glance at his clerk, who waited patiently to be noticed, and stalked off towards the stairs. 'Certainly, certainly,' he said, marching up them.

He shut the door behind his unwanted visitors the moment they were inside, with just a hint of a slam. Konrad watched as he crossed to his desk, and sat behind it. Perhaps he felt more powerful there. 'Very well, then. What—' His eye fell on the pipe, and he stopped. His frown deepened.

'Something wrong, sir?' said Alexander.

'No,' said Tsevar shortly, but his frown did not lessen. He stalked back to the door, and rang a bell-pull; a clanging sounded distantly, somewhere below.

The clerk appeared twenty seconds later. 'Yes, sir?'

'What is this doing in here?' said Tsevar, picking up the pipe and brandishing it in some irritation.

'I couldn't say, sir. Shall I take it?'

'I want to know how it came to be in here. We can't have—' He broke off again, staring at the pipe. Konrad felt a moment's unease; had he noticed the damage? But the businessman's face slowly turned white, and he put the pipe down on his desk as if he did not want to touch it anymore. 'Verinka?' he gasped. Then a spasm of anger wiped away whatever else he had been feeling; he rounded on Konrad and the inspector. 'Did you do this? Did you put this here?'

'I did,' Konrad admitted. 'I wanted to know if you had seen it before.'

'Spirits, man, why did you not just ask me?'

Konrad said, as delicately as he could, 'People are not always forthcoming.'

Tsevar gave a great sigh, and sagged into his chair. In response to the clerk's repeated offer of assistance, he waved him away with an impatient gesture, and sat staring at the pipe. 'She was betraying me,' he said at last.

Konrad's brows rose; unexpected. 'How so?'

'That pipe. She begged me to involve her more in the business — wanted to see the offices, the warehouses, the stores. Wanted to know all about what we do. I did not trust her, I confess, for she had never shown any interest before. But I chose to hope...' He shrugged. 'Well. That pipe is one of mine, but I didn't give it to her. She must have taken it. And you know what?' His brow darkened still further. 'She took it to *him*, didn't she? Kristov. That sneak. He—' Words failed him, apparently, for he subsided into seething silence.

'It was found in your sister's possession when she died,' said the inspector, and hesitated. Probably he was wondering how to broach the topic of the secreted diamond.

Konrad interrupted. 'How did you know Verinka took it?'

Tsevar shifted in his seat, and would not meet Konrad's eye. 'I... guessed.'

'Or you *saw*. Some sense of her lingers there, does it not?'

Tsevar met Konrad's gaze then, but briefly, and with a shade of alarm. 'That is absurd,' he muttered.

'Not to the spirit-sighted.'

'I have no such sight,' snapped Tsevar.

The inspector interpolated, 'Rest assured, sir, it is in no way a crime.'

That prompted a gusty, irritated sigh. 'Very well. Yes, I can sometimes get a sense of such things. Though I do not understand how it is that any part of Verinka lingers around this pipe.'

'She is mostly liberated by now,' Konrad said. 'Only a trace or two left.'

Tsevar blinked at him in what appeared to be genuine incomprehension. But he had overdone it, and Konrad had not missed the quick, sharp glance that preceded this display of ignorance.

'I beg you would be straight with us, sir,' said the inspector. 'We are not here to accuse you of anything. We are here to find out who killed your sister.'

Tsevar, remembering perhaps that he was devastated by his sister's death, capitulated. He picked up the pipe and brandished it in the inspector's direction. 'Have you any knowledge of this kind of article?'

'Pipes?' said Alexander uncertainly.

'No. Mourning jewellery. And other such objects.'

Alexander, blinking, cast a sideways glance at Konrad.

Who recalled, from some distant part of his memory, a snippet of an old story he'd never given much credence to. 'Go on,' he said.

'Long ago, it's *said*, it used to be the custom to keep some memento of a deceased loved one, as a remembrance. Necklaces, bracelets, pins, that kind of thing. Pipes or watches, if either the deceased or the mourner was a male. They were said to keep the loved one near — never truly gone, you can imagine the kind of sentiment.' The scornful twist to Tsevar's lips suggested he did not know what sentiment was. 'Some nonsense about clear diamonds and ghosts—'

'Except it is not nonsense, is it?' Konrad said. 'It is truth. That's why you looked so shocked just now. Did you manufacture this to sell to the credible among your clients? A high-priced article for a grieving widow; a way to keep hold of some scant trace of her lost spouse. Only, it can work, to an extent. You realise that now.'

'You suspected, though, didn't you?' said Alexander. 'Or why include the diamond at all? It's concealed. You could have left it out.'

Tsevar looked from Konrad to Alexander and back, trapped and profoundly irritated by the fact. 'I thought it an idiot's dream,' he snapped. 'But people pay a lot for dreams. It's a new line; we haven't even launched it yet.'

He wouldn't be launching it. The Order would be obliged to put paid to the scheme. 'Why do you think your sister was taking it to Mr. Balandin?' Konrad asked.

'Because the two of them have been thick as thieves for months,' growled Tsevar. 'And in that time, the damned fool has been constantly getting ahead of us, somehow. Buying up stock ahead of me. Luring my artists away from me. Undercutting my prices. Where was he getting his information, if not from my sister?'

Alexander gave a slight cough. 'You did say you and your sister were very close, sir.'

For the first time, a note of genuine sadness crept into Tsevar's voice. 'We were, for most of our lives. Kristov changed all that. I don't know how he did it, but...' He shrugged. 'Since he began courting her, she has been different. Puffed up, guarded. Coaxing and disdainful by turns. And there can now be no doubt that she was a traitor to me. I didn't want to believe it.'

'Clear motive for murder there,' Alexander said, half apologetically. 'Cannot help pointing it out.'

Tsevar scowled. 'I'd never have killed her.'

'I'm sure you didn't, sir, but nevertheless I'm obliged to ask: have you ever had any dealings with certain, ah, women's facilities in the lower town?'

'What?' Tsevar looked at the inspector as though he had run mad. 'Women's— what sort of man do you take me for?'

A possible murderer, thought Konrad, but Alexander merely smiled. 'Never mind. Thank you for your time.'

'It could be him,' said Konrad soon afterwards, when they had left — or been thrown out of — Tsevar's office. 'He had reason, and an opportunity, and Verinka strongly distrusted him. Have your men managed to wring anything out of the waiters yet?'

'Not that I've heard. They are still denying all knowledge. It might not have been one of them slipping the weed into the wine, remember. Indeed it might not have been administered during those weekly lunches at all.'

'When, then? She seems to have prepared her own food at home; there's no sign of a cook in her employ. We found nothing in her house that might have been contaminated with widow weed. And as far as we've discovered, the only time she ate anywhere else was at that same club.'

'I have no idea,' said Alexander thoughtfully. 'I am looking forward to your conversation with the mysterious Kristov, though. If he was a competitor of Tsevar's, and cheating to boot, that explains the man's distaste. I wonder why he was courting Verinka?'

'If he was getting information out of her, that's probably reason enough.'

'Nothing sincere about it then, you think? Poor woman.'

Konrad shrugged. 'She seems to have been easy to corrupt, for all her former closeness to her brother. I do not know how much sympathy I shall feel for her.'

'We only have Tsevar's word for any of that, too,' Alexander reminded him.

7

'Konrad.'

It was Tasha, climbing in through his study window, attended by a blast of cold air.

Konrad, startled out of the reverie into which he'd fallen, sat up with a jerk. '*What* are you doing?'

'Breaking and entering,' said the little lamaeni, planting both feet upon his fine carpet and dusting snow off her dark jacket.

'I can see that. May one ask why you found it necessary to enter that way, instead of via the front door?'

'Gorev would've sent me away if I tried to come in that way.'

'And why is that, pray?'

'Because last time I was here I went into your kitchens and stole half of your cook's fresh batch of pastries.'

Tasha said this serenely, but with an impish twinkle lurking in her eye — the kind that begged to be taken up for it, and argued with, all her sauciest wit at the ready.

'I hope your boots are clean,' was all Konrad decided to reply. 'Or my housekeeper will have your guts.'

'Of course they aren't clean. Where do you think I've come from?'

'The filthiest spot you could find in the whole of the undercity.'

'Correct. Don't you want to know why I took the pastries?'

'Not particularly.'

'I was feeding the street children.'

'How altruistic of you. I suppose it would be too much generosity if you'd had to pay for them yourself as well.'

'Redistribution of wealth is important.'

'No doubt. Do feel free to redistribute mine anytime you feel so inclined.'

'Oh, I do,' Tasha assured him.

'Did you come here for a reason, besides the daily torment I've come to know and love from you?'

Tasha grinned at that. 'There was that. Also, I wanted to ask you a question.'

'All right.'

'You shouldn't be asleep in the middle of the afternoon, you know. Only old men doze off over their newspapers like that.'

'I am an old man, and I wasn't asleep. I was thinking.'

'You can't be more than, what, five-and-thirty? Six-and-thirty?'

'I *feel* at least twice that. What was the question?'

'Oh. I want to know where Verinka lived.'

'Ask the inspector, then. He has all the details, and he's responsible for you, spirits help him.'

'I did. He refused to tell me.'

Konrad raised a brow at that. 'And why did he refuse to tell you?'

'He said I was going to meddle.'

'Are you?'

'I'm a police ward. I'm *meant* to meddle.'

'Your immediate superior disagrees.'

'What am I there for if I'm not to do any detecting? I need training.'

'Is that what you want to be when you — ah — don't precisely grow up? A detective?'

'*You* seem to enjoy it.'

'Do I? Appearances can be deceiving.'

Tasha's gaze sharpened. 'So you don't like it? Really, really?'

Konrad shrugged, experiencing a moment's irritation. 'Does it matter?'

'Yes, actually.'

'Why?'

'Can't tell you.'

'Right.' Konrad got out of his chair, and retrieved a memorandum book from a drawer in his desk. 'If I give you Verinka's address, will you get out of my house?'

'And your hair,' Tasha said. 'Promise faithfully.'

'Your promises mean virtually nothing,' Konrad said, scrawling Verinka's address on the next blank page, and tearing it out. 'Don't go bothering the inspector,' he recommended, handing it over to Tasha.

'You mean don't tell him you gave me this? I might, if it suited me.' She glanced at the paper, folded it, and tucked it into her jacket.

Konrad sighed. 'You're the worst person I know.'

Tasha doffed her cap at him in thanks, and launched herself out of the window again. Konrad heard a muffled thud.

'Still alive?' he called.

'You do realise what you just said?' Tasha yelled back.

Oops. Tasha hadn't been alive in a while. 'Right,' he called, but there came no reply, and he received the impression that she was already gone.

He wasted some little time trying to imagine what the wretch might be getting up to in Verinka's neighbourhood, and what worried Alexander about it.

Mischief, was the inevitable answer. But since Tasha could take care of herself better than anyone else he knew, he wouldn't waste his time worrying.

Nanda, though. He would waste his time worrying about Nanda, and gladly. And he needed to finish this case in order to find out how he could help her.

His ruminations had resulted in one conclusion, if a vague one: the biggest questions remaining about the case of Verinka Tarasovna revolved around Kristov Balandin. They had gleaned some information about Verinka's suitor, if not much. He was a competitor of her brother's; he had some money, and liked to flash it around; he had some kind of interest in Verinka herself, possibly romantic but possibly only opportunistic; and, if Tsevar's story proved true, he was a little short on moral fibre.

Some of those questions could prove vital. *If* Tsevar's story was true, Kristov was no candidate for the murder. If he was using Verinka to such excellent effect, he must have been making a lot of money out of her. Why would he kill her? Unless he had reason to think that relations between the siblings had deteriorated to the point where he might no longer be able to make use of her. But that still wasn't motive for murder, especially not the kind conducted over several weeks.

If he had a motive at all, Konrad couldn't imagine what it might be. Tsevar still looked by far the likelier culprit. But Konrad had no evidence of Tsevar's guilt, without which he could not act. Might Kristov have some light to shed on the story? Might he even have evidence of Tsevar's misdemeanours to share?

Konrad needed to find him. He could wait until tomorrow, and corner him at the club. But that meant wasting the rest of the afternoon, and the night, and most of the following morning, with nothing much to do and no particular leads to follow. He'd waited at home in hopes of word from the inspector: a confession from a bribed waiter, perhaps, or some new insight into the identity (and motive) of the woman who'd bought the widow weed.

But nothing came, and Konrad grew more impatient. At last he abandoned his vigil. No sense in retracing the steps already trodden by the inspector's men; they knew their work. Konrad held out little hope of somehow succeeding where they had failed.

No, instead he would find out where Kristov Balandin might be hiding. Alexander had already discovered his place of business, but when he and Konrad had gone there that morning he'd been reported absent. For the whole day, on business, sorry sirs, he will not be back until tomorrow. Or the day after.

The serpents having confirmed that he really was not on the premises, Konrad and Alexander had been obliged to take a cursory look around and go away again. Until the morrow.

Or not. Perhaps Konrad could find him. There was one advantage he did have over the police: he knew where the social elite spent their leisure time, or those who aspired to be admitted into their (supposedly) exalted ranks. Given Mr. Balandin's habit of patronising the Larch Club, and of making a display with his wealth, Konrad guessed that he was not above a little social-climbing.

In which case, he had an idea. There were not all that many gentlemen's clubs in Ekamet, and most were very exclusive: memberships were given out only to those who met the club's stringent requirements. But one could sometimes get around them. Not through bribery; oh no, that would be inappropriate. But if you could persuade an existing member to take you along as a guest, well then.

Kristov Balandin had already proved himself adept at making the right kinds of friends, and charming the most useful people. Perhaps the kind of "business" he was conducting that afternoon was more of the same.

Despite Konrad's confidence, his tour of the better clubs proved fruitless. As did his subsequent exploration of the poorer grade. No one recognised the name of Kristov Balandin, or would admit to doing so. The man himself certainly was not to be found at any of them, ensconced at his ease by a blazing fire, or engaging in conversation with the club's members.

A waste of an afternoon, he thought bitterly as he abandoned the endeavour. He had missed dinner, unwilling to halt the search earlier for fear that the *next* establishment would prove to be the one he sought. At length, though, he ran out of options; and being by then chilled through to the bone and heartily bored, he permitted his coachman to drive him home. There was always the possibility that word from Alexander would await him there, containing just the breakthrough they needed.

If not, well, there was still the lunch-club tomorrow, where he would at last encounter his quarry. And he might have an opportunity to investigate the waiters, too, while he was at it. If they wouldn't talk to the inspector's men, he would just have to terrorise them a bit, and see what happened.

Such ruthless plans being evidence enough of his being thoroughly out of humour, he prescribed himself a hearty dinner and a large glass of brandy, to be taken forthwith. Perhaps even two glasses. He stepped down from his carriage at his own front door, heartened by these reflections, but before he had taken two steps, Ootapi shattered his peace with a single word, uttered like the crack of a whip.

Master!

Yes?

He is in there.

Konrad stopped in the street, to the irritation of a passing woman, who almost collided with him. *In there? In my house? Who?*

The one you seek. Ootapi seemed pleased.

Konrad was not. *Kristov Balandin is in my house? Are you certain?*

Ootapi did not precisely answer. Konrad experienced the serpent's degree of certainty by way of a wash of sensation: predominantly, dithering.

'Well,' Konrad said aloud. 'Let's find out.' He strode up to the door and let himself in without hesitation, determined not to be cowed by this unlikely and unpromising development.

Gorev stood in the hall.

'You have a visitor, sir,' said he gravely. 'I have put him in the library.'

Which said much. A better class of guest — or one who was at least expected — would be shown into the best parlour, or even the drawing-room. No one was ever abandoned in the library. 'His name?' said Konrad.

'Balandin, sir.'

Konrad paused a moment. How could it be, that the man he had spent the afternoon chasing all over the city had beaten him home? A stranger, too, who could have such reason to seek Konrad as Konrad had to seek him? His skin crawled with misgiving. Something was not right.

Well, nothing would be resolved by hovering in his hallway. 'Thank you, Gorev,' said Konrad to his butler, permitting himself to be divested of his hat, cane and coat. 'Have you sent in refreshments?'

'Not yet, sir.'

'We should at least feed the fellow, should we not? Have Mrs. Aristova send up a few things, if you please.'

'Not the delectables, sir?' Gorev seemed mildly appalled.

'Yes, why not? Let us not be accused of lacking in hospitality.'

Gorev bowed stiffly, and withdrew, leaving Konrad to wonder just what manner of person awaited him in his library. Gorev was not usually such a high stickler.

He braced himself for some unknowable trouble, and walked quickly into the library.

His guest had not chosen to take a seat. Whether that was because he had only just arrived, or whether because he scorned to lounge at his ease in Konrad's house, there was no saying. He ignored the hundreds of cloth-bound books packed into the carved bookcases and stood instead at a far window, staring out at the drifting snowfall, his hands clasped behind his back. Gorev had at least ordered a fire to be lit, and the wall-sconces; a pleasant glow filled the room, affording Konrad more than sufficient light by which to scrutinise his guest.

Kristov Balandin was a big, big man: that was the first impression Konrad received. Taller than Konrad by half a head, at least, and broad; his bulky shoulders strained at the seams of his coat. Intimidating. Not at all what one expected in a man of business. Little could be determined about that coat save that it bore a suitably dark hue, and was well-cut. Probably not the height of fashion, but respectable. He had a thick head of hair, black but going to grey, and rather unkempt.

'Mr. Balandin, I understand?' said Konrad, when the man did not turn around. Had he not heard Konrad come in?

'Aye,' said Balandin in a low growl, still without moving. 'I am pleased to make your acquaintance, Mr. Savast.'

'Are you? But you haven't, precisely, so I must ask what you are doing in my library.'

'I would have preferred a decent parlour myself,' said Balandin, turning about at last. 'Your butler had other ideas.'

'I'm afraid you did not present a very promising appearance,' said Konrad, and found himself surveyed with the same keen curiosity with which he was examining Balandin. The man had the weathered face of one given to striding about outdoors a great deal, and could not be below forty-five or so years of age. He stood with proud posture and even a faint air of menace; some very tall men sought to mitigate the effects with a slight stoop, but Mr. Balandin clearly took pleasure in looming over all those around him. Especially Konrad, perhaps. His narrowed eyes were steely in expression.

'Not fine enough for your servants, am I?' said Balandin. 'I don't see what is wrong with my appearance.'

Nor did Konrad, in truth, for nothing in his attire seemed amiss. But his manner — nothing about *that* spoke of the gentleman. He gave off the appearance of a thug dressed up in fine clothes.

'It is not your garments,' said Konrad, advancing into the room. 'It is your obvious intent to present a threatening appearance. Why exactly am I to have the pleasure of your company this evening? I don't believe you have yet explained that.'

'You've been asking for me all over town.'

Konrad's eyes narrowed. 'So I have. How did you come to know of it?'

'And you have spies on me at this very moment.' Balandin cast a scornful glance towards the ceiling, where the serpents hovered.

Incorporeal. Invisible. Supposedly.

'They are not here to spy on you. They are here to attend *me*.'

'And what an ordinary toff wants with a pair of bonded spirit-slaves is beyond me.'

'They are not slaves,' Konrad grated. If the man had the power to charm the likes of Verinka, he had yet to see any sign of it. 'And I might ask how an ordinary man of business has any idea of their presence. Are you a ghostspeaker, sir?'

'No. Only a man with eyes to see.'

'Like your rival, Tsevar Tarasovich Manin,' said Konrad. 'And, I begin to imagine, his sister.'

Balandin inclined his head. 'You've been seen with a police inspector,' he said abruptly.

'I am friends with a Mr. Nuritov, yes.'

'You appear unusually hand-in-glove with the police, sir, if you are doing their work for them.'

'I do my own work.'

'Oh? And what is that work?'

Konrad did not know how to answer. The silence stretched a fraction too long, and Balandin gave a bitter, mocking smile.

'Just why would an idle gentleman such as yourself do investigative work? There are other pursuits, better suited to a bored toff.'

'That's twice you've called me a toff, and you appear to be casting aspersions upon my motives—' Konrad broke off, interrupted, perhaps fortunately, before he could work himself into a rage, by the arrival of a maid with a tray. Mrs. Aristova, he saw, had obeyed his directions and sent up her best: a delicate array of pastries and cakes, each one exquisite, occupied a tiered porcelain stand.

Balandin's only reaction to the delicacies was a sneer. That, or he took exception to their being delivered upon a silver tray, courtesy of a paid servant.

Konrad, tiring of Balandin's attitude, and content for the moment that he stood in no immediate physical danger, threw himself into a chair by the fire and gestured to the one opposite. 'We can continue to bristle at each other from opposite sides of the room, or we may finish this conversation in something resembling comfort.'

His guest looked disconcerted, his mouth opening and closing again in silence. With that stature and the demeanour to match, he was doubtless used to cowing people into deference.

After a moment, he consented to come away from the window and install himself in the proffered chair, though he continued to disdain Mrs. Aristova's work.

Konrad didn't. He was starving, and if this irritating brute of a man proposed to keep him from his dinner then he would take what he could get. Four of them, in fact.

He was halfway through the second buttery something, aware the while of Balandin's scrutiny, before his guest spoke again.

'Who are you?' said Balandin, and this time at least he sounded more confused than angered.

'Konrad Savast,' said Konrad, swallowing a mouthful. 'Not quite so idle toff of Ekamet. I had the misfortune to discover the body of Verinka Tarasovna this week.'

Perhaps the man would conclude that to be reason enough for Konrad's interest in the case and he need answer no further probing questions.

Alas, no.

'This is not the first case in which you've taken an interest,' said Balandin.

Konrad irritably flicked pastry crumbs off his waistcoat. 'You've been very curious.'

'If you may ask questions about me, I may do the same about you.'

'I suppose that's fair. Why exactly did you come here? If we could establish what you were hoping to get out of the visit, we may be able to draw this interview to a close a little sooner.'

'I came to tell you,' growled Balandin, 'that you are wasting your time. It is of no use investigating me for the murder of my beloved Verinka. I did not kill her.'

'*Was* she your beloved?' said Konrad. 'It is convenient that she happened to be the sister of your nearest rival.'

Balandin snorted. 'Manin is a paranoid fool. He is successful, I grant you, but he is *not* my nearest rival and I had little interest in his doings beyond what was public knowledge.'

'So he was wrong to think that Verinka was spying on him at your behest?'

'Yes. Oh, she was spying on him, but not because I asked her to. She thought she could please me by bringing me information — all of it useless, I'm afraid. No doubt she, like you, was influenced by his absurd ideas. He would make an enemy of me, but I had no interest in him.'

Konrad said nothing.

'Even if I had,' added Balandin. 'Why would I kill Verinka? What could that possibly have accomplished?'

Since Konrad had asked himself the same question, he had no retort to offer. 'The pipe Verinka had with her,' he said instead. 'Do you chance to know anything of it?'

'A graceless filigree thing? If it is the one she tried to give to me, then I know of it. I bade her return it to her brother.'

Konrad looked at him, nonplussed. It was hard to doubt him; what reason could he have for lying? His possible espionage via Verinka did not seem to have any bearing on the case. If anyone had killed her over it, it would far more likely have been Tsevar.

Perhaps it had nothing to do with her death at all.

'Did you know that she was ill?' he said, his thoughts taking an abrupt swerve in direction.

Balandin's brows rose. 'Of course I knew. I saw much of her. I took her to the best doctors. No one could help her — but no one imagined her to be in such danger, either.'

'You speak of her death with remarkable composure,' Konrad noted.

'Whatever my feelings are, I need not make a theatre-display of them.'

'You had no reason, then, to think that she was being poisoned?'

'How could I?'

A fair question. Konrad took another pastry, and sat munching upon it in glowering discontent. The case positively *refused* to afford him a break. He wanted to believe that this brute of a man was guilty. Because he looked like he could be, as though that had ever meant anything. Because he was rude and boorish and had irritated Konrad. Because then the case would be over and he could get back to Nanda.

In truth, though, he had no good reasons to suspect him whatsoever.

'Right,' said Konrad. 'Setting aside for now my right, or lack thereof, to ask questions. Will you tell me one thing?'

'If it will get you off my back.'

'You seem to have known Verinka very well. Do you know of anybody who might have wanted to harm her? Anybody she quarrelled with?'

'She hated Tsevar,' said Balandin.

Konrad blinked. 'Tsevar claims they were close, at least until recently.'

The bitter smile returned. 'Until I got hold of her, you mean? Yes, so he has said to me. Actually, he is a blind fool. Verinka always despised him. He thought of nothing but money, she said, and patronised her daily. They were never close. *He* could have done it.'

Konrad felt like hurling something at… something. Pure frustration. Why did he have to care about the convoluted rivalries and affections between these three? None of their accounts matched up with one another. If Verinka had always hated her brother, she certainly hadn't behaved like it. How could Tsevar genuinely believe they'd been close if she had? Then again, why would she imagine her brother capable of her murder if she hadn't despised him?

Had she just said those things to Balandin because it was what he wanted to hear? He'd said she was a pleaser.

Konrad did not care who loved or hated whom. He did not care whether Balandin was a canny sneak, using Verinka for her connections, or a man in love; he did not care whether those two wretched siblings had adored or hated one another. He didn't care.

He thought back to Tasha's questions. *Do you like being a detective?* Whether he did or no, he wasn't a very good one. Not if he couldn't take the right kind of interest in these kinds of details.

'Anyone else Verinka fought with?' he forced himself to say. 'Or was it love and peace with all the rest of the world?'

Balandin shrugged. 'Not that I— wait, though. One day when I arrived to collect her, she was having some kind of quarrel with a woman who'd stopped in front of her house. She seemed very angry.'

'What was the fight about?'

'She wouldn't say.'

'All right. Describe this woman.'

'Will you take this information to the police, and stop hounding me?'

'That will be up to the police.'

'I asked if *you* will stop hounding me.'

He wasn't angry again, precisely, but some kind of peculiar

emphasis lay behind the words. Konrad looked long at him, and saw a shadow of something behind his eyes. Fear perhaps.

And that put the fear into Konrad, too, for why would a man like this fear a mere Konrad Savast, unless he had asked himself why such a man might chase all over town in search of a killer, and come up with an answer uncomfortably close to the truth?

'I am just assisting the police,' said Konrad evenly. 'The inspector makes all the decisions.'

Balandin shook his head, showing some of the same frustration Konrad felt. 'As you will. The woman was stout, older than Verinka. Same colouring as half the city. Nothing much out of the way about her.'

'And you have no idea how Verinka knew her?'

'No. Verinka would not speak of her.'

Konrad, recognising the moment when the interview must draw to a close, waved a hand in irritation. 'I *should* find another hobby,' he muttered.

Balandin regarded him with a curious tilt to his head. 'Is this how you spend much of your time?'

'Assisting the police, or eating pastries by the fire?'

'The latter,' said Balandin.

'Yes,' Konrad said, it being, after all, the truth. At least since Nanda had become a regular part of his life.

'No bad thing, independent wealth.'

That, thought Konrad sourly, depended on how you came by it. And he'd done worse things with his time. Far worse. 'I cannot promise that I won't have more questions,' he warned. 'Or the inspector might.'

Balandin rose to his feet. 'That's as maybe. But you'd better have a good reason, Mr. Savast. If you keep asking questions about me, I'd have to keep asking questions about *you.*'

On which happy note, he left. Konrad did not trouble himself to get up, or show his unwanted guest out. Balandin was a clever man; he could find his own way to the front door.

The interview left him feeling, above everything else, tired. Exhausted. Wearied to the core of his bones with the whole mess of it all.

That was the drawback to developing something like a life, he thought sourly. He'd developed the power of contrast, and a divided personality with it. The Konrad who gloried in quiet nights by the fire with his favourite people around him couldn't help but detest the other Konrad. The one who had to get up at the eerie hours of the morning and go chasing after miscreants with a sharpened bone in hand. The one who had to spend his afternoons haring all over the city, asking stupid questions of people who didn't want to talk to him and probably hadn't committed a crime anyway.

Grumpy, Master, chided Eetapi, floating down from the ceiling and draping herself around his neck.

'It is my very favourite mood.'

Yes, but how tiresome you are when you're in it.

He needed Nanda to jolly him out of it. Or mock him out of it, that usually worked as well. But she had enough troubles of her own, and a real friend would not needlessly burden her with his trials as well.

Stifling a sigh, he hauled himself out of his chair with two errands in mind. One: send a note to the inspector. They sought an unnamed woman of unknowable abode, stout and middle-aged and looking like half the rest of the women in the city. Good luck with that.

Two: finally get his dinner, if his cook hadn't given up on him altogether. Perhaps his mood had soured because he was half starved. That was often Nanda's theory, anyway. Perhaps that was why she was always pressing food on him: *she* found him a tiresome grump, too.

Meat, Master, recommended Eetapi. *And lots of it.*

Konrad exited his library, with the intention of applying himself to just that.

At one of the aforementioned eerie hours of the following morning — approximately three o'clock, to be exact — Konrad was roused from a mildly drunken slumber by the freezing wind to outdo all other freezing winds. The bone-chilling current drifting suddenly through his room brought him awake with a start, greeting him with the sensation of having been entombed in ice.

A familiar, if ghostly, visage hung over him.

'Finally,' Tasha snapped. 'You shouldn't drink so much, Konrad.'

'Why, because it's harder to wake me at inappropriate hours of the morning? Did it occur to you that I might prefer to sleep?'

'You are meant to sleep when the work is done.'

'I did.'

'There's more now.'

Konrad sat up with a groan. 'Would you mind turning off the winter routine? I cannot feel my feet.'

Tasha's incorporeal face stretched in a sadistic smile. 'I will turn it off when you get up.'

'I'm not getting up until you've turned it off.'

'What if I told you I've found your murderer?'

8

'Impossible,' said Konrad.

'Fact.'

'Well then, where is he?'

Tasha rolled her eyes. '*She* is... not here.'

Did Konrad imagine the abrupt shift from exasperation to shiftiness? Guilt, even. 'Where is *she*, then?' Konrad said. 'For that matter, who is she?' His thoughts flew back to Balandin's description of an altercation in the street. Stout woman. Middle years. Was that who Tasha meant? But how could she possibly have found a woman so imperfectly described — and whose description she hadn't even heard?

'Fine,' said Tasha. 'I've found your murder*ess* and also lost her, but you can get her back, can't you? You're the Malykant. You can walk faster than most men can run. There's no getting away from you.'

'You lost her.'

'I spooked her,' Tasha admitted. 'She ran away.'

'From *where*?'

'She's Verinka's neighbour, who hated her, and she's off her rocker if you hadn't guessed that already. *She* bought the widow weed, and she used it, too.'

'Slow down. How did you figure this out?'

In the long-suffering tones of all-knowing youth, Tasha said: 'The two of *you* were so set on the idea that some man must've sent my weed-buying woman, you didn't even consider that she might have been acting of her own accord. Just because Verinka pointed the

159

finger at her brother—'

'She *did*,' Konrad objected. 'Quite clearly.'

'The woman didn't even know she was being poisoned. How was she supposed to know who did it?'

Konrad opened his mouth, and shut it again, finding himself without argument. 'Well, and?'

'I went back and got some more details out of the woman who sold the jar of widow-weed. Not that she had much. But she remembered what one might call a distinguishing feature — a mole in a prominent place on the woman's face. So then I asked myself: if this woman wanted to poison Verinka, she must've been acquainted with her, and how would she have been? This Verinka divided her time between her home and that stupid lunch-club, so it had to have been at the one place or the other. And if I was wrong about that, well, finding out more about her habits would help.

'So I harassed all the neighbours until someone told me that Mrs. Usova, five doors up, was always sneering about Verinka for giving herself airs and being aloof and acting above her station with her wealthy brother and her suitors in fancy carriages — typical ill-natured stuff, one *would* think, only when I went to see her she matched the description, down to the mole and everything—'

'Stout?' asked Konrad. 'Middle-aged, nondescript?'

'Yes, and also well able to put on the kindly act, because she did that at first. Me being a sweet, appealing young lady, you understand.'

Konrad had trouble picturing Tasha putting on any such act, but kept that to himself. 'So, what then? You confronted her about it?'

'I did.'

'You should've come to me, or the inspector. Preferably both.'

'I know, but I got carried away. My first case! *I* solved it, me, while the two of you were trailing about after the brother and the suitor and who knows who else. I wanted to bring her in myself.'

'I fail to see how she could have got away from you.'

'She... locked me in her cellar,' Tasha confessed. 'My body's still there.'

Wearily, Konrad hauled himself out of bed. The bone-shattering cold had ebbed, thankfully, perhaps because Tasha was too busy talking to think about it. 'You are certain of her guilt, yes?'

'Quite. She had a lot to say about it, once suitably motivated. Sent Verinka little "gifts", apparently, supposedly from her admirer, but nicely dosed.'

'But why didn't the inspector's men catch on? They talked to all the neighbours, I thought.'

'Didn't you hear what I said? The woman's full of all the usual neighbourhood gripes, admittedly with an extra layer or twelve of malice. Nobody would take it as reason for murder, not without the other information. And only I had that.'

'Tasha, I respect your abilities, but are you certain? You are right: nobody could take all this as justification for murder.'

'No one reasonable could, but in case you had not grasped the facts here, this woman is not reasonable.'

'They did argue, once,' Konrad said, and told her about his conversation with Balandin. 'Perhaps their relationship was venomous on both sides.'

'And what were you doing with that information? Sleeping on it?'

'Some of us still require sleep, Tasha.'

'How sad for you.'

Konrad had by this time disappeared into his dressing-room, and saw no occasion to reply.

The house of Verinka's disgruntled neighbour proved to be very similar in character to Verinka's own. Not just in the proportions and exterior décor, either; walking soft-footed through Mrs. Usova's hallway, parlour and kitchen, Konrad felt as though he might have entered the wrong house by mistake. The two women had much the same taste in furnishings, a similar dislike of ornament, and as far as neatness and cleanliness went, Mrs. Usova differed only in being even more scrupulous about it than Verinka. The house was so clean, in fact, that it bordered upon sterile; any signs of ordinary inhabitation had been ruthlessly scrubbed and wiped and polished away.

The stairs down to the cellar lay in a corner of the kitchen. Only a trapdoor led down, these houses being too modestly proportioned to permit of the space for stairs. Konrad, wondering why Tasha's skills with inconvenient locks seemed to have deserted her, found the answer to this question in the large, solid oaken chest that had been dragged into place atop the door. Even if she had manoeuvred the lock — which she had, he discovered upon pulling away the chest — she could never have got the door open. Lamaeni or no, one of the few things Tasha lacked was sufficient brute strength to hurl chests through the air, especially when they were filled with something heavy... a stray thought had him browsing briefly through the contents.

A thick glass jar occupied one corner, filled with a dried leaf of some kind. Konrad procured a bit, and wrapped it in his handkerchief. In case there was any doubt about Mrs. Usova's guilt, it would be useful to be able to check the identity of the herb with Nanda. Nobody had an innocent explanation for harbouring so large a jar of reasonably fresh widow weed.

'Tasha,' he called, hauling open the trapdoor. A palpable darkness greeted him, unbroken by so much as a sliver of light. His own lantern could illuminate little but the top two stone steps leading down. 'Tasha, hurry up or we'll never catch her—'

Tasha rose, corpse-like, from the darkness, her white face stark in the ghostly lamplight. She rose with a hoarse scream.

Konrad screamed back.

'Heh,' she said, and clambered out. 'Did you bring the snakies?'

'That was horrible.'

'We're a lamaeni and a Malykant. *One* of us has to be horrible, and if you aren't going to do it then it has to be me.'

'I am going to do it,' said Konrad grimly. 'Just as soon as we find your kindly friend.'

'The snakies?' she prompted.

'Say hello, serpents,' Konrad called.

Twin lights bloomed in the air over Tasha's head: sickly white for Eetapi, a diseased green for Ootapi.

'Ooh, that's very horrible,' said Tasha, and gave them a jaunty salute.

We like her, Ootapi informed Konrad.

Which he ignored. To Tasha he said, 'Tell me at least that you fed off her. Sumptuously.'

'I thought you disapproved of my doing that.'

'On ordinary people innocent of murder, yes. In her case, draining her energy might slow her down.'

Tasha patted her stomach, not that she used it for this particular kind of feasting but the gesture served. 'She's too stout to go far anyway,' said Tasha.

'Just because she's— never mind. Serpents, spread out please. Any

162

hint of her passage at all, you tell us.'

Yes, Master.

'As for you,' said Konrad to Tasha, fixing her with a stern eye. 'We'll talk later about your chatting with the suspect without me, but did any part of this ill-executed conversation include some hint as to where she might run to?'

'No.'

'Excellent.'

'She really just rambled about how horrible Verinka was, how unfair it was that she had all these rich friends and an admirer and so on, and how she'd got what she deserved now that she was dead.'

'Charming woman.'

'Accused her of being aloof, snobbish, too good for her company — I could go on. She never even invited her neighbours in for tea! Not even once! *Not good enough* for her, were we? No! Not when she had the likes of the Gentleman coming calling!' Tasha put on a shrill voice, and shrieked the last few words.

'Did she really say it like that?'

'No, it was more just venomous. But I thought it sounded good that way. Also, I think she may have had a thing for the Gentleman in question. She did rather dwell on his finer points. And what did Verinka have that she did not? And so on.'

Konrad had by this time paced his way back to the front door, Tasha trailing behind. He'd hoped for a quick response from the serpents, if she really hadn't gone far. But there were only two of them, and there was only so far they could sense.

He hesitated, genuinely at a loss. He knew nothing about the woman, and neither did Tasha, save that she had malice enough for twenty people and a vindictive nature. Where might she go? If she'd merely stumbled off through the streets and made a run for it, the serpents should have found her by now. If they hadn't—

Master. This way.

You've found her? Konrad hurled himself out of Mrs. Usova's house and took off down the street, following the beckoning sense of Ootapi.

She went this way, Ootapi said, which meant no. But a trail to follow was better than nothing.

Few streetlamps lit the narrow streets in this part of the city, and they were turned very low at this hour. Konrad plunged into thick darkness, only intermittently illuminated by a guttering glow. Twice he stumbled over uneven patches in the snow, swearing horribly the second time, and abandoning his ordinary sight. He let his spirit-sight swamp his vision, and the darkness leapt into shadows etched starkly against ghost-white. *Ootapi,* he called. *You'll have to guide us.*

Ootapi did not reply, but his ethereal coils blazed in Konrad's altered vision, a beacon by which to navigate the winding, night-dark streets of Verinka's neighbourhood. Her flight had taken her by a tortuous route, perhaps by design, perhaps out of panic. Konrad, with his lengthened, ground-eating stride, had covered at least a half-mile before he began to recognise his environs. Mrs. Usova was heading into the heart of the city.

If anything, he might have expected her to flee the city altogether. A flight out into the Bones at this season bordered upon suicidal, however; if she had sense enough, even in her disordered state, to realise that, then perhaps she had some other means in mind of departure. A coach south. A sleigh north. But she was not bound for the north gate, it seemed, nor for any coaching-inn, for Ootapi passed three of the latter without pausing.

They seemed to be bound unerringly for the police house, but that could not be—

She is in there, said Ootapi, stopping at last.

Before Konrad, Ekamet's primary police house rose, tall and shadowed. *Here?* he demanded. *She cannot be in there!*

Why not?

No fugitive from justice would run to the police!

Ootapi's silence said enough. A lone light burned somewhere above. Konrad would have put money on its being Alexander's office.

Tasha caught up, panting for breath, and ran straight into the police headquarters without stopping.

'Er,' said Konrad, and hastened after her.

Inside, he found only silence and darkness. The entrance hall, all white stone and carpets in the daylight, was a mass of shadows at this hour. He stood inside the door, listening, but heard nothing.

Where in here, Ootapi?

Left, answered the serpent. *Down the corridor. On the right there is a door.*

There was. Konrad stopped, and put out an arm to hold Tasha

back. He could not really suppose her to be in any danger from such a woman, but it did not pay to be careless. Or reckless, was that not what Nanda had called him?

Tasha furiously shook her head, pointing at nothing in particular.

He admonished her with a finger to his lips and a quelling frown, and softly went through the half-open door.

And collided with a person barrelling out of it, who stopped with a shriek and stared up at him.

'Are you the police?' she said. 'Finally! I wish to make a complaint. Your *ward* has invaded my home, and made such accusations against me as I can barely stand to repeat! She ought to be sent back to the streets, where she doubtless belongs—' She broke off when Tasha herself appeared — in a flare of ghost-light provided by Ootapi.

Tasha gave a ghastly grin.

'This ward?' said Konrad politely.

Mrs. Usova faltered, but made a recover. 'Yes, this one. She...' Trailing off, she gazed doubtfully upon Tasha, who looked at that moment like anybody's worst nightmare, and took a step back.

'You shouldn't have run,' said Tasha. 'And you *really* shouldn't have thrown me into your cellar.'

Konrad watched the woman's face, marvelling. He had seen real fury there, and a deep fear, but only momentarily. Now she was transformed: a good, respectable woman, outraged and appalled by indecent treatment, seeking refuge with the police. As any good, respectable citizen would do.

'I know you'll help me,' she said warmly to Konrad, somehow managing to seem both motherly and appalled in one.

'He is not the police,' said Tasha, with a relish he privately thought a fraction unseemly.

Mrs. Usova at last paid him attention enough to realise that he was not quite the vision of a typical policeman. 'Who are you, then?' she said, her outrage melting into a heartrending vulnerability. Her lip trembled.

'He's—' Tasha began, but Konrad clapped a hand over her mouth and another to the back of her head, bottling her up until she capitulated, and sagged in his grip.

Carefully, Konrad released her.

To his relief, she said nothing more.

'Did you kill Verinka Tarasovna?' he said to his quarry.

165

'Of course I did not.' Mrs. Usova gave a little laugh. 'Why would I?'

Tasha spoke up then. 'That isn't what you said before.'

'Nonsense, child.' Mrs. Usova directed a stern look at Tasha, who folded her arms and stared right back. 'Children do have fevered imaginations, do they not?' said Mrs. Usova to Konrad. 'This one is clearly running wild, and ought to be contained. I came here to inform her superior—'

'At this hour of the night?'

She blinked in smiling incomprehension. 'But of course. There must be someone here. People do not only need the police during the day, do they?'

As if summoned by these words, Alexander appeared behind Konrad, heralded by his characteristic measured footsteps. 'What is afoot down here— oh? Konrad?'

'You think no one ever believes *children*,' spat Tasha, and Konrad realised she was genuinely incensed. 'But these two do. *He'll* believe me.'

'Tasha?' said the inspector.

'Your ward, sir—' began Mrs. Usova.

'She killed Verinka,' said Tasha at the same time.

Alexander blinked myopically at Tasha. 'But what would she be doing here, then?'

If Konrad had doubts left, they were banished by the gleam of triumph in Mrs. Usova's eyes. 'Dissembling,' he said. 'Playing a role. With great skill, I admit. An innocent person could have no qualms about entering the police house, hm?'

'I am innocent,' said Mrs. Usova, but something was slipping behind her façade. Konrad caught a glimpse of rage.

He withdrew his handkerchief, the one with the widow-weed wrapped up in it, and gave it into the inspector's hand. 'I found this in a jar in her kitchen. In the chest there. If you test it, I am convinced you will discover it to be widow-weed, and any one of your men will soon discover the rest at Mrs. Usova's house.'

'It is a medicine,' said the woman quickly. 'I use it myself.'

'It is a discredited medicine, rightly banned, and even if it were not you could hardly be in need of so large a supply.' Konrad watched the woman's face closely as he spoke; he needed to be certain of her guilt. 'You bought the jar some five or six months ago from a women's facility in the lower town. The woman who sold it to you will confirm the date.'

'And that she sold you a *full* jar,' Tasha put in, with a quick, questioning look at Konrad.

Konrad nodded. 'The one in your house is much depleted. What happened to it, if you have only been taking small, safe quantities yourself at intervals?'

'I— I shared it with some other women of my acquaintance—'

'Indeed you did. Specifically, Verinka Tarasovna. Whom you hated.'

Mrs. Usova, damn her, had control of herself again. She smiled benignly upon Konrad, and said in a sweet way: 'Who could have hated poor Verinka?'

'That isn't what you said earlier, either,' said Tasha furiously.

Konrad gave an inward sigh. Tasha had uttered the words "properly motivated", too. What had she done to *motivate* so wily a woman to speak openly about her hatred, her guilt? It did not bear thinking about.

Having temporarily bested Tasha, the dratted woman had guile enough to try to rescue herself even after so damning a tirade. And she was convincing. Konrad did not know quite how to proceed. He did not doubt Tasha's word, for surely she would not invent such a story — and it did dovetail with a few other scant facts Konrad possessed about the case. But it wasn't proof. Much as he would like to skewer the woman then and there and be done with the matter, he had to be certain beyond all doubt that he had the right killer.

'Can she be locked up for the night?' Konrad said to Alexander. 'Perhaps in the morning, someone can investigate the herb. If it is widow-weed, there can be little doubt of her guilt.'

'*My* guilt?' snapped Mrs. Usova. 'I have explained the herbs! What about your filthy ward, breaking into people's houses at night and accusing them of crimes! I demand assistance!'

The inspector pulled his pipe from a pocket, and lit it. 'See,' he said to Konrad. 'This is why I didn't give her the address.'

'I stand rebuked.'

'I *did* find her, though,' said Tasha staunchly. 'You have to give me credit for that.'

'I do,' said Alexander, fragrant smoke pouring from his lips. 'Madam, if your intent was to discredit a girl you took for a jumped-up street orphan, you have badly miscalculated. Any story of Tasha's is considered credible, and she can have no reason to lie about you.'

'But she has,' insisted the infernal woman. 'And really, what could one expect?'

Pitting her carefully cultivated air of respectability against Tasha's obvious lack of it? Konrad shook his head, privately wishing Tasha a thousand miles away. Yes, she'd found their killer — probably — but with such infernal complications, he did not know how to proceed.

'The weed,' he said. 'Tomorrow. And if Balandin can be found to identify this woman as the same one he saw quarrelling with Verinka, that would help, too.'

'Right,' said Alexander.

Mrs. Usova's mouth dropped open. She stood frozen in indignation, or horror, or both — and then made a break for the door.

Konrad was ready for that. He stepped smoothly to block the doorway, seeming, suddenly, taller. Darker. More menacing. She could not have said why, later, she had shrunk from an ordinary man, wearing a pleasant smile as he barred the door before her. But she saw something in him that terrified the small, primal part of her soul that knew when to run.

Konrad made sure of it.

'You'll remain in police custody,' he told her. 'If you are indeed innocent, you will be released soon.'

'And if not?' she said, her wide, horrified eyes fixed upon Konrad's face.

Konrad had no answer to offer her. He turned away, leaving the inspector and Tasha to deal with her between them.

Quietly, he stole up to Alexander's office, and took up a station in his usual chair there, waiting.

Some quarter of an hour later, the inspector returned.

'Got her into a cell,' he reported. 'She isn't happy.'

'If she said half the things Tasha claims, I struggle to believe she is ever happy,' Konrad replied.

Alexander grunted. He did not sit down, hovering instead near his desk, still clutching his pipe. 'Anything I can do for you, Savast?'

'It is an ungodly hour, isn't it? I was wondering what you were doing here at such a time.'

Alexander fiddled with his pipe, perhaps in order to avoid meeting Konrad's gaze. 'I am often here late.'

'I know it,' Konrad said. 'But there is late, and then there is four in the morning.'

No reply came.

'I am... concerned,' Konrad persevered. 'Why do you not go home?'

'Perhaps I am simply dedicated to my job.'

'There can be no doubt of that.'

Silence.

'Is there no one waiting for you at home?' Thinking back over the course of their friendship, Konrad realised — with some shame at his obliviousness — that the inspector had never spoken of his home life. Nor of his family, if he had any.

'There isn't,' said Alexander, more or less neutrally, but Konrad sensed that there was more.

'Will you tell me?' he said. 'I am ready to help, if I can.'

'You cannot.' Alexander took a seat at last, and sat there with the slumped posture of a man without hope, as though half the animating life force of him had vanished with the words.

'Tell me.'

Alexander was silent for some time. Konrad would not push him again. He would speak, or he was free to hold his peace.

Finally he said, 'I had family.'

Konrad, noticing the past tense, said nothing.

'My wife died many years ago. And my daughter — Magriet — last year.'

'She— was she—' Konrad swallowed the word *killed*.

'Sickness,' said the inspector. 'A fever. She was — about Tasha's age.'

Konrad was silent, putting pieces together in his mind.

'Tasha appeared here a few months after Mag died,' Alexander continued. 'She needed a place, and I... hadn't the heart to turn her away.'

'I did wonder about that.'

'Well.' Alexander finished cleaning his pipe, and put it back in his pocket. 'The house is so empty, I... prefer it here.'

'I'm so sorry,' Konrad said. 'For the loss. I can't imagine...'

Alexander looked up at last. 'Never had children?'

'No.'

He smiled faintly, a pained smile, and said nothing else.

Konrad struggled for something else to say, something that might express the way his heart hurt for the inspector's pain. But he came up with nothing. No mere syllables could ever make any difference to him.

But there was one thing he could do.

'It's still early,' he said. 'Why don't you come back for breakfast with me? Mrs. Aristova says you're her favourite guest.'

That brought a spark of amusement to the inspector's eyes. 'Why should I be?'

'Because you're so appreciative. Always a clean plate, she says, and always a kind word sent down to the kitchen.'

'Konrad. You aren't trying to set me up with your cook, are you? I'm sure she is a lovely woman, but—'

'No, no,' Konrad said hastily. 'Just with her fresh-baked bread, her excellent coffee, those perfect eggs she does, perhaps a bit of that smoked fish you like…'

'Now you sound like Nanda. Trying to mend me with food.'

'Not with food,' Konrad said, rising from his chair. 'Maybe with company.'

Alexander thought this over, and eventually stood up. He moved slowly, heavy with weariness and grief and lack of sleep. Watching the play of exhaustion and pain across his face, Konrad chided himself for his inattention. The inspector had been grieving for months, and he hadn't known. Yes, he was a private man; he hadn't chosen to confide in Konrad about his life, for reasons of his own. But Konrad ought to have seen. *Something.*

'If there's going to be smoked fish,' said Alexander, 'I daresay Mrs. Aristova could persuade me to a bite.'

'Right.' Konrad donned his hat again, and collected his cane. 'Breakfast's this way.'

9

Strange, to set off for "work" at a reasonable hour later that day, his destination the police house. Especially considering the nature of the work that awaited him there.

The inspector had departed an hour or two before, having disposed of a hearty portion of smoked fish and a variety of other delectables. He had not spoken again of his family, or his home, and Konrad had not asked. The silence had been a companionable one, though, and by the time Alexander departed the house again, well fed if not well rested, it seemed to Konrad that he was in a better frame of mind.

So was Konrad, at least until he was called upon to set off after Mrs. Usova. The woman bothered him, in some obscure way. He had taken an instant dislike to her, and for reasons he could not decipher. It was not, he thought, because she was almost certainly a murderer, though that was more than cause enough. Her affectations offended him, her deceit, her spite, her comfortable conviction that she could say anything and be believed.

What had Tasha done, to win (if it could be termed a victory) some part of her true thoughts and deeds regarding Verinka Tarasovna? Needled her into it? That was likely. The girl could goad a rock into losing its temper, if she so chose.

But she was lamaeni, too. Perhaps she'd done a lot worse.

Konrad could not feel that he much cared.

Alexander was not in his office when Konrad arrived, but a note lay waiting on his desk, inscribed with a large "KS" in black ink.

Konrad opened it.

Called away, but go ahead. Karyavin found the jar you mentioned. It's widow weed. And some of the neighbours vouch for some part of Tasha's story. Seems Mrs. Usova has let fall some malicious remarks about Verinka before. - AN

It was thin, Konrad acknowledged to himself. Possession of a jar of widow weed did not absolutely prove that the woman had used it, though its presence in her house was highly suspicious, and he did not buy her explanation at all. Perhaps he just struggled to believe that anybody could commit murder with so flimsy a motive. Had anybody malice enough to slowly poison a fellow human being to death, just because she took exception to the woman's attitude, or style of living, or connections? Or over envy, at perceived admiration or advantages that did not seem deserved?

Apparently. Given his line of work, he ought not to be surprised by the depths of depravity to which humankind could sometimes fall. Particularly when the fragile balance of sanity slipped.

'Mrs. Usova,' he said a few minutes later, having, with the use of the key the inspector had left him, let himself into her cell. She'd been put well below, in a cell a little separate from the rest. That lying tongue of hers had prompted Alexander to keep her apart from other prisoners, perhaps, though the entire floor proved to be deserted except for her.

That was... convenient. Thoughtful of the inspector, Konrad mused; he had ample peace and quiet within which to work.

He had with him the bone he had harvested from Verinka's torso.

'You are no policeman,' she said, with an attempt at her former cajoling manner. But sleeplessness and fear had worn away some of her powers to dissemble, and her voice shook. She darted a look at the door as Konrad closed it, but did not attempt to escape. 'Have you come to help me?'

Konrad ignored the sweet smile which accompanied these words. 'You can hardly suppose it likely,' he said. 'You should know that the inspector has found your jar of poison, and confirmed its contents as widow weed. The same herb used to kill Verinka Tarasovna. Is that a coincidence, madam?'

'It— of course it is. One of her gentleman did it, or—' She had no other theories to advance, for she fell silent.

'I did favour the brother, myself. His motive still strikes me as sounder than yours. But the signs all point to you. You were witnessed fighting with Verinka, outside her house. Some of your neighbours have confirmed that you felt a great deal of resentment towards her, and had frequently expressed your disapprobation of her conduct. It *seems* a poor reason to kill someone, but then I have rarely heard of a good one.'

'They are liars,' she said, smiling, but Konrad could see that she was sweating, and a desperate gleam had come into her eyes. 'They have always disliked me — all of them.'

'Oh?' said Konrad politely. 'But how could anyone dislike so kindly a soul as yourself?'

Her smile fell away. She had run out of lies to tell, or she simply saw the implacability in Konrad; he'd taken no trouble to hide it. She stood up from the bare bench upon which she'd been sitting, and advanced towards him, hands clasped, her expression pleading. 'You must see how it was, sir. She— she hated me, she would have harmed me if I had not done something—'

'But that is not true either, is it?' Konrad said coldly. 'You told the truth to our ward, madam, late last night. Why deny it now?'

'That— that *rat*,' spat Mrs. Usova, anger darkening her face. 'She goaded me, taunted me, threw insults and accusations — slapped me! *Me!*'

That sounded like Tasha. *Not* exactly police approved methods, but then his weren't either. 'And when you realised what you'd said, you set out on this absurd masquerade to discredit any tale she might carry to the police. Yes?'

'I tried to kill her,' snarled Mrs. Usova. 'I thought I had. But she— laughed at me.'

'Tasha's close to unkillable,' Konrad agreed, unwrapping Verinka's bone. Cleaned, sharpened, it shone dully white.

Verinka's killer took a step back. 'Wh-what is to be done with me?'

'The usual fate of murderers, madam,' said Konrad. It did not feel right, to conduct such business down here, inside a locked cell. He was used to a fevered chase through the night, the triumphant apprehension of a fleeing killer, and the inevitable end to the hunt. Or laying a trap, into which a murderer walked through their own greed or arrogance or destructiveness. This felt... cold. Clinical.

But she had built this trap herself, and pure arrogance had taken her there. Arrogance, malice, envy, and perhaps an inability to grasp certain facts of reality. She lived in her own world, a place where all those about her were villains and deserving of the worst punishments. A world where she alone was righteous and justified.

A world where everyone was a fool, to be taken in by her superior cleverness.

Another stain upon the world, in short. She deserved the torments her victim and The Malykt would visit upon her in the beyond.

Konrad ceased his dithering, and got to work.

'Verinka is waiting,' he said, and struck.

10

When you are ready, Konrad had written in his note to Nanda, *I await you.*

He did not need to specify where; she would remember. He bade his coachman drive him to the city gate, and from there he made the rest of the journey on foot. No gentleman's attire today, to his relief. For a venture into the enchanting dangers of the Bone Forest, he wore the simplest of garb: stout boots, a waxed great-coat, layers against the cold. Always he donned these with relief, for thus attired he felt like himself again.

Whoever that was.

Nanda laughed at his hut. It *did* make a comical sight in some respects, hiked up on its leggy stilts above the treacherously ice-wreathed swamp-water beneath. The hut itself looked overlarge, perched up there, its weather-darkened wooden slats extending a fraction too far on either side. However ungainly it looked, however, it was stout and stable. However much it might shake and rattle and sway in winter's winds, it had never betrayed Konrad yet, and stood firm against every attempt to dislodge it.

Konrad strode through the thin, pale Bone-trees with a confidence and an ease he rarely felt in the city. Here was his element, out here in the wilds. Nobody to expect anything of him, save that he mind his own business, and leave others to theirs. No masquerade to maintain, no horrific duties to perform, no — he shuddered — social events to attend. Or worse yet, *host.*

The cold, though. As he swung himself up the ladder and through the trapdoor into the belly of his hut, he had in justice to reflect that his fireplaces at Bakar House were worth a fair degree of torment. The wind sliced mercilessly through his wool and waxed layers, and while the onslaught largely ceased once he shut the trapdoor behind him, a persistent, icy draught swirled around the room.

Hopeless, expecting to light a fire in here. He'd burn the place down. Instead, he sat on his makeshift rushes-and-cloth bed, wrapped every blanket he owned around himself, and waited for Nanda.

He had plenty of time to reflect as he sat there alone, for she did not come for some hours. He'd thought to bring food, thankfully, a quantity of pies and preserved fruit; this he devoured, saving one or two of the choicest morsels for Nanda.

What could she be preparing to tell him? He'd spent countless hours ruminating on the topic of her mysterious illness, ever since news of it had first reached him. Not from Nanda. From a former case. A killer with unusual senses. He'd known, somehow, that Nan was ill, and had told Konrad only to spite her.

Nanda hadn't denied it. But though Konrad had watched her closely since then, he had detected few signs of deterioration. Yes, she was less energetic than once she had been. She tired more easily, and sometimes she wore such a wreath of shadows around her eyes as to elicit all of Konrad's worst fears.

But nothing more. Nothing, save the hints her bedroom had offered: restless, tormented nights.

What happened when Nanda slept?

No answer came to his mind, only purposeless, absurd speculation. He got up a few times, and strode about the hut, walking the cold and the stiffness out of his legs. When the thin afternoon sunlight began to falter, and dusk gathered itself to descend, he knew a moment's fear.

What if she did not come?

He was halfway to the trapdoor, hardly knowing why; would he hurtle down it again, run all the way back to Ekamet, and invade Nanda's house? But to wait grew intolerable. To sit, heart pounding with a growing fear, head full of tormenting ideas, and with no power of action; he could bear it no longer.

The trapdoor flew open, hurled with some energy — or irritation

— by someone below.

Nanda's head appeared moments later.

'Going somewhere?' she said, eyeing him. She had a lantern, judging from the shivering streaks of light splashing into the gathering darkness.

Konrad hastened forward to take it from her. Setting it on the floor, he helped Nanda into the room, and firmly shut the trapdoor behind her. Night brought a deepening of the piercing cold, and he wished again that he could contrive some means of bringing warmth to his otherwise perfect hut.

He settled for enfolding Nanda in a tight embrace, for she was warm, and maybe he felt so to her, too.

He *felt* her eyebrows go up, pressed though her face was against his shoulder. 'What's this about?'

'I'm glad you came,' he said into her hair.

'I did say I would.'

'I know.'

'You cannot have doubted me, surely.' She spoke with a trace of humour, and when she pulled away Konrad had leisure to admire the familiar twinkle in her eyes.

'Never,' he said stoutly. 'Or at least, not much.'

Nanda sat down at the foot of his bed, and purloined half of his blankets. 'These are still warm,' she said, wrapping them around herself.

'I have been here a while.' He did not immediately join her, but stood watching her face. The lamp's soft glow softened any darkness there, for she looked pale and hale and much her usual self. Too pale, perhaps?

Nanda chuckled. 'You've been giving me that mother-hen look for months. I don't suppose it has helped.'

'You don't really look ill,' he allowed.

'It isn't quite a usual sickness.'

'I suppose I'd guessed that.'

She fell silent, and if she sought for words to begin she did not find them.

'Just tell me, Nan,' he said at last. 'It may be difficult, but perhaps I can help.'

Her expression turned baleful. 'That is the most annoying thing of all. You might be able to help, otherwise I'd never dream of

177

humbling myself like this.'

'Humbling yourself?' he repeated blankly. 'How are you humbled by contracting an illness?'

'If I brought it upon myself, through my own stupidity? My own arrogance? What then?'

'I'd suspect you are being far too hard on yourself—'

'I'm not, Konrad. Everything I just said is the plain truth.'

'And you think I won't love you anymore, if you've been foolish? Done something wrong?'

She just looked at him, and everything in her face said: *Yes, of course I think that.*

He laughed.

'I don't see what's funny,' said she with asperity.

'You say that, while you're sitting here with *me*. Konrad Savast, slayer. Serial killer, if you like. And how did I get into this position in the first place? Because I did the mother of all stupid, reckless, *terrible* things, but you haven't washed your hands of *me* yet.'

Nanda sniffed. 'It's those gentry-togs. They dazzle a girl so, I hardly know what I'm thinking.'

He managed a faint smile, and took a seat next to her, stealing a blanket to ward his feet against the chill. 'Right, I'm ready,' he said. 'Confession time. What wretched things have you done?'

Nanda said nothing for a moment. The lantern-light shone eerily upon her face, and shadows seemed to leap in her eyes. 'I'd better show you,' she decided.

Konrad had no time to reply, for already something was happening. There *were* shadows in her eyes; shadows etched in light, like the spirit-lands, and those shadows spread to engulf Nanda's frame. She shone stark-white, like a spirit herself, and Konrad's heart plummeted and began to race, for she wasn't *dead* surely, she couldn't be—

He grabbed her hand, and felt a moment's relief to find it warm and solid in his own. Not dead. Something else.

A low, grating chuckle sounded, startling him, for it could not possibly have come from Nanda. Following the sound, his eye travelled to the dusty slats beneath his feet, and the lantern there.

'Fae?' he breathed, wondering, for half-hidden in shadows of its own making stood a twisted little spirit-creature, a goblin in common parlance, or a ghoul, or a wraith; he hardly knew. It twined about

Nanda's feet with some mockery of affection, for its presence was anything but loving. Everywhere it touched her, it stole from her: her vitality, her energy, her life itself. Bit by bit.

There were more, he saw. If only it had been just the one, Nanda could have borne it; nothing so small could bring Nanda low. But there were more.

'I can hold them at bay when I am awake,' she said. 'To a certain extent, anyway. And I can hide them from... well, from everyone, but especially you.'

'Not at night, though,' Konrad said, realisation dawning. 'Not when you sleep.' What nightmares would such contorted creatures bring? How much did they weaken her, night after night? How had she borne it, month after month? A lesser person would have foundered long ago.

'You're wondering how this happened,' Nanda said, a faint smile curving her lips even as another grubby fae romped repulsively through her hair. 'That is the stupid part.'

'You didn't... Nan, you didn't treat with these creatures?'

'It was just one at first,' she said wearily. 'One pact. My mother needed — more than I could give at the time. It was worth it, and so easily borne that the next time it was... easier, to take on a second.'

'How many do you have now?'

'Five,' she whispered, with a quiet desperation which cut Konrad to the quick.

'But—' he said. 'But why, Nan? What could have been so important that you'd risk so many?' Pacts with spirit-fae were the province of spirit witches, and many, he knew, held some agreement with one such familiar. The fae lent their peculiar abilities to the witch, in exchange for some small piece of her soul — so went the lore, at any rate. Looking at Nanda, he thought it was not quite accurate. They were taking *everything*, by slow degrees. What would be left of her, by the time she finally died? Would any of her spirit remain, to pass into The Malykt's care?

'My mother's work, for one,' she said. 'She uses some part of her Oracle's powers to avert disasters, when she can, and sometimes she has need of me.'

'Does she know what you've been doing to keep it up?'

'She's an Oracle,' Nanda said tartly.

'Right.'

179

'Then sometimes there are — customers, I must call them — who come to me seeking remedies. I can heal some of their complaints sometimes, if I am suitably assisted. I've saved lives that way. It was worth it, Konrad,' she said, before he could speak.

'That was all five?' he said, instead of the objection he'd been planning to utter.

'No. Three was bad enough, and the last two…'

'Yes?'

'It was at Divoro. I cannot ordinarily Read anything from a deceased corpse, not once the spirit has fled. But I can if… with help. And there were other things.'

Konrad had frequently wished that the expedition to Divoro had never been made at all. He should have been there alone, doing his Malykant's work as he must, but without endangering either Nanda or Alexander. He wished it again now, so fiercely.

'Mother told me I should not go,' Nanda said with a wry smile. 'Why don't I ever listen to her, Konrad?'

'Who ever listens to parental prohibitions?' he said.

'Fools certainly don't.'

'You haven't been a fool, Nanda.'

'I have. Only a fool overestimates her abilities, imagines herself invincible, refuses to accept the consequences of proceeding down a certain road—'

'Your motives were excellent. Unselfish to a fault.'

'Were they? Yes, I helped some people. But there is always selfishness in that. The satisfaction, of sending an ailing patient away healed. Of averting some catastrophe, half-glimpsed in my mother's sight. Of helping to avenge Eino, and the others. It made me feel good, too. Like a hero.' Nanda passed a hand over her eyes, and the crawling creatures around her faded from sight. 'Pure ego.'

'We could argue all night about that, but I propose we instead consider the question of how to extricate you from these pacts.'

'If there were a simple way to do so, believe me I'd have done it.'

'So I supposed. Is there a complicated way? A difficult and dangerous way? I like those.'

'I did say you were reckless. You really should not be, on my account. I've been reckless enough for the both of us, and allow me therefore to apologise for reproaching you on that topic. It was hypocritical of me.'

'I like feeling like a hero too, Nan.' So much humility, apology and self-reproach from Nanda was unsettling him. It spoke more eloquently of her deterioration than anything else could. He wanted his proud, self-assured, somewhat righteous Nanda back.

'I refuse to play the damsel while you heroically set forth to rescue me,' Nanda retorted, which was more like her, and Konrad's heart eased a little.

'How about we heroically rescue you together?'

'Maybe we could do that.' Nanda gazed wistfully at him, looking as though she strongly doubted the possibility of their success.

'Can I speak with them?' Konrad said. 'Can you bring them back a moment?'

Nanda shook her head. 'They aren't here, precisely. What you saw are their... shades, or some such thing. They attach to me, attend me everywhere. They're here to collect what's owed. Those with whom I formed the pacts remain in the spirit-lands.'

'They can't be persuaded to relinquish or break the pact?'

'Pacts are absolute. They only dissolve once the agreed-upon price is paid. And I don't mind paying it, Konrad; I *did* agree. But I think that it will kill me.'

'Then we need to... reduce the impact, somehow. Break one or two of them.'

Nanda shrugged. 'There is no way to break them, Konrad. None.'

'What if we found some other way to pay the price?'

One eyebrow went up. 'Such as?'

'Such as... such as, me. Give them me.'

'Those were not the agreed terms.'

'Do you think I care?'

'I do,' said Nanda simply. 'And they will. And you have enough to deal with, Konrad, without—'

'Without what? Helping you? It won't kill me.'

'I don't know of any way to accomplish a— a transfer of debt, like that.'

'We can find one.' He hadn't released Nanda's hand, preferring to keep it safe in his own. He captured her other hand, too, and held both close. 'Have you any more objections to raise? Let's get them all out of the way now. And just to save time, the answer to them all is: "so what".'

That prompted a smile from her, a real one. 'No. I suppose I

181

don't. I… can't think of another solution.'

Konrad could. But it was a bloodthirsty, ruthless, Konrad-the-slayer solution and he knew Nanda would never consider it.

He didn't have to give her the option, though. Let her put her mind to the question of how to transfer some part of her burden to him. If she succeeded in that, well, excellent; problem solved. Konrad would bear the torment very willingly.

But if she didn't…

Serpents, he said silently. *You've heard all this?*

Yes, Master, they said, with a hissing disapproval from Eetapi. *Filthy sneaks.*

What would you have us do? said Ootapi. *We are eager to assissst, Master.*

Willing? You? No objections?

We are willing, repeated Eetapi.

You like Nanda, hm?

No one with any sense can fail to, Master, said Ootapi, which restored much of Konrad's flagging faith in the serpents' own sense. If they could be said to have any at all.

Find them, then. These creatures holding Nanda in thrall. Find who they are, and where they are, and bring this news to me.

What then, Master?

Then, Ootapi? We will do what we do best. We will go hunting.

His snakes twitched with a glee he might once have found repulsive, and he felt a surge of fierce, blood-hungry joy from them both.

Then they faded away, crossing in the space of a breath into the spirit-lands.

Konrad gently squeezed Nanda's hands. 'Shall we go home? Tormented by ghouls you may be, but you don't have to be cold and hungry while you do it.'

She smiled faintly, and rose to her feet, drawing Konrad with her. 'I don't know why, but I feel better in your house. Perhaps less alone.'

'It's at your service,' he promised. 'Every inch of it, for as long as you need. And so am I.'

Nanda looked him over, that beloved spark of mischief lighting her eye. 'Every inch of you?'

Konrad blinked, and failed to come up with a ready answer. *Yes* hardly seemed appropriate, but *no* would be falsehood—

Nanda's laugh echoed off the bare walls of his frigid hut, and she bent to haul open the trapdoor once more. 'Maybe we can discuss it,' she said, disappearing down the ladder. 'Somewhere warmer.'

Konrad collected the abandoned lantern and swung down the ladder in her wake.

THE MALEFIC CURSE

1

A knock came at the door of Bakar House.

Konrad, ensconced in the best parlour with Nanda, did not move so much as a muscle. He had a butler for a reason. Hopefully the caller would prove inconsequential, and easily fobbed off; Gorev was good at that kind of thing. At three in the afternoon on so foul a day, sleet driving down from the skies in great torrents, and the streets awash with the half-melted snows of early spring, he rather wondered that anybody had troubled to travel to his door at all.

'It seems our reverie is at an end,' said Nanda. Resonant footsteps were indeed approaching the parlour; Konrad heard them as clearly as she, though he toyed briefly with denial.

'Come in,' he sighed, when his butler's discreet tap sounded at the half-closed door.

Gorev entered, and bowed with an apologetic air. 'It's the inspector, sir. He's—'

Konrad sat up. 'What? Well, let him come in! He need not stand on ceremony.'

Gorev cleared his throat. 'I meant to say, sir, that the inspector has sent someone. A policeman. Shall I say that you are at home?'

'Is it Karyavin?'

'That was the name given, yes.'

'Send him in, quickly.' If the inspector had sent a human being rather than a note, then the matter was of some urgency. If he had not come himself, doubly so.

Gorev withdrew, and a moment later Karyavin came in. A young man, he was high in the inspector's good graces, a consequence of his quick wits, level head and obliging nature. Konrad rather liked the man himself. He was everything Konrad might have liked to have been in his own youth. 'Sir,' said Karyavin, with a bow for Konrad and a smile for Nanda. 'There's been an, ah, incident...' Karyavin's eyes wandered about the parlour for a moment, dwelling on the majestic carved fireplace with its enormous mirror, and travelling to the silk-upholstered couch and armchairs. He had not, perhaps, expected to find Konrad surrounded by such extravagant splendour.

'Nuritov sent you?' Konrad prompted.

'Yes, sir. He's down by the river. He asked that you come as soon as possible. And,' the young man added, his gaze turning on Nanda, 'Miss Falenia as well, if you're at leisure, ma'am.'

Nanda, slouching in her chair in a half-doze, blinked and awoke. 'Me? He asked specifically for me?'

'Yes, ma'am. The incident is of an unusual nature, and he thought perhaps your unique abilities might be of use.'

Nanda exchanged a look of mild disquiet with Konrad. 'Just what is the nature of this incident?'

'There's been a death.'

That got Konrad's attention. A death? Murder? No. Were it murder, surely he'd have heard by now. The serpents were vigilant about that kind of thing. But if it were a natural death, or some accident, why summon Konrad?

Serpents? Konrad called. *Have there been any murders in the city today? The kind that I ought to know about?*

No, Master, they chorused.

Yesterday? Last night?

No, Master.

Konrad, at a loss, asked no further questions. He set aside the book he'd been pretending to read, and rose. 'Give me a moment to change, Karyavin, and we will be with you.'

'I'll await you in the porch, sir.' Karyavin, discomfited perhaps by the grandeur, made his bow and withdrew.

'Curious,' said Nanda.

'Before you ask, no, the serpents are aware of no murders.'

'Can they be wrong?'

'I haven't known them to be.'

'Right.' Nanda hauled herself out of her chair, causing Konrad a moment's concern in the evident effort it cost her to do so. Last night had been especially difficult for her, he judged; not from anything she had said, but from her pallor when she had arrived at the breakfast-table, and the air of heaviness and lethargy she'd displayed all day. Her unwelcome entourage had subjected her to a special depth of torment, he supposed. Nightmares of the very direst.

He had his serpents scouring the spirit-lands at every opportunity, seeking out the wretched fae with claims upon Nanda. When they found them, his displeasure would be... violently expressed. The errand had distracted them, possibly, from their regular duties, for the spirit-lands were wide and complex, and the search occupied a great deal of their energy and time. He may arrive at the river to find that the case was one of murder after all.

But still, the serpents were not given to mistakes. Their purpose was a simple one, and they performed that duty with enthusiasm.

Why, though, was Nanda also summoned? That was the most intriguing part of the business.

To his own surprise, he felt his disinclination to leave the house — and to engage with another horrific murder case — lifting a little in the anticipation of an interesting problem. The worst part of Assevan winters, arguably, was the utter boredom of it all.

Half an hour later, Konrad ducked under the dripping frame of Parel's Bridge, and inched his way underneath. The river's waters were on the rise, swollen with melting snow and sleet. A strip of sodden earth only a few feet wide served as the bank, upon which Konrad found the inspector.

'Savast,' said he grimly. 'I wouldn't have wasted your time, or Nanda's either, only we've... got a problem.'

Konrad tried to see past him, to whatever it was he'd been guarding. But the daylight was fading fast, the underside of the bridge was not illuminated, and Alexander seemed to be trying to block his view of whatever it was.

'Well,' said Nanda, coming up behind him. 'What is it?'

'What it is, chiefly, is messy,' he replied, and stepped aside.

Konrad moved forward, stooped over, but managed to strike his head against the damp, oozing boards of the bridge anyway. 'Ow,' he muttered, but the slight pain in his head vanished from his thoughts upon beholding Alexander's "problem".

A man lay there, or so Konrad supposed from the figure's general proportions. Few identifying features were left, for the body had been brutally savaged. Half the face was missing, dissolved into a bloodied pulp; the deathly pallor of the rest was marred by great, blood-soaked gouges. The rest of the body was in much the same condition, the chest broken open, and the inner organs lacerated. Konrad had not light enough to determine whether any were missing, but he thought not. This had not been done with the precision of an organ-harvester. This was a frenzy of pure violence.

That did not preclude the possibility of someone or something's having... eaten them, however.

Some*thing* indeed, for nothing about the man's state suggested that ordinary mortal weapons had been used. 'Those look like claw marks,' he said.

The inspector nodded. 'Or— or teeth.'

'Nothing human, anyway.'

'That's what I thought,' Alexander agreed. 'But is it an ordinary beast, either? I cannot think of any dog or — or even a wolf or something, that could have done this kind of damage.'

'Is there something else?' Konrad asked, for nothing that he'd seen or heard yet explained the inspector's insistence on Nanda's presence. Given the choice, Konrad himself would rather have protected her from such a sight.

'Karyavin?' said Alexander.

'I was the first one on the scene, sir,' said Karyavin. 'A beggar found the body, and came to the police house to report it. When I got here, the corpse was thick with crows. Feasting, as you'd imagine; it is their nature. Only, they didn't fly away.'

'They aren't here now,' Konrad said, confused. 'What do you mean, they didn't fly away?'

'They... dissolved, sir. Vanished. Faded out like shadows at dawn. I don't quite know how to express it.'

Konrad drew in a breath. 'You mean either that they were not ordinary corporeal crows, or that they departed by some means more ethereal than physical?'

'I don't know as to which of those might be the truth, but yes. Something of that kind. I'd swear to it.'

Konrad believed him. The young policeman was steady, and had never given any sign that he was prone to wild imaginings. And

Alexander relied enough upon his testimony to bring Nanda and Konrad running.

'Nan?' said Konrad. 'What do you think?'

Nanda had ceased to examine the unfortunate victim, and instead wandered along the width of the overarching bridge, running the fingers of one hand lightly over the boards. 'The old stories say that bridges are places of crossing,' she said. 'Not just from one side of a body of water to the other, but in other ways, too. Crossing from one realm to another. One land to another. Long ago, the spirit-witches of Ekamet used to keep a close watch on Parel's Bridge, for it was once known as the source of many a strange, creeping thing bent on causing havoc in the city.'

'Not now?' Konrad asked.

'Their vigilance was such that the bridge fell increasingly into disuse, at least for that purpose. So it's said, anyway. And so, they ceased to watch it so closely. This, perhaps, is the result.'

'You think something has used the door,' said Konrad.

'So to speak, yes. Those crows certainly did. Whether they came out of the spirit-lands in the first place, or merely fled that way when disturbed, one thing we can conclude is that a door was recently wrested open at this bridge, and *something* has used it.'

'Is it closed now?'

'Now it is,' said Nanda, with a brief smile for Konrad. 'I've made sure of it. I can't say, though, that another might not be created. This is the kind of place that lends itself to such portals.'

'Do they open up on their own,' said Alexander, 'or does someone have to make one?'

'The old stories say they do open on their own, at certain times of the year,' said Nanda. 'I'm not sure that is true, however. It's my belief that the barriers grow *thinner*, if that is a fair way of describing it, but they do not disappear altogether, only to obligingly reform themselves the next day. I think the formation of any portal has to be, at the least, helped along.'

'So someone has done this.' The inspector stood looking down at the ravaged corpse, an expression of bleak distaste on his usually mild-of-expression face.

'That is hard to say. Someone made a door here, yes. Whether they did so in order that something capable of *this* should come through it, I couldn't say.'

'Do we know who this man is?' Konrad asked.

'The beggar identified him,' said Karyavin. 'A friend of his. Known only as Matenk. If he had a family name, or indeed a family, our informant knew nothing of it.'

Konrad had already surmised his beggar status, judging from the filthy and ragged state of his shredded garments. Many such folk used the shelter of the bridge at times of inclement weather, though it was riskier to do so at this time of year, with the waters rising. 'Not murdered, exactly,' he mused. 'At least, not by a human hand. Which counts me out, in the regular way. This is not in my purview.'

'Konrad,' said Nanda severely. 'If you mean to say that you're going straight to bed and leaving Alexander to deal with this alone, I'd think that impossibly shabby of you.'

'While I can't deny that I am tempted by the idea, no. What I was actually doing was congratulating myself on the prospect of—' He was going to say, *of not having to slaughter someone at the end of this,* but remembered Karyavin's presence just in time — not to mention the other two police officers he did not know, both stationed some little distance away. 'Of an unusual and intriguing problem,' he finished.

Nanda gave him a wry look, which declared her perfectly aware of what he was actually thinking. 'I'm minded to brush up on my folklore,' she said. 'I cannot immediately think of anything commonly dwelling in the spirit-lands that might make this kind of a… mess.'

'Or want to,' said Konrad. 'Spirit-fae and the like have found their way here before. They may make mischief, and sometimes they're known to cause harm, but what they are *not* known to be in the habit of doing is running rampage like this.'

'Which is a horrid thought,' said Alexander. 'Is it running rampage? Shall there be more such victims?'

A good question. Had the thing vanished back whence it had come, along with the disappearing crows? Or had it attacked this unfortunate soul, and then ventured out into the city?

Was it somewhere out there, preying upon more of Ekamet's unsuspecting citizens? Or had it come here with some other errand in mind, and this frenzy of violence was not like to be repeated?

The latter questions could only be answered with time; sadly, little could be done but wait, and hope there came no reports of further such incidents.

Unless.

'Nan, you can't trace it, I suppose?'

'I have no way of doing that.'

'Nor your... er, friends?'

Nanda gave him a sour look. 'My *friends* have enough of a claim on me already, wouldn't you say?'

'I would,' he hastily agreed.

'I don't believe they can help, though. They cannot magically sense each other's passage any more than humans can.'

Serpents? Konrad tried. *Anything?*

No answer came from Ootapi. He had gone back into the spirit-lands himself, Konrad supposed, in pursuit of that other errand. But Eetapi answered. *I sense nothing,* she reported. *If it is neither dead nor human, I am not interested.*

Or capable, I take it.

Silence.

You have spent much time in the spirit-lands lately, Eetapi. Have you seen anything there that could do this?

She took her time in answering, and Konrad felt a faint chill as she wafted down to inspect the remains for herself. *No, Master,* she finally decided. *Not quite. But— there may perhaps be—*

Yes? He prompted, when she fell silent.

I will investigate, she said, and faded away. Back, presumably, into the spirit-lands, by some door ever-available to her. The Malykt's gift. Konrad enjoyed such privileges himself, though rarely used them. The spirit-lands were no pleasant place to while away the time.

Konrad wanted to investigate, too, but could not do so while Karyavin and the other policemen stood there. His presence here at all might occasion remark, for who was he to advise the police? His friendship with the inspector might prove explanation enough, just about, for Alexander Nuritov was known to value his insights (such as they were). But if he were to fade out like a shadow at dawn — as Karyavin had put it — striding into the spirit-lands like a wisp of smoke himself, *that* would not pass without comment. And suspicion. City gentlemen did not ordinarily have the means or the inclination to go waltzing about in the ethereal realms.

So Konrad bided his time, joining in with speculation and surmise but without offering much by way of his true expertise. Let Nanda take the lead. Later, he would follow his serpents into the spirit-world and see what else he could see.

He wouldn't tell Nanda, either. She would insist on going with him, and in her weakened state that must be dangerous to her. She had borne enough from the tricksy spirit-fae as it was; let the rest leave her in peace.

2

Konrad had intended to conduct his explorations somewhere during the night; nearing dawn, perhaps, when the creatures that swarmed those hazy lands were beginning to think of rest. But urgency left him no peace. The case presented an interesting problem, but no mere academic one; the city's people stood at risk, whether because the creature that had killed the unfortunate Matenk was still at large among them, or because whatever had permitted it to enter the city in the first place might occur again.

So Konrad waited only until darkness had swallowed Ekamet, and the hour grew enough advanced that the inspector's men must have completed their work, and left.

Then he stole back to Parel's Bridge. He had with him his snake-headed cane, more for confidence than because it could serve much useful purpose. He was dressed for the cold and the damp and the dark. He had a lantern, much good it might do him.

He made his way back to the spot in which Matenk had died, stepping carefully in the drowning dark. He did not wish to be fished out of the river in the morning, sodden and lifeless. What an ignominious way to end his career as the most dangerous person in Assevan.

The body was gone, removed to The Malykt's temple by now. Nothing remained of the tragedy that had there occurred, save perhaps bloodstains. A hush reigned, and nothing moved. Word of Matenk's fate had spread, Konrad guessed, and beggars had sought a safer shelter for tonight.

He did not know in precisely which spot the door from the spirit-lands had opened, but it did not matter. He was close enough. Summoning his eerie, Malykt-gifted senses, he let the corporeal world fade from his sight, and mustered his spirit-vision in its place. This strange sight offered him a blended view of the world: the familiar contours of his home city, in all its streets and bridges and buildings, plus the ethereal spirit-plane that lay just behind everything, in which the mundane faded and the strange stood etched in brilliance.

He saw nothing out of place; nor had he earlier. The same hush prevailed, the same stillness.

A single step carried him over the threshold, landing his physical self on the *strange* side of the divide. Parel's Bridge dissolved into the darkness. He saw instead a different landscape, still waters etched in stark white and edged in shadows. Dark trees rose like grasping hands on either side of this other river, decked in leaves of shadow. Rain fell, but a rain of glittering light rather than water, for no fresh deluge soaked Konrad's coat.

He paused, motionless, every sense alert for sound — movement — anything that might herald danger. That, or the presence of the creature he sought.

Nothing.

Serpents. Konrad sent the call out far, and waited as it reverberated through the eerie silence of the spirit-lands. Ootapi, he knew, would be far away, probably beyond reach.

Eetapi, though, soon answered. *Master? What are you doing here?*

Investigating.

But I was investigating.

We can both investigate, cannot we?

Yes, said Eetapi, but dubiously.

I take it you have not discovered anything of note, or I would already be hearing about it.

But I have. Unabashed glee in Eetapi's whispery words. *I have been following a trail. Go you over the bridge, Master, and you will see.*

The bridge in question arched over the eerily still waters, not dissimilar in shape and proportion to Parel's Bridge below. Konrad had not ventured upon it yet, for its surface did not display the comforting solidity of the other bridge. Like the rain, it bore a peculiar insubstantiality about it; Konrad caught glimpses of the water's silvered surface, shining straight through it. Built for spirit-feet. Could it bear Konrad's ordinary mortal weight?

He set forth a foot, and planted it upon the bridge. Shadows blossomed where his boot fell, boiled alarmingly around his foot, and streaked away in wisps.

Strange. But the bridge held, and Konrad took another step.

'Konrad,' came Nanda's voice behind him, the word uttered in tones of exasperation. 'I might have known.'

He whirled. There stood Nanda, wrapped in her red cloak (her current favourite, judging from the frequency with which she wore it). He could see little of her face, muffled as it was with scarves as well, but the eyes fixed upon him were lacking in such pleasantries as welcome or delight. In fact, she looked thoroughly annoyed.

'What?' he said. 'Coming here must be a good idea, because here you are yourself.'

'I at least have some passing familiarity with this place, and a vague sense of what I'm doing here,' Nanda retorted. 'Can you say the same?'

'I have been here before.' That was truth. He'd had to pursue a murderer through the spirit-lands, once. A member of The Malykt's Order, with some ambitious ideas about enslaved spirit-creatures. He had pulled it off with credit, hadn't he?

'A lot?' Nanda said, striding toward him with the brisk step of a woman who knows exactly what she is doing. 'And recently?'

'No, but—'

'Then you'd better let me lead.'

'But you're already—'

'I *know*, but which one of us is the spirit-witch here? You or me?'

'You.'

'Which one of us, then, is better suited to, for example, *not die* up here?'

'I am not without my abilities—'

Nanda interrupted this protestation with an inarticulate noise of disgust, swept past him, and marched off over the bridge without the smallest hesitation. Konrad watched, fascinated, as those odd wafts of shadow formed around her every footstep, and went sailing off into the night.

He hastened after her, half ashamed now of his own creeping, cautious progress. But then, she had just chastised him for what she evidently saw as another piece of recklessness, hadn't she? Caution was good. Caution kept people alive.

Nanda displayed none of it whatsoever, for she was already disappearing into the looming trees on the other side of the water. A narrow path led the way into a close, shadowy thicket, one which Konrad would hesitate to enter with impunity had he any sense at all. Nanda evidently didn't. He began to see how she had got herself into so tangled a mess with her pacts and her spirit-fae. She moved like she was a denizen of the spirit-lands herself, and perhaps she saw herself that way.

But she wasn't. She was as mortal as he.

Konrad hurried after her.

He caught up with her just inside the sinister wood, for she had stopped in the middle of the pale little path, and crouched down to inspect something.

There you go, Master, said Eetapi, as proud as though she had created whatever it was herself. He hoped she had not.

'What have you found?' he asked, bending over Nanda's crouched form.

'A trail, I suppose,' said she. 'Our mysterious creature passed this way, one concludes.'

So it seemed, for discarded among the moon-bright moss at the side of the path lay the broken remains of some creature to which Konrad could put no name. Humanoid in shape, it had once had two arms and two legs, he judged. Two of them were missing, torn off by gigantic claws; he saw one lying some distance away, but could find no sign of the other. The thing looked tiny and forlorn, lying there, its withered white face drained of life, its black eyes staring in death. It lay liberally covered in its own blood, which was not red in the way of humans but some odd, paler hue.

'Goblin,' said Nanda, regaining her feet. She barely paused, but went on again into the darkening depths of the wood, dauntless, despite this macabre evidence of recent dangers.

Konrad knew better than to remonstrate with her. Instead, he kept as close to her heels as he could, and bade Eetapi remain alert for any and all threats.

Nanda, though, did not give off the impression of a woman in any danger. She could not possibly have *grown* since entering the spirit-lands, but Konrad could almost swear that she was taller. She radiated power, confidence and magic, and Konrad began to reconsider his assessment of a moment before. Human she might be, but she was in her element here.

How much time had she spent, walking these eerie paths? Was this where she had so often vanished to, when he could not find her, and did not know where she was?

That might explain a few things.

The woodland grew thicker, darker and stranger as Konrad followed in Nanda's wake, and the path more winding. Sometimes it swerved abruptly, left or right, and appeared to double back on itself in a great loop. Black tree-boughs hung and swayed over the path, attended by the occasional, deep *toll* of a mournful bell. Once, something whisked about his feet, leaving an icy trail and a sensation of wetness behind.

Twice more, Nanda halted over the remains of some hapless, shredded thing lying by the roadside. If they were the kinds of things that had names, he knew none of them, but he pitied them all. Black blood spilled over pale grass; the meat and bone of fae-things opened wide to the lightning sky; these were the impressions he carried with him as he walked on.

'Who is to avenge these creatures?' he said at last, struck by the thought.

'I beg your pardon,' said Nanda, only half-listening.

'These slain fae. They are murdered, just as surely as Matenk at the bridge. Whose task is it to avenge their deaths?'

'I don't believe that person exists.'

'Why not?'

Nanda raised a brow. 'Should they be avenged, in the way that you mean?'

'I... well, yes. If humans deserve such vengeance—'

'Do we, though?'

He stopped. 'What?'

Nanda spoke carefully, without looking at him. 'Some might say that the Malykant ought not to exist. That it's a justice too harsh, too unforgiving.'

'Some *might* say. You mean some *do* say that.'

'Yes, some do.'

Struck by a terrible suspicion, Konrad tried — and failed — to get a look at her face. 'Are you among them?'

'I couldn't wish you out of existence.'

'If it wasn't me?'

'In the more abstract sense? Perhaps. But I am of the Shandral, recall. We take a different view of things.'

'And you've had your interfering fingers in the Malykant pie for some time.'

He almost left the words unsaid, afraid that they might offend. But Nanda grinned. 'You are much improved by our interference, admit it. Ah— now.' Three quick steps took her off the path, and she plunged headlong into the gnarly trees. No lantern, no guide.

'Nan!' he called, uselessly, and plunged in after her.

Lights bloomed among the dark, dank trees, but not the kind anybody would wish for. Pallid things, these, floating at eye-height and above, or inches from the ground; bobbing and twisting, beckoning with ghostly promise. Konrad altered his bearing to follow one, only half aware of what he did; his reward was a faceful of something wet and somehow dusty and foul-smelling, and a sharp drop from which Nanda saved him at the last instant.

Her scolding words died away, mostly unsaid. 'Oh,' she said instead. 'Very well done, Konrad.'

'Thank you,' he said dubiously, staring down at the abrupt descent that fell away before him. He stood atop something of a cliff, about as high as Konrad was tall, and had almost plummeted over the edge. Below, another path wound away into a steep valley, crowded on either side by trees as bone-white as their fellows above were black. Creatures passed this way, evidenced by the jagged stairs that offered passage down — to those sharp enough to spot them in time.

Konrad thought he saw, in the near distance, a house huddled beneath the white boughs.

'That looks promising,' said Nanda, and started down the steps.

'Just what are we doing?' Konrad called, hurrying after. 'Are we looking for something in particular?'

'Yes. That house, I imagine.'

'Er?'

'Someone opened a way through Parel's Bridge. Someone from the spirit-lands side, I surmise. That someone had a purpose. It may have been the same person — or thing — that tore up Matenk, but then again it may not.'

'And that someone lives here.'

'The trail leads in this direction. What does your detective brain tell you?'

'That the evidence is circumstantial.'

'True, but that does not mean that it is incorrect.'

Konrad ceased his protests, keeping a weather eye out instead for creeping things in the ghost-light. But nothing moved, in fact the woods seemed bare of life altogether. An impression Eetapi unwittingly bore out in saying, *Master, I sense nothing.*

Nothing relevant, or nothing at all?

Nothing at all. It is as though everything has fled from these parts.

Interesting.

Or... died. Is everything dead?

Konrad did not dwell on the unseemly relish with which she posed the question. *I don't know. Are you finding a great many dead things?*

Some, Master. Some.

The house grew more distinct as they approached, and the vague sense Konrad had received that it was made of ice proved to be the literal truth. From a distance, it had shimmered blue-tinged white, as though lit with its own ghost-glow. Up closer, the radiance faded. Konrad beheld a round-walled structure of uneven construction; not built with bricks or stone blocks or anything that might make sense to Konrad, but asymmetrical, listing to one side and haphazard. Quite as though rain or some other fall of water had poured out of the skies and frozen into this shape, thoughtfully forming a ragged-edged window or two as it did so. And a door.

A deep, bone-aching cold radiated from the wintry house. Konrad felt that to set one's hand to that ice-frosted door might prove a terrible mistake; the flesh would freeze from his fingers, his bones would crack and break under the intense frigidity, and he would leave half of his arm behind him.

Nanda, either less fanciful or more experienced than he, simply kicked it open, emerging apparently unscathed from the procedure. 'Hello?' she called, upon marching inside, and her voice echoed off the glittering ice walls.

The house consisted of only one room, and it bore no furniture at all, or nothing that deserved the name. A pallet of woven white branches huddled against one wall, padded high with goose down and rags, and canopied with strands of ice-drops. No firepit or hearth in a house made of ice, of course. Detritus lay piled in heaps here and there, dark and rotting, though the smell these unappealing stacks emitted wasn't half so malodorous as might appear. Slightly sweet, and herby.

'I've heard of spirit-witches living out here,' said Nanda, when nothing answered, and nothing moved. The place was empty.

'Nothing human could live here,' Konrad objected.

'That depends. No, you may be right — but not quite all spirit-witches are human.'

'What *is* a spirit-witch, then? I thought it referred to a human with some rapport with the spirit-fae.'

'That is its most commonly used definition, though not absolutely comprehensive. We shall see. Whatever lived here, though, is gone. And...' Nanda crouched over something, and brought Konrad's lantern to bear upon it.

Expecting another torn-apart fae, Konrad approached with caution. But it was only blood, black blood, albeit in sickening quantity.

A trail of it ran from the bed to the doorway, and beyond.

'Something was injured,' said Nanda. 'And fled.'

'Injured by the same thing we are hunting?'

'Maybe. We—'

A tearing shriek struck Konrad's ears with the force of a blow, and a wraithlike shape erupted from the shadows. So fast, too fast; darkness came at him in a blur, engulfing him in shadow, smothering the shout that tore from his throat. Talons raked over Konrad's arm, splitting apart his coat, leaving stripes of burning fire behind, and bile filled his mouth. He spat, or vomited. Black blood poured in gouts from between his lips.

He heard Nanda scream, though not an inarticulate sound, not the cry of alarm or terror that he had been trying to make. There were words in it, method to it; white light, lightning-bright, flashed through the house, and Konrad heard the ominous crack of shattering ice.

Quiet, then, and stillness. The wraith-thing was gone.

'Nan,' Konrad muttered, and hauled himself up. He'd fallen onto that ice-hard floor in the tumult, and he slipped now in black blood and bile as he tried to rise. His head spun, his arm burned, and he was colder than he ever remembered being in his life.

Then Nanda was there, steadying him. Her hands burned with intense heat — a good heat, *nice* heat, not the searing stuff that went through his arm like acid — and his wracking shivers eased. She looked at him, and he thought maybe her eyes were glowing with an ice-light of their own, but he was probably delirious.

'I did tell you this was a bad idea,' she said calmly. 'Inkubal, the arm, please.'

'Wha—' Konrad's words dissolved into an inarticulate hiss of pain, for some merciless thing had hold of his arm, and was industriously tearing at it. 'No!' he cried. 'Don't take it off, it can't be that bad, I'm going to need it—'

'Inkubal does not perform amputations, as a rule,' said Nanda. 'Don't so insult his capabilities, if you please.'

'*What?*' Konrad gasped. Dizziness swamped him, and he shook his head, desperate to ward off a fainting fit. How *embarrassing*, especially in front of a lady, and with all that mess on the floor to fall into—

'Ouch,' he croaked, insufficient utterance, to say the least, as his arm went into ice-water up to the shoulder, or something that felt like it, and for a horrid, unbearable second he'd rather have been set on fire.

Then the pain vanished. All of it.

'Thank you, Ink,' said Nanda. A suggestion of a bow, sketched upon the bright air in shadow, and then they were alone again in the ravaged ice-house.

Konrad fought for breath. 'Was that — one of your —'

'Pacts? Yes. Ink has been assisting me with healing for some years now.'

Konrad's brain whirled with conflicting impressions. Somehow it had not occurred to him that Nanda's spirit-fae — the ones who drained her of life and vitality day by day, and would surely kill her in time — were not merely faceless embodiments of evil, but living creatures, at least of a sort. Capable of good as well as bad. That she'd formed those pacts because they were useful.

Business relationships, if you will, if paid for in an unusual currency.

That made them much the same as humans, in essence, and Konrad's plan to mercilessly tear them all to shreds in Nanda's name fell into tatters.

Especially if one of them had now saved his arm.

He flexed it, experimentally, and found that his fingers worked. Marvel.

201

'You'd have lost that, if Ink and I hadn't been here,' said Nanda coolly. 'And the rest of you shortly after.'

'What was that *thing*?' Konrad said, too appalled to bear with merited told-you-so logic.

'A pertinent question. I don't know.'

'I was vomiting blood.'

'Yes.'

'Black blood.' Konrad swept out a hand, indicating the gore all over the floor.

'And I think that is the fate that befell whoever lived here.' Nanda spoke calmly, but her eyes betrayed her: wide and horrified, and she breathed too fast.

'It was not my own blood. It's as though I was a — a conduit for something else — infected by it—' Konrad forced himself to breathe, and tried to dismiss from his reeling thoughts the impressions left by the last few minutes. Agony. Death. Merciless evil.

'By nightmare incarnate. I don't know, Konrad. This goes beyond my knowledge. It— what? What is it?'

For Konrad had gone very still, eyes wide in horror. For half a minute, he did not breathe. At length he said: 'When I first became the Malykant, I was told a story. The story of why Assevan must have a Malykant, or specifically what happens if those duties are not tended to. I do not know that I paid it much heed at the time, or have ever thought of it since—'

'Go on,' said Nan.

'It's said that deaths The Malykt calls *Unclean* leave a… residue, behind. A poison, a corrupting influence — a nightmare, if you will. An evil only purged by justice, however harsh. If that doesn't happen, it — builds. That's why people used to ward against things creeping through from the spirit-lands. It wasn't ordinary fae they were worried about. It was these… *things*. Nightmares. Evils. They don't have a name, or a soul, or anything that might seem— they're just death incarnate. All they know is blood and bile and decay, and they will kill anything living, indiscriminately.'

'But—' said Nanda. 'But there is a Malykant. There has been one for a hundred years — hundreds? I don't know. Too long to permit of such an abomination to form again, no?'

'Not every murder can be solved, Nan.' Konrad took in a deep breath, and another. 'Spirits above, I try. My predecessors tried. We do the best that we can, but some elude us; some escape justice, and it is the cumulative effect of *those* that now forms the danger. We have not escaped entirely from these corrupted things. But they've become so rare that we have forgotten them. The first one in a hundred years, perhaps.'

Nanda blinked, and breathed, and looked helplessly around at the destroyed winter-house. 'But what can be done about it? Do you mean to say that it is unstoppable? Out there somewhere right now, killing fae — or in Ekamet, killing people?'

'Probably not the latter,' said Konrad. 'At least, not now. Because I rather fear that the thing is following *me.*'

3

It made sense, after a macabre fashion. A thing formed of death itself, of killings and hatred and evil, would naturally enough be attracted to the same. And what was Konrad? Death's tool, formed of its essence, a creature who existed for the sole purpose of dealing it out again.

In a sense, the Malykant existed so that these other, worse creatures would not. Or, not so often.

'I don't think I believed the story, quite,' Konrad said later, restored to the questionable comforts of Bakar House. Questionable, because short-lived. If Konrad was correct, and the creature was drawn to *him*, he could not stay long among other people. He endangered everyone nearby. 'In my early days among the Order, I was given such a wealth of information, I doubt I registered half of it. I thought this titbit nothing but a nursery tale, most likely. A pretty piece of mythology to justify the existence of so foul a role.'

'Nursery?' said Nanda blankly. 'Not quite a bedtime story, Konrad.'

Ordinarily by now they would have retired to the parlour, and comfort, and warmth. Or indeed to bed, and the same. But today was different. Konrad, still reeling from the attack, still dizzy, his thoughts in a whirl, could not even think of rest. Nanda, drawn and wan, her exertions having for the present exhausted her, was doubtless sorely in need of slumber; but she, too, was restless. They had proceeded as far as Konrad's elegant tile-floored hall, and had got no further. Konrad paced back and forth, still clad in his coat, his hat torn off and relinquished absently into Gorev's care. Nanda stood with her back against the closed door, as though such a posture might ward off anything minded to come through it.

Futile. Such a *thing* did not use doors. Not that kind.

'I must go to the enclave,' said Nanda. 'Gather some others. The bridge must be warded, the door sealed, a watch posted—'

'Enclave?' said Konrad, pausing in pacing and ruminations both. 'What enclave?'

'In the Bones. There's a hidden village there, an enclave of spirit witches. I went there not long since; it's where I found Lady Lysak. She bade me come back sometime, if I needed help.'

'I wonder if this is what she meant.'

'No. No one could have foreseen this. But I *will* need help, Konrad. I cannot keep fending that thing off alone.'

'No, no. You must have help. I'll go with—' He broke off. 'I mustn't go with you, must I? Not unless we can be certain I don't endanger you by doing so.'

'I am not sure if you're right about the nightmare. Is it drawn to you? Why would it follow you?'

'Like is drawn to like.'

Nanda's face darkened. 'You are *nothing* like that thing,' she said, with a vehemence Konrad found comforting.

'In too many ways, I am. Anyway, which is the better alternative? That I should be attacked like that, quite far from the scene of Matenk's death, is puzzling. Either the creature followed me there, or there are at least two of them. One still at large in Ekamet, and one that we ran into face-first in the spirit-lands.'

'Two,' gasped Nanda, turning paler than ever. 'Horrid thought.'

'Quite. I cannot decide which horrid thought I prefer.'

'There is another possibility,' said Nanda.

Konrad leapt on that idea. 'Tell me.'

'In which order did those deaths occur? Did the creature originate somewhere at, or near, that ice-house, kill all those fae, and then cross over to kill Matenk? Or was it the other way about?'

'How could such a thing manifest in Ekamet? Surely it must originate from the spirit-lands.'

'I would have said so myself, but I cannot be sure. Who can? We have not seen such a thing for a century. Also, it may have made more than one passage. Begun in the spirit-lands, passed through into the city, and then retraced its steps.'

'Following me,' said Konrad.

'Maybe.'

Konrad sighed, and rubbed at his burning eyes. 'In short, we can draw no sound conclusions. Yet. If you go to the enclave and recruit assistance, I must go to the Order. If anyone knows more about this nightmare of a thing, it must be they. I'll see Diana.' He did not want to see Diana. Hadn't, ever since she had told him she had asked for his "retirement". He did not know how to face her after that, or what to say in the wake of what felt like a personal betrayal. But he must. This was more important.

'In the meantime,' said Nanda, 'we... hope, that it will not kill again.'

'A faint hope, Nan.'

'Bordering upon non-existent, I should say.'

News travels fast, Konrad recalled as he arrived at the Temple of The Malykt soon afterwards. Ill news travels faster still, and here was the proof of it, for bursting with tidings as he was, he found that he had been preceded.

His first hint of it being that the temple was in a state of some uproar. Usually ordered, placid and soothing — in its cold way — Konrad entered at the hour of only quarter past seven to find the entire Order gathered there, or so it seemed. The great, double doors of grey stone were closed, as expected, but beyond was chaos. The moment Konrad set foot into the entrance hall, he heard the babble of voices, near and distant, the sharp sounds of footsteps echoing upon tile and stone, and glimpses of his fellows among the Order as they dashed about, carrying tidings or orders or simply panicking, for all he knew.

It was news to panic over.

He hesitated in the hall, uncertain what to do, or where to present himself. Was Diana here? If so, where?

Footsteps approached again, the quick, staccato sounds of someone in a hurry. A figure entered, and stopped dead upon seeing Konrad.

'*There* you are,' said the man, though it was no one Konrad recognised by sight. Grey-headed, weathered, uniformed and harassed. 'The entire Order is searching for you, did you not know?'

'They would have found me at home.'

'Someone has been dispatched there, yes, and also into the spirit-lands in pursuit of you. They'll have to be recalled. Could you *not* have sent word?'

Strain was behind the man's rudeness, Konrad knew. Strain, and fear. So he forbore to return a snappish answer, and said mildly: 'How did you know I was in the spirit-lands at all?'

'Go up to the second floor,' said his interlocutor without seeming to answer. 'They're in the embalming rooms.'

Was someone being embalmed? Konrad, mystified, took himself up the nearest flight of stairs without further comment, and entered upon another scene of chaos. The embalming rooms, normally white, pristine, stark and serene, were full of people. He put his face around the door of the nearest of two large chambers, and almost withdrew again.

If someone was being embalmed, the process was proving unusually bloody.

'*Konrad*,' said Diana, from somewhere within a small throng of people gathered around the bloodied corpse. If corpse it was. 'Thank goodness.'

That, at least, was more welcoming. He stepped fully into the room, and the little crowd parted, making way for him.

Lying upon one of the embalming tables was a figure, human, but with some fey quality about her... she lay alarmingly still, white as the moon, her hair also, save that it was as liberally daubed in blood as the rest of her. Red blood, darkening as it dried, and also thick, black fluid. Aged, probably serene in temper at better times, her face was calm enough, but her eyes when they met Konrad's were dark with pain.

Something about her spoke of winter's chill, a deep, slaying cold Konrad could almost feel as he approached her.

'The house of ice,' he said. 'That is your abode, is it not?'

'Yes,' came the answer, in a cracked whisper.

'You're alive. I thought whoever lived there must be—'

'Konrad,' interrupted Diana. 'She's very weak. Don't pester her.'

'It attacked you,' Konrad continued, largely ignoring Diana. The woman wanted to speak; let her speak.

'Nearly killed me,' said she, with the ghost of a smile. 'I am not so easy to kill.'

'This is Talin,' said Diana. 'She is one of the Order's wardens for the spirit-lands. She brought word of the manifestation, nearly at the cost of her own life, so please do not tire her.'

'I came,' said Konrad, controlling his irritation with an effort, 'to report this news, had you not already heard of it—'

'*Very* late, Konrad, and since your idea of dealing with the catastrophe appears to have been to go after it alone—'

'I did not *then* know what it was!'

'How could you possibly fail to realise what it was? Have we taught you nothing?'

Konrad swallowed another sharp retort. Diana, too, was in a stew, for her position at the pinnacle of the Order must be chafing her today. A genuine disaster, and everyone looked to *her* for a solution. One she hardly knew how to provide, for neither she nor generations' worth of her predecessors had ever had to deal with such a nightmare.

He did not envy her. He was feeling some of the same heavy responsibility himself.

'I came to find out more about that *thing*,' said Konrad, as calmly as he could. 'The world at large has forgotten these creatures, but I am sure the Order has not.'

'The term, once, was malefic,' said Diana. 'For that is what they are. Deeply malefic, and that is *all*, they have no better side, no redeeming qualities.'

'So I had surmised,' said Konrad, a vision of his own attack at the nightmare's hands flashing through his mind. He had sensed nothing about the creature but darkness, and evil.

'You were hurt,' said Diana, seeing him at last, for she focused upon his torn coat, and particularly the ragged shreds of his sleeve. Konrad had the gratification of seeing her rise to her feet, and run over to him, her concern palpable. 'Spirits above, Konrad, you should have said — here I've been haranguing you—'

'I am all right,' he said quickly, interrupting her flow of self-recrimination. It soothed, but it could help nobody. 'Nanda sent it packing, and patched me up.'

'Irinanda Falenia?'

'Yes.'

'She fought off a malefic?'

'Yes.'

Diana blinked, nonplussed, her tongue momentarily silenced. 'Can we get her here? Is she with you? We are going to need skills like that.'

'She has gone to muster assistance from the spirit-witch enclave in the Bones. She can't fight it off alone, Diana. This one intervention almost finished her. She's already weak—'

Diana waved this away. 'Naturally not. No one can easily destroy a malefic, certainly not alone. Let them come here, those who are willing to help.'

That Diana seemed to know all about the hidden enclave did not much surprise Konrad. He wondered if any of those who dwelt there were among the Order's members, too. More of them were Shandral, most likely.

'She may take them to The Shandrigal's Temple,' he suggested.

'That will do as well. And— *spirits*, yes. The Shandrigal's Order. We'll need them, too.'

'Diana,' said Konrad. '*Pause* a moment. Do we know how to defeat this thing? Is that still written somewhere?'

'We have... ideas,' said Diana.

'Ideas? That's it? Wasn't the Order chief among those who hunted the malefics, once upon a time?'

'With The Shandrigal's Order, yes. One thing you may not know about, however, is the fire.'

'The fire?'

'The great fire, must be seventy years ago now. More. The Temple was almost entirely destroyed, and all its records with it. What we are now standing in is its replacement.'

Words failed Konrad.

'And of course those specific records have never been replaced, because by that time hunting malefics had become an obsolete art, and the arm of the Order devoted to that kind of peace-keeping was long since disbanded. So we'll have to ask the Shandral,' said Diana grimly. 'Though I do not know how much help it will be to *us*, for their methods must of necessity be very different from ours. Still, we will take any information we can get.'

'So,' said Konrad slowly, 'we have no idea what to do about this thing.'

'Truthfully?' said Diana. 'No. Not much of a one.'

Talin made a sound, a choked cough. 'I have been aware for some time of a… wrongness, growing,' she said faintly. 'I took measures to draw it to me, when it came. I succeeded.'

'Too well, nearly,' said Diana, with a tenderness that surprised Konrad, coming from her. The Order's cold, lamaeni leader returned to the older woman's side and bent over her in concern. 'You did not tell me.'

'I had nothing to tell. I hardly knew what I was seeing. I could have been wrong, senile…'

'Never senile. You were right. You should have trusted your instincts.'

'And I knew,' Talin continued, her pale eyes focusing on Diana, 'that you would recall me as warden, if I told you.'

'I would have been right to!' said Diana. '*Look* at you.'

'I am not finished yet.' Talin's odd eyes flashed fiercely as she spoke, and she half rose from her recumbent posture upon the hard table-top.

Diana pushed her back down. 'I know. Dauntless to the end, but I pray that the end shall be some ways off yet. Rest, won't you? You have done enough.'

Talin sank back obediently, but her ferocity vanished; despair came instead. 'And what is it that I have done? Only drawn its ire, almost at the cost of my life. I did not prevent it. I could not stop it. I do not even know where it has gone.'

'We will soon know that,' said Diana bleakly. 'You brought us word, Talin.'

'He would have done just as much, if I had not got here before him.' The *he* in question referred to Konrad, for she looked dispassionately at him.

'Yes. Konrad. Let's hear your story. What exactly happened? How did you come to be up in the ice-house?'

Konrad recounted everything that had happened, beginning with the appearance of Karyavin at his house, and the summons to the scene of the malefic's first human victim. At least as far as they knew. The room grew quiet as he spoke, the gathered Order as well as Diana listening attentively. Talin's sharp, fey eyes rested upon him throughout, intent, almost unblinking.

'It attacked you, too,' said Talin when he had finished speaking. 'Why you, and not your companion?'

'I had thought… it follows me.'

'Follows *you?*' said Diana, frowning. 'Why?'

Konrad related his theory as to that, too, though his confidence in the idea faded with every word. Diana's frown only deepened.

'Forgive me, Konrad, but it is very like you to find an explanation centring especially around yourself.'

That stung. 'I may well be wrong,' he conceded. 'I hope I am.'

He did not miss the worry in Diana's face. She thought, feared, that he might be right after all. 'We will soon know that, too,' she said wearily. 'You had better take care, Konrad. And keep that spirit-witch with you.'

'I cannot ask her to keep defending me.' Not at such a cost to Nanda.

'One of the others, then. Go to The Shandrigal's Temple, and wait for them. That would probably be best.'

'And if it is following me? Shall I not endanger any others there?'

'The Shandrigal has ways,' said Diana mysteriously. 'Wards. It might prove to be the safest place in the city for you, if your surmise is correct.'

Konrad bowed. 'And what will you do?'

The hollows beneath Diana's eyes seemed to deepen and darken as she spoke. 'I had better try to talk with the Master.'

Konrad did not envy her that duty.

4

Nanda had never imagined she might be retracing her steps to the enclave in the Bones so soon, but now she blessed that earlier venture. Her feet remembered the way, and moved the faster for it. The snow, lessening in impact now that it melted day by day, impeded her much less than before, and she arrived at the twist in the bone-white trees sooner than she had ventured to hope. The air was still, at so early an hour. All she heard was the occasional, soft *drip* of melted sleet or heavy dew falling from bough to earth, and the faint crunch of thinning ice beneath her own feet as she walked. Her breath misted in the still morning air.

She did not waste time on pleasantries. Announcing her presence in some subtle way, waiting for someone to answer her call, and open the way between the trees — these things she did not have time for, today. Urgency wrest all thought of etiquette away.

She set a hand against the trunk of the nearest guard-tree instead, its frosted bark shivery-cold and rough under her fingers, and let its gentle, natural magics elevate her own.

A deep, deep breath.

'Ware!' she cried. 'Wake! Danger! The enclave is sorely needed, and I bid you, *wake*.'

Her words rolled and boomed through the tree-tops, setting the boughs to shaking, and the lofty eyries with it. Leaves and lichen and shattered ice rained down, dislodged by the thunder of her voice.

They did not take long to rouse, after that. Soon a low, thrumming, *creaking* sound split the air, and the twined trees before her unwound themselves, and broke apart.

Lady Lysak, or Rita, stood waiting.

'I thought it was you,' said she. She was dressed for the weather, wrapped in soft layers, no late riser here. Her hair, though, was not yet dressed, and hung in a dark mass down her back. She looked Nanda over, bright with alarm. 'When I spoke of help—'

'No time,' Nanda said quickly. 'I would not so rudely rouse you without good reason. I come bearing ill tidings.'

Rita beckoned her into the enclave, and the trees instantly snapped shut behind her. She stood in a large clearing, bare earth beneath her feet, a ring of close-knitted tree-trunks surrounding it. The settlement lay above, in the mass of withy-built treetop dwellings only half-glimpsed among the boughs. They were good at hiding, these witches. She wondered briefly why.

A *thud,* and a large-framed man landed beside Rita, having tumbled down from some way above with surprising grace. Niklas, his hair as white-blonde as Nanda's own, but eyes clear grey rather than blue. He had not greeted her with much warmth the last time they had met, nor did he do so now. He merely watched. Waited.

Nanda told her tale. She did so as quickly, but as clearly, as she could, unwilling to waste time repeating herself, or answering questions, for every moment's delay could mean another death, human or fae. Her nerves jangled, more shattered by the nightmare creature's attack upon Konrad that she had wanted to admit. Too alert, restless, she struggled to stand still where she was, and speak in measured tones. Her ears strained, expecting every moment to hear that tearing *shriek* again, to see the flash of bright-dark talons, see the spray of red blood. Konrad's. And the flow of black, bloodied bile that had streamed from his mouth...

'Konrad said—' she began, when her narration was over. 'It's been said that the witches of Assevan used to ward the bridges for a reason. Not just the bridges, either, but everywhere the doors used to open long ago. And *this* was the real reason, not just that the fae sometimes wandered in. Is that so? I must know. *Can it come through without that someone has opened a door?*

'I don't know,' said Rita, wide-eyed. 'I know nothing of such a creature. Niklas?'

The big man silently shook his head.

'If it is true that you — that *we* — used to hold fast the doors

213

against these things, then someone must know. There must be someone who remembers. Or a book, something written. Anything.'

'What do you hope to do?' said Rita.

Nanda groped for words — ideas — something. 'I do not see how such a thing can ever be destroyed,' she said. 'It is so strong. I could not fight it, I could only deflect it, for a time, and that cost me—' She broke off. Less rambling, Irinanda. *Think.* 'I want to contain the danger,' she said. 'Keep it from wandering at will between spirit-lands and the city, thereby to reduce the number of its victims. *There* I think you may help me, if you will. How to overcome it after that, well, that I cannot guess at now.'

Rita made no answer. She exchanged a look with Niklas, a look both thoughtful and profoundly disturbed. 'I wish that we had more to tell you,' said she at last. 'How was it that you deflected it, as you say? Was it through our magics, or something else? For I cannot think how that may be done.'

'Ours,' said Nanda rapidly. 'Ours, and something more, for I am Shandral.'

'Then you will want Inia and Mili, for they too are Shandral.'

Nanda vaguely knew an Inia, among the Order. A slight woman, if her recollections were correct, and very young — barely twenty, by appearance. A shrinking creature, but shyness did not denote a lack of heart or courage. Mili she did not know.

'I will accept their help very gladly,' she said. 'I had hoped—'

'We will all attend you,' said Niklas, to her surprise.

Rita shot him a sharp look. 'All?'

'It must be so,' he said. 'And she must also see Anouska.'

'Anouska? Can she...?'

'She is stout enough for this.'

Nanda looked from one to the other, confused. Their conversation excluded her entirely; they seemed absorbed in whatever their shared reflections were.

Finally, though, Rita returned her attention to Irinanda. 'You take her,' she said, presumably to Niklas. 'I will muster the village.'

With which words she nodded to Nanda, and leapt. She caught hold of a low-hanging bough, or something, and swung herself up; instantly, she vanished into the canopy, as thoroughly disappeared as though she had never been there at all.

Leaving only Niklas.

'Come,' he said, still all ice, not a shred of warmth in his manner at all.

Nanda set aside her cares. As long as he did what she needed, he may speak to her as coldly as he chose.

A small shriek escaped her, hard upon the heels of this thought, for her feet came off the floor and suddenly she was shooting up, *up* into the canopy, following the way Rita had gone. Her passage was neither smooth nor straight; she shot this way and that, turning and tumbling, threading her way through branch and leaf and tangling plant, plagued by the sensation of myriad tiny hands clutching and hauling and releasing her.

Stopped, at last, far above the ground, she balanced atop a platform of woven sapling-boughs, dizzied and trembling. A peep below punished her with no glimpse of the far-off ground, but an impenetrable thicket of pale leaves and ivory branches. How there came to be so much leaf at such a season, she only then thought to wonder.

'Anouska tires easily,' said Niklas from behind her.

Nanda spun about. He stood, unruffled, a few feet away, on the other side of the platform. Near at hand was the stout walls of a withy-hut, a latticed door built into its façade. He glanced only once at Nanda, perhaps assuring himself that she had survived the passage in one piece, and then knocked firmly upon the door.

Rattling reached Nanda's ears, a sound as of a basket of dry bones being shaken.

She heard nothing else, but apparently the signal to enter had been given, for Niklas unlatched the door and pushed it open.

A gesture ushered Nanda inside first.

The room beyond was tiny, the woven floor uneven; Nanda pitched sideways upon entering, her foot inadvertently set down upon a rupture in the ordered tangle of the withies. A powerful melange of aromas assaulted her nostrils: pungent, herbal smoke, stale sweat, and the indefinable scent of sickness.

In a chair tucked into a shadowy corner sat the woman Anouska, her thin fingers clutching the chair's protruding arms so tightly her knuckles gleamed white. An emaciated, shrunken figure, she must have been three, four times Nanda's age — easily over a century old. The relentless passage of years may have stolen her vitality away, but

215

the withered husk left behind had life to it yet, chiefly in the hard pair of eyes which took in Nanda's entry. Pale, yes. Paler... as Nanda stared in growing disbelief, those eyes drained of all colour, turning stark, ghost-white.

'Malefic,' she hissed, and her hands gripped her chair-arms so hard the wood creaked in protest. 'I smell it on you, woman.'

'Malefic?' echoed Nanda, disturbed in spite of herself. 'Is that what they are called?'

Anouska did not answer. She watched Nanda with those eerie eyes, unblinking. Was she even breathing? Did Nanda imagine the distrust, fear even, that she saw in their expression? Perhaps she suffered some delusion. Such advanced years frequently brought senility with them, a cruel reward for a life lived long and well.

'It is not me,' she said, as calmly as she could. 'I am no malefic.'

'You have been near,' hissed Anouska. 'Near... did it strike you?' She sat up as she spoke, leaned toward Nanda with an odd, hungry ferocity Nanda knew not how to interpret. 'Did it?' she repeated.

'No, I—'

'Good.' Anouska sank back into the embrace of her chair, some of her strange energy deserting her. Too much. She shrank back into a faded shadow of a woman, diminishing in her every aspect. 'Better you had died, than that.'

'What?' Nanda whispered. 'Why?'

A sniff of disdain. 'Need you ask? Has the whole world forgot?'

'We... have not been obliged to deal with them in many years.'

Anouska shook her head. Her mouth stretched into a death's head grin, no mirth in it. Disdain, again. Mockery. 'Forgotten,' she spat. 'And you are come here for help, is that it?'

'We are in dire trouble without it, ma'am.'

'Do not *ma'am* me, young woman.' Anouska bristled, and for a moment Nanda thought she would spit at her.

Nanda hoped Konrad was meeting with more success, at The Malykt's Temple. Surely he must. 'You warded the bridges, once,' she tried. 'Why? Was it because of these malefics?'

'Much good it did us,' growled Anouska. 'Still they came, thick and fast. Close one door and another opens, and another...' Her eyes turned distant, remembering.

'They open by themselves, then, these doors?' Nanda persisted.

Anouska's distant look faded. 'No,' she snapped. 'By themselves?

How should they?'

'Then who opened them? Who would facilitate the passage of such a thing?'

'Who?' Anouska shook her head in slow despair. 'You remember the question I asked you when you came in?'

Did it strike you. 'I do,' Nanda said.

'There is your answer. Can you not manage so simple an equation?'

Nanda thought, and... blanched. '*I* might?' she said. 'I? Were I struck?'

'It is always better when they kill,' said Anouska, as if that was an answer. But then, perhaps it was, for she added, 'When they did not... we had to do it.'

'Kill?'

'Death is not the worst of all possible fates,' hissed Anouska.

Nanda fought her way through the convoluted alterations in subject with an effort. There was a thread here, a line of argument making sense in Anouska's aged mind, filled as it was with so many years, so many memories, so many thoughts... her mind obliged her with a sudden memory of her own: Konrad doubled over in agony, black bile or blood or *something* pouring from his mouth, a flash in his eyes that was nothing of his: darkness? Rage?

Had he used the word *conduit,* or had she?

'It... corrupts,' she said shakily, her stomach churning. 'Is that it?'

'How could it not?' said Anouska simply. 'You have seen it. You know.'

Nanda had. She did. Such a nightmare must spread itself, could not touch without destroying — one way or another.

'Spirits above,' she breathed. *Konrad.* Was he irrevocably marked? She had healed the physical damage to his body, purged the taint from his blood — or had she? She had not known then what she was looking for. If there had been a touch of darkness in him, well... that was Konrad. How could she have known to look for more?

'A lucky escape?' Anouska's hard stare returned, and those eyes... they sent another shiver down Nanda's spine. 'Or something else?'

'A friend was... struck.'

'Then you will have to kill them.' Anouska spoke simply, matter-of-fact, as though she had not just condemned a living man to an abrupt death at the hands of his own loved ones.

'I cannot.'

'There is no other way. Only death will purge the foul touch of a malefic from the blood.'

A year ago, a few months ago, Nanda could have welcomed such news, for Konrad alone had the power to die — and live. And die again.

Not now. He couldn't die, not *now,* not when it meant a final end.

'There must be a way,' she said stoutly. 'To save him.'

'You lose sight of the problem,' said Anouska, brisk now. 'To lose a friend, yes, that is a pity, but as you hesitate and keen over it a malefic remains abroad. Killing more. Corrupting more. What shall you do, witch? Have you the strength to fight it? Or shall you lose your chance to sentiment, and grief? You cannot afford such weakness now.'

Nanda shuddered inwardly at such words, wondering at the life this woman had led. What had turned her so hard, so cold? Had it been the malefics?

'What did *you* do?' said Nanda, taking hold of herself, and shoving down the wild panic surging up in her. 'When the malefics came? How did you fight them?'

'Me, nothing,' Anouska said. 'I was a mere child, the last time a malefic manifested in Assevan. My father was struck. My mother slew him. Another witch slew her in her turn. Both were lost, the moment that rot touched them.'

Nanda's nausea grew. *Spirits help me, what a history lies behind this woman. What an impossible duty lies before me.* 'And the malefic?' she persevered. 'How was it subdued?'

'No ordinary weapon can slay a malefic,' said Anouska, confirming Nanda's worst fears. 'If you can get near enough to one to wield it, which is doubtful.' Raking Nanda with a disdainful glare, she made her feelings as to Nanda's probable valour clear.

'What, then?'

'There is one entity whose Will can oppose such evil,' said Anouska, hoarse now, dry as paper. She gave a cough.

'Shandrigal,' breathed Nanda. *Say it is so. Give me one weapon in this war, one I can wield.*

'Aye,' said Anouska, but not quite as though she was answering Nanda's question. She nodded to herself, and that rictus split her face again, a grin gone horribly wrong. 'Smelled that on you, too.

Shandral, are you? They do not make them the way they used to.'

Nanda wished, for one selfish moment, that she had met this woman in her earlier years — before she was spirit-drained, before she was diminished. At the height of her powers. *Then* the gritty, grimy old woman might have been impressed.

Never mind what she thought. 'I am Shandral,' Nanda said, lifting her chin. 'And if my Mistress has the means to counter this threat then I shall bear Her banner proudly.'

'I wonder,' mused Anouska distantly, 'if they are still there?'

'What?' said Nanda, breathless. 'What, and where?'

'There was a blade,' said Anouska. 'There were three. Brightness itself, all of them, the Shandrigal's gift to our benighted realm.'

'Two were lost,' said Niklas, the first time he had spoken since entering Anouska's house.

'Then but one remains,' said Anouska. 'Shall it be enough?'

'It must be,' said Nanda. 'Only tell me where to find it.'

'You imagine yourself saving your friend, do you?' said Anouska, and gave a dry, deathly chuckle. 'Walking away a hero? No one battles a malefic and lives. That is the nature of it, Shandral. There was a sacrifice. Always.'

Nanda swallowed. She had seen the nightmare Anouska called malefic, seen the frightening speed with which it moved, the merciless onslaught it brought. Too fast, too brutal, for study; she could not even say what it had looked like, quite. All that she had taken away was a confused jumble of impressions: darkness, glinting talons, impossible speed. Blood.

Whoever slew the malefic could hardly hope to do so without being *struck*, as Anouska put it. And to be struck was to die.

To wield that blade, then, was to die — whether or not she took the malefic with her. And Konrad's life, too, was forfeit.

For a moment, courage failed her. She quailed, despair overwhelming her in a rush. What nightmare was this? She'd had hope, only a few scant hours ago. How long ago it seemed. Her only problem then had been her surfeit of spirit-pacts, the slow drain on her health that would, at last, kill her. Her hope had come out of Konrad's ready offer of assistance, the belief that somehow he would help her free herself of the consequences of her own folly.

Now they were both doomed.

Chin up, Irinanda Falenia, she scolded herself. Despair killed as surely as any malefic.

Oddly, it was a recollection of Tasha's existence which saved her this time. That sardonic grin, the eye-rolling insouciance with which a child turned *lamaeni* far too young defied everything the world had to throw at her. What would she say to this news? How would she respond to the challenge?

Do your worst, then. Nanda could almost hear her say it.

'The blade,' Nanda said, more steadily than she would have thought possible a moment ago. 'Where is it?'

Anouska looked to Niklas.

'We have custody of it,' he said, reluctantly. 'It is here.'

'Give it to me,' said Nanda. 'Please.'

But Niklas shook his head. 'That is not for me to decide.' He, too, looked Nanda over with — not disdain, but something tending in that direction. She knew how she must appear, to those with senses enough to see. A drained spirit-witch, caught by her own ego, her too-comfortable belief in her infallibility. A woman who had put herself in such disorder could not be trusted with such a mission. She had not the strength left for it.

Well. If death was in Nanda's near future anyway, what better use to make of it than taking a malefic with her? 'I can do this,' she said. 'And I will.'

Niklas shook his head again. 'It is not for me to decide. We will consult.'

'But—'

'We will bring the blade,' he said, talking over her objections. 'To The Shandrigal's Temple. It shall be decided there.'

That would be enough, for a beginning. Nanda nodded. 'Bring everyone you can,' she said. 'I will not accept that there is nothing to be done for those struck. There must be something. If we all work together—'

Anouska fell to hoarse cackling. 'You think that was not tried?' she wheezed. 'You think we would have fallen to slaying those we loved, if there had been any alternative?'

'We must try,' said Nanda doggedly. 'I cannot simply accept—'

'*Accept,*' snapped Anouska. 'Accept what you must. Life demands that of all of us. Accept, and *do*. But do not *dither*, or more of your loved ones will die around you.'

Life demands that of all of us. So it did. Konrad had been forced to accept the upheaval of his life, long ago, the loss of the person he had been. The role that had been thrust upon him. He had borne it, borne all of it, year upon year, performing his harsh duties with more honour than Nanda had imagined possible. He did not deserve such an end. Life had demanded too much of him already.

Nanda thought of Tasha, and the inspector, and steeled her nerve. She had allies in this. She had options.

The way forward would not be easy, but a way *must* be found.

'I will find you at the Temple,' she told Niklas. 'There are things I must do, first.'

'Stubborn,' muttered Anouska. 'You will see. You will see.'

'When hope fails, at least there is the stubborn refusal to accept defeat,' said Nanda, with a flash of her impish smile. 'It has got me out of trouble more than once.'

'And into it, too, I'll wager,' said Anouska.

5

The Shandrigal's Temple occupied a spot so close to that of The Malykt, Konrad marvelled at himself that he should never have set foot in it before. Both constructs were given prominent positions at the very heart of Ekamet, and a mere two minutes' walk carried Konrad out the grand double-doors of the one and into the equally majestic entrance of the other.

He entered cautiously, not for fear of the malefic leaping out at him from some shadowed nook, but out of a feeling of wrongness. *He* was the wrongness here, a creature belonging so utterly to The Malykt that he could have no business placing himself under The Shandrigal's roof. This was why he had never come here before, despite Nanda's influence over his life. He was the opposite of everything her Mistress stood for.

He paused in the entrance hall, half expecting a smiting for his presumption.

Nothing came.

In its essential design, this second temple was surprisingly similar to The Malykt's. Both were built from solid, ash-grey granite; both possessed the soaring height, the grandeur, the handsome, imposing façades lit with improbably large windows. The tall roofs and coloured domes. They had been built at the same time, in all probability, and bore all the prevailing architectural conceits of their era.

Their interiors differed. This hall, similar in proportion to The Malykt's, and with the same echoing hush courtesy of marble and tile, differed in its details. The carvings adorning the central pillars, the mosaic images set into the floors, bore The Shandrigal's symbols in a riotous tangle, possessing in consequence a liveliness missing from the Temple of Death.

How fitting, Konrad thought. Of all the things one would expect of the dead, liveliness wasn't supposed to be one of them. Even if his experience had sometimes been rather different.

He was the vanguard. Hard on his heels came Diana, attended by, in all probability, most of the rest of the Order. When had these two Orders, devoted to such opposite principles, worked together in this fashion? Had it occurred in living memory?

Some quality of the brightness in that hall stirred his disgust. He preferred the sobriety and deep silences of his own Temple; the celebratory atmosphere of this one was unseemly, vulgar, detestable— he raised his hand, the one that held his heavy, silver-topped cane, with some half-formed thought of beating the life out of those repulsive pillars.

The intensity of this thought shocked him, and he lowered his hand again. The thought was gone, so completely he wondered that it had entered his head at all. What bizarre impulse had gripped him? He stood in silence for some moments, breathing too hard, and felt it again: a stirring of something ugly in his soul. Something he would not have been eager to acknowledge as his own.

'Welcome to the Temple of—' Someone had come in, unnoticed by Konrad in his momentary self-absorption. A woman, smiling. But when she caught sight of him, she stopped smiling, stopped talking, stopped everything. Her face registered shock, dismay — and alarm. 'Sir?' she said, visibly gathering herself. 'Are you—'

'Forgive me,' he said, pushing down that inexplicable ugliness, drawing his civilised habits back around himself. Like armour. 'I come from The Malykt's Order; the rest will soon arrive, and numerous others as well. There has been — there is an emergency.'

She was young, this Shandral, with some quality that reminded him of Nanda. Not her appearance: she had typical Assevan features, the pale colouring and dark hair, and a freshness about her that could belong only to extreme youth. An acolyte, of some sort? Had she even achieved her eighteenth year, yet? Perhaps it was that penetrating stare that put him in mind of Nanda, the intense focus, that indefinable suggestion that she saw right through him.

223

What, he thought, *did* she see? Nothing she enjoyed.

'You are the Mal—' she began.

'Best not to say it out loud,' he interrupted hastily.

She nodded, regaining her composure. 'What is the nature of this emergency?'

'Malefic.'

Her eyes widened. 'No,' she breathed. 'That cannot be—'

Tumult cut her off, the clamour of many arrivals. Konrad heard Diana's voice rising above the hubbub. 'A place of comfort for Talin please, at once. No, I would not have chosen to move her just yet, but leaving her behind is unthinkable, and this is by far the better place to prepare for this war. Ah! You.' This last was directed to the woman he'd just been speaking with, Konrad surmised, and so did she, for she started at Diana's words and hurried over. 'Where is Katya? If she is not here, she must at once be summoned. There is no time to lose.'

'It's true, then,' said the acolyte, staring ashen-faced as the majority of The Malykt's Order shattered the silence of her Mistress's Temple, pouring grim-faced into the echoing hall.

'Konrad,' said Diana, stopping as she made to pass him by. An odd, searching look directed at him; it made his guts churn. What was *she* seeing, now? 'Are you well?'

He swallowed, and nodded. Was it a lie? He felt well.

He saw disquiet in her face, and her gaze passed from him to Talin, who was then being escorted out of the hall and into some quieter, more comfortable spot.

'What is it, Diana?' he said, though it cost him to ask the question. He was not sure that he wanted to know the answer.

'Nothing,' she said shortly, and turned from him. She was gone the next instant, bustling away, already calling instructions or orders or reprimands to somebody else.

Konrad retreated until his back hit the wall, and stayed there.

'Konrad,' hissed a young voice, and he looked down to find Tasha half concealed in the shadows at his elbow. 'What's going on?'

'How did you find me?'

'Eetapi fetched me. Something about nightmares.'

'Oh? Why did she fetch you?'

'She said you were going to need me.'

Konrad's brows rose at this idea. 'In what way?'

'I was hoping you could tell me that. What in the Spirits' name is going on here? Why is everybody forting up in the temples?'

Forting up. Diana had used the word "war". Konrad's head spun. He made himself speak calmly to Tasha, recounting everything that had happened since that fateful knock upon his door.

Tasha, as always, took it in stride, reacting with a low, impressed whistle. 'Excellent,' she said.

'Excellent? Tasha, the thing could kill half the city.'

'Don't exaggerate. We'll probably manage to destroy it before it kills *half*. Quarter, maybe.'

'We?' said Konrad, ignoring the rest.

'I did say I was here to help?'

'You've some manner of expertise regarding malefics, I suppose?'

She shrugged. 'As much as anybody else, right?'

Fair point. Expertise was exactly what they lacked.

A brightness entered, bringing with it a penetrating, commanding voice to rival Diana's. The hall was thinning out by that time, half of The Malykt's Order having dispersed into the Temple. Still, though, people enough remained to obscure Konrad's view of whoever had come in, save for that indefinable lightening that she brought with her.

Until the people melted from her path like snow, and she stood in uncontested possession of the centre of the hall.

Katya, as Diana had called her. Ekaterina Inshova, seventy years old if she was a day, but utterly unbowed by time. She stood several inches shorter than Konrad, rather shorter than Nanda too, but her presence in no way gave that impression. She stood tall in power and authority, radiating that sense of hope and light, the soft lines on her face in no way marring her beauty. Her wealth of hair, white with age, was neatly coiffed, and she wore a plain, dark green gown under a heavy black cloak.

Nanda's superior, Konrad mused. Chief among the Shandral, a real avatar of her Mistress's power. And just the person wanted in this calamity, besides Nanda herself.

She'd asked for an explanation. Diana having gone out of the hall, and no one else seeming much inclined to answer her, Konrad took the risk of approaching her.

Only to see her eyes widen slightly, and narrow again as she looked upon him.

Konrad bowed. 'I am—'

'I know who you are.'

The words lacked warmth, but her tone did not. She looked on him with the same, odd wariness Diana had displayed, but with approval also. No enemy of the Malykant here.

Encouraged, he went on. 'There is a malefic loose in the city,' he said quietly. 'Or the spirit-lands, we are not at present certain which. It has killed in both.'

'It has come, then,' she said, in no wise as shocked as he had expected.

'You anticipated it?'

She bowed her head. 'Diligent as you are, it could not be avoided forever.'

Konrad felt a new burden of guilt settle over him. It blended perfectly with the rest. 'I'm sorry,' he said helplessly. 'I've tried—'

This she waved away. 'Were you and your predecessors less diligent, it must have come all the sooner. This is not the time for self-reproach.'

True.

'Tell me everything.'

Konrad, wearying of repeating so horrific a chain of events, nonetheless did so in as much detail as he could remember. The success of this war, if war it would be, must depend to a fair extent on this woman's understanding and support. Without the full and knowledgeable assistance of her Order, little could be done.

He had not fully finished this latest narration when Tasha stiffened beside him, and drew in her breath in a sharp hiss.

Konrad broke off. 'What is it?'

Tasha, after a long pause, relaxed. Mostly. 'Nothing, I think,' she said.

Then Nanda was there, rushing headlong into the Temple with another army at her back. Spirit-witches. Konrad recognised none of them, but he knew who they must be. They came prepared, he saw, if only in resolve, for in their faces — male and female, young and old, from all levels of society — he saw the same bleak determination, the same fear suppressed.

Nanda split away from this group, her gaze alighting immediately upon him. She approached at a near run, filled with an urgency, and an anxiety, that Konrad could not make sense of.

'Don't say there's been another death,' he said, catching the two hands she instinctively held out to him.

'It isn't that. It's— oh, Konrad, do you feel well?'

'Well? I am perfectly well.'

'Are you *sure*? There is something you don't know. About— the malefic, and being struck. It corrupts, Konrad. If we want to know who opened a door at the bridge, we need only find whoever lived in that ice-house, I think—'

'Talin?' Konrad snapped. 'Nanda, what madness is this? She's been with the Order her whole life through. She couldn't have done such a thing.'

'Not normally, no, but she is not quite Talin anymore.'

Konrad's sense of crawling unease grew. 'But that means…'

'Yes,' said Nanda, her anxious eyes searching his face.

'*I* would never—'

'It struck Konrad?' Tasha said abruptly, sharply.

'Yes. I healed him, but I cannot know whether the poison persists.'

'There's—' began Tasha, but then Konrad heard it too. A distant *shriek,* a tearing sound fit to turn the guts to ice. It echoed off the cool stone walls of The Shandrigal's Temple, and was then repeated.

An ordinary, human cry followed. Then a scream.

Konrad was running before the first shriek had faded, unsure of where he was going in that unfamiliar place. 'Talin's here,' he said to Nanda, on the other side of the hall by then, following the distant sounds of distress. 'Injured. They took her somewhere—'

'There's an infirmary,' she said, and took the lead. 'It's this way.'

Down a corridor, feet pounding on the cold tile as another scream echoed down from above. Up a flight of stairs; left; someone passing in a headlong flight, bloodied, vomiting black bile—

'Stop *him,*' Konrad shouted, willing only to pause.

'Got it,' said Tasha, and tore off after the beleaguered man.

On again, and then Nanda burst through a door into a quiet infirmary, beds laid out in neat, white-blanketed rows. Or it had been quiet, once. Chaos now reigned, and blood, and *bile,* such wet redness and glistening blackness, flowing in streams and tides all over the cool floor.

Talin was on her feet. Not in any strength; she swayed, white as death, ready to topple at an instant's notice. Her white, white eyes

227

were not as they had been. She was emptied of Talin, become something else, at least in this moment.

Nanda hissed. 'There's a door here,' she gasped. 'She's opened one.'

'And the malefic came through,' said Konrad, though there was no sign of it now. Only the destruction it left behind it, in the form of two attendants, bent on caring for Talin in her distress and now cruelly punished for their solicitude. One lay huddled against the far wall, her hair spread out in the pool of black bile she'd fallen in. She was dead, eyes blank and dark.

The other sat on the edge of one of the beds, leaking blood onto the pristine blankets, his shirt and coat dripping black fluid. His wounds were not such as to kill him, but he appeared dazed, staring at nothing.

Konrad approached the woman who stood, alone and terrible, gasping in air. 'Talin,' he said. 'Tell me. What has happened?'

She turned her terrible eyes on him, and he saw in them the same ugliness he had felt astir in his own soul. A bleak, blank cold.

Then a cry tore from her throat, and she collapsed. Not dead, despite Konrad's immediate fear. Weeping. Tearing, heartbroken sobs.

'It seemed a nightmare,' she said indistinctly. 'I thought I remembered — I thought I had — and I *did.*'

'The bridge?' said Nanda softly.

Wordless, Talin gave a single nod.

Nanda sighed, a soft, weary sound, and turned to face those who had found their way into the room. Tasha was there, hauling the malefic's other victim with her. He did not look long for this world, Konrad thought dispassionately, and that was possibly for the best.

Diana stood there, too, looking from Talin to Konrad with a look of utter heartbreak in her face.

At last: something that could touch The Malykt's chief servant. Diana Valentina had a heart after all.

'Talin,' she said, and took a step towards her friend.

Talin erupted, pushing herself off and away from the bed — and away from Diana. She backed up until she hit the wall, and stood there, trembling. 'Give me a blade,' she said.

Diana's eyes filled with tears; but only for a moment. Then they were gone, and her mask was back in place. Cool, cold, unbreakable.

Wordlessly, she retrieved a short-bladed knife from some pocket in her clothing, and gave it to the nearest man to her. She could provide the knife, then, but she had not the strength to give it into Talin's hands herself.

Her deputy performed that office for her, his own face expressionless. Konrad realised that he knew this man: Lev Antonov, a necromancer of the Order.

He stepped back, returning to Diana's side: a solid, perhaps comforting, presence.

Diana did not turn away her head. Konrad stood, watching her as her friend died, and she betrayed nothing. Not a flicker of emotion.

No one spoke into the silence that followed, not for some time. The only sounds came from the wounded: faint moans of distress, too-quick breathing.

It was Nanda who spoke at last. 'Anouska, of the Enclave, spoke of this,' she said. 'She said— that—'

She could not finish the sentence. Someone else did it for her: one of the spirit-witches, Konrad guessed, a big, broad-shouldered man with Nanda's own icy colouring. 'She is the eldest of us,' he said. 'She remembers the malefic. She spoke of the fate that has overtaken Talin.'

Diana turned her cold, dead eyes on the man. 'And what does she say is to be done about it?'

'They must die. There is no other way.'

A tremor passed over Diana's face, nothing more. 'Well,' she said softly. 'What are we, the Order of Death, if we cannot die in our turn?'

To Konrad's horror, her attention turned then to him.

'Not—' he began.

You are the Order's executioner, her face said. She would not speak it aloud before so many strangers, but he heard her clearly all the same.

I am not, he wanted to cry. That was a part of his duty only, and only when it was merited. He did not kill innocents. He could not.

And what of himself? He, too, had been struck. Must he not also die?

Was that also there in Diana's gaze? Did she expect him to follow Talin's example, and turn the knife next on himself?

He backed away, hardly knowing where he thought to go, or what he imagined he could do. He was out the door, halfway down the corridor beyond, before thought caught up with him at all. He could not stop shaking.

Nanda had followed him. She was there when he slowed, her presence the only comfort that could reach him. 'Tasha's already on it,' she said.

'Tasha?' he repeated numbly.

'Dispatched the fellow she brought up here in one knife-thrust. She was after the other one when I got out.'

His mouth tightened, revolted in spite of himself. Tasha. Such an appearance of youth, and so ruthless a soul. She'd have been twice the Malykant he was.

And she was what they needed now. She had all the resolution he had not; lacked all the sentiment that so impeded him.

'What now?' he said, looking into Nanda's eyes, hoping desperately for an answer there.

He saw only fear. 'I— Konrad, I don't know if you are safe. I don't know if I healed everything the malefic did to you.'

If it were possible to heal that kind of damage, Konrad guessed, the witches of the enclave must know of it. This elder, Anouska, must have known of it. There was no way.

'But,' he said. 'I feel— there is *something* that isn't right, but it's a small thing, Nan, I swear. I'm me. I am still in control.'

Nanda nodded slowly. 'Of all people, you are perhaps the best to bear it,' she said, with a trace of her mirthless, unamused smile.

'I am deathly enough as it is?' he said, trying to see the humour of it. 'It must be hard to turn a deathbringer any darker.'

'I'll talk with Diana,' she said. 'She cannot possibly—'

'She's already ordered my execution, in effect,' said Konrad. 'What makes you think she will hesitate to hasten it along?'

Nanda had no response to make to that, could only look at him with great, frightened eyes.

'I've got to go,' he said, already backing away. 'If they find me here, I'm done.'

'Tasha would not hurt you.'

'You are sure of that?'

'Not like *this*,' she amended, and there it was: she was as unsure of Tasha's capacity for mercy as he was.

'I'm going,' he said again. 'To the Bones. The spirit-lands. Anywhere but here.'

'I go with you.'

'Nan—'

'Don't even bother,' she said, crossly, as though he had come home late for dinner and tried to fob her off with an excuse. 'You know it's futile.'

He smiled, faintly, at that. 'I might hurt you,' he said, serious again.

She shrugged. 'Then I'll have to kill you.'

'Or I will,' said a new voice. Tasha. A composed Tasha, not wielding a naked knife-blade, not leaping upon him with his death in her sights.

Konrad looked down at her. Not a speck of blood on her, somehow. '*You* can't come. You are what we're trying to run away from.'

'That's Diana, no? Don't worry, Konrad. I won't kill you unless I have to.'

'That hardly seems fair. Look what you just did to my fellows.'

She shrugged. 'I don't care about them.'

'But you do care about me? *You?*'

'Hard to believe, isn't it? Are we going or not?' Tasha marched off down the corridor. Konrad, hearing the approach of voices, hurried after her. If he did not make himself scarce right away, he would lose his chance.

6

Later found Konrad, Nanda and Tasha secreted deep in the Bone Forest, in hiding.

Not, to Konrad's regret, in his own, familiar hut. He had made his way there on instinct, but Nanda had stopped him partway there with a vicelike grip upon his arm.

'You're going to your hut.'

'Where else?'

'Konrad. Nobody but the three of us knows about that place, right?'

Konrad had given it due thought. 'How could they?' he had concluded.

'I don't know, but people have learned unwelcome truths about you before. You need to be *sure,* Konrad. Do I need to remind you that your life literally depends upon it?'

In the end, he had only been nearly sure. Nanda was right. For all his caution, he had at times been caught out. Followed, out-guessed, pre-empted.

'Where else, then?' he'd said again, standing there in an indeterminate spot in the Bone Forest, sleet-soaked and exhausted and afraid. Night fell early out in the Bones, and the shadows already loomed and leapt and flickered among the pale trees. Ordinarily this had no effect on him, but today was different. Today, he started at every shifting shadow, jumped at every sudden noise, even the sound of twigs breaking under his own feet.

'Come with me,' she'd said, and then led them by a winding route to a different part of the forest, one Konrad rarely ventured into.

And then down, into a hole in the ground. Down through the stout, twisting roots of a cluster of three ancient trees, down into the cold earth.

'Nice place,' said Konrad, taking a long look.

Nanda snorted in response. The abode had promise, perhaps, but little of that had been realised. The bare earth walls were densely packed and sound, but empty and damp. Ditto, the floor. Nanda — or someone — had built rudimentary furniture at some point: a species of couch, woven from felled branches, and a pallet for a bed, not dissimilar to Talin's in its general appearance. Only the canopy of ice-droplets was missing.

Konrad left this superior comfort to the ladies, and reposed himself upon the couch. Wrapping his coat more tightly around himself, he shivered deeply, and sighed. It was cold that made him shake like that, he told himself. Just the bone-deep cold.

Silence reigned for a time. The shocking events of the day had to be absorbed, thought about, reconciled to. Or simply stuffed down somewhere where they could not, for the present, cause trouble. Konrad attempted the latter, and found it difficult. He kept seeing Talin's white face: as he had first seen her, injured and regretful and frightened, in The Malykt's Temple. Then as he had seen it again so soon afterwards: twisted, marred by a cold evil. Then, heartbroken.

Was this the fate that awaited him? Would he, too, succumb, and turn loose a malefic upon the city he loved so well?

There would be no living with oneself afterward, Konrad knew. He understood Talin's feelings exactly.

He ought to destroy himself over the mere possibility of it, but he could not. He was not yet finished. He still had so much to *do*.

'Right,' said Tasha after a time. 'What are we going to do?' She alone of the three seemed scarcely touched by the horror and the tragedy of the past two days. She'd sat very still as Nanda thought and Konrad brooded, looking at nothing, motionless and emotionless. Could she be so very implacable? For once, Konrad was not the murderer in the room. Tasha had actually outdone him in death, today.

'The malefic,' said Nanda. 'We need to find it.'

'It could be anywhere,' said Konrad, for that was a thought that had been plaguing him, too. Where had it gone, between attacking him at the ice-house and entering The Shandrigal's Temple at Talin's instigation? What if there were several other knots of tragedy all over the city right now? Others who'd died? Others who'd been struck, and now colluded in the destruction of their friends?

Spirits above, what of the inspector? If more had died, the police would be summoned all over the city tonight. Summoned into fresh danger, perhaps. He wrestled with an urge to get up at once, run back to Ekamet and retrieve Alexander. Bring him down here, where he would be… safe.

Safe? No one was safe. Were it possible to protect him, the rest of his men remained in danger, along with everyone else. And if Konrad's instincts did not lead him awry, wherever Konrad was could be the most dangerous place in the city.

'Maybe it will find me,' Konrad said. 'Even down here.' He was hoping for that, in truth, for out here there were far fewer people to be endangered by its presence.

Only his maddening and maddened friend Tasha, together with the person he loved best in the world.

'All right,' said Nanda. 'Supposing that's true, we need a way to fight it. And there is a way.'

Konrad sat up, 'There is? What way?'

'There were once three blades, blessed in some way by The Shandrigal, that could destroy them,' said Nan. 'Two are lost. The third is now at the Temple.'

'The Shandrigal's Temple?'

'Yes. The enclave brought it — it's been under their guardianship — but I don't know which of them is carrying it or I'd probably have taken it.'

'Taken as in stolen?' said Tasha with a gasp. 'I am impressed.'

Nanda responded with a grave little bow. 'Thank you.'

'Pity you couldn't carry out this admirable plan. You don't have any notion which of them is most likely to have it, by any chance?'

'Possibly Niklas. He's the big, cold, silent one with my hair colour. Alternatively Lady Lysak, or…' she shrugged. 'Whoever is the leader of their enclave. I have no idea who that might be.'

Tasha subsided into silent reverie. Konrad could almost see the thoughts flashing through her mind. 'While our favourite kleptomaniac arranges her ideas, what do you think are the chances of finding those other two blades?'

'About nil. I got the impression they were lost long ago, as in, the last time malefics roamed Assevan. If not, we have zero clues as to where they might be or how they got there. The only other possibility I can think of is somehow making another one.'

'How possible is this possibility?'

'Also about nil.' Nanda sighed. 'I did not get a chance to see the blade, so I can only guess at what makes it… potent, when other blades are not. It's the property of the spirit-witch enclave, but they were clear enough that it was made in partnership with The Shandrigal's Order. Some combination of spirit and Shandral magic, then? I thought to consult my Mistress. Perhaps She can help.'

Konrad's smile was crooked, thinking of his own Master. 'Is she prompt to answer entreaty?'

'No.' An answering smile flickered over Nanda's face, soon gone. 'I feel terribly out of my depth, Konrad. It isn't a pleasant feeling.'

'It really isn't. What's worse is knowing that even Diana and Katya are similarly outfaced. What's anyone supposed to do?'

Nanda hesitated. 'The other thing about the blade…'

'Yes?'

'It's— Anouska, the elder, said that nobody fights a malefic and lives. You can't get near enough to it to use the blade without being struck, and you know what that means.'

'So it's a suicide mission for whoever expects to dispatch it.'

'Exactly.'

He stared at Nanda. 'Nan, tell me *you* aren't proposing to wield it.'

'I am not in the best health anyway—'

'No. I should do it.'

'*You* of all people cannot be permitted to die. Not now. What are we even doing down here, if you're that resigned to a speedy trip into the hereafter?'

'I've got two different death penalties on my head right now,' said Konrad. 'Diana's personal curse, and the malefic. I can't dodge them both forever. But perhaps I can take the malefic with me when I go.'

Nanda stared right back at him — and then, surprisingly, laughed. 'Listen to us. What a pair of tragedy queens. Are we in so great a hurry to martyr ourselves?'

'Someone has to do it.'

'Maybe someone will. Someone else. Maybe when we walk out of here, we'll find that the malefic reappeared, was duly skewered by

Niklas or someone else unspeakably brave and self-sacrificing, and it's all over.'

'Chance would be a fine thing.'

'Wouldn't it?' Nanda abandoned the daydream with a sigh — and then a gasp. 'Where's Tasha?'

'She's—' Konrad broke off, the inescapable fact of Tasha's absence hitting him forcibly. 'How did she do that? She was right here.' *Right here* being a mere few feet away. 'Tasha?' he called.

Silence.

'She's gone to steal the blade,' said Nanda. 'Konrad, I am not persuaded that's the best idea.'

'Wasn't it what you wanted?'

'It...' she hesitated. 'Anouska wasn't exactly overflowing with confidence in me as a possible vanquisher of malefics.'

'So what? Who is she to judge?'

'She wasn't wrong, though, was she? Look at me. I am not exactly at my best. Maybe someone else would be better.'

'Like me.' Konrad smiled. 'I can do it. I'm good at killing.'

Nanda regarded him gravely. 'So you are.'

'Also quite good at dying. Admit it, I've had more practice than most people.' Konrad spoke lightly to hide the sinking dismay doing terrible things to his insides. He didn't want to die. He knew it with a vehemence which might have surprised him, a few dark months ago. But he was running out of other choices.

'What's it like?' Nanda said. 'Dying?'

'It... um, it's...' Konrad groped for words.

'Unspeakable?'

'Best if you only do it the one time,' he said, but he was aware that Nanda was no longer fully listening. Hard to say what it was that gave him that impression, for she was still looking at him. A slight shift in focus, a faint glassiness to her attentive gaze...

He stopped speaking, and waited. Would she notice? She did not. She sat still, taking in slow, shallow breaths, as though her mind were somewhere else entirely. Not just her thoughts, but her whole mind.

Then, shadows lurched and tumbled at her feet, and something else was there. It snarled something.

Nanda sat, gripping the edge of her branch-woven pallet and trembling so hard her teeth chattered. The bones of her face protruded through her paper-white skin, as though she had lost a portion of her bodyweight on the spot.

Perhaps she had, for the something at her knee took shape, growing more solid by the instant. Konrad was reminded of Inkubal, only this being was more distinct, more substantial, for all that it looked wrought from shadows. Eyes of dirty gold glinted from within a dark little face, teeth flashing in a too-wide smile. It stroked Nanda's knee, prompting a renewed shudder from her.

'Mistress,' it said silkily.

'What is your name?' said Nanda at once, gaining some degree of mastery over herself. She sat up, willing herself to strength and calmness. Konrad watched her do it, wondering and appalled.

'I am called—' said the creature, and uttered a stream of incomprehensible syllables.

'You shall be called Stev,' said Nanda, picking only the first of them.

Stev smiled. 'And what is my task?'

'Guardianship.' Nanda pointed at Konrad. 'Something evil stalks that man and you are to keep watch for it.'

'Evil?' said Stev, head tilting. 'More evil than me?'

'Much more. Will you do it?'

'What is to be my payment?'

'The usual.' Nanda uttered the word firmly, and would not meet Konrad's eye.

'Nanda,' he said. 'This is not— tell me this is one of the five.'

She said nothing.

'*Nan*, you cannot take on a sixth pact. Please don't do this. We can manage without it—'

'How?' she snapped, rigid with exhaustion and wrath. 'How, Konrad?'

He was silent, for he had no answer.

She turned back to the thing called Stev. 'Are we agreed?'

'I will pay it,' Konrad said. 'The price. You'll take it from me.'

Stev regarded him in a silence which seemed to Konrad disdainful, but at length nodded. 'So it shall be.'

And Konrad felt it at once: a slackening of energy, a rush of tiredness, as though a weariness long-suppressed caught up with him all at once. The effect was, briefly, intense, and then it faded — leaving him indescribably lessened.

'Good,' he said thickly, trying unsuccessfully to shake the sudden fog from his thoughts. 'This thing. A malefic. You—'

'You may sense it on us,' said Nanda. 'We have both been near it.'

Stev did not move, but Konrad felt a sensation as of tiny hands crawling all over him, or intense little eyes subjecting him to a palpable scrutiny.

Stev's dirty-golden gaze grew wider. 'That,' he hissed.

'Yes,' said Nanda. 'Don't get too near it.'

'And what would you have me do?'

'Watch for it. Warn us of its approach. Find where it has gone, if you can.'

'I cannot do all of these things at once.'

'Find it, then,' said Konrad. In answer to Nanda's half-uttered protest, he said: 'The serpents will watch.' Already he had called them, before he was fairly out of The Shandrigal's Temple. He felt their approach: they had gone far from him, but they drew rapidly nearer.

'Can they?'

'Eetapi followed its trail, through the spirit-lands.'

'She wasn't just following the trail of corpses?'

'Perhaps. But, Nan, that thing will leave a trail of corpses wherever it goes.'

Hideous thought, but inarguable. He saw her swallow.

'Go,' said Nanda to Stev. 'Waste no time. Bring us the first news of it that you find.'

Nanda tore open a door, small but potent: the thing Stev fell into it, and disappeared.

'Now what?' said Konrad.

'We wait. Either for the malefic to find us, in which case we await death. Or for Tasha to come back with the blade, and Stev to return with news, in which case we hunt.'

'Three of us against a malefic,' said Konrad. 'Madness.'

'It's the only way.' Nanda spoke with resolution now. 'The Order, and the enclave, will shore up the passages between Ekamet and the spirit-lands, reducing its options. And if any more have been struck, and are liable to prove a danger, they will deal with that, too. As will *your* Order. But to have so many set out to kill the thing — numbers can only give it more to destroy.'

'There's nothing else the witches can do, to fight it? Nor the Shandral? You deflected it—'

'Yes; perhaps they can do as much, and keep themselves safe. Perhaps others, too. But we don't want to deflect it again, Konrad. We want to kill it.'

With which words, she sealed her own fate, and Konrad's too.

Konrad felt emptied of the necessary energy to care, at least about his own fate. Nanda's, though. That could still prompt an emotion: a bleak despair.

Right, then. He took a slow breath, meant to be steadying, and tried to ignore the sudden tremor in his hands. After all these years, that it should still horrify him so...

Master, he called into the aether. *Master. I beg You, attend to me.*

Silence stretched, a peculiar frozen silence as of suspended time. Konrad held his breath, torn, as ever, between hope and fear of success...

Then came the wave of knee-weakening terror, and the blast of killing cold that heralded his Master's presence. *You call upon Me?* said The Malykt. *Again?*

7

Konrad swallowed, did his best to gather his thoughts, too aware of Nanda's white, frightened face across from him. She had scooted as far back on her pallet-bed as she could get and sat plastered to the wall, as though she'd gladly fall through it given half the chance.

He'd like to do that, too.

'Master,' he said aloud — no sense now in concealment, Nanda might as well hear what he had to say.

And whatever response he was given.

'A malefic has manifested,' Konrad said.

'Yes,' said The Malykt.

Nothing else.

Konrad licked dry lips. 'It is— beyond our knowledge, Master. What might we do against this foul creature?'

'Nothing.'

'N-nothing?'

'It is a duty belonging to My Sister. Why do you trouble Me with so inconsequential an occurrence?'

'Inconse—' Konrad stopped, and swallowed. 'Your Sister? But I thought— The Malykant's duties—'

'It is your *duty to see that such manifestations occur infrequently,'* said The Malykt, and with every freezing word Konrad shivered harder. *'It is the duty of Her followers to remove the problem when they do.'*

The Master spoke as though Konrad ought to be fully aware of all this, as though it were common knowledge. Well, once it was. The Malykt had not kept up with the changing times.

Konrad, gathering himself, resolved upon one more try. 'Master. If You would but help us, there is nothing I would not—'

He did not even get to finish the sentence. The Malykt thundered, *'You have already promised to die for Me, Malykant. What more can you give?'*

What more indeed. Konrad felt the confirmation of his worst fears like a block of ice in his gut. 'I— I see,' he said.

'And I am still waiting,' added The Malykt.

Then He was gone, His dread presence fading away between one breath and the next.

Konrad required several breaths before he could speak again.

'I am intended to die, then,' he said.

Nanda just looked at him, white still, and drawn. Then the fear left her. She sat up, drawing herself away from the wall, drawing herself up to her full height. Her chin came up, the fire of resolve flashed in her eyes, and she set her lips tightly together: all signs Konrad knew well.

'Right,' she said. Only the one word, but uttered with a firmness which proposed to defy the whole world if necessary.

Konrad waited for more, but nothing came. 'So,' he said, trying unsuccessfully to still his trembling, 'While it is apparently a Shandral problem, it appears it would be best if *I* take on the duty of slaying the malefic.'

Nanda was not looking at him. Her gaze was fixed somewhere over his shoulder, fixed upon nothing, most like, but what was passing through her mind. He could guess at none of her thoughts, watching her face. 'Yes,' she said slowly. 'That would likely be the best thing.'

Konrad could not suppress a startled exclamation. Of all possible responses to his dreadful statement, he had not expected that one. Would she not even try to talk him out of it? Did she accept the prospect of his demise with such equanimity? Her mind turned on the problem of the malefic; that resolve of hers, that was Nanda laying the burden of obligation squarely over her own shoulders, Shandral that she was. She had no thought to spare for Konrad's fate in the midst of such a crisis, and that was right. Konrad ought not be so distracted by it, either.

Unbecoming of a hero, to worry so much about the miserable self. He never had been much of a hero, had he? But he could try. How would a hero think, in this moment?

If I must die, best that I do so in a worthy cause, and take the infernal malefic with me.

Konrad replayed the sentence a few times, until he found that he could accept it.

Only, he worried — for Nanda the most. Perhaps Alexander would look out for her, and Tasha. Would it be enough?

'Tasha,' said Nanda, as though echoing his last thought. 'I need her. Serpents, Konrad, quick. Is she coming yet?'

'With the blade,' he said. Yes, best to get the business over with quickly. 'Eetapi?'

No answer came. She was yet too far away, and her brother too.

'They are close,' he told Nanda. 'But still a little beyond reach.'

'Why?' said Nanda.

He blinked, nonplussed. 'What?'

'Why are they out of reach? They are never far away from you.'

'I... sent them on an errand. They have been seeking the malefic.'

'Is it like to be so far away as all that? I think not.'

He could not tell her about the serpents' other errand, not without revealing the terrible plan he had come up with for freeing her from her own troubles. So he shrugged. 'I do not control their every move, as you know.'

A copout, and Nanda knew it. But she said nothing else, for a little while. Then: 'Either this malefic is not following you, or we are better hidden here than I expected.'

Konrad had been thinking the same, in the intervals between his various existential crises. Perhaps he had been mistaken on that point — *How very like you to find an explanation centring especially around yourself* — Diana's words echoing through his thoughts, harsh but fair, much like the Master Himself really.

He regretted it, overall, because in that case where had the malefic gone, and how were they to find it?

A clanking noise interrupted him, and a scuffling, and a soft rain of dirt and ice and other detritus from above.

Then Tasha dropped into the middle of the dank, makeshift room. 'Still sitting here?' she said. 'Some conquering heroes you make.'

'Heroes with any sense do not hare off into battle without either information, a plan or a weapon,' Nanda informed her.

'Well, I have one of those things sorted. Here.' Tasha

unceremoniously dumped a dully glinting object into Nanda's hands.

She held it for a moment, tracing her fingers over the polished blade of a long knife. Where her fingers passed, pale fire briefly blossomed.

Then she leaned forward, and put it into Konrad's hands.

Konrad stared dully down at the implement of his own demise. It had beauty, this weapon, he noted with surprise. That something designed for destruction could exhibit such grace did not strike him as fitting. What use the look of the thing, when all it would ever do was rend apart those at whom it was directed? Nonetheless, a smooth curve to the blade; etchings, light and exquisite; and that pale fire, which bloomed in response to his touch just as it had to Nanda's.

'I suppose I thought you'd have to be Shandral to use this effectively,' Konrad said.

'Well,' said Nanda. 'You more or less do.'

Konrad looked up. 'Then I cannot wield this.'

Nanda just nodded at the blade, still gleaming under Konrad's touch. 'The blade thinks otherwise.'

Konrad frowned down at the thing, his mind flying back to a recent conversation with Nanda. She'd posited that he was no longer entirely The Malykt's creature; since his resurrection by The Shandrigal he was partly Her creature, too.

Here was evidence for it, of sorts.

'Good,' he said briskly. 'Let it be done soon, then. The thing's disappearance will be causing all manner of panic at the Temple.'

He expected a wisecrack from Tasha in response, but she said nothing. She was looking at Konrad, then at Nanda, a frown creasing her forehead.

Nanda looked steadily back.

'They won't be pleased,' Tasha agreed. 'But they weren't doing anything with it anyway. Dithering about wasting time, rather like you are doing.'

The words sounded like her, but Konrad could not shake the feeling that she was distracted — nor that something had passed between her and Nanda just now, a wordless exchange of some profound meaning to them both.

He didn't like it. Secrets? *Now?*

Useless to enquire, though. Nor had he the right, being fond of secrets himself. He stood up with a sigh, and busied himself with the finding of some safe place to stash the knife among his clothes. Nowhere it would stand out, shining like that, and nowhere it would stab him if he moved unwisely.

He trusted, by the time he was finished, that Nanda and Tasha had concluded their secret counsels and could now focus on the matter at hand.

'No further word of the malefic, while you were there?' he asked of Tasha.

'It hasn't appeared again, that I heard. And I think I'd have heard.'

Where was it, then? Somewhere about the city, or the spirit-lands, tearing apart more hapless victims — or hiding somewhere, biding its time until it chose to strike again.

'You are planning to use it, I suppose?' said Tasha, and again he felt that the question was not so idle nor so teasing as it seemed. Deadly serious, in fact, judging from the dark gaze she directed at him.

'Yes,' said Konrad.

'Whatever the consequences?'

'Yes. Need you ask?'

'Actually, I did need to ask.' Tasha beamed at him, and then at Nanda, and gave a curiously satisfied sigh. 'Excellent. On with the show, then.'

'The show?' said Konrad. 'The kind no one in their right mind would go to.'

Tasha's grin widened, and he was reminded that she could not quite be said to be in her right mind. 'Right then,' she said. 'See you later.' Without further comment, she swung herself up and out of the subterranean hut again, and disappeared into the gathering darkness.

'Where—' said Konrad, too late. He directed a puzzled look at Nanda, who shrugged.

'Some errand or other, I daresay,' said she.

'*Errands*? Now? We might be needing her.'

'Yes,' said Nanda. 'Exactly.'

Konrad shook his head, electing not to try to unravel this mystery. He had other things to think about. For example—

Master! Eetapi's shivery tones, thrilling through the air. A quantity of fractured ice split apart above and fell with a *whump* onto the dirt floor, narrowly missing Nanda.

Konrad straightened. 'They're back,' he told Nanda. 'Eetapi, have you news?'

I have something better than news!

She paused; apparently Konrad had to ask. 'All right, what is it?' he snapped.

A trail, Master. Like before.

He winced, torn between relief and disgust. They needed a trail to follow, if they were to catch the malefic, but if it was like the last one, a trail made up of dismembered and bloodied corpses...

All the more reason to hurry, of course.

'The hunt's on,' Konrad said to Nanda, and immediately followed Tasha's path up and out of the cavern. *Where does this trail begin?*

Ootapi answered. *In the city, Master. In the Darks.*

The Darks. The slums, or the darkest, most miserable part thereof. Curious. Was that coincidence, or among its other attractive qualities did the malefic have a taste for such wretched places? Formed of despair, and drawn to the same...

Less fanciful musings, he chided himself. The time now was for purpose, and resolve, all those things Nanda was so good at. He was, too, ordinarily, but he spared a moment's regret — odd, this — that he was not now embarking on the usual kind of hunt, a hunt for an ordinary murderer, one to be expediently dispatched by the usual methods and then home for tea.

His own words of the previous day came back to him. *I was congratulating myself on the prospect of not having to slaughter someone at the end of this.* Hah. How life did taunt one, sometimes. He'd got what he'd wished for: he wasn't going to slaughter a *someone* at all. How gladly he would trade this new duty for all those old ones, however deeply resented.

Nanda clambered out behind him, and stood shivering.

'You should wait here,' Konrad told her. 'I had better do this alone.'

'Do you want to do it alone?'

Nanda had a way of asking those unexpected questions, the ones that cut through the nonsense he told himself and exposed all the idiocy of it. 'No,' he said, choosing to give her an honest answer. 'But why endanger you?'

'Then it's goodbye,' she said composedly. 'Right now, in this moment.'

Konrad hesitated, torn between his better impulses and his

unworthy ones. He didn't want it to be goodbye, not now, not for a long, long time. If he had only a short time left, a few short hours at most, he wanted Nanda by his side. He wanted to savour every last minute with her, and part from her only when he had to.

But to carry her with him was to put her in grave danger. Would she emerge unscathed from the encounter with the malefic? Doubtful. She had been lucky to do so once; nobody could expect to manage it a second time.

He wished she might betray some emotion at the prospect of an abrupt, final parting, but this was Nanda. Ever had she walled her tenderer feelings behind solid ice. She would do so now, more than ever.

Konrad did not have to do the same, however.

He swept her up in his arms, and held her very close, his cheek against her hair. 'Irinanda Falenia,' he whispered, and kissed that soft, smooth hair, savouring her warmth, inhaling the scent of her. 'Goodbye.'

Even this was not enough. Before she could answer — before she could devastate him by choosing not to — he drew back just enough to take her pale face in his hands, and press one, fervent, long wished-for kiss to her soft, cool lips. He felt her stiffen, hopefully only with surprise and not with distaste, but what did it matter now? He was a dead man.

He released her with the greatest reluctance — or he tried to. He was pulled back, fiercely kissed, and released just as abruptly. 'Go,' she said.

Konrad paused just one moment more, trying to embed every detail of her face and form upon his memory. Trying, perhaps, to detect even a glimmer of sorrow in her demeanour.

There was none, only that cold, implacable resolve.

'Bye, Nan,' he said softly, and somehow he managed to turn away. He lengthened his stride, putting as much distance between himself and her as he could, before he had chance to weaken and change his mind.

Soon enough, he permitted himself one look back. He could not help it.

She was gone. Nothing met his eye but unforgiving, bone-pale trees frosted with ice, shrouded in a gathering gloom.

8

That was touching, said Eetapi, as he strode on into the chill embrace of the Bone Forest.

'Could you try at all to develop something resembling a heart?' Konrad retorted.

We were not made for sentiment, Master.

Didn't he know it. Konrad maintained a dark silence as he followed Eetapi's lead ever on towards the city, ignoring one or two commonplace remarks of hers. He needed his concentration in order to keep moving as fast as he could go; his supernaturally fast Malykant's stride was useful, but the darkening forest posed many dangers to an unwary Konrad. He ducked and swerved around the trees looming out of the shadows, and arrived at the city gates in one piece.

He maintained that pace through the streets and on into the Darks, uninterested now in attempts at concealment. What did it matter if someone saw him? Who cared if people guessed who, or what, he was? His time as the Malykant was over. Soon someone else would guard Assevan from the malefic curse, and Konrad would be gone.

That being the case... Konrad, almost gleefully, threw off every concealment he possessed, and let his true nature blaze through. He'd only ever done so while on the trail of a confirmed murderer, preparing himself to strike, a nightmare to strike terror into the hearts of the guilty.

Let everyone see him now. They would talk of it, later; those harrowing days when death stalked the streets of Ekamet, and no one was safe. Those days when one nightmare had slain another, and wiped them both from the world.

Or perhaps they would put his passing down as a fever-dream, a hallucination brought on by fear and darkness.

There was a relief in showing himself as he was, just this once. No more secrets. No more fumbling attempts to fit in with a society that would recoil from him, if they knew the truth. No more skulking. Konrad would face his death in all his dubious glory, and damn the consequences.

Here, Master, said Eetapi. *Here it begins.*

The serpents had led him deep into the Darks, and the light being almost gone, the narrow streets were living up to their name. He paused at the entrance to a foul-smelling alley, peering doubtfully into the gloom.

Slick blackness spilled in a dark pool over the filthy ground. There: near one wall, almost indiscernible in the deep gloaming. A shadowed shape, too still. The smells of fresh blood and — disturbingly — seared meat hung strong in the air. Something burned?

Konrad swallowed rising bile. The regular kind, he hoped, not the foul black filth he'd hoped never to encounter again. 'There are more, I take it?' he said softly to the night.

Many more, said Eetapi, and sailed on.

Konrad followed.

Fresh kills, these; the malefic had not long since reappeared. Konrad passed two more pitiful corpses, torn apart, one of them still bleeding. He began to see policemen rushing to each fresh scene of death, and pitied them: helpless as they were, still they must respond to the frightened cries of the citizens of Ekamet, still make some futile attempt at the restoration of order.

He wondered how Alexander was, and where he was, and what he made of all of this. Pity that he had not had any opportunity of bidding him farewell, too. But he did what he could, in ridding the city of a problem the inspector, with all his diligence, could not solve.

Serpents. You are sure that we are going the right way down this trail, I suppose? Having gone some half-hour expecting to encounter the malefic at any moment, his nerves thrumming with tension, it had occurred to him at last to wonder whether they were not in fact walking *away* from the thing.

Yes, Master, said both the serpents together, and Ootapi added, *These deaths are fresher. Newer!*

They would know about such things, of course. Konrad suppressed an urge to duck into a doorway, or cloak himself afresh, in order to avoid the notice of the police who dashed helplessly past, taking a grim pleasure instead in the stares he attracted. Word of this might reach the inspector's ears yet, and he'd know where Konrad had gone, and why.

Eetapi came to a stop, and Ootapi with her. *It is gone,* she said blankly.

What is gone? The trail?

Yes, Master.

Why, then it must be nearby. Konrad prepared himself for a scream, a cry, that fearsome *shriek* that still, sometimes, shot through his memory, and searched the shadows with a keen gaze, hand ready on the hilt of the knife he carried.

No, Master. The malefic is gone.

What? How can you be sure?

He felt the mental equivalent of a shrug from Ootapi. *The taint is gone,* said he helpfully, as if that explained anything.

Gone where?

Somewhere.

Somewhere.

Think, Konrad. Where could it possibly go? If it had vanished from the city so abruptly, it must either have been destroyed — surely impossible, when he had custody of the only blade acknowledged capable of such a feat — or it had gone Elsewhere. Meaning, into the spirit-lands.

Konrad did not hesitate. He ripped the aether apart and strode through, leaving the darkened, panicked streets of Ekamet behind him. The spirit-world blossomed around him with all its jagged edges, blazing lights and fathomless darks. Impatient, he jerked shut the door he'd made behind himself — no sense leaving it open for just anything to wander through, not that the malefic seemed to be short of options there — and stood for a moment, inhaling the silence. Peaceful, in a way, after the shattered mess he'd come through to get here. No palpable sense of fear; no police, no Shandral running here and everywhere, uselessly seeking an enemy no one could kill. Quiet.

Quiet, but no true peace, for a crawling sense of menace assailed his senses. *It's here,* he whispered to his serpents. *It has to be.*

No answer came. He felt, shockingly, that they were gone, blended into the aether like a pair of insubstantial shadows. Hiding, in short.

'Come out, then,' Konrad said, drawing free the Shandrals' knife from its own hiding place. It lit up like a beacon, taking him by surprise, blinding him in a haze of clear, impossibly bright light. He blinked away the watering of his eyes, straining to see past the absurd thing; it confirmed that the malefic was near but how was this *helpful*—

The shriek came, piercing his defences, swamping him with such fear he could neither move nor breathe. Shadows shifted and roiled. A shriek again; a hunting call of its own, he thought, a declaration of imminent attack, Konrad braced himself—

A sudden flurry of movement to his left, and shadows leapt at him, screaming. He shouted something inarticulate in response, slashed blindly with the blazing blade, hit nothing. Spirits above, how did one fight an insubstantial thing that came out of nowhere, consisted of nothing? He moved, supernaturally fast, Malykant-quick, and still his blade came down upon empty air. Fear faded in the wake of urgent necessity, a grimness settling over Konrad, muting every unhelpful sensation. He would *not* go without taking the malefic along; *not* permit himself to be slaughtered like every other of its hapless victims, uselessly, senselessly torn to shreds, dead and helpless to prevent its ongoing rampage—

Master. Eetapi manifested before his face, mere inches from his eyeballs; startlement merged with all the suppressed fear within him, and he stumbled back with a shout.

Sorry, said Eetapi guiltily. *Master, it is gone.*

'Gone?' he gasped, and stared blindly about. Darkness gathered about the ground, and an eerie-pale sky. Trees grasped for him with silhouetted fingers, black and menacing, but for all that essentially mundane. No movement, save the drifting shape of Eetapi before him. 'How can it be gone?'

Ootapi floated up, following his sister. *Master. I do not think the thing is following you.*

'You think not? Why?'

Has it not occurred to you, said Eetapi, *that the thing is in fact running away?*

'From me?'

Yes. From the Malykant.

He pondered that, turning the idea about, fitting it in with everything else that had happened.

It could be the truth. Had Nanda deflected the malefic, or had it fled of its own accord — finding itself facing the Malykant? Had it sensed something in him that had repelled it?

'But why?' he said. 'Why? How? I am no danger to it. Not without the blade.' And he hadn't had the knife with him, back there at the house of ice.

Maybe you are, said Eetapi.

'The Master said it has nothing to do with me.' But he remembered, as he spoke, the other things The Malykt had said. Things that revealed how much Assevan had changed, apparently outside of the Master's notice. Was He right about this?

Harrowing thought, that The Malykt Himself could be wrong.

You are not the typical Malykant anymore, Eetapi pointed out. *Are you?*

No. He was the Malykant, and he was also a shade or two Shandral. A blend of the two things that had any power to threaten a malefic at all: one whose daily efforts erased the existence of most malefics by destroying the very filth from which they formed. And one who, suitably empowered, could tear it out of the world.

He looked thoughtfully down at the blade, its light ebbing now, and wondered. Did he truly need such a tool? Did anybody?

'Right, then,' he said to the empty air. 'If it runs from me, then I must hunt it down. Nothing has changed.' He was a good hunter, and chasing down the evil things that ran from him... this was familiar territory.

It is too fast, Master, said Ootapi. *Even you cannot hope to catch it.*

He might be right, curse it all. Konrad thought...

...and a new idea flickered to life in his mind, and took root. Perhaps, after all, there was one thing he could do; for even the worst of curses might be turned to a blessing, given the right circumstances. And had not Konrad curses enough?

Letting his awareness of the external world go, Konrad sought inside himself instead, dug deep into his grubby soul in search of that seed of ugliness. The malefic had planted it there, the touch of its rending talons sufficient to poison the spirit. He'd striven to suppress

251

it, ignore it, pretend he was unchanged; but to no real avail. There it still was, unfurling greedy, unclean petals deep in Konrad's soul.

It had not grown much, in the past few hours. Scarcely at all. What did that mean? The foul taint had taken Talin much faster, conquered her with unseemly ease. Was she less resilient than Konrad? Or had it been Nanda's intervention after all? She could not save him, but perhaps she had been able to give him time.

Shame to waste that, now.

Konrad caught hold of that blackened, burnt space in his heart and pulled. Careful, careful. A delicate balance, for this: he did not want the malefic's curse to overwhelm his will, not the way it had with Talin. He could never, then, have the strength to slay it.

But to make himself enough like it to attract its notice? Yes. That could be productive enough. He opened up a window, and invited the malefic to come in...

Master? Eetapi's high tones, as he had never heard them before. Shrill with distress, a thin whine of fear. *What are you doing?*

I rely upon you, serpents, said Konrad. *If I should blunder, and lose myself, you two must put it right.*

And... how are we to do that, Master?

You must kill me. And quickly.

The expected shrill of delight did not come. Eetapi said nothing, nor did Ootapi, and the silence stretched.

Can you? Konrad prompted. *You must. Do not let me down.*

But... said Ootapi. *But you do not want to die, Master.*

Few people do, Ootapi. But we must.

I could kill you if you wanted it, said Ootapi.

Very well, then, believe me to be eager to hasten my journey into the beyond, if it will make you happy. Only do as I say.

He felt a palpable wave of misery emanating from the pair of them, engulfing him in shades of their twin despair. *Never tell me you do not want me to die?* he asked them, in some surprise.

You are a good Master, said Ootapi at length.

Nonsense. Half the time you have despised me.

But there was also the other half, said Eetapi.

Konrad sighed; what a moment for a display of loyalty. *All of this is neither here nor there,* he said firmly. *Shall you perform this last duty or not?*

Reluctantly, the words came. *We shall, Master.*

Thank you.

No use letting himself feel warmed by this unlooked-for reluctance. If he judged right, he had, at best, minutes to live...

Master, said Eetapi, turning shrill again with panic. *It—*

She vanished in a waft of despair, melding into the shadows, drawing Ootapi with her.

Good, Konrad thought as disaster approached. Well, then.

He stood, very still, knife in hand, watching for the malefic's appearance. There: a patch of shadows beneath a trio of craggy trees, deeper and darker than the rest, every other pale and wan in comparison. A roiling, boiling disturbance there, and a palpable malevolence; Konrad felt it touch his skin, reach grasping fingers into his thoughts. Nausea crept over him.

Now. It would have to be now.

He leapt, blade flashing in the moonlight, leapt into those roiling nightmares and stabbed down with all his strength—

Wait, whispered a dark voice.

And Konrad stopped, stopped dead, the wicked blade of his blessed knife halted inches from its target. He did not know why he stopped. The one word had penetrated his heart, frozen his limbs, robbed him of his will. He knew despair, but so distant a sense was it that it could have no power to influence him.

'Why,' he managed to spit out, 'am I waiting?'

You wish to destroy me?

'I had thought about it, yes.' Blood leaked from Konrad's lips with every word, for he had to tear each one free from some deep part of himself, some place the malefic had yet to conquer. Pain lanced through him with every breath.

Why?

The question interested him, in spite of himself. Why did he wish to destroy it, considering the cost to himself of doing so?

'You... destroy others,' he managed.

So do you.

'The— only those who deserve it.'

Who is to say that my victims do not?

Konrad, bewildered, tried to fix his thoughts upon Talin, lost in the worst way to this monster's predations. A faithful warden, she'd spent long years guarding the spirit-lands from just such a menace as this — and what a reward for her labours. She could not possibly have deserved it.

Then again, what did Konrad know? He had never met Talin before yesterday. He did not know what else she had done with her life, what crimes she might have committed.

And he knew nothing about the malefic's other victims, either.

Except — himself.

'Are you— telling me you prey upon the guilty?'

We are alike, you and I. The malefic drifted closer, a foul wind to choke Konrad's breath. He gasped for air, retching up blood — and black bile.

'We are — not,' he ground out.

You have felt it, whispered the malefic. *You know it to be true.*

Konrad felt his resolve disintegrate, tattered shreds of it melting away like snow in the sun. What if the thing was right? If he, Konrad Savast, Malykant and serial killer, deserved to exist, why not this extension of his essential darkness? Why not?

His right arm shook with the effort of holding it, and the knife he held, aloft. And then it fell, the knife tumbling from his grip. He had not the strength to speak, barely enough to breathe; he sat, dazed and befuddled, conscious of a terrible despair opening up within him but powerless to respond to it.

The malefic smiled. Not with its face, for it had none. It smiled with its soul, supposing it had one. Konrad felt the waves of its horrid satisfaction bathe him in something like... peace. The peace that comes of total surrender.

'*Konrad.*'

Nanda's voice, sharp as a whiplash, and as sudden. His head came up, eyes straining for a glimpse of her. *Where* was she? He saw nothing, nothing but darkness and a thick white mist boiling up from the ground.

A hallucination, then. Fitting that he should experience her contempt as well, here at the failure of everything he was.

Tasha's words came then, lacerating. 'Told you he couldn't do it.'

'He can,' said Nanda, grim as winter. 'He will.'

And something shifted. Only the slightest lessening of the black despair that had swallowed him, a crack in the mockery of peace he had been so ready to embrace. But it was enough. One swift, hard-won motion, muscles shaking with the effort: he reached into the dank mist, and his fingers closed around the hilt of the discarded knife.

254

And now, to kill. Just one more death, one more stab of a sharpened blade, one more soul — if such it was — sent shrieking into the darkness.

One more, and he could rest.

The malefic sensed the weakening of its terrible grip; it would not sit quietly as it was ushered out of the world, could not accept the prospect of its destruction as meekly as Konrad had. And Konrad discovered the truth of the spirit-witches' bleak pronouncement: *nobody survives a fight with a malefic.* As he stabbed down, completing the merciless motion he'd begun a scant few minutes before, the malefic thrashed and *shrieked,* the sound splitting his mind apart. Those unearthly, lightning-bright talons raked lines of black fire across his face, his neck, his torso; Konrad screamed, too, ablaze with agony.

But his own knife flashed bright, twice, thrice, and a searing light tore the malefic into pieces. Tattered ribbons of shadow thrashed, groping for him, lashing him with fresh pain—

—and then, with a final, blinding flash of the Shandrigal's light, the malefic sank into nothingness and was gone.

9

'Konrad.'

The hallucinations were not gone, then. How sweet of them to linger, and keep him company as he died. He did not know that dreams could be so kind.

Konrad managed to smile at it, this vision of Nanda bending over him as he lay in a puddle of black bile. He felt it seeping through his coat, burning the fabric away, searing his skin, its foul smell assaulting his nostrils.

None of that mattered now.

'I love you,' he said to the dream-face, and tried to touch it. His arms wouldn't work.

Ah, well.

'Never mind that now,' said Nanda, which was *too* like her, and Konrad felt a momentary pique. Could not this dream of his *behave* like a dream, just for a moment? While he died? Could it not say something soothing to his rended soul, for example *I love you too*, maybe even shed a sparkling tear?

Nanda was Nanda to the end, even in his imagination. Irascible in the face of sentiment, ruthless in pursuit of her goals, brisk and practical and allergic to wasted time.

'It isn't a waste of time,' he told her. 'Not now. There isn't any anyway.'

'Exactly,' said the Nanda-dream, and then Tasha was there, too, her small, pale face coolly professional as she looked him over.

'Mortal wounds, most likely,' said she with a clinical air. 'But better not depend upon it.'

Nanda's attention had slipped from him for a moment, she'd turned away. A glimmer of clear light flickered at the edges of his vision: the Shandral-knife, retrieved, secreted somewhere among her clothes.

Why did he have to bother with that detail? Who cared what became of the knife? He was *dying*.

'You don't have to watch,' said Tasha. 'If you don't want.'

Konrad floundered, grasping at the edges of this peculiar dream, and failing to restore his flagging grip upon it. The two characters in it continued to talk as though he were not even there, chatting amongst themselves on incomprehensible topics while his life's blood slowly drained away.

Tasha's face again. He thought she would say something more, but she did not.

A knife flashed. The knife again? Not again. Hadn't the Nanda-dream—

—*pain* tore his torso apart, a new, fresh pain, a searing agony that tore another scream from his raw throat. Blood spurted and spilled — *his* blood, spirits above, had he actually had any of it left?

'Wasn't,' he gasped, 'a dream, was it?'

His heart pulsed once, twice more and then — stilled.

He heard, dimly and distantly as he faded, one final word from his loved ones.

Tasha's voice.

'*Idiot.*'

***

Nanda, alone suddenly with Konrad's murderer and his corpse, felt less than she had expected to feel. Numbness, primarily. Shock? Denial?

What had they done, the two of them? The enormity of it hovered just beyond the range of her comprehension, comfortably distant. A dark cloud on her horizon, preparing to strike her down but not yet. *Not yet.*

'He *is* an idiot, I grant you,' she said dispassionately, staring blank-eyed at Konrad's bloodied, still face. 'But did that have to be the last word he heard in life?'

'I knew you were going to be weird about it,' said Tasha, sitting back on her heels. She squatted there, next to the remains of Konrad, like some oversized crow with the delectable stench of carrion in its nostrils. Its... beak. Did crows have nostrils? No. Beak.

With an effort, Nanda collected her scattered wits. 'I knew you would not be,' she said. 'Did you enjoy it?'

Tasha stared at her, her eyes dark hollows in her white, white face. 'That is hardly a helpful question to ask, is it?'

'But did you?'

'I will admit to feeling an urge to stab Konrad on more than one occasion, but no. Monstrous I may be, but stabbing my friends to death doesn't number among my favourite amusements.'

Monstrous. Konrad had said that of himself, numerous times, and not without justice.

Tasha, though. Tasha was something else.

'You are sure about this?' said Nanda.

'It's a bit late to change my mind.' In answer to Nanda's questioning look, she made a small sound of annoyance and shook her head. 'I am sure. And speaking of that, I had better get on with it, hadn't—' She broke off, looking down with distaste at the thing that had appeared at her knee. 'What do you want?'

Stev. Nanda had forgotten the sixth pact. 'My price,' said Stev, and looked pointedly at the dead body of the one who had pledged himself to pay it.

'I'll pay it,' said Tasha.

'You are unsuitable.'

'Right. Lamaeni. Sorry, Nanda.'

Nanda resigned herself. Some part of the fae's blood-price it had already taken from Konrad, she judged, for this new burden did not weigh her down as much as she had expected. Hardly noticeable, really, on top of so many ingrained layers of exhaustion.

Regaining her feet cost her a bit more. She stood, head swimming, breathing deeply until she steadied, and her vision cleared.

When she opened her eyes again, Tasha and Stev were gone. She was truly alone with Konrad, now; could feast her eyes on their handiwork without either interruption or judgement.

He made an ugly corpse. She had seen some blessed, privileged souls, the ones who had passed away while they slept. In death, at least at first, they looked serene and composed, with a strange kind of beauty about them.

Not so Konrad. It wasn't just the mess the malefic's wounds made of his body, or the quantities of crimson blood and dark bile that covered his cooling skin. He'd died with a grimace upon his face, almost a snarl, a rictus of pain perhaps. His staring eyes held all the ferocity he'd shown, again and again, in his life as the Malykant. He had been torn from the living against his will, and it showed.

Nanda bent, and gently closed those eyes. It did not help.

A moment's work summoned all of her five — no, six — fae friends to her side. Friends? Could they be called such? No, but it was a pleasant word.

'Friends,' she said aloud. 'I have one last boon to ask of you.'

Six small faces gazed up at her — or down, in the case of Hreejur, winged and wispy and upside down just out of her line of sight. 'There is a dead man here,' said Kulu.

'Yes. I need you to keep him alive.'

'But he is dead,' Kulu said.

'His spirit is gone,' added Hreejur in his icy whisper.

'I need you to keep his body alive. Inkubal, mend what you can of his wounds. All of you, please, keep his heart beating and his blood flowing, for as long as you can.'

'What shall be our reward?' Nanda did not know which of them had said it, but the question came from them all. Six bright, avaricious pairs of eyes asked it of her.

'That shall be arranged,' she said. 'Trust me. You know I shall not cheat you.'

They accepted this, for while no one answered her, they gathered around Konrad's corpse, half a dozen bright-dark little shapes, hands and eyes and senses taking possession of him. Nanda caught one more glimpse of his dear face before he faded from view, whisked away by her friends to some safer spot. So she hoped.

Well, then. Only one task remained before her, the hardest she had ever faced, but only the one. And when it was done...

No use thinking about that, yet.

She drew a slender gold ring from a pocket in her skirt, and slipped it onto her finger. A simple piece, she had inherited it from her grandmother some years ago. The elegant swirl of metal bore but one adornment: a tiny, clear diamond, faintly aglow now in that chill, eerie fashion Nanda had seen once before. Not long ago, either, a matter of a pipe with a hidden resource.

Nanda touched one finger lightly to the jewel, and it pulsed.

The only way Nanda knew of to travel into the Deathlands was to die — at least, supposing one chose to do so from the mundane world, from one's own home, for example. The spirit-lands, though, were different. Some said they were the space between: a hazy middle ground, with the cities and towns and forests of ordinary mortality below, and the enigmatic stretches of the Deathlands somewhere above. To a mortal deranged enough, desperate enough, a shorter series of steps might carry her from the spirit-lands into that misty grey space, and all the dangers it held.

'Well,' said Nanda aloud. 'And am I mad enough?'

The question was rhetorical. Of course she was. Gathering what was left of her strength, she took hold of The Shandrigal's knife, and carved a brutal slice across the fabric of the world.

A door opened in keening tatters, and a dark mist wafted through, carrying with it the stench of… flowers.

'Curious,' said Nanda, and stepped through.

***

The Temple of The Malykt was deserted.

Tasha had hoped for just that, though hardly dared to expect it. When was so populous and so important a space ever empty? Even in the small hours of the morning, some devotee of The Dark Master lingered there, either in performance of some leftover duty, or in search of the serenity only the Temple of Death could bring.

Today was different. Today, every member of The Malykt's Order was either at The Temple of the Shandrigal, or spread out across the city, seeking the malefic. They did not yet know that the creature was destroyed. Tasha's first task was to dispatch letters to that effect, one each to Katya of The Shandral and Diana Valentina. Thus they would be informed that the knife had been stolen to good effect, the deed performed, and the realms safe once more.

This duty Tasha had carried out on her way through the city. A convenient post-box received the two missives; in they fell with a satisfying rasp of paper.

A third went in, too, this one with the words *Alexander Nuritov* emblazoned on the front. Tasha did not know what Nanda had

260

written to the inspector, and had not chosen to ask. Not her problem.

Next.

At the heart of The Malykt's Temple lay a room only the few had ever been admitted to. Fewer still had forced their way inside, as Tasha proposed to do. This chamber was sacred, so the Order said. Sanctified to The Malykt in some indefinable and uninteresting way, a place where the most sacred of rituals or ceremonies were performed in His honour, blah blah. To enter without invitation or permission was to offend against The Malykt himself, so they believed. Even Konrad had likely only seen that room a time or two.

Having availed herself of Diana Valentina's keys during the chaos, Tasha let herself into this "sacred space" with scarcely a sound. The door was cleverly hidden, after a fashion she actually admired: not concealed in some obvious way, but camouflaged as nothing at all. From the outside, the unassuming door might be taken for the entrance to a closet, or some such uninteresting thing.

Tasha closed it behind her, and took the precaution of locking herself in. Not that she expected to be interrupted, but disruptions enough to her plans had occurred already. The malefic, for one. Abominable timing! Konrad had needed to be slain much sooner than planned, before she'd had time to get everything in place. And Nanda, instead of having a suitably monster-sized diamond with which to manipulate Konrad's immaterial existence, had been forced to use the only one she had to hand. A tiny sliver of a thing, only just enough to absorb a wisp of Konrad's fraying soul. Hopefully it would be enough.

Shame, too, for Tasha had been looking forward to the challenge of divesting some self-satisfied nob of a prized diamond. Maybe she would do it anyway, later, just for fun.

But first.

Hurling herself dramatically face-down upon the floor of The Malykt's sacred room — an underwhelming place, all told, nothing but a shadowed altar near the far wall, and a set of iron sconces — Tasha offered up a prayer.

'O Malykt,' she intoned, enjoying the way the words echoed off the stark walls. '*Your humble supplicant would have speech with Thee.*' Such ancient beings liked old-fashioned conceits such as *thee* and *thou*, did They not? '*Hear me, I beg Thee, for I offer Thee my service and honestly, it's a great deal.'*

She went on in this way, wondering after a time whether she ought to have lit the sconces, or sacrificed something small and bleeding on the silent, looming altar, or whether His Malyktship was simply busy — Konrad complained sometimes that the Being could be distant and unhelpful, well small wonder, Great Spirits were like that sometimes, too high and mighty for Their own good really—

You may stop, came a deep, shattering voice, emanating out of the air and the floor and the altar and everything all at once. *Beseeching,* added The Malykt, and Tasha did, for she had stopped breathing, too, and speech could be difficult under those conditions.

She fought for air, noting with bemused detachment the raging winter going on in her insides under The Malykt's cold stare. Spirits above. Konrad hadn't even been exaggerating.

'M-Master,' Tasha managed after a moment, and bowed her head again. She'd tried for a glimpse of The Malykt but no luck: He was immaterial. 'I bring news.'

You are not one of Mine, said that dark voice.

'No, but I am hoping to change that pretty soon. And I'm bringing you news of one of Your most loyal servants.'

Silence. He was a hard sell.

'Your Malykant,' Tasha added helpfully.

Silence — but a palpable one this time, *arrested.*

'As You are no doubt realising at this moment,' said Tasha, sitting up, for her neck was starting to ache, 'He is dead.'

Why?

Tasha had not anticipated such a question, and knew a moment's pause. But she went smoothly on. 'It *was* the terms of that pact you made a while back, was it not? He has died as You commanded, his debt to You is paid, and the position of Malykant now being open—'

She'd rushed her fence. The Malykt was not listening. *I commanded no such thing. Yet.*

Tasha blinked. 'What?'

It was not yet time.

'Not yet *time*— there was a set time?' Tasha gabbled. 'When was that supposed to be?'

This is the doing of My Chieftain. Has it been ordered by her?

'You mean Diana? Sort of. Well, no, not exactly, though she *did* say Konrad should retire—'

She may have been right. But The Malykt did not sound certain of the fact. A cold fury laced the words; black ice shot across the floor and up the walls; and Diana Valentina might be in for a bad morning.

And Tasha herself might need to do some very fast talking.

'It was what Konrad wanted,' she said quickly.

She was beginning to hate these long silences, for how could an absence of sound — of everything — feel so suffocating? *Was it?* said The Malykt finally, and Tasha drew in a huge gulp of air.

It was important, now, to be truthful, she knew. Fast talking was all very well, but for once in her life, she was dimly aware that what was at stake was infinitely more important than she. And, moreover, had nothing to do with her.

Was it what Konrad had wanted? She had been poking at him about it for some time, trying by oblique means to get at Konrad's true feelings about his role as the Malykant. She hadn't dared ask direct questions for fear of tipping him off about what she meant to do. Nanda and Alexander had taken the same approach, she knew, and the consensus among the three had been that Konrad was weary of the appalling duty laid on him by The Malykt, ready to stop, desperately in need of peace.

Which wasn't quite the same thing as being ready to *die*, indeed volunteering himself for a speedy murder at the hands of one of his few friends. But she needn't go into that.

'He was tired,' she said. 'He wanted to resign his duties.'

Then why did he not?

Tasha swallowed. 'Because...' A difficult question, this one, for she had wondered the same thing herself. Konrad had often given the impression of a man wearied of life itself. Hating his existence as he had, why hadn't he ended it long since?

The entrance of the inspector — and, if she could so flatter herself, of the inspector's ward, too — might have had something to do with it. Friends made life just a bit less execrable, on the whole.

But that wasn't enough by itself. The real reason Konrad hadn't wanted to die, not even when it was the means of extricating himself from his detested life as the Malykant?

'Because he was in love,' she said.

And now he is dead.

'Yes...' Better get it over with, make a clean breast of it and all that. 'I killed him.'

No doubt you have some excellent explanation for this decision.

'He was mortally wounded anyway,' Tasha said quickly. 'I was just helping things along. Look, can we put this aside? The facts are that You're short one Malykant, which I imagine to be pretty inconvenient.'

Extremely.

All the air whooshed out of Tasha's lungs again, squeezed as though by an icy, incorporeal hand, and she hid her own, traitorously trembling hands behind her back. A small voice somewhere deep within said, *spirits above, what have we done,* but she ignored it.

'I offer myself as replacement,' she said in a rush.

Indeed? And what qualifies you for this role?

'I am good at killing. Haven't I proved that?'

The Malykt said nothing, which Tasha took as an encouraging lack of opposition. She soldiered on. 'And I have experience at solving crimes. I'm a police ward, I've been working with Konrad for a while now, in fact I solved a case for him not long ago.'

Formidable.

Unmistakeable sarcasm to the word; not a good sign. Tasha swallowed. 'I will do a good job,' she said. 'I swear it.'

This is not the way such matters are usually handled. The Chieftain of My Order—

'Condemned Konrad to retirement-by-way-of-death, left him to deal with that alone, and apparently hasn't yet found a replacement for him. Has she?'

No, acknowledged The Malykt. A flare of anger followed: a fresh coat of ice covered the walls, and Tasha's coat too. And her face. The ice burned. *This is not how I prefer things to be done.*

Tasha, aware that her weakened knees would give out on her any moment, took a deep breath. 'Look,' she said coolly. 'Do you want a new Malykant or not?'

✳✳✳

Konrad knew cold.

He would have said that without hesitation, once. A life lived in Assevan gave a person an intimate knowledge of winter, in all its frigid cruelties, its unforgiving, icy beauties.

A decade, or near it, in the service of The Malykt resulted in the

264

same.

But all that had been nothing.

Bodiless, dazed, he now felt that cold was *all* that he knew, perhaps all that he had ever known. No heart beat in his chest, for he had neither torso nor heart. No blood to carry warmth and life to his head and limbs. No face to smile with.

He remembered love. Hate, too. Warming emotions, both of them, in their different ways. He felt them now as a distant echo, deprived of all their power, turned to naught but the dead ash of regret. He had failed at love, succeeded too well at hate.

Eternity drifted by.

This was death, he realised, this hazy existence. He knew serenity, the kind that came from nothingness. He knew calm. Could not muster feeling enough even for distress, despite the loss of — everything. He existed, a shade of himself, waiting.

Waiting?

For what?

He felt, in some dim way, that this was not yet the end. Not for him, yet, the blissful, utter nothingness of The Malykt's embrace. He... waited. Not quite ended, nothing begun, a thin sense of wrongness his only company.

Wrongness.

He ought not to have died, yet. That was the truth of it. He had been dispatched into the Deathlands before his appointed time, before The Malykt had yet expected to receive him. A *wrongness* had done this.

And until that wrongness was righted, Konrad must wait.

Wait.

SHANDRAL

1

At the door of a certain luxurious study at Bakar House stood Inspector Nuritov, hatless and bemused.

'Tasha,' he said. He paused, and looked behind himself as though he suspected life of playing some prank upon him. 'Have you seen Konrad?'

What puzzled the good inspector, Tasha realised, was twofold. The absence of Konrad was half of it. The other half was Tasha's emphatic *presence*, for she was not only occupying space in Konrad's private study, she had taken possession of it. She lounged at her ease in Konrad's favourite chair — a respectably well-worn article with wide arms, smooth leather and plentiful stuffing — and in her hand she held Konrad's snake-headed cane. It felt rather like wielding the royal sceptre. If only she'd been able to avail herself of one of his tall, glossy hats, too.

'Not lately,' she answered, which was sort of true depending on your definition of *lately*. Two whole days had passed since she had last exchanged words with Konrad, and that was a long time, wasn't it?

'He isn't here?' said the inspector, venturing a step or two beyond the threshold.

'No,' said Tasha. 'But you can relax. I'm the new Konrad.'

'The new...?'

'You did come here looking for the Malykant?'

'I... a case has come up, yes, and I wondered—'

Taking pity on her erstwhile superior's bewilderment, Tasha smiled. 'Wondered why Konrad wasn't already all over it? He—' She stopped, for doubtless if Konrad was present he *would* have already been all over it, and therefore why wasn't she? 'How did you find out about this case?' she said abruptly.

'I *am* the police,' he reminded her, gently enough.

'Yes, but Konrad always gets there before the police. What am I not... oh.' Her eyes narrowed. 'Eetapi!' she yelled. 'Ootapi! Get down here.'

A long silence followed, so lengthy and so pointed she wondered if she was to be obeyed at all. She tried not to look too closely at the inspector while she waited; the look of befuddlement was fading fast, replaced by narrow-eyed comprehension laced with disapproval.

'Eetapi!' she screamed.

Cold descended, wrapping around her shoulders — no, her throat, icy draughts slipping over her neck, and down her back. Deep, dark winter took hold of her, and squeezed.

Was there something? hissed Eetapi.

'Yes!' choked Tasha. 'Manifest, please. Do I have to talk to empty air?'

She regretted her insistence at once, for bright bands of ghostly energy wound around and around her throat; Eetapi, her incorporeal serpents' form locked in an icy death-grip. 'Stop that,' she gasped, swallowing down a slight tremor.

Eetapi ignored her command. If anything, the cursed creature's grip tightened; Tasha choked, and shivered.

'Why,' she gasped, 'have you not reported this death to me?'

'To you,' said the inspector. 'Why should she?'

'Because I— am the Malykant, now.'

The inspector, to do him justice, did not waste time on futile questions or exclamations. He was silent for a short time, no doubt putting the pieces together in his mind.

What death? whispered Eetapi, innocence itself, but Tasha heard the echo of a harsh laughter behind the words.

'That death,' she said furiously. 'The one the inspector is here to report. Unless it is more victims of the malefic?'

'Not unless the malefic has taken to blinding its victims and then stabbing them to death,' said the inspector, watching Tasha with calm, sad eyes. 'And you know there have been no further sightings of the malefic in two days.'

'Before you ask,' said Tasha, 'which I know you are dying to do, yes, Konrad is dead.'

'I see,' said the inspector.

'He died... slaying the malefic. That's why no one has seen either of them in two days.'

Yet, hissed Eetapi, *his was an unclean death. I felt it.*

'The—' Tasha swallowed painfully. 'The malefic wasn't too *clean*, was it?'

It was not like that. He died by the hand of another mortal. Like you.

Tasha, catching the inspector's eye, hurried into speech. 'He died a heroic death, isn't that great? Saving the city and the spirit-lands alike from the predations of an ancient curse — selflessly sacrificing himself for the greater good—'

'So you mean you were there?' said the inspector.

'Um. Yes.'

'You've known for two days he was dead, and did not tell me?'

'I... was going to.'

'When?'

When she was ready to reveal herself as Konrad's replacement. Her first plan had been to do so at once, not only to the inspector but to the Order of the Malykt as well. Only, it had proved difficult. Something had kept her hesitating, postponing the moment. She ought first to familiarise herself with The Malykt's Temple, had not she? So she'd done that. And then someone ought to keep Konrad's seat warm at Bakar House...

In truth, she had been a coward. The enormity of what she had done had only hit her when it was far too late. And wasn't that just the way of things? It didn't matter what you thought you were ready for. You never were.

'I was there,' she acknowledged again. 'So was Nanda.'

'Nanda?' Misdirection successful: the inspector was entirely diverted. 'What was she doing there?'

'Helping... Konrad.' Sort of.

'Is she all right? Where is she?'

'She isn't dead,' said Tasha hastily. At least, hopefully Nanda wasn't dead. Where she had gone, there was no saying for certain. 'She will be back soon.'

'Back from *where*? Tasha, if you will not be honest with me—'

Tell him the truth, hissed Eetapi, and a needle-sharp pain blossomed suddenly in Tasha's ear. The filthy creature had bitten her! *Tell him the truth or I will slay you where you sit.*

'You can't slay me, I am lamaeni,' said Tasha. 'Not that we cannot die, but that isn't how you go about it—' Her words failed as the pressure on her throat increased, cutting off her air.

271

Tasha flailed.

'Eetapi,' said the inspector sharply. 'Please, leave be.'

Somewhat to Tasha's surprise, the serpent obeyed this request, slinking sulkily away from Tasha's throat and taking up a position near the inspector's left shoulder instead.

Two sets of eyes — one mortal, one ghostly — stared balefully upon Tasha. How could she suddenly feel so small, when half an hour ago she'd felt the size of a house?

'Fine,' she sighed, sitting up. Massaging her throat did not help, damn the serpent. 'I killed Konrad. I think. He went up to the spirit-lands in pursuit of the malefic, and Nanda and I followed him. He fought it, and killed it, but it injured him — again — and you know they said anyone marked by the malefic has to die? Well, Konrad would probably have died of the wounds anyway, they were *quite* bad I can tell you, but I had to make sure, so I killed him the rest of the way.'

'Why?' said the inspector, in a low, ominous tone Tasha had never heard from him before. Not even when she had broken the framed miniature of his wife he'd once kept on his desk.

'I told you. Those struck have to die—'

'You planned this *before* the malefic appeared. Did not you? Did not we?'

'There was the small matter of that bargain with The Malykt,' said Tasha quickly. 'And Konrad's misery and how he was losing his marbles. *You* agreed that something must be done.'

Some of the indignation went out of the inspector in a rush, leaving him weakened, for he sank into a chair. 'I did not think it would be like this,' he said simply.

'Well, neither did we. You can thank the malefic for that.'

He said nothing.

'Anyway,' Tasha said crisply. 'Never mind all that. What was this about a corpse?'

'The Malykt accepted you as Konrad's replacement?' said the inspector, looking sharply at her.

'He did.'

'Then why is Eetapi enraged with you?'

'She disagrees.'

'And Ootapi?'

'I don't know where he is.'

He is gone into the Deathlands, said Eetapi, in an oddly small voice. *In search of the Master.*

'He is not your master anymore, Eetapi. That's what I am trying to tell you. You work for me now.'

The Malykt has not said that this is so.

'I'm sure He is just busy.'

'Where is Nanda?' said the inspector, and Tasha wished fervently he wasn't so tenacious of mind.

'I shouldn't say this part out loud,' said Tasha. 'If it were to be known what she's trying to do—'

'You can tell *me*. And you will, or I will haul you before Diana by your hair and let her deal with you.'

'Oh, she knows about me already,' said Tasha airily. 'She's completely in support of this. Said I'd be a great Malykant.'

'All lies.'

Tasha growled. 'Nanda's gone into the Deathlands to fetch Konrad back. Which is in total contravention of all natural laws about Life and Death set down by The Malykt and The Shandrigal both, so if she gets out alive They will probably skin her to death.' She directed a dark glare at Eetapi, which the serpent returned with a snippy hiss.

'*What?*' gasped the inspector, and shot out of his chair. 'And you let her go alone?'

'Someone has to mind the shop while Konrad's gone. We worked it all out between us.'

The inspector actually clutched at his hair, a procedure Tasha watched with interest. She did not think she had ever seen anyone literally do that before. 'She'll die,' he said. 'She'll die too. They will both be dead.'

'I think you underestimate Nanda.'

'You said it yourself, three seconds ago. *If* she makes it out of there alive, the Great Ones will kill her.'

'Maybe I underestimate Nanda, too. Look, will you settle down? We can't help her now, but she is not alone. She has Ootapi, apparently, and she's a witch. She has resources of her own. Our job is to keep things in order down here, so will one or both of you *please* tell me who's dead out there.'

'So you are a temporary caretaker?' said the inspector, after a moment, and a few deep breaths.

'Maybe. We'll see, when Konrad gets back.'

'We'll see what?'

'Whether he wants the job back. And whether The Malykt wants him to have it.'

'You think you'll be so much better?'

'Of course,' said Tasha, which was a barefaced lie. Nanda had said, more than once, that The Malykt did not appreciate what he had in Konrad, and neither did Diana Valentina. Tasha would never admit it, but privately she agreed. So did The Shandrigal, apparently. Well, maybe The Malykt needed a reminder.

By the time Tasha was finished, He would be begging Konrad to come back.

And the power of saying yes or no would rest, as it ought to, in Konrad's hands.

The inspector looked at Tasha out of red-rimmed eyes, which surprised her rather. Had he been so attached to Konrad? Or Nanda either? The man was sentimental to a fault, an odd quality in a police inspector. The next breath he took was shuddery, as though there were tears behind it, but he got a grip on himself after that.

'I'm still here,' Tasha offered.

A thin smile. 'Disaster, I name thee Tasha.'

'Charming. Thank you. For what it's worth, I believe that Nanda will make it back, too.'

'And Konrad?'

Tasha shrugged. 'That I don't know. One could say with some truth that it's in the lap of the Gods.'

'Are you sure he was blinded by whoever killed him?' said Tasha half an hour later. 'Maybe someone else poked his eyes out.'

'That is possible, yes.' The inspector stood with his hands in the pockets of his shabby, oversized coat, looking down at the mutilated corpse before him.

Death was so undignified. Here sat a man, old but not infirm yet, the respected elder of his household most likely, in what was probably the best chair in the house. He had that poor-but-respectable look about him, befitting the meagre, well-swept cottage they had found him in. Coat with a patch at one elbow. Some indefinable curve to the lines on his face gave him a kindly air, or might have when he was alive. Grandchildren probably played about his knee, disporting themselves before a blazing late-winter fire while their elder looked benevolently on.

And now he sat with his torso split open, a knife still embedded in the depths of a few vital organs, and a face bloodied and soiled from the wreck someone had made of his eyes.

'Maybe he put his own eyes out,' Tasha added, after a moment's thought. 'That's possible too.'

'Is that something you would do?' The inspector gave her a sideways glance.

'Take a sharp object to my own eyes? Don't be ridiculous. I might manage to put out one eye, in a moment of madness, but it's the second one that's the more chilling thought. The *pain*, Nuritov. Imagine the agony.' Tasha did so herself, receiving as usual an odd thrill at the prospect. Not the good kind of thrill, quite. This was not a pain she would seek for herself.

'That seems to put paid to that idea, then,' said the inspector, moving off to explore the scene.

'I was speaking of me. Who knows what this man was capable of.'

'If there's a person alive who could stab out both their own eyes, it would have to be you. I think we can rule out the self-blinding theory.'

'Fine. So, then. Why would someone bother to blind him, only to then kill him afterwards?'

'Unless they killed him first, then blinded him afterwards.'

'That makes even less sense.'

'Yes, at present it does. But you must keep an open mind, Tasha. If you become too certain of a particular set of events, without sound reason, that can blind you to the real truth. And as Konrad would tell you, the real truth can sometimes be far stranger than you would imagine possible.'

'Cannot argue with that.' Tasha took a turn about the room, questing for clues. She found… none. Some blood had descended to the floor, not surprising, a lot of it had come out of the man after all. Enough of it had poured everywhere to suggest that he had been stabbed where he sat, and died there. The room contained little else of interest. The house was tiny, containing only three rooms in total: a rough kitchen, a bedchamber behind, and this front chamber overlooking the narrow street. The harbour lay not far beyond; Tasha could smell the sea, an occasional wisp of salt-tang.

'What information do we have about him?' she said.

'He was found by a passing costermonger, who, she says, happening to glance through the unshuttered window, saw his body and summoned the constable. His neighbours named him as Rodion Artemo, a former potter, though he had not engaged much in the trade since the rheumatism set into his hands. He has one daughter, Agasha, from whom he is estranged.'

So much for the grandchildren playing around the fire. 'That's it, then?' said Tasha. 'Nothing else to work with?'

'Not yet. I was hoping Konrad would be able to extract something... more.'

'How would he have done that?'

'With, er, the serpents' help...'

'Oh. I see what you mean. Eetapi, can you...?'

No. His spirit is long gone.

She uttered the words ungraciously, but at least it was a prompt answer. 'Eetapi says not,' Tasha reported. 'It's too late.'

'That suggests he was killed some time ago, then. Early in the night, perhaps? Or even yesterday.'

'If it was so easy for the costermonger to spot him through the window, surely he hasn't been there since yesterday, or someone would have seen him much earlier.'

'Perhaps. But not everyone is observant enough, or nosy enough, to notice much beyond the sphere of their own business.'

The hapless Rodion Artemo had the look of a man deceased for some little time. All the blood was dried to a deep brown colour, almost black, and he had the stiff, frozen look that only sets in once every lingering trace of life is drained from the body.

'Nobody saw anything, I suppose?' said Tasha.

'Karyavin is working on that. So far, the neighbours have nothing to tell us.'

'Right.' Tasha stood, not at all enjoying an unusual helpless feeling. How did Konrad trace a killer who'd vanished into the night, leaving no convenient clues behind them? How did Nuritov proceed, if his men came back with no real leads and no obvious direction to go in next? Yes, she had solved one case herself, but luck had played a large part in that. If luck refused to favour her... what then?

'I suppose,' she said doubtfully, 'we could try to find the daughter?'

276

'That must be done anyway; she ought to be told that her father is dead. By all accounts, though, she had not been seen in this neighbourhood for some years.'

'So she probably isn't the killer, and she's unlikely to have much idea of what was going on in her father's life either.'

'That is about the size of it, yes.'

Tasha gave a sigh. 'Is detecting always this frustrating?'

'Always.'

'Then why by all the spirits were you mad enough to pursue it as a profession?'

The inspector shrugged, and put the stem of his pipe between his teeth. 'A man must have a purpose,' he said around it.

'You could have picked anything.'

'Not really. For better or worse, I have a knack for this one.'

'A knack. All right, what is your knack telling you right now?'

'That it might be interesting to know why Rodion Artemo was estranged from his daughter.'

'How's that likely to be relevant?'

'It might not be, but it is a question to ask.'

'And how are we going to find her?'

'We ask around, consult those records we have at our disposal, and... hope for some luck.'

'Luck,' muttered Tasha sourly. 'Always it comes back to that.'

'Is that so bad?'

'I am pretty sure The Great Spirit of Luck hates me.'

'There is no such being.'

'Then I am just cursed.'

The inspector's lips curved; he was laughing at her.

'You on the other hand are swimming in luck, right? All the time. A whole ocean of luck all to yourself.'

The inspector's smile abruptly faded. 'No,' he said quietly. 'Luck hasn't favoured me at all. Not when it mattered.'

Aware that she had strayed into something serious, Tasha hastily backtracked. That solemn quality to Nuritov's tone threatened a return of the tearfulness, and nobody wanted *that*. 'So we find the daughter,' she said quickly. 'What else?'

The inspector looked at her in silence.

'What?'

'You volunteered yourself for this role, Tasha. You are a detective, now. What would you do next?'

'When I did that I was thinking more of the executioner bit. That part I can handle.'

'No doubt, but first you must find out who is to receive the honour of the executioner's attention. Think. What would you do next?'

'*Do*? I have no idea.'

'Alternatively. What questions might you ask?'

Questions. Tasha stared sightlessly at the mess someone had made of Rodion Artemo, and cudgelled her reluctant brains into action. Questions. She could do that. 'That knife,' she said. 'It is made of bone. Is that bone?'

'Good. Yes, it looks like bone to me. An unusual weapon, no? What does that suggest to you?'

'Nothing, because I am an ignorant lout.'

'Yes, but it suggests further questions, does it not?'

'What kind of a knife is made all out of bone? Where would somebody get something like that? And why would it be used like this?'

'Exactly. It is likely to be a rare piece, possibly expensive to procure. But this man was poor, and those he knew probably were poor as well. Surely a cheap, simple knife would be a more likely weapon, then. Why this one?'

Tasha nodded along. 'Good. Right. In that case, if it was rare and expensive, why did someone leave it here?'

'Such a piece ought to be a prize, oughtn't it? It is engraved, too — patterned with etchings. And yet it's been left here as though it's valueless. An important point, possibly.'

Tasha began to feel less at sea, the world firming again beneath her feet. Ask all the questions! And then ruthlessly scour the city until answers presented themselves. That was how they did it. That was the essential process she had followed herself, when she had sought the source of a rare poison, and deduced her way to a sensible solution.

Sensible. The word had passed seamlessly through her mind and she'd scarcely noticed. Tasha the Sensible. How Genri would have laughed.

'Another question! If he couldn't work, how did he live? Why isn't he on the street? This house is small and mean but it still cost money

278

to live here.'

Nuritov looked at her with a twinkle lurking at the back of his eyes. 'Getting into it, now, aren't you? Another good question. He received some small charities from his neighbours, here and there, but we don't yet know how he paid rent, or how else he acquired or paid for food. What can we do about that, do you think?'

'Talk to the landlord. Who owns this place?'

'We will certainly do that. I would like to know if he was in arrears. If he was not, was he ever late with payments? How did he pay?'

Listening to so drab a list of questions, Tasha felt her heart sink a little again. Combing painstakingly through the intricate details of so ordinary a life, that was detecting. Those were the kinds of questions one had to concern oneself with. How had Konrad stood it? The inspector, that was no surprise; he was a good man, and she was fond of him, but he was not overflowing with vivacity or imagination. She could picture him, plodding his methodical way down the growing list of minutiae until he uncovered something relevant.

Konrad was more like Tasha herself. He'd prefer to hack and slash his way to a solution.

'Wondering when you'll get to the violent part?' said the inspector.

'I was rather.'

'It's like everything else in life. Labour comes first, the sweets later.'

'I *really* don't see why everyone doesn't just go straight to the sweets.'

'I don't suppose you would, at that.'

'Wait.' Tasha, suddenly electrified, leaned closer to the corpse. Close enough that her nostrils filled with the odours of blood and torn flesh, and she could feel the murdered man's absence of life like a palpable chill. Such a mess had been made of those eyes, so bloodied and blackened and torn were they, that a feature of the blinding had hitherto escaped her attention. 'Nuritov. Where are the eyes?'

He nodded once. 'It appears they were removed.'

Twin emptinesses stared vacantly back at Tasha, dark holes in a ruined face.

Tasha's grin broadened. 'Why might someone take out their victim's eyes, Nuritov?'

'No reason I want to know about, but that, too, is a question that must be answered.'

'That,' said Tasha with deep satisfaction, 'is much more like it.'

2

The lingering pungency of a thousand flowers embraced Nanda like... like a punch in the face.

She had found it pleasant, at first, an unexpected scent to lift the heart. She had stepped into the Deathlands expecting to find it like The Malykt Himself: dark, bleak and without mercy. Instead she had encountered an airy lightness buoying to the spirits, and received the sensation of drowning in an ocean of flowers.

Well, drowning was never pleasant in the end, whatever one chose to drown in. Fragrance turned to stench in her estimation, her head ached, and she would almost have cut off her own nose if that would take the abominable reek away.

Staring now at a warped blossom for which she had no name — because it could possess none, inside-out as it was, and twisted out of recognition — she fought with a crippling sense of weariness for some clarity of thought.

Think. Where would Konrad be, in this nonsensical place?

She had hoped that she need only step through the divide, and find him waiting there. He had died right beside her, after all; perhaps he had only faded through the invisible veil, and fetched up, figuratively speaking, a bare few inches away. She could reach out, and find him there, and haul him back through.

But when she had completed the passage from the spirit-lands into the Deathlands, a harrowing process she did not care to remember in too much detail, no sign of Konrad had she found.

Space there had been, and plenty of it. The sky, for a start, went on forever. Most skies did, of course, but this one gave off an impression of so deep an endlessness, Nanda felt dwarfed to nothing beneath it. How a fathomless sky could contrive to be both night-dark and searingly bright at the same time was beyond her comprehension, but one did not ask such questions of the Deathlands.

Then there was the landscape below, which was sharp and jagged and crisp, like the air at the top of a mountain. Or it was oppressive and deep, shimmering glassily like the bottom of the sea. Or suffocating and hot, like the high summers of Kayesir that Nanda had never known, the air drenchingly damp or bone-dry or— Nanda had to close her eyes for a long time, her mind turning itself inside out with the futile effort to comprehend the Deathlands. They defied logic, sense and reason, and to cross those lands safely and return with Konrad, she would have to find a way to accept that.

She did not know where the stench came from. Besides their muddling contradictory qualities, they were marked primarily by a lack: a lack of anything alive (or dead); lack of verdure; lack of definition; lack of... impact. Once she knew that Konrad was not near, Nanda walked and walked, and she did not grow tired. Neither too hot nor too cold, but she was not comfortable either. For an hour at least she walked on, stride after stride, and went nowhere.

'Right,' she said to the air at last, coming to a halt. Speaking aloud helped, somehow, the sounds a grounding influence even if she had made them herself. And it made a pleasant change from the hollow, barely perceptible whistle of a wind that wasn't there. 'One goes nowhere in the Deathlands by walking, then,' she added. At least, not if you were alive in this unliving place. What became of the dead? Where did they go, and how? For the thousandth time, Nanda scanned the horizon and found it lacking.

She might have expected to encounter *someone* by now. Were these lands not the ultimate destination of all deceased souls? They ought to have been crowded with thousands upon thousands such souls by now. Yet alone she stood, isolated and cold — no, not cold. Still not cold. Just with the lingering sense that she ought to be.

'Konrad!' she shouted, knowing it to be futile. The two crisp syllables split the air like a bolt of lightning; for one, hazy second she thought she saw something else hidden behind the lifeless atmosphere, a glimpse of structures rising tall and dark...

'Konrad Savast!' she shouted again, louder still, and there it was again: a flash, a glimmer—

'You will not find anybody *that* way,' said somebody. Dry words, uttered like the crackle of dry paper. For the first time since stepping into the Deathlands, she *felt*: wisps of air wafting past her face, a kind of movement if not exactly a breeze, and an aroma that had nothing to do with flowers.

She whirled, but saw no one.

'Help me, then,' she demanded. 'How do I find my— friend?'

Slowly, a figure materialised before her. At first glance, this soul — whatever he, or she, or it was — satisfied every idle speculation she had ever formed about the inhabitants of the Deathlands, for the figure was a motley collection of shadows streaked with light. A dark mist boiled upon the air and wafted away, pouring from everywhere and nowhere, and within its depths Nanda saw quite another being. He — she thought — sat cross-legged upon the empty air, elbows planted upon his knees, a cloak of dark nothingness billowing around him. He had a pleasant face, no deathly cadaver at all: smiling even, skin of indeterminate colour, if it *was* skin at all, and eyes of clear black.

Nanda's words deserted her, leaving her staring. Not out of fear, for while the shadow-bound figure exuded an intimidating aura, she did not find that it affected her. It reminded her of— of Konrad. 'Who are you?' she finally mustered wit enough to ask. 'Are you... are you The Malykt?'

A faint, faint smile came in answer; she would swear to it. 'They call me the Gatekeeper.' He put his chin in his hands and stared back at Nanda, a hint of curiosity lightening an expression of otherwise unbroken bleakness. 'Or the Guide. If that answers your question.'

'Not even a little bit.'

'So,' he said without moving. 'I am forgotten.'

'By whom?'

'The living. I had colour about me, once.'

'You serve The Malykt?'

The Gatekeeper merely blinked slowly. Assent, of a sort.

'I'm looking for another of His servants,' said Nanda more briskly, setting her fascination aside. Time was wasting, and Konrad was dying ever more permanently with every minute she lingered in this empty place.

'I had supposed you to be in search of somebody,' said the Gatekeeper. 'It was the shouting that gave it away.'

'Will you help me find him?'

The Gatekeeper dropped one hand into his lap, his head tipping sideways upon the other. He regarded Nanda like this with solemn attention. 'What I don't understand,' he said, 'is why you appear to be alive.'

'Because I am.'

His wide nostrils twitched, as though he inhaled her. 'These are the Deathlands.'

'I am aware.'

'And you are alive.'

'For the moment. I would like to get on with retrieving my friend, while I can still say that.'

'This friend.' He sat up suddenly, and his bones — had he bones? — loudly cracked. 'Is he alive, too? Are there more of you adrift?'

'No. He is dead.' Nanda said it quickly and evenly, suppressing as she spoke the image her ready mind presented to her of Konrad so. Felled like a tree, torn apart, face a rictus of agony as his blood spewed all over the ground and Tasha looming over him like Death itself, knife in hand—

'Then you cannot take him,' said the Gatekeeper, interrupting this happy flow of thought.

'Why not?'

'Because this is the final destination.'

'And?'

A blink. 'Final.'

'There is another place. Isn't there?' Nanda jabbed a finger in the general direction she'd seen that city materialise, if city it had been, and for however brief a time. 'Konrad must be in there, but I cannot reach it. Please help me. He did not deserve to die yet.'

'Who does?' said the Gatekeeper, with a simplicity that briefly silenced Nanda. He was right. How many people truly deserved to die?

Well, everyone Konrad had slain. That was the whole point. 'Killers,' she said firmly. 'The Malykt says so, and Konrad is the one who is responsible for dispatching them here. Is that not important?'

'The Malykant?' The Gatekeeper woke up a bit more at that, his sleepy eyes widening. 'Another one?'

284

Nanda's turn to blink. 'What?'

'You are careless with them.'

'They— how many *have* there been?'

'All of them were glad to arrive here,' said the Gatekeeper. 'Grateful to die, and this friend of yours can be no different.'

'What if he is?'

A wave of an insubstantial hand dismissed this point as immaterial. Or improbable. 'Always it's the same. Go home, while you still can. Find another friend.'

'Wait,' said Nanda, aware that he was preparing to leave. To abandon her to this hopeless nothingness, with no Konrad in it. 'What would it take, to get you to help me?'

The Gatekeeper climbed slowly to his feet, still impossibly aloft, and looked down upon Nanda from a great height.

She stood quietly, looking up and up into that shadowed countenance, jaw set, heart hardened.

'You,' he said, 'can have nothing to offer.'

'You spoke of colour.'

'What of it?'

'I will bring you colour aplenty, if you get me my Konrad.'

'Will you?' he said softly. 'How?'

'I do not yet know, but I pledge myself to perform this task.'

An infinitesimal nod answered her, and her heart leapt. 'Thank you,' she said, weak with relief.

'Do not thank me. You have no idea what you face.'

'You are the Guide,' Nanda replied. 'Guide me.'

An eyebrow went up. 'You ask more?'

Nanda folded her arms, and stared hard at the sorry creature. Honestly. 'Are you not bored?' she said. 'When was the last time you had any company in this heartless place?'

'The Gatekeeper needs no company.'

Her brows rose. 'Mhm. The Malykt told you that, I expect. Have you been at this a while?'

'Half of eternity, or thereabouts.'

'I offer you an interlude. Keep *me* company, and remember what life was like. You were alive once, I presume?'

His eyes grew distant. 'Was I?'

'Try it out, for a few hours. You might enjoy it.'

Slowly, the Gatekeeper descended from his lofty height, until he was eye level with Nanda. More or less; still he towered some little way over her head. He did not speak, only studied her face, quizzical.

'What is it?' she said, feeling the stirrings of impatience. Konrad was waiting.

'You are trusting me.'

'Were you planning a double-cross?'

'I might be. I am the Gatekeeper. My role is to open the gates so that souls can pass through — and then close them again, forever.'

'But you won't do that with me, because I am not dead. Don't tell me I am the only person who has ever come up here looking for a friend.'

'It has happened before,' he allowed. 'Most of them were tattered shreds within minutes. This place is not forgiving to the living.'

That disconcerted Nanda. 'And why am not I?'

'Perhaps it is because you come bearing *Her* protection.'

'Her— oh.' Nanda remembered the blessed knife she still had in her possession. It was by the knife's penetrating blade that she had torn a way through into this place; had its Mistress's touch also shrouded Nanda herself, keeping her safe?

Thank you, My Lady Shandrigal, Nanda prayed, and added another silent prayer that the effect, wherever it came from, would last long enough. 'Do I pass, then?' she said aloud. 'Will you open the Gates?'

The Gatekeeper, shockingly, grinned. 'I think I may be going to enjoy this after all,' he said.

'I'm not turning into tattered shreds for anybody's amusement.'

The Gatekeeper did not reply, but turned away from Nanda and swept out an arm in a smooth arc across the sky. In his hand, dark fire burned, leaving in its wake a jagged-edged rupture in the world, like torn fabric.

Through it, Nanda saw the city she had glimpsed before; saw it clearly now, nothing wavering about it at all. Gut-wrenchingly solid. Unspeakably vast.

'Do you want to go in?' said the Gatekeeper.

She lifted her hand, the one upon which she wore her simple ring. The sliver of diamond embedded within the golden band glinted with a nauseating pallor. 'No one in their right mind wants to go in there,' she retorted. 'But nonetheless, lead on.'

3

Tasha left the unfortunate Rodion Artemo's place of abode with a bone knife in either pocket. One was the pretty engraved specimen which had done for the victim. The other was the stoutest of his ribs; not strictly a knife yet, but soon she would sharpen one end and make a blade of it.

She had tried not to enjoy the process of its removal, not too much. The inspector had withdrawn, taking Karyavin with him, on the pretext of further enquiry with some nearby soul. He'd given orders for the removal of the body to the morgue beneath The Malykt's Temple, to be carried out shortly. In the intervening time, Tasha had found her opportunity to procure her weapon. Considering the mess of the man's torso already, she'd had an easy time of it. Beginner's luck.

She walked away from the humble cottage, hands in her laden pockets, whistling in her own mind if not aloud, and picturing the moment when the second of those two knives would puncture some scoundrel's heart and send him twitching into the afterlife.

First, though… the inspector was right. She would have to do some of the dull work.

She had a little hunch about the knife — the engraved one, the murder weapon. If Artemo had died by the hand of someone he had known, and the inspector claimed that most murders were committed by some connection of the victim's, then that presented a puzzle. Who among Artemo's likely social circle, poor as he had been, might possess such an object? And where had they got it?

The second question might be the easiest to answer first; and answering it might produce a solution for the first, too. Tasha knew the poorest regions of Ekamet well. When families fell on hard times and needed fast money, there was always a pawn-broker at hand to purchase their remaining articles of value for a fraction of their worth. The brokers did not always know what it was they had bought, and considering the low cost of purchase, said articles were frequently sold for a fraction of their value, too. Had somebody parted with the pretty knife in exchange for some quick cash? The murderer might have bought the thing nearby, in that case, and need not be rich to have done so.

Two minutes' walk brought Tasha to the nearest pawn shop. She went in, and presented the knife — carefully cleaned of blood already — to the shopkeep, a rotund woman with round cheeks and lank hair.

'I'm not selling,' Tasha quickly explained, when the woman barked an offer at her. 'I want to ask if you've seen something like this recently, or sold one perhaps?'

'No,' said the pawn-broker. 'But if you're interested in knives I got three others here, good nick, cheap—'

'I don't want to buy a knife,' said Tasha. 'I just had the one question.'

The pawn-broker responded with a flat, unfriendly stare. If Tasha was neither buying nor selling, what was she doing in the woman's shop?

Tasha stared right back. Was this what Konrad had to put up with? Small wonder he'd killed a lot of people. Tasha suppressed an impulse to "lose" her pretty knife in one of the woman's steely eyeballs, and satisfied herself with a quick snack instead. Greasy the woman may be, but she had vitality aplenty. Tasha inhaled, and received a dose of the objectionable woman's energy. Intense. She swallowed it down, enjoyed the brief elation that always followed a good feed, and smiled benevolently upon the aggravating woman.

The pawn-broker looked a shade paler than she had a moment before, and rather drawn. Tasha left the shop, satisfied that the woman would suffer a dragging, inexplicable weariness for the rest of her day, and possibly tomorrow too.

She deserved it.

Her trip around the woman's competitors availed Tasha very little.

Few were so rude as the first woman, but none had any information of use to offer. No one had seen or sold any such knife, not recently and not ever.

Except for one, the furthest away from Artemo's house. Quite on the other side of the city, in fact; Tasha arrived there some three hours later, footsore and chilled and heartily bored. Her inclination was increasingly to pack the venture in and go home, and let the inspector's men finish such dull duties as this. But her perseverance was rewarded — slightly — when the last broker on her list, an elderly, desiccated man with a single, blackened tooth surviving in his wizened jaw, tapped a finger against the knife's smooth hilt and said, 'Pretty thing, ain't it? I seen one like it afore. Give 'ee a good price for this one.'

'When did you see one before?' said Tasha quickly, her heart leaping.

'Long ago now, missie. Long afore you were born.'

'Oh.' Twenty years or more, then? It did not seem likely to have any bearing on the case at such a distance of time, and Tasha's hopes sank again. 'Um. Still, do you know anything about it?'

'Know anything?' echoed the broker, blinking rheumy eyes.

'I mean, about where it might have come from, or why it's engraved. Things like that.'

The broker blinked slowly, and was silent so long Tasha began to suspect him of a profound simplicity of thought. 'It's old,' he said at length.

'I had imagined so.' The knife was neither damaged nor stained — someone had kept it in good condition — but it bore a well-worn smoothness to it suggestive of some age, and an indefinable air of antiquity.

'Out of Marja, mebbe,' said the broker. 'Had me some bone jewellery of theirs, a time or two. Not much of it about now.'

'Engraved, like this?' Tasha traced a finger over the swirling patterns embedded into the blade.

The broker nodded, head bobbing upon his skinny neck. 'Something a bit like.'

'You don't happen to have any examples in the shop right now?' Tasha crossed her fingers, unconsciously holding her breath.

'No,' said the broker, dashing her hopes. 'You selling that one, missie? I'll take it off you.'

'I can't,' she said with a moment's regret, for it would probably fetch a bit. Enough for a new cap, at any rate. 'It isn't mine. I was just trying to find out about it.'

'Well, you change yer mind, you come back.' The broker grinned, awarding Tasha a beautiful view of his sole, rotten tooth.

Tasha grinned back. She liked the old man, for all that he stank of mildew and mould. Quite the contrast with that awful woman at the first shop.

He looked tired, though. Small wonder at his age. Moving stiffly and carefully, he regained his seat upon the high stool behind his shop's counter and sat gulping in air.

Hm.

Tasha reached within, to the core of vitality that kept her sundered body and soul more or less together. It burned strong and clear, thanks to the snacking she'd indulged in on her way across the city. She could spare a little. She caught at it, exhaled; several potent wisps found their way to the pawn-broker across the counter, and he breathed them in.

She fancied he looked a little brighter right away.

'I'll come back,' she promised. 'Probably not with this knife though.'

'Anything else you like,' said the cheerful fellow, and waved her off.

Tasha went out, whistling. Next time anyone happened to mislay something vaguely valuable in her general vicinity, she would certainly keep that man in mind.

As for what he'd told her: that could prove of interest. Did it mean that the murderer was from Marja? No, not necessarily. Anybody could get hold of a Marjan artefact. But it did give her an idea.

'Nuritov,' said she a little later, bursting into the inspector's office with the Marjan knife in hand. 'Help me with something.'

He was sitting, not in the chair behind his cluttered desk but on the edge of the desk itself, still wearing his coat. Only just returned, from whatever investigative activities he had gone off upon? He looked up as she bustled in, but half his attention was still on the paper he held. 'What's that?' she said.

'In a minute. What do you need help with?' He looked at the knife she wielded in her left fist, and his brows went up. 'If you're asking for help committing murder, I am too busy this afternoon.'

'Not just yet. That comes later.' The inspector winced, and she grinned. 'Too easy, Nuritov.'

'I never learn, do I?' He drifted back to his letter.

Tasha brandished the knife, producing a satisfying *swish* as it sliced through empty air. 'This is from Marja,' she said.

The inspector looked up again. 'Oh? How do you know that?'

Tasha explained, and had the satisfaction of winning all of his attention away from the missive. He actually put the paper down. 'That's very interesting,' he said, and Tasha beamed.

'And I have an idea of where to ask next, but that's what I need your help with.'

'You *need* my help? Something exists which you cannot handle yourself?'

Tasha made a rude gesture. 'There's a shop in the posh part of town. Art, jewellery, that kind of thing — all from Marja. Proprietors are Marjan too. I bet if you ask them they'd know something about this thing.' Tasha swished the knife again.

'A canny thought, but why can't you ask?'

'Fancy place,' said Tasha.

Nuritov palpably failed to catch her drift.

Tasha sighed, and gestured down at herself. Patched black coat, never cut to fit her frame in the first place. Shabby garments beneath. Nondescript cap. *She* loved her clothes, for they were well-worn and practical and she could do anything in them. But the proprietors of an establishment for wealthy customers would not love them at all, or her either.

'Oh,' said the inspector. 'I see.' His smile appeared, briefly. 'Konrad's whole Bakar-House masquerade makes sense, doesn't it?'

'It has its uses,' she allowed. She offered the knife to the inspector, not without a certain reluctance, for despite its prettiness it was a well-balanced piece and it had a nice heft to it. She'd like to stab a person or two with such a prime weapon.

Still, needs must. The inspector took it, and Tasha put her hands behind her back before she could snatch it away again. 'If you ask, I bet they'll talk.'

'I'm only a policeman.'

'A respectable policeman, and you have a right to ask questions about murder weapons.'

'True.' Nuritov set the knife down on his desk, and dithered over picking up the letter again.

'So what *is* that?' Tasha asked. 'Besides riveting, which is clear enough.'

'It is from The Shandrigal's Temple.'

'That... was not what I expected to hear.'

The smile flickered again. 'A love letter, was that what you thought? Sadly not.'

'One can always hope.'

'And one does. But no. This is from Katya Inshova, the—'

'—head of The Shandrigal's Order. I know.'

Nuritov nodded. 'She writes to me to express her private concerns about two members of her Order, whose whereabouts are, um, indeterminate at the moment—'

'Missing persons!'

'Yes.'

'Tell me one of them's Rodion Artemo.'

'One of them is indeed our unfortunate victim of this morning. The other is called Timof Vak, a young man quite recently joined, but whom Katya felt had promise.'

'But Rodion Artemo only died last night.'

'Yet no one among the Order had seen or heard from him for weeks, which I gather was unusual.'

'So why didn't someone just go to his house and talk to him?'

'Several attempts were made to find him. He was never at home.'

'Curious. Did the neighbours mention that he was absent?'

'No, but it doesn't appear that he was regularly in touch with any of them. They might well have noticed nothing.'

Tasha whistled. 'So he goes missing for weeks, then turns up last night at his own house again — dead, and with a matching set of missing eyeballs.'

'Nicely summed up.'

'Thank you. What about Timof Vak?'

'Same scenario. He has not been seen at the Temple — three weeks, for him — and he hasn't been heard from. She says she is unsure whether there's reason for concern, so she writes to me privately.' He waved the letter. 'But she has a *bad feeling*.'

'Why the bad feeling?'

'She didn't say.'

'Well, she was not wrong. One of them's dead. What's the betting Mr. Vak is, too?'

Nuritov nodded, retrieving his pipe. That meant an interval of deep thought was coming. 'We will visit his house, soon. Perhaps he's there.'

'Eetapi?' Tasha called. 'Any more unclean deaths in the city today?'

'Or yesterday,' said the inspector. 'Or this week, for that matter.'

Eetapi did not answer.

'Snakie?' Tasha yelled. 'Are you even there? I can't tell.'

Nothing.

'She's gone,' said Tasha. 'Either that or she's punishing me for something.'

'Proceeding without the snakes, then,' said Nuritov. He spent a few minutes in a brown study, a process which Tasha watched in fascination. He looked miles away when he disappeared into his own mind like that, and failed to notice that the pipe in his mouth was not lit, and emitted no smoke.

Then he would abruptly come back to himself, focusing on his surroundings again with the sleepy look of a man waking from a refreshing nap.

And the eyes would fix upon Tasha with the faintly startled look. *Ah. Tasha. Are you still there?*

He did all of this again. Once he had returned from his ruminations, Tasha watched as he absently returned the pipe to his pocket. She hoped he did not tend to do the same thing when it *was* lit. 'Shall we go?' he said.

'Where to? The shop!'

'Later. First, to see if Timof Vak has also arrived home in the night.'

'And mislaid his eyeballs.'

'That, too.'

4

It was his youth and wasted vigour that made the vision of Timof Vak more disturbing, Tasha decided.

Vak, of a more affluent background than his Order-mate Artemo, lived in a small but sumptuously fitted-up house about ten minutes' walk from the harbour and Artemo's cottage. He'd been engaged in the fur trade, just starting out in the business but already successful. Several specimens of his wares lay strewn about his house: a large, velvet-brown fur covering a wide window-seat, and another of black tints cast over the tall-backed chair in which the man himself sat.

They'd arrived to find the house locked up. Vak must have had a servant or two to look after him, but no one was home; Tasha had at length been given leave to practice her lock-picking skills upon Vak's stout front door, a task she fell to with relish. She had it open inside of two minutes.

They'd found Vak's corpse in less.

Silence reigned between the two of them for some time as they took in the grisly scene. Vak was not yet thirty, smooth-faced, with a thick, dark brown beard. His shirt had been fine, once, a pristine white garment sewn of an expensive fabric. Now it was ruined, torn and blood-drenched, gaping in two halves around the deep wound in his chest. Someone had not merely stabbed him, but carved him open; exposed bones gleamed wetly. A bone knife, slightly larger than the first but otherwise its twin, crowned the gory mess.

Empty, black sockets marred the handsomeness of his face, great gouges where his eyes once were.

Uneasy in ways she had not been when confronted with the corpse of Artemo, Tasha maintained her silence. Why was it melancholy, this tableau, when the other had not struck her at all that way? Was it only this man's youth, the sense of wasted potential? Absurd. No one deserved to have their chest carved open and their eyes hacked out, whatever their time of life. Did Rodion Artemo's advanced age change anything? Just because he was unlikely to have many more years left to him, did not mean that Tasha ought to pursue his murderer with any less zeal.

The arrogance of youth, Genri would call it.

She chose not to find out what the inspector might call it.

'Well,' she said at last, loud and heartily, to cover her unease. 'What do you make of all this now?'

Nuritov did not move. 'I wish Nanda was here.'

'I miss her too, but—'

'No. The only connection we know of between these two men was their membership of The Shandrigal's Order.'

'Oh. Yes. And they had both been missing.'

'For two, or three weeks respectively. Vak must have died last night as well, that's my guess. Both arrived home after weeks of absence, unheralded — the servants have not been called back, you see — and both died before morning.'

'It's the eyes that interest me,' said Tasha.

'Me, too. And those knives.'

Tasha said nothing for a moment. A strange, stray thought had just darted across her mind, prompted somehow by the inspector's words. Those knives. She thought of her walk across the city earlier that day, a bone knife in each pocket. One taken from a human body, and the other... 'Whose bones are they made from?' she said aloud.

'What? The knives?'

'Yes. Do you think they are human bone?'

'They could be,' said the inspector slowly. 'They are small enough to be carved out from a thigh bone, say, or something of that size.'

'What if it's something a bit like... what I do? What Konrad did?'

Nuritov glanced at her, and said sharply: 'Just what are you saying?'

'The... the knives Konrad made out of the victim's bones. They were intended to— to bind the two souls together in the Deathlands, were they not? Murderer and victim, for the one to wrest their own justice from the other. What if these knives are also forging some kind of link between souls?'

'The souls of these two men, and whoever's bones the knives were cut from?'

'Exactly.'

'But why?'

'I don't know. And the first knife at least is quite old, the broker told me that, and it looks it. So it must have been made from someone who lived at least a few decades ago. But...'

Nuritov was nodding. 'It could be,' he said slowly. 'There must be *some* reason why a bone knife has been used in each case, specially selected over more convenient choices.'

'Maybe whoever used them knows whose bones they were.'

'And knows something about these two men that we do not.'

'To the shop!' said Tasha.

'Right. Yes. Hm.' The inspector dithered about for a bit, investigating who-knew-what, apparently without achieving very much. Tasha waited with barely suppressed impatience. Alight with the fire of speculation, she wanted to rush off at once, and pursue her theory. Timof Vak was dead, and he'd stay dead. Did Nuritov have to faff about like this now?

'Can't you send Karyavin down here?' she finally said.

'Yes, and I will. Look, though.' The inspector stooped, and picked up something from the floor near the fireplace. It was a sliver of black charcoal, chalky, disintegrating in Nuritov's palm. 'What do you suppose that is doing there?'

'It's a fireplace,' said Tasha.

'And this is not coal.'

'Then it's wood. So what?'

In answer, Nuritov merely nodded his head in the direction of a large, black receptacle standing to one side of the fire. A coal-scuttle. 'Oh,' said Tasha.

'Either something wooden was burned in a fire there last night, and left some residue, or this was brought in from outside. Perhaps on somebody's shoes.'

'Might have been Vak who brought it in.'

'Or it might have been the murderer.'

'All right. Duly noted. *Now* can we go?'

'Not yet.'

Tasha gritted her teeth. 'What *now*?'

Nuritov cleared his throat, and jerked his head towards the remains of Timof Vak. 'Um. Don't you have something to do first?'

'Aha. Yes. I was... forgetting.' The rib bone. She eyed the protruding knife with a touch of distaste. The damned thing was in the way — but then again, it was sharp. Wrapping her fist around the hilt, she pulled it out in one swift motion and went speedily to work. Quickly, before unhelpful reflections had time to take hold of her mind.

Somehow, she didn't enjoy this butchery at all. It only went to show: the novelty really could wear off absolutely anything.

Strange, to walk nonchalantly into a shop with the blood only just wiped from the hands, and wrists, and coat. Tasha was not yet a neat butcher; practice would help. She shoved those hands into her pockets and tried to look inconsequential. Not too difficult, being much shorter than the inspector, and female, and grubby; the people who kept these types of shops would look right past her, with someone both much taller and much more respectable to talk to. And nobody would guess how she'd spent five minutes of her life, only a short time ago. Up to her elbows in a man's carved-open chest, hacking out bones.

The shop was not merely posh but *posh*, dripping in grandeur and jewels. The contents must cost a fortune. Tasha looked everywhere with the eyes of pure greed, mentally calculating the value of those diminutive statuettes, that graceful, glimmering necklace, the miniature in oils by the door... her fingers twitched, and she thought of the friendly pawn-broker. Come back anytime, he'd said, with anything.

No. Today was no day for being light-fingered. She was a responsible police ward — and a sensible Malykant, hah, how bizarre a combination of ideas was that — and she would not disgrace herself or the inspector by purloining, say, that small ring from a high side-table, the kind that slipped onto the smallest of the fingers, coppery and set with an emerald. Easily swiped, easily secreted in her pocket...

'...these rather fine knives,' the inspector was saying, his voice breaking in upon the flow of Tasha's reprehensible thoughts. 'I wondered if perhaps you might—'

'Where did you find these?' interrupted the shopkeep, in an arrested tone.

Tasha turned her attention away from the tempting ring, and began to listen.

'I... cannot immediately say,' said the inspector. 'They are rare, I take it?'

'Extremely. Rare, and... precious.' The shopkeep, a tall, willowy woman with Nanda's icy-pale colouring and a faint Marjan accent, bent over her counter to examine the knives more closely. She was exactly the type to keep a place like this: refined, just the right air of snoot but nothing supercilious, a serenity that might make anybody feel more comfortable about expending vast sums of money on trifles.

She'd said the word *precious* with emphasis, as though she was not talking about their mere monetary value at all. Precious. Precious how?

'They are...' she straightened, and eyed the inspector doubtfully. There was the snoot, all right: the assumption of superiority. 'Do you know much about Marjan traditions, Inspector?'

'Very little, I'm afraid.'

'Some of them are not so different from your Assevan notions,' she said. 'Death, for example. We have our rituals, our ceremonies, for those who have passed on. There is something... extra, for those taken early. Deliberately, and by the hand of another. You comprehend.'

'You mean,' said Nuritov, 'that for those who have been murdered, these knives are made.'

'For them, and from them,' she said, picking up the smaller of the two knives. 'This little one. So slim, so delicate. Perhaps it would not even require the big bone, of the thigh?'

'What are they for?' said the inspector, with deceptive mildness. Tasha heard the tension in his tone.

The shopkeep set down the knife again, carefully. 'It is believed that the knife will find the one who slew its... original owner? That it will avenge the poor slain soul, and that justice will be found in the beyond.'

'It,' repeated the inspector slowly. 'The knife will do that, will it? All by itself? It does not require a guiding hand?'

'Like your Malykant, you mean?' She shrugged. 'It is not of much relevance, how the knife shall be delivered. It is only known that it will happen.'

'But,' Tasha put in, approaching the woman. 'They're supposed to be rare.'

'It is a tradition little observed, now. Only in some parts of distant Marja, where savage ways still hold sway...' Her demeanour plainly showed what she thought of such brutal notions, dispensing with the Assevan tradition of the Malykant along with them. Tasha sniffed. Who knew? Someday she might require such *savage* services herself, and then she'd be grateful.

The woman's attention moved to the second of the two knives, the larger, so recently removed from the gaping torso of Timof Vak. Frowning, she picked it up, and carried it close to her face.

'Something amiss with that one?' said the inspector.

'It is quite new. Look.' She proffered it for the inspector's perusal, her slender fingers pointing out disparate parts of the bone blade and handle. 'No wearing along the blade's edge, or around the hilt, that might suggest a long life. Only one trifling little bit of damage, here, an indentation — a nick — it has not long since been fashioned, I imagine, and used only once.'

'It has indeed been used once,' said Nuritov, and the grimness with which he spoke perhaps tipped off the oblivious shopkeep, for she paled, and quickly set the knife down.

'You do not mean to say...'

'It was found, not two hours ago, hilt-deep in the chest of a very dead young man,' said the inspector. 'So I must ask you again, madam. According to this tradition, who is supposed to wield these knives?'

She was shaking her head, her eyes wide. Frightened? Perhaps just because of her sudden proximity to a violent death, or those who had recently left such a scene. Maybe because she'd dismissed the quaint tradition of her people as fanciful and inappropriate nonsense, and must now consider the idea that it was not. 'No one,' she said. 'There is no such person. To have a designated wielder of such a weapon — that is pragmatism, not? That is Assevan. You will not trust to destiny, to fate, to right these wrongs. You must take care of it yourselves. That is not how it is in Marja.'

'Fate?' sighed the inspector. 'Fate's of no use to me, madam. Destiny did not use these knives to slay two Assevan men last night.

A real, human hand did that.'

A strange look came into her face. 'Of this you are certain?' she said.

And the inspector, oddly, hesitated. 'Yes,' he said, but not before an awkward pause.

Tasha, in her own mind, snorted. Dull pragmatism, was it, to put the bone-knives and justice both in the hands of a real, solid person? More rightly say that they were a bit odd, up in the far north in Marja. Wishy-washy ideas. Even Nanda could be a bit that way, on occasion.

Nuritov was right. Whatever force wielded those two knives was mortal.

'So do we have any reason to think either of our two victims were killers?' said Tasha shortly afterwards, as the inspector, with a curt word of thanks to the shopkeep, led the way outside. 'I don't hold with the notion of destiny, but I might have competition. And if the second knife is new, it might have been made from some victim of Timof Vak's, despite his youth.'

'Speculation,' said the inspector. He held up a hand to forestall the objections that began to spill from Tasha's lips. 'But that, too, is a question that must be asked.'

5

Konrad sat under a tree.

He had spent some little time attempting to determine — or to remember — what kind of tree it was. He did not know how long. Once, it had been possible to count time into little pieces and watch each one pass, the way he did now with a fall of the tree's leaves. One — two — three — leaves went floating away upon the dry air, cast up one after another, and let fly. He had measured time that way, once, seconds drifting past one after another, turning into minutes and hours and dying away.

The tree. The tree was everything and nothing. Old, for its trunk and branches twisted and turned like logic, like supposed facts in a thorny case, convoluted and fathomless. Young, for the leaves — those airy, drifting leaves — were fresh and bright and vivid, though their colours changed with every glance Konrad bestowed upon them. Green. Indigo. Crimson. Rose. Fading, always, into the same dead, dull black, or featureless white, before vanishing altogether.

He had a seat under the logicless tree, a cold one made of nothing, but solid enough. It bore his weight as he sat there, at least, sat and threw leaves away and waited.

He was waiting. What for? He no longer knew. Nothing. Everything. Only faint, disjointed impressions penetrated the haze of his thoughts: the flash of brightness, followed by agony, and redness, and a sense of drowning. A face before him: one he knew, and loved, but who did not seem to love him. A darkness somewhere near at hand, and another love, and—

Nothing. He remembered less and less with every discarded leaf, as though he stripped himself of memory when he plucked leaves off the tree, and threw them carelessly into oblivion. Perhaps he did.

Eternity had crawled sluggishly past before a change occurred. A ripple came, like a hand plunged into cold water, and nothingness was gone for the present. A leaf, a pretty frilled-edged specimen he had been preparing to cast aloft, was plucked from his fingers.

'You should not,' said someone, without specifying what it was that Konrad should not.

Konrad looked, observing with scant interest the figure of another soul before him. Or... not a soul. A thing. Insubstantial and black and white and strange, not unlike Konrad himself, a solidity among the nothing.

It had a face. Konrad watched the face, and the lips moved.

'Someone is looking for you,' said the thing.

'Looking,' Konrad repeated. 'For me.'

'The Malykant, as was. Another one.'

The face, Konrad thought. He had seen it before. Forever ago, or only recently, or both. This face, and its attendant body (if such it could be called, being a construct of smoke and cruelty and absence) had appeared before him, and bowed, and had then torn him away into nothingness and — left him there. Here. Under this tree. 'You,' he said slowly. 'The Gatekeeper.'

'You remember. That is a good sign. I did not like to tell your friend, how little survives the — passing.'

'My friend.'

'Remarkable,' said the Gatekeeper. 'Someone wants the Malykant back.'

The Malykant. The word spoke to him with its own cadence, setting off an echo deep within. *Malykant.* He knew the word. Hated it? Loved it.

There was no deciding, not with the tree arching above him and the leaves all around. He took another one.

'Stop that,' said the Gatekeeper, and took it away from him. 'Dead people. Have you no sense?'

Konrad said nothing.

'Do you wish to be found?' said the Gatekeeper.

The word *friend* touched him, too, and he almost remembered — a glimpse — paleness — anger?

302

Nanda, said something in his heart, and he sat up, blinking. 'Is it Nanda?'

The Gatekeeper bent down and down, studying Konrad like a specimen of some remarkable and peculiar thing. 'That, I think, was a clear memory,' he said.

It was. Konrad *remembered*. Paleness: white face, ice-blonde hair, pale blue eyes. A twinkle of humour there, the quirk of her lips into a mischievous smile, a set look of anger. Warmth. 'Nanda,' he said again, clutching hard at the vision, before it could fade back into the soup of nothing in which he drifted. 'Yes. I wish to be found.'

The Gatekeeper floated up to a great height, until his feet cleared the top of Konrad's head. He hovered up there, a mass of smoke and shadow, looking down and down upon the felled Malykant before him. 'I have a feeling,' he said, 'I am going to be in trouble for this.'

And he was gone.

Konrad remembered trouble, too. He had always been getting in trouble, for nothing was quite right with the way that he was. He felt too much — then too little — then, again, too much; he had too little conscience, or an excess of it; he performed his duty with unseemly zeal, or with a deplorable lack of enthusiasm. Whatever balance The Malykt, The Shandrigal and Diana between them had expected of him, he had perennially failed to strike it.

Perhaps someone else would do a better job.

Nanda.

He let the thoughts go, watched them fade into the nothing without regret. What did it matter now? He was dead. He would never have to care for, or worry about, or regret, anything ever again.

Yet somehow, he did. One thing, one face, one name. *Nanda.* He let those things go, too, but slowly, reluctantly, clinging onto them until the last possible second.

The leaves. He took another from a low-hanging bough, and put it in his mouth. It tasted... cold.

Ouch, said something, cross and prickly.

Konrad spat. Out of his mouth came the leaf — no, not a leaf. A wisp. Smokely and dark — pale — everything? Nothing.

Master, said the same voice, still cross, and the wispy, smokely thing stretched itself out. Stretched and stretched into a long, thin thing, with lambent eyes — everything — and a palpable chill, like a pint-sized winter. A serpent. Sort of.

The serpent-thing shook itself. *Master! What are you doing up* here?

Konrad stared.

Dead, said the snake crossly, the tip of its tail lashing. *Dead, dead, dead.*

'You... like dead things,' said Konrad, memories wafting up out of the soup again. 'Ootapi?'

I love dead things, grinned the snake. *But not a dead you! Master! What possessed you?*

'To what? Die?' He frowned. 'I can't remember. Did I have a choice?'

You did some stupid things, said Ootapi, and with a sudden, darting movement, sank its fangs into Konrad's — what? Soul? He had no body now, and neither did the snake, but the teeth penetrated anyway. Penetrated something.

Ouch.

'That does not sound impossible,' Konrad allowed. He remembered — vaguely — doing a great many foolish things. Nanda had often told him of them.

Nanda.

'Is it true?' he said. 'Is Nanda coming?'

She is here, confirmed the snake. *Somewhere.*

She'd met the Gatekeeper. Did that mean... 'Is she dead, too?' Distress, faint but potent, shredded his befuddled serenity.

Not dead. Which means she is stupider than you. What a feat.

The snake bit again, and again, and Konrad found himself driven to his feet, and out from under the leafy tree.

Up, said Ootapi. *Fool. The longer you sit here, the less of you will be left when Nanda arrives.*

Konrad stumbled beyond the edge of the canopy, and stood blinking in a light that hurt his eyes. He could see nothing beyond the blaze of it, sense nothing. 'But,' he gulped. 'Where are we going?'

We are going to meet Nanda. Or did you plan to let her do all the work?

***

'Where did you get *that*?' said Fros, eyes wide, her hand darting towards the exquisite bone knife Tasha had unwisely withdrawn from her pocket.

Tasha snatched it away. 'Don't touch it. It isn't mine.'

'Of course it's not yours,' said Fros, rolling her eyes. 'They're never yours. What do you think it will fetch?'

'I didn't steal it and I'm not selling it.'

'What did you bring it here for, then?'

Why had she, in fact? She had wanted to tell her old friends about it. About her new role, her new life. Fros was her best friend, wasn't she? Had been ever since she had arrived at Noster House five years ago, soon after Tasha. Shouldn't she be the perfect confidante?

But Fros sat with her back half-turned to Tasha, ensconced on the divan before the fire, flicking her pale hair and glowering into the flames. Her lack of interest in the knife, or anything Tasha had done to procure it, could not be more obvious.

'Better hide it,' added Fros without turning her head. 'Genri will have it if you don't.'

Tasha restored the knife to her pocket. She had retained the smaller of the two, the larger remaining with Nuritov. She was supposed to be researching the thing, seeking more information as to who might have wielded it. Or what any of the knife's strange history might have to do with the stolen eyes.

Instead, she'd come home, gone into her room on the fourth floor and shut the door. She had intended to copy the inspector's trick of deep thinking, shutting herself away from distractions and bending all her mental powers upon the problems of the case until some new idea occurred to her.

She'd sat shivering and brooding for a whole hour, and nothing had occurred to her.

Some Malykant she made.

Tiring of this process, she'd ventured down into the girls' parlour, hoping to find Fros at home. Which she was, garbed in a frilled gown she'd stolen out of somebody's laundry and with her hair in ringlets. Waiting for Androniki, probably. She talked of little else, now.

Tasha turned to leave. She should have gone to Bakar House in the first place. It wasn't the same without Konrad there, but it felt more... hers.

Idiot. It is not yours.

Bakar House would never be hers, Malykant or not. So if the home of her lamaeni years no longer felt like hers either, where could she now go?

Nuritov. She could consult him. Her new life had begun a year

305

ago, when he'd adopted her into the police. Perhaps he would be willing to help her find somewhere to go.

Or maybe she could stop being feeble and solve the problem herself. Scowling, Tasha marched out of the parlour — and stopped just short of running full-tilt into Mother Genri, coming the other way.

'Tasha,' said Mother Genri, with her sweet smile. 'How charming to have you among us.'

Carefully smoothing the scowl from her face, Tasha adopted a neutral expression. She could read the subtext to Genrietta's words perfectly well. She had absented herself from the House a great deal in the past year, more and more every month. Mother Genri did not like it.

'I've brought stuff,' she said shortly, and emptied the contents of one of her pockets into Mother Genri's waiting hands. A pair of gold rings fell into the broad, white palms, purloined from a dozy couple lingering too long in one of the pawn-brokers' shops. A brooch, missing a jewel but the silver was still good. A handful of coins extracted from pockets and bags in one shop or another.

Mother Genri took her time in scrutinising this haul. She was young, or at least appeared to be, but then the lamaeni often did. Tasha had no notion how old she was; plenty old enough to have developed an expert eye for valuable trinkets. She wore her glossy brown hair in ringlets, like those Fros now affected, and her gowns were always first-rate.

'Is this all?' Mother Genri looked up. 'This is a month's worth, at best. And the brooch, Tasha, is inferior.'

Tasha took a deep breath. 'I'm leaving tomorrow. No, tonight. You can keep the extra.'

'Leaving.' Mother Genri went still, her smile vanishing.

'Any minute now.'

'You cannot leave.'

'Why not?' Tasha drew herself up, cursing her diminutive height. Couldn't Mother Genri have had the courtesy to wait until Tasha was fully grown before making lamaeni of her? She was stuck forever at five feet. Well, four feet, eleven inches and a bit — but who was counting?

'I have not given you leave.' The smile was back. Tasha had once been deeply affected by that smile, and Genrietta's air of sweet, motherly concern. It was what had taken her off the streets and into the welcoming embrace — hah — of Noster House.

She saw through it, now.

'I've paid my way for years,' said Tasha firmly. 'Often I've paid extra. I have stolen plenty of choice trinkets for you, and now I choose to go.' Without giving Genri a chance to reply, Tasha pushed past her and into the hall. She hadn't quite meant to leave yet — certainly not today — but now that she had said it, it felt right. Time to go.

'Tasha,' said Mother Genri, before she'd reached the stairs. The word rang out like a whiplash, halting Tasha in her tracks.

She turned.

Mother Genri stood, her hands full of Tasha's stolen jewellery, looking after her young protégé with an air of tender melancholy. 'You will be missed,' she said, much more softly, and without the smile.

She seemed sincere. Maybe she was. Something tugged at Tasha's cynical heart, and for a moment she weakened. Whatever her faults, Genri was the only mother Tasha had ever had.

But she knew better than to rely on Genri's seemings. Without answering, save for a tip of her black cap, she turned away from the mistress of Noster House and launched herself at the stairs. Her few possessions awaited her in her garret chamber, and then — the future.

'Nuritov,' said Tasha, bustling into his office. A small something slipped from within the tightly-wound bundle of clothing in her arms, and fell clattering to the floor. 'I hope you— oh. Don't mind me.'

Two faces turned to look as she came in: Inspector Nuritov's, registering mild surprise at her laden appearance, and an unfamiliar woman of middle age, the plump, respectable type with sober taste and a disdain, apparently, for ornament.

'Tasha, this is Mrs. Yuriena, the daughter of Mr. Artemo.'

'Ohh.' Tasha dumped her bundle in a corner and approached the desk. 'I am sorry for your loss,' she remembered to say.

Mrs. Yuriena murmured a 'Thank you,' so quietly Tasha barely heard her. A swift look seemed to dismiss Tasha on the spot.

'Tasha is a detective apprentice,' said Nuritov. 'She has been assisting me on the matter of your father's death.'

This did not impress the woman much either, but she accepted it, returning her attention to Nuritov. 'I had not seen him for more than twenty years,' she said. 'Still, when I saw the report in the evening paper I was — I felt more than I imagined possible.' She did have the reddened-eye look of a woman suffering some emotion.

'And why was it — if I may ask? — that you had lost contact with your father?' said Nuritov.

She hesitated, and glanced, for some reason, at Tasha. 'We had not been close since I was a child,' she said. 'Mother died when I was only seven years old, and father... did not take it well. Three years later he left Ekamet, to go travelling, he said. I was sent to school. After that I saw him only three more times. Once six years later, once when I was married, and the last time some twenty years ago.'

'Travelling,' said Nuritov, echoing Tasha's thoughts. Her ears, too, had pricked up at the word. 'Do you happen to know where it was that he went?'

'Oh, everywhere. Some years in Kayesir, in Marja, in Balgrand. It is the only thing he ever talked of to me.'

He'd been in Marja. Interesting.

But something did not ring true, for his neighbours had described him as a potter. Perhaps he had given up travelling, somewhere in the twenty years since he had last seen his daughter, and settled down to the trade. But years of travel such as Mrs. Yuriena described cost money. Had he been conducting some kind of trade across these various countries, that had financed his journeys? He was more than a simple potter, that much was obvious.

The inspector's next questions revolved around the same topic, but to no avail. Mrs. Yuriena, too poorly acquainted with her father to have any inkling as to how he lived, could not help.

And then she was leaving, rising from her chair, making some excuse about her husband, her children — when would her father's remains be released for his funeral?

Nuritov stopped her before she had made it out of the door. 'One more question, madam, if I may.'

She paused. 'Yes?'

'Your father was murdered. Do you know of anyone who might have held some kind of grudge against him?'

'You mean, do I know who might have done it? No, Inspector, I don't. I knew almost nothing of my father's life.'

Away she went, taking Tasha's hopes of a lead with her.

'She wasn't much use,' she said, hurling herself into the chair Mrs. Yuriena had just vacated.

'She did confirm the Marjan connection, though,' said Nuritov.

'True, for what that's worth. You think he might have killed somebody up there, and someone's taken revenge?'

'I don't yet know enough to form a coherent theory. It's possible.'

Tasha nodded, thoughts awhirl. 'Talked to Katya at all?'

The inspector's brows rose. 'Katya? Why?'

'He seems to have lived a varied existence and we can't get a grip on what kind of man he was. If he was Shandral, maybe Katya knows more. She noticed him enough to write to you about it.'

'Yes,' said Nuritov slowly. 'That's a good thought, Tasha. Do they — what do people — I mean, what do you *do*, as a member of such an Order? Are there duties, tasks? Was Artemo employed upon something particular?'

'Or do people just show up at the Temple on ritual days and otherwise go about their lives? Maybe both. Konrad and Nanda had a lot to do.'

Had. She shouldn't have used the past tense. Nuritov noticed, and winced. 'I wish we could ask Nanda,' he said.

'We can ask Madam Inshova.'

'And we will. Meanwhile.' Nuritov dragged himself out of his chair and crossed to the corner in which Tasha had discarded her bundle of possessions. 'What's this about?'

'I, er, need somewhere to stay.'

Nuritov responded with a look of enquiry, tinged with suspicion.

'I don't want to talk about it,' she said quickly. Trying to explain Mother Genri and Noster House could only be futile. 'I was hoping you could… help me?'

'You're asking for help.'

'Right.'

'*Tasha* is here in my office as a supplicant, admitting to a problem she can't solve without assistance and asking for help.'

'I *can* solve it myself,' Tasha muttered. 'I just think you can probably solve it… better.'

Nuritov grinned. 'My own lodgings are… insufficient for a second person, or I could solve it on the spot. But what of Bakar House? It has room enough for twenty.'

Tasha stirred uncomfortably in her chair. 'Not when Konrad's not there.'

'That didn't stop you yesterday.'

'That was bravado, all right? I sat in Konrad's chair for a while and pretended I was him. It's not the same as *moving in*.'

'I am fully convinced that Konrad wouldn't mind.'

Tasha eyed him doubtfully. 'You think he wouldn't?'

'You know he wouldn't. If he was here, he'd have you installed in your own room already, with Gorev and Mrs. Aristova at your beck and call.'

Tasha grinned. 'And he'd regret it by the end of the week.'

'It's not a long-term solution, mind,' Nuritov cautioned. 'The Order will probably sell or reassign the house in due time. But for now, I think you can make use of it.'

Tasha retrieved her bundle, which felt pitifully small now she came to think of it. She hefted it as though it weighed three times as much, bestowed upon the inspector a jaunty grin, and took herself off. 'Thanks,' she said. 'Good luck with Katya.'

'Back here in the morning, nine o'clock sharp,' Nuritov called after her.

'Wouldn't dream of being late, sir,' Tasha sang back, and guffawed.

6

Tasha considered entering Bakar House her favourite way (through the back window in Konrad's study, ridiculously easy to break into). Or possibly via her second favourite route (glide in through the servants' door, past the kitchens, and up the stairs; nobody down there was too likely to challenge her anymore). But both of these would be cowardly, wouldn't they? And she would need Gorev and Mrs. Aristova's support if she proposed to stay beyond her usual short visit.

So she went up to the front door, and rapped upon it with the heavy cast-iron knocker. She stood shivering a little — she should have dined on the way over, too late now — and rehearsed her speech as she waited for the butler to answer.

It seemed to take a long time.

Then came the familiar crisp, echoing footsteps approaching, and the rattle of the door opening.

'Gorev,' said Tasha at once. 'I—'

'Miss Tasha,' said he, with... relief? 'Come in.'

Tasha obeyed, wondering. 'Something gone awry?' she said, as the butler closed the heavy door upon the fading light behind her.

'No, miss, nothing like that. Only there's a visitor here for Mr. Savast, and seeing as he's not expected back yet—' Here he paused, and bent upon her a look of stern comprehension which Tasha did not at all like, '—I hardly know what to tell her. The matter seems quite urgent.'

'What's it about?' Tasha set her bundle down in a discreet corner, aware that Gorev missed nothing. He did not comment on it.

'A recent case, I understand,' said Gorev, and waited.

He didn't add that he knew, somehow, that Tasha had taken over this "hobby" of his master's, but that was obvious enough. Had someone overheard her conversation with Nuritov?

Just how much did the servants of Bakar House know about their master, anyway?

'Er,' said Tasha. 'I might be able to help there, yes.'

Gorev bowed. 'It's Ekaterina Inshova, miss. She's in the best parlour.'

'Interesting,' said Tasha, and took herself off to the parlour at once. She had vanity enough to feel brief regret over her shabby appearance: she did not make a good Konrad substitute, certainly not for holding an audience in the best parlour.

Ah, well. No quantity of fancy suits ever helped anybody solve a mystery, or dispatch a killer either.

Katya Inshova sat in the chair Nanda usually occupied, ignoring the tray of refreshments at her elbow, for her thoughts were elsewhere. Tasha had to say her name twice before she looked up, and then she appeared startled by the interruption.

'But where is Mr. Savast?' she said.

'He is… indisposed,' said Tasha glibly. 'But perhaps I can help?'

She received a look so doubtful, she wished she *had* taken a moment to change first. Not that she possessed anything much better than what she already wore. 'You?' said her reluctant guest. 'Who are you?'

The words were rude, but spoken more in puzzlement. Not unjustly. 'You could think of me as Mr. Savast's replacement,' she answered. 'My name is Tasha.'

She was gambling on the extent of Katya Inshova's knowledge. The woman must know of Konrad's real identity, or what was she doing here? And as the head of The Shandrigal's Order, it made sense that she would.

'Replacement?' said Katya, by no means reassured. 'I did not know there had been any change.'

'It's of recent date.'

'Does Diana know?'

'Yes,' said Tasha quickly.

She was not believed.

'Listen,' she said, cutting across whatever objection Katya Inshova intended to raise next. 'There's a killer on the loose, so how about we talk all this over later once the case is solved? Did you come here with information? Inspector Nuritov was just on his way to see you.'

'Yes,' said Katya, but hesitantly. 'Possibly. In fact, I came with — questions.'

'Answers would be better, but ask away.'

'I understand that my two missing Order members are deceased.'

'Yes, ma'am, I'm afraid they are.'

'Please explain to me the condition in which they were found.'

She sat, straight-backed and silent, while Tasha related the particulars of both death scenes. Nothing appeared to shock her; either that or she hid her feelings perfectly. When Tasha had finished, she said: 'Their eyes were… taken? Not merely blinded, but absent?'

'Yes.'

She nodded. 'And what of Irinanda Falenia?'

'I…' Tasha paused, taken aback by the abrupt shift in topic. 'I'm sorry, what about her?'

'She, too, is missing, and I now begin to fear—'

'Oh!' said Tasha. 'No! It's not the same thing at all. Nanda's fine.'

'*Is* she?' said Katya Inshova, and stared imperiously at Tasha. 'How is it that you know?'

'Well— I— I know *where* she is, and why, and it's nothing to do with whatever happened to Artemo and Vak.'

'You had better tell me where she is.'

'I can't tell you,' she said stoutly. 'Nanda would not want me to.'

'She could not wish you to keep secrets from *me*.'

See, there was the problem. Tasha didn't know. *Would* Nanda want her to tell the truth to this one person, if no one else? What if Katya Inshova could help, somehow?

'I collect that it has something to do with Mr. Savast's "indisposition",' said Katya coolly.

'Erm.'

'You may not be aware that her spirit-companion, Weveroth, arrived at the Temple this morning in a state of some distress. Typically, such an animal displays this kind of behaviour when their bonded companion has died, and so you will understand my concern. If you know what has become of Irinanda Falenia, you will tell me.'

Tasha swallowed. Dead? Was Nanda dead? She could be. After all, who expected to march into the Deathlands and come out alive? Shoving down a spasm of fear — she hadn't felt *that* in a while, what a pleasure to be reacquainted with the feeling — she said staunchly: 'Nanda isn't dead. I would put money on it.'

Katya Inshova surged out of her chair and stood towering over Tasha, her composure vanished. 'Then *where is she?*'

And Tasha thought she'd got the easiest job of the lot. Stay in Ekamet. Talk The Malykt into accepting her as the new Malykant. Solve any mysteries that came up, while evading the notice of people like Diana Valentina. Dispatch a killer or two, hopefully she would still get to do that part. And bang the drums in triumph when Nanda returned with Konrad. Above all, *keep a low profile.*

She'd reckoned without Katya Inshova.

'Right,' she said. 'I'll make you a deal. Tell me everything you've got about Rodion Artemo and Timof Vak, and I'll share what I know about Nanda's whereabouts.' She wanted to add *don't tell Diana,* but that sounded so unprofessional, and besides it was too late for Diana to do anything about it anyway. Wasn't it? Hopefully.

Katya took a breath, and sat, and nodded once. 'You may begin.'

'How about we get the case stuff out of the way first?' said Tasha. Once she shared the crazy extent of Nanda's mad plan, she doubted Katya would have much thought to spare for bone-knives and missing eyeballs anymore.

'Very well,' said Katya, with a trace of annoyance. 'Rodion Artemo and Timof Vak were both Shandral, as I gather you know. Rodion had been a member for many years, but Timof was quite new to us. They were both part of a sector of the Order that we call Warders. Irinanda is also a member of that faction. Their purpose is to watch for… threats, disturbances, in the fabric of the living world. The recent trouble with the malefic is an example.'

'Oh, that's dead, by the way,' said Tasha quickly. 'Just so you know.'

'You are certain of that, too, are you?'

Tasha nodded. 'I was there. Anyway, carry on.'

'What—'

'I'll tell you about it in a minute.'

Katya's eyes widened. She had not guessed, then, that Konrad and Nanda's joint disappearance had anything to do with the malefic. 'Mr. Artemo and Mr. Vak had both been out of communication with the

Order for weeks,' she continued. 'As I indicated to Inspector Nuritov. They did not arrive for scheduled meetings among the Warders, and those sent, after a time, to enquire with them at home found them absent. They had not been sent on any errand by the Order.

'About two hours ago, I was given this.' Katya Inshova held up a grubby letter, wrinkled as though it had endured long travel in poor conditions. 'It is a report from Mr. Vak, dispatched from Marja. He says that he... sensed a disturbance, of alarming enough a nature that he followed it. My thoughts went first to the malefic, as you may imagine, but I do not think it has anything to do with that at all.'

'No,' Tasha agreed. 'Far too early.'

Katya nodded. 'And he speaks of a— man, though not an ordinary mortal. Someone who had gone beyond the borders of life, and also of death. Someone who had killed, and killed, for he wore those deaths like a mantle — fanciful language, I know, but Mr. Vak was not a fanciful man. And he offered me a concrete comparison with a concept I am of course familiar with. He suggested that this man's aura was not dissimilar to that of the Malykant, but he did not get close enough to this person to confirm his real identity.'

Tasha's breath stopped. 'Wha— no. It wasn't Konrad that he saw, if that's what you were thinking.'

'The notion had crossed my mind.'

'If I understand you rightly,' said Tasha coldly, 'you came here expecting to find an out of control Malykant, fresh from a random killing spree. Did Diana put that idea into your head? Was it *she* who told you Konrad had snapped?'

Katya Inshova held up both hands in a pacifying gesture. 'It was not she, or not precisely. It has happened before, you know. More than once. Or why do you imagine we would assign one of our most brilliant members to the guardianship of the Malykant?'

'She's done fine work, if you mean Nanda. There's nothing wrong with Konrad.' Honesty compelled her to add, 'Well, nothing much. He's a bit frayed around the edges, but who isn't?'

'Tasha,' said Katya seriously. 'Where is Mr. Savast?'

'He certainly hasn't been swanning around in Marja lately. Ask anybody. And he *definitely* wasn't available to be killing those two men, however similar a method it might appear—'

'It is quite similar, isn't it?' Katya mused. 'Those knives — they were bone?'

'Human bone. Yes. But it wasn't Konrad.' She laughed, taking herself by surprise as much as Katya. 'Or do you think the manner of his madness has taken a creative bent? Did he do those pretty engravings himself?' Tasha took out the knife she'd retained, and all but threw it at Katya. 'Take a look.'

Katya examined the knife in silence. 'I think it's time you told me what has really happened to Mr. Savast,' she said, without commenting on the weapon.

Faced with the suspicions now mounting up against Konrad, Tasha revised her ideas as to how much to tell. So wrong, that he should have to be defended against such allegations. Who that knew Konrad could imagine he would run rampant like that, and kill without discrimination? But that was the problem. None of them had taken the time to get to know Konrad, not really. Probably they assumed he wouldn't last long in the role — few of them did — so why bother? Put Nanda on the job, listen to her reports from time to time, and otherwise forget it.

Diana had done the same. Kept her distance, so she could order Konrad's replacement in due time without undue struggle. Sound enough as a policy, Tasha was forced to acknowledge, given a job like hers; but the consequence was that she was clueless. They all were.

So Tasha told The Shandrigal's chief handmaiden everything she knew. Not just about Konrad's recent fate, but everything. About Konrad himself, about the ways in which he went about his duties. How he felt about them. His friendship with Nuritov and herself. How he felt about Nanda, embarrassingly obvious as it had always been. How he felt about Diana's easy ordering of his "retirement". What he'd done about the malefic, and what Tasha herself had done, and where Nanda had gone.

'So you see,' she said, with some venom, when she'd finished her lengthy recital. 'This is not a crazed serial killer we are dealing with here, whatever he might sometimes say about himself. He's as mortal as it gets, easily as confused as the rest of you, and no more a stone-cold monster than you are. I don't think he was ever like that at all.'

'He has certainly earned your loyalty.'

Tasha rolled her eyes. 'Not easily done, granted, for I detest most people. Including you at this moment. Konrad isn't your killer. Honestly, the person you'd more have to worry about where that's concerned is me. *I'm* the type to go maverick and kill people just for the fun of it. Konrad... no. Just no.'

Katya Inshova had gone from suspicious and wary to thoughtful, which seemed like a good thing, though Tasha didn't altogether enjoy the scrutiny she was receiving. 'And you are our new Malykant, hm?' said she.

'For now. I'm sort of hoping Nanda will be bringing Konrad back.'

'Tasha,' said Katya, and her tone had changed. Sympathy and understanding had crept in. 'You must realise — I am sorry to tell you, but it is not possible for her to bring Konrad back.'

'She's not planning to attempt necromancy on him, or anything like that. She's got a plan.'

'And what is that plan?'

'She had more sense than to bore me with the details. Don't worry though, I'm sure it's a good one.'

Silence fell between them, a silence which Tasha expected Katya to break. But wherever the woman had gone in her mind, she did not seem to want to share her thoughts.

'You can tell Diana if you want to,' Tasha said after a while. Silences always made her nervous. 'She can't stop Nanda now.'

'You imagine she will want to?' said Katya, snapping out of it.

'She wanted Konrad gone.'

'I don't believe that was ever what she wanted,' said Katya gently. 'Not as you imagine. But let us set the matter aside. If Irinanda is indeed wandering the Deathlands, she may need assistance coming back, and the Order may be able to provide it.' She rose from her chair.

'Wait,' said Tasha. 'Was that everything? About Artemo, and Vak.'

'Yes. The Order can do nothing for them now. That duty, I gather, lies with you.'

Great. Tasha planted herself in the doorway, talking fast. 'Was there anything else useful in that letter of Vak's? Why did he send it? And why did you ask about the eyes?'

'He writes that he was afraid,' said Katya. 'He was on the point of journeying home, but he had not succeeded in answering the questions that plagued him, or in eliminating his quarry. The man had... disappeared, leaving Mr. Vak with a sense of personal danger. That is why he chose to send a written report, in case he did not have the chance to make it in person.'

'He was followed home,' Tasha guessed.

'So it appears. I have received no reports from Mr. Artemo, but I must guess that he engaged himself on a similar errand. With, alas, the same result.'

'So that man, who or whatever he is, might still be loose in Ekamet.'

'I fear he may be.'

'But why did either Vak or Artemo go to their own homes, on arriving in Ekamet? Why didn't they go straight to the Order?'

'Perhaps they tried. The Temple is closed at night, naturally. If they arrived in the pre-dawn, perhaps they had intended to make contact with the Order in the morning.'

'And were prevented,' Tasha said slowly. 'And the eyes?'

'Ah. I don't precisely know what that might have been about, but it puts me in mind of… this link with Marja, it is persistent. You have consulted Marjan folklore?'

'Didn't think of that,' said Tasha. 'But now I will. I have one more question.'

'Ask it, and quickly. Time presses.'

True; Tasha wanted all the help for Nanda that Katya could muster. Hastily she said: 'The bone-knives must be significant. Do you think it probable that our two victims might ever have — well, murdered anybody?'

Katya's face darkened. 'They were not merely "victims", they were good men. Among the best. They could not possibly have committed such a crime.'

'Ah,' said Tasha. 'Forgive me, but… hardly anyone or anything is just evil. Crimes are committed by people, all kinds of people. Even good ones, under the right (or wrong) circumstances.'

'Nonetheless, most people are *not* capable of murder, and those two men certainly were not. It is inconceivable.'

Tasha said no more. She might privately disagree with Katya's personal belief — everyone was capable of murder — but her answer was emphatic enough. And she'd known both men, Artemo especially.

Katya waited for further comment, and when Tasha made none, she nodded. 'I wish you luck, Malykant,' she said. 'Avenge my men for me. They did not deserve this.'

318

'I'll do my best,' said Tasha.

'Do better,' Katya snapped. 'The Malykant does not fail.'

7

The Gatekeeper vanished mid-sentence, again.

He'd often done so. Nanda had found it startling, at first — rude, even — until she recollected that people did not cease to expire, just because she personally had need of their Guide into the Deathlands. He had, at intervals, to go and intercept some freshly-deceased soul, and dispatch it to its destined spot.

It, no. He, or she; these were people, or recently had been. They were not featureless objects. But it could be hard to keep hold of such mortal concepts in the city of the dead. The longer she wandered those hushed streets, the more her own life receded from her mind and heart, and the more she felt like a shade herself. Insubstantial, detached, ethereal.

She had, sometimes, to remind herself why she was there at all. Konrad. She was there for Konrad.

The city was of no help. It lacked substance or continuity, shifting with every step she took. She passed an occasional soul, adrift about the city on some business of its — *no,* his or her — own, and the buildings around them rippled and altered in response. Did anything here have a fixed character of its own, or did it change moment to moment, sensitive to the memories of those who inhabited it? On one occasion, halfway along an endlessly curling street, she saw a small house tucked into a connecting alley. So similar was it to her mother's erstwhile abode, the same house in which Nanda herself had grown up, she changed direction at once, and all but ran down the alley to reach it. But once she arrived upon its doorstep, the familiar dark brick walls and small, thickly-glazed windows were gone; she stared up at a simple white-washed structure which did not speak to her at all, and wondered if she had imagined it.

This, above everything else, put the fear of the Deathlands into her. For if it was responding to her as it responded to its ghostly inhabitants, did that mean that she, too, was losing her grip on life?

'Might we hurry?' she said, the next time the Gatekeeper reappeared.

'We are hurrying,' he said, walking along beside her again with his too-long stride.

'You cannot whisk me away with you, the way you do with the dead?'

His sideways glance was amused. 'Not unless you, too, would like to die.'

'Oh.'

'The living have too much...'

'Substance?' Nanda guessed.

'Yes. That.'

'Where *is* Konrad, then, and how far is it to get there?'

'You grow impatient.'

'Unsettled, perhaps.'

'That is wisdom. Your "Konrad" waits at the Tree.'

'The Soul-Tree?' Nanda said, startled. 'It is real?'

'I do not know what the living say of it.'

'Many conflicting things, but the tales I have heard say that it harvests memory.'

'It has been known to do that.'

'And once all the memories have been taken, and weighed, then a soul may pass on.'

'Weighed?' said the Gatekeeper. 'Judged? No. But the memories are taken, yes. Or what else did you think this place is made of?' He swept out a long, thin arm, indicating the entire city of the dead in its eerie half-light.

'If we do not hurry, Konrad will have no memories left.'

'We are hurrying,' said the Gatekeeper again.

And his body will die, Nanda added privately to herself. Her fae would do their best to keep his mortal shell from succumbing to decay, but they were but minor spirits, not gods. There was only so long they could hold him.

'I do not think the concept of *hurrying* exists here,' she said, tension making her snappish.

'Ordinarily,' said the Gatekeeper, 'I go nowhere, save to fetch and carry. This is refreshing.'

'You are sight-seeing.'

'Are not you?'

She had been; she could not deny it. 'Where is the Tree?' she said.

'I believe we will reach it in a year of your days.'

'A year!'

That amused, sideways glance again. 'Or perhaps an hour.'

'You do not know?'

'Perhaps I don't. Perhaps there is no such thing as distance, in the Deathlands.'

That made a horrible kind of sense. Nanda's heart sank.

'Or perhaps I indulge myself at your expense.'

'You are teasing me.'

'I admit to amusing myself. I have not had company in some time, either.'

Nanda, swallowing a rising wrath, reminded herself that she was dependent on this odd person's goodwill. 'I am grateful for yours,' she said, instead of the curses that had risen to her lips.

'My what?'

'Company.'

'Oh.' He seemed startled at that, for his glance this time was surprised, and then appraising, and he said no more.

She sought for something else to say, some other way of hurrying him along without simply repeating *might we hurry*, for that had done no good. But a wisp of light caught her eye, a familiar glimmer; how could that be? Nothing could be familiar to her in this place.

But it was. A clear, ghostly light, and with it a sickly green glow...

'Eetapi?' she gasped. 'Ootapi! Say that it is you. I do not imagine this, too, do I?'

The twin lights drifted nearer. *You give yourself too much credit,* said Eetapi tartly. *Could you imagine anything half so beautiful?*

We are *beautiful,* said Ootapi, with a kind of wonder, as though the idea had seemed impossible to him before. *And so are you, Nanda.*

Not knowing how to take that, Nanda let it pass. Whatever these bloodthirsty creatures considered beauty to consist of, probably it was nothing she wanted to resemble. 'Tell me Konrad is with you,' she said.

He is! carolled Eetapi.

But Nanda looked and looked, and did not see him. Ahead of them stretched yet another bland street, cobbled and wide and winding, and empty.

He was, said Ootapi, stopping in mid-air. He turned about, and soared back down the street. Eetapi followed.

Abandoning all thought, Nanda ran too.

She found him almost at once, just around the next turn in the road. There was not much left of him; as a ghost, he did much resemble the person he had been when he was alive. But she knew him anyway, would know him anywhere.

He had turned aside, and stood staring up at the façade of a humble house. Out of step with those around it, this house was shorter, narrower, meaner, shabbier; a meagre abode for an impecunious dweller. Konrad, though, was arrested by it. Before Nanda could reach him, he had drifted through its front door — which, suddenly, hung open — and faded from view.

Nanda dashed after him.

'Konrad,' she panted, reaching the bottom of a narrow set of stairs. She set her foot upon the first step — and the stairs dissolved into smoke. The air shimmered, and reformed itself. Where a narrow passage had been, there now came another house, another hall: her own mother's. Nanda had strayed into her own memories, and had lost Konrad to his.

'Konrad!' she shouted. 'Konrad.' She stopped, breathless and exhausted and weak, and laid her forehead against the cool wood-panelled wall of her own childhood home. 'Konrad,' she sighed. 'Do not *again* go wallowing in the past, I beg of you. Not now.' Regret would strand him in the Deathlands forever, for the one place Nanda could not follow was into the depths of his own past — those years before she had ever known him at all.

You lost him, she heard Eetapi hiss. *How could you lose him?*

I didn't, snarled Ootapi. *YOU lost him, you were—*

'Serpents!' Nanda snapped. 'This isn't the time. Can you get him back?'

The Gatekeeper, absent a moment before, was at her elbow. 'It takes people that way,' he said, making her jump.

'What does?'

'Memory.'

'Regret,' said Nanda bitterly. 'Konrad is amazing at it.'

'A singularly futile pursuit.'

'Try telling him that.' She paused, drew in a breath. 'Maybe you *can* tell him that.'

'Me?'

'Yes. I cannot follow him, but you can. Please. Go drag him out of the ocean of self-reproach he's hurled himself into.'

'I cannot,' said the Gatekeeper.

'But all this way, you've—'

'I cannot, unless he wants to be retrieved.' The Gatekeeper shrugged, looking curiously about at Mother's house. 'If he has found his appointed place here, I cannot change that.'

'You're the Gatekeeper. Of course you can.'

'You must have me confused with someone else.' The Gatekeeper, or the Guide, turned cold eyes upon her, and she remembered that, whatever his manner, he was not her friend. He was not even human. 'I am not The Malykt, only His servant. I ensure the deceased reach their appointed places in the Deathlands, and that is all.'

'This is not his appointed place.'

'He seems to feel differently.'

Nanda abandoned the argument. *What if he's right?* whispered her heart. *What if Konrad doesn't want to come home?*

What if, this time, he truly wants to die?

Nanda squashed the traitorous voice. 'Serpents,' she said. 'It's down to you. I cannot follow Konrad, but maybe you can. You've known him for longer than I have.'

'And you are dead,' softly said the Gatekeeper. 'This place has no love for the living.'

We will try, said Eetapi.

'Don't try,' said Nanda tightly. '*Do it*. Find him. Bring him back.'

***

'Konrad,' said a dear, dear voice, achingly familiar, so long lost as to be almost forgotten.

Almost, but never quite.

He'd looked up.

There she was, leaning out of an upper window in the house they had once shared. Enadya. Her hair, black and wavy like mother's, hung in a loose, tangled mass; she was always impatiently scraping it back, binding it up, and still it fell down. She wore her favourite shade of red, and it became her, but her dress was faded and beginning to fray. He ought to get her another, somehow.

'Kon!' she said, waving and smiling, and he smiled back, feeling the weight of too many years drop away like empty air.

'Ena,' he whispered. 'You're — all right.'

'Of *course* I am all right,' she'd said, laughing. 'Though I've missed you. Are you coming in?'

Was he? Yes, of course. Why not? Had he been doing something...

The door of the little house swung open, and he heard his sister's voice again, calling him from within.

Konrad went through the door.

She waited for him at the top of the narrow stairs, the wooden ones that creaked with every step. And her arms went around him and he held her again, little sister, whom he had so terribly failed. Apologies spilled from his lips, and the tears would have poured from the eyes he no longer possessed, had he substance enough to make them.

She said nothing. Why wasn't she saying anything? He pulled back to look at her, and wished he had not, for all her laughing welcome was gone. 'Where were you?' she said, cold now. 'Where were you that day? How could you leave me alone? How could you let them hurt me?'

The same words he had so often reproached himself with, only in *her* beloved voice, her beautiful dark eyes hard and unsympathetic as she looked at him.

'I didn't mean—' he gasped. 'I had no idea— if I'd known I never would have left you alone—'

She said nothing, only looked at him.

It wasn't enough. Whatever excuse he came up with, it was *his* fault she had died. He'd stolen and he shouldn't have. He had transgressed, and she had paid the price.

He had avenged her, but it hadn't mattered. Nothing had changed, and nothing ever would.

Master, shrieked a distant voice, incongruous in the midst of this house, this pain. It was... other. It did not belong. Jarred and disoriented, he blinked and stared, turned about. Where had it come from?

Master! came the shriek again, thin and distant, and the floor shook under him.

Two shapes shot out of the skies — skies where the ceiling had been — twin shapes like blazing arrows, bound straight for him.

Twin impacts, knocking him sideways, driving the non-existent breath from his incorporeal lungs. Silly, that, he distantly thought. Dead, and still he tried to breathe.

The floor shook again, and the walls, and when he turned in a panic looking for Enadya, he found her gone. 'Ena!' he screamed.

It isn't her, shrieked the shrieking thing. *Master, come with us. Come now!*

'It is her,' Konrad wept. 'It has to be.'

Why, so you can wallow in misery forever? A different voice, that. The other one. The tones chimed in Konrad's mind, splintered ice and funeral bells; distantly, they struck a chord. *How refreshing,* said the second voice, with a scorn to cut Konrad to the quick.

Nanda's waiting, said the first voice, still at screaming volume. *She's waiting and she has risked everything to bring your sorry hide home and you are coming. WITH. US!*

Konrad wanted to speak, to say — something — protest — memory — apology — no time. Twin forces, freezing and implacable, took hold of what passed for his limbs and walked him back down those narrow, creaking stairs and out into the street, and no matter how he called for Enadya she did not come back, and she did not stop them.

Nanda was indeed waiting. She looked... wondrous. Brimming with life in so pale a place; vibrant with colour; all red-rimmed eyes and drawn face and an expression of thunderous fury.

'Do you *have* to make everything so impossibly difficult?' she said.

He swallowed something bitter. Regret. 'Yes,' he said. 'It seems I do.'

Nanda held out her hand. She wore an ornament there, a jewel that shone like the sun. Mesmerising. Familiar.

'You're missing a bit,' she said. 'Do you maybe want it back?'

Konrad stretched out a hand. His fingers did not, could not, touch hers, but something else caught at him. A little bit of himself, tangled up in the jewel there.

Knowing Nanda, she had probably saved all the best bits.

'Are you coming home?' said Nanda.

'If— if you are going to be there.'

'No ifs,' she said sternly. 'No buts. Are you coming or not?'

Better say yes, Master, said Eetapi. *Or she'll kill you herself. Again.*

I'll help, added Ootapi.

'Yes,' said Konrad. 'Let's go home.'

'Good,' said Nanda. 'It's never going to get any easier, you know. Living, I mean. But it's infinitely superior to the alternative.'

He smiled at that, then winced as his snakes disentangled themselves from whatever was left of him. *You are hard work,* muttered Eetapi. *But you're ours.*

Nuritov found it first.

'Curse you,' scowled Tasha, slamming down her much-resented tome. 'What was I even here for?'

The inspector simply put his book into her hands, amid soothing noises. She liked those no better than she'd liked his infuriating cry of jubilation. Victory for the dull, old policeman! She should've left him to get on with it, while she did... something more useful. And maybe entertaining.

'Look,' said Nuritov, pointing to the musty page before her.

'This isn't about Marja.' Tasha flipped it upside down, glowering at the title inscribed upon the cover. *Death Rites and Rituals.*

'No,' said Nuritov. 'I knew you had that covered, so I chose a different topic. Read it.'

His experience was showing. Well, just because she hadn't set foot in a library in years... 'I knew it,' she said. 'I *knew* there had to be some advantage to being old.'

'There are a great many, which I hope you'll have the opportunity to learn for yourself. Meanwhile, read.'

'Couldn't you just—'

'*Read.*'

Tasha sighed, turned the book right way up again, and applied herself to its contents.

She turned a page, and then another.

'Eyes,' she said, looking up. '*In the hands of a gifted ritualist, the eyes See far beyond the mundane. They may See beyond the borders of life itself, and glimpse into the shadowed realms of the Great Spirits of Death.'* Tasha looked up. 'Spirits above, is that what Eetapi and Ootapi have been doing?'

'I don't think they have been harvesting eyes, if that's what you mean.'

'Are you sure? I wouldn't put it past them.'

'It's more that I don't think they need to. Their eyes, such as they are, See beyond the borders of life already, courtesy of The Malykt. They don't need to borrow and bewitch someone else's.'

'True. But all this rubbish — rites and ritual burnings and Seeing beyond the borders — do you think this is it? Really?'

'The language is somewhat dry and obscure, but my reading of it is this: we already knew that in *some* traditions, including among some Marjan communities, the idea of an unclean death prevails as much as it does in Assevan society. That being, an early death, someone hastened out of life before their time, and by the hand of another. But for all that shopkeeper's words about destiny or whatever it was, it *seems* that there are rites to — detect traces of this. To see, as you say, whatever it is Eetapi and Ootapi are seeing when they look at a recently murdered corpse.'

'That's my understanding too,' Tasha said. 'But harvesting and empowering eyes? Really?'

'The eyes of murdered corpses,' said Nuritov. 'There's an odd kind of symmetry to it.'

'A creepy kind of symmetry. So somebody killed our two gents because they'd killed some people themselves — Konrad-style — and then whoever did it took their eyes so they could use them to find the next crime?'

'It fits, doesn't it?'

'It might, though Katya swears blind neither of them could possibly have killed anyone. But who are we dealing with, then? Some twisted kind of would-be Malykant, with no dead and deranged serpents to assist him?

'And no mandate from the Great Spirits, either, is my guess,' said Nuritov.

'Great. A plain old serial killer, in other words, but one with delusions of grandeur and a knack for creepy Marjan death-rites.'

'A fine challenge for your first job.'

Tasha scowled. 'Katya seemed really certain that these two couldn't have killed anybody.'

'She could be wrong. Why did Artemo and Vak go to Marja in the first place? They followed — *something* that felt wrong to them. Perhaps they... dispatched whomever it was, after Vak had sent his letter to the Order. Depending upon one's perspective, that is murder.'

'That's a thought.'

'Or possibly our serial killer was wrong.'

'You mean... Artemo and Vak might have been wrongly identified as killers?' Tasha thought about that, and went cold. 'Spirits. Nuritov, do you think — you don't think *Konrad*'s ever killed the wrong person?'

Nuritov didn't answer immediately. 'I have total respect for his abilities,' he finally said, which wasn't at all the same thing as an emphatic *no.*

'No one can be right all the time, can they?' said Tasha faintly.

'Let's hope Konrad can.'

'And me, too.'

Nuritov looked gravely at her. 'It is a serious responsibility.'

Tasha swallowed. She had known it was, of course, when she volunteered herself to take it on. But somehow, that aspect of the role had not occurred to her before. Perhaps because Konrad always had such certainty about him, such a cool efficiency as he dispatched killer after killer that she hadn't...

Spirits above.

'We are going to need Konrad back,' she said.

Nuritov didn't disagree, but he said: 'Now is not the time for a crisis of the confidence, Tasha. All right? We have work to do.'

'Right. Yes.' She sat up, dismissing her disquiet. She was starting to sound like Konrad in his maudlin moods, and that would never do. 'How does this help us?' she said, tapping the book before her.

'It is pertinent information we didn't have before.'

'Yes, but how does it help us find our killer?'

'Maybe it won't. In fact,' Nuritov tapped the bowl of his pipe absently against the topmost page, thinking. 'In fact, there is a real possibility that our killer is already gone back to Marja. We may never find him.'

'No! He has to be punished.'

Nuritov raised his brows.

'Well,' Tasha persisted. 'Isn't that what we do here?'

'Do you think anyone has ever felt that Konrad ought to be punished?'

'Only if he was ever wrong.'

'Oh? What about all the times he was right? Do you think no one has ever resented his actions, even when they were justified according to The Malykt's law?'

'You mean to warn me that widespread resentment lies in *my* future, too.'

Nuritov shook his head. 'Not precisely. But it's worth remembering that Konrad had good reason to keep his identity secret.'

'Fine, fine. I won't barrel in like an idiot and give myself away.'

That won her one of Nuritov's rare smiles. 'Won't you?'

'I'll *try.*'

***

Extracting Konrad from the city of souls proved easier than Nanda had feared, despite the Gatekeeper's utter uselessness.

'I cannot,' he said, when Nanda turned to him for her passage out.

'What? Why not?'

He took a seat upon empty air, cross-legged, chin in hand. 'Letting a living person *in* was transgression enough. I cannot also let a deceased soul *out.*'

'He is not deceased,' said Nanda quickly. 'His body still lives.'

'Oh? Then what is his spirit doing here?'

'The two are temporarily sundered.'

That irritating, head-tilting glance, curious and vaguely mocking, set Nanda grinding her teeth in frustration. 'It is beyond your power to reunite the two. What, then, are you planning to do with this soul you've retrieved?'

'Forgive me, but that is my business and can hardly be considered relevant to you.'

The Gatekeeper grinned, showing too-pale teeth. 'You will keep it, I suppose, like a pet.'

Nanda folded her arms, and stared at him in silence.

'The truth is,' said the Gatekeeper conversationally, 'what you ask is beyond my power. I can bring a soul *in*, but no part of my duty involves taking them out again.'

'Ah,' said Nanda, her heart sinking. *That* presented a problem. 'Snakes?' she called. 'You do not have a solution, by any chance?'

We do not, Eetapi confirmed.

Through this discussion, Konrad stood quiet. Nanda might have appreciated a thought or two from him, supposing he had any, but his silence and docility was at least better than the tearful (and misguided) protests of shortly before.

No use asking him. He, too, dealt in sending souls into The Malykt's city, not in getting them out.

She thought about how the Gatekeeper had opened a way in: a slash of his hand, a ragged tear opening up in the barriers between the Deathlands and the spirit-lands — or the Deathlands and that featureless, fathomless in-between place she had first arrived in.

And she thought about how she had contrived to step from the spirit-lands into his deeper, higher, stranger plane in the first place.

'I wonder if this would work,' she said, taking out the knife her Mistress had blessed. It glimmered in the light, in a colour Nanda had never witnessed in it before: vivid green, like spring grass.

The Gatekeeper recoiled.

'Don't you like it?' said Nanda, letting the point drift in his direction.

'It's — anathema,' said the Gatekeeper, keeping a close eye on it.

'What I suspect you mean is simply that it's potent. It could slice through you like butter, could it?'

The Gatekeeper's eyes narrowed. 'The Shandrigal is not The Malykt's enemy, you know. Why would Her weapons harm me?'

'I wonder if it differentiates?' Nanda said mildly. 'It went through the malefic like butter.'

'Malefic? What, are they returned?'

'Just the one, for a bit. It's gone now.'

The Gatekeeper was silent, visibly disquieted. His dark eyes moved from the knife to Nanda's face and back, and he said nothing.

'We need *him*,' Nanda said, pointing the knife at Konrad. 'To keep the malefic curse at bay. Our Malykant.'

'There is always another Malykant,' said the Gatekeeper.

'Yes. Another new, traumatised, poorly trained and poorly supported Malykant. The world might like to keep the same one for a bit longer, this time. Who knows? Maybe we can have a world with no malefic, ever again, for always.' And he'd have time, Nanda thought, to mentor his own replacement. Whoever finally took over from Konrad would do so from a position of knowledge, confidence and stability, with all the support from *both* Orders that Konrad (and his predecessors) always should have had.

A woman could dream.

'It is still beyond my power to free him,' said the Gatekeeper.

'I know. I was just hoping you might stand aside and play dumb while I do this.' Nanda lifted her arm, and swept The Shandrigal's knife through the air in a great, smooth arc, mimicking the Gatekeeper's own gesture.

A rift opened.

The Gatekeeper folded his arms, mimicking Nanda's own posture from shortly before. 'You still *owe* me.'

'I do. Don't worry. You like company, no? I'm going to send the most colourful person I know up here.'

She chose not to wait for a response, but turned at once to the serpents. 'Eetapi, Ootapi. Get him through, will you?'

The dread snakes went to work at once, binding Konrad's soul to their own will. Under their influence, the vague look did not fade from his dead eyes but his limbs moved, and that was all she wanted at present. He walked inexorably towards the rift she had created in the fabric of the Deathlands, and vanished through.

'Thank you,' she said to the Gatekeeper, and bowed. 'I am much obliged to you.'

He gave her in response a crooked smile, and a dismissive wave of one insubstantial hand. 'Give The Shandrigal my regards,' he said. 'Somehow I think She is no match for you.'

Nanda smiled, too, in a small, secret way, and followed after Konrad.

'Madam Inshova?' she said in surprise, for awaiting her on the other side of her green-glittering rift was her Order superior, wearing a look of irritation.

'Quickly,' said Katya, though the word emerged more as a growl. 'It will close on you, you know.'

Nanda hastened her steps, keeping a close eye on what was left of Konrad. 'I don't— what are you doing here? Not that I am ungrateful, for I perceive you've been—'

'*Quickly,*' said Katya again. 'Or did you want to finish this alone?'

The fae had cleaned up Konrad's mortal remains. Nanda had not expected that, but she experienced such a rush of gratitude upon seeing him — free of blood and bile, his skin clear, his flesh still plump and blooming and *not* desiccated in death — she could almost have kissed every single one of the slippery creatures.

'He is sound enough,' said Inkubal, upon enquiry. 'His heart beats, his blood flows.'

'And his injuries?' They had, more oddly, discarded Konrad's own clothing, and dressed him instead in some of their own garments. Perhaps his clothing had been too dirtied and insanitary, to leave in place. The replacement robe (woven, for all she could tell, from light and tears and dark dreams) shrouded his form too thoroughly for her to discern the state of his flesh beneath.

'Healed,' said Inkubal. He wore shadows of his own, primarily around his penetrating eyes; the tasks she had set him had wearied him. Wearied them all, no doubt.

A heavy reckoning lay before her.

'Good,' said Nanda crisply, and took the one, small liberty of touching Konrad's hair. He lived, but he was so cold.

No time to waste.

The fae had not tried to move him far. He lay still in the spirit-lands, no longer prone in the pool of his own blood in which he'd fallen, but not far distant from it. He lay in cool, ice-touched grass, a canopy of withies laden with leaves arching above. The ethereal thing in some manner deterred the wind, for nothing stirred beneath it. Kulu sat at Konrad's left ear, staring into his left eye with a fierce, unnerving level of concentration. Why his left eye was open, when the other was closed, Nanda did not know, but that Kulu bent all her small but potent powers upon Konrad's being she did not doubt.

At times, she had resented the price they demanded of her for her aid. Especially late at night, drowning in visions — *their* visions, glimpses of the lives they led and the deeds they'd committed, so alien to her simple way of life.

Today, she grudged them none of it.

What now? Eetapi demanded. She detected strain in the serpent's words; holding Konrad bound took its toll on them, too.

We cannot put him back in, said Ootapi.

'I know,' she murmured.

Neither can you, he added, helpfully.

'I *know*. Hush.'

The Gatekeeper was right, the serpents were right: recombining the sundered halves of Konrad's being, body and soul, lay beyond the power of any mortal. Only the Great Spirits had ever been able to do that.

Well, then.

Nanda took up the knife — no longer glowing green — for what she hoped would be the last time. The knife had dispatched a malefic, and carved a hole in the Deathlands; such power ought not to rest in the hands of a mortal, either, except at dire need. The first use that had been made of it surely counted. She must make the second and third count, too — and now it was time to turn its powers on herself.

Gritting her teeth, Nanda carved a long, shallow cut down her own arm, elbow to wrist. Quickly swapping hands before blood loss could weaken them, she performed the same procedure upon her other arm. Her blood flowed, mingling with The Shandrigal's verdant magics as it trickled in a slow stream over her fingers, and onto the ground.

She had expected pain, but not agony. She fell to her knees, swallowing a cry, as agony flared and *burned* — and faded, taking with it everything in her that was unworthy of Her Mistress. Every lingering trace of the darkness she had lately fallen into, in her life at Konrad's side.

She let some of that blood fall into Konrad's hair, onto his face. *Pity,* she thought with distant irrelevance. *And they cleaned him up so nicely...*

After that, nothing remained but to pray.

'Mistress,' she said aloud. 'I know I have become a nuisance with my — my failures and my requests and my need for favours, but nonetheless I have another such to ask of You.' She swallowed, and breathed, aware abruptly of an infinite weariness. 'It is one I've asked of You before and You have granted it before. Grant me this thing one more time. Bring Konrad Savast, the Malykant, servant of Your Brother The Malykt, back to life.'

Something stirred at last in the lifeless air beneath the canopy: a faint breath of wind, a gentle current that told her The Shandrigal listened.

'In return I offer You... well, my life in exchange, if You want it. Also Konrad's, not in quite the same way. He is The Malykt's creature, but I think he should be Yours, too. The Malykant serves both, doesn't he? He punishes transgressions against The Malykt's laws, and in so doing he defends and celebrates life. He has come to value his *own* life, at long last, thanks in part to Your interference and in part to mine. It's too cruel that he should have to relinquish it now, and in such a cause. And it would be a cruelty to Your people, too, who've benefited from his work, and his predecessors' work, for years — the malefic proved that — and —' Breathless, Nanda stopped, swallowing down a wave of dizziness. 'Bring him back. Please. Take him into Your service, as well as Your Brother's.'

Split him between Us? Her Mistress's voice, thrumming deep in Nanda's heart.

'Why not?' she said lightly. 'Already that's been the case, near enough.'

Since the last time I knit body and spirit back together, and turned him loose upon Assevan.

'Yes. And he's been… better, since then. I've seen it.'

Why has My Brother not already revived His own servant?

Nanda, deprived of her small hope that The Shandrigal would not ask certain inconvenient questions, sighed. 'Konrad has been the Malykant for nearly nine years now.'

Then it is his time. The words were not encouraging, but the faint suggestion of a question lingered behind them. Nanda seized upon it.

'It *isn't* his time. It doesn't have to be! He is *good* in the role, and *not* losing his wits, whatever Diana Valentina may say of it — what does she know? She hardly sees Konrad. I see him every day. He is not mad, he is *not* corrupt, and we need him.' Tears gathered at the back of her eyes, tightening her throat, and Nanda paused for another steadying breath. Tired. She was just tired. 'Please,' she said.

Why does it matter so much to you, Shandral? The voice was curious, mild, probing. *Is it for Assevan you plead?*

'No.' Nanda took a shaking breath. 'I am not so unselfish. I want him for myself, too.'

Nothing more was said, for a time, and Nanda used the interval to gather herself. She was conscious of her pact-bound fae, silent and cowed by The Shandrigal's presence, making themselves small and invisible. Nanda did not blame them. The Great Spirit's attention was no easy burden to bear.

She was also conscious of Katya Inshova's presence at the edge of

336

the ethereal clearing, silent and watchful. So far, she had not chosen to interfere. Would she? Or did her mere presence here offer her tacit support to Nanda's plea?

What do you think? said The Shandrigal at last.

The question was not directed at her, nor even to Katya. The Shandrigal spoke to Konrad himself, and Konrad felt the shift of Her attention, for he woke from whatever dreaming reverie he had lost himself in, his wavering spirt seeming suddenly more substantial, more present.

I...

Konrad's voice was so distant, so thin, that Nanda's heart quailed. Had he come back with her at all, or was it only a shadow? Did he linger still in the Deathlands, his mind and heart held there in spite of all her efforts?

I would like to live, he whispered. *For just a bit longer.*

And what, answered The Shandrigal, *will you do with this time?*

Konrad's reply was immediate.

Everything.

Nanda did weep, then, tears drowning her cheeks and trickling, cold and salty, into the hollow of her throat. Just exhaustion. She didn't remember ever being even half so tired before, not in the whole course of her life.

You are replaced, however, said The Shandrigal. *As the Malykant.*

I... am? said Konrad.

'That's all in hand,' said Nanda quickly.

She felt Konrad's attention fix upon her, sensed the questions he wanted to ask. The only word he managed to utter was: *Who?*

Nanda swallowed the rest of her tears, and got to her feet. 'How about I tell you later?' she said. 'I am not altogether sure you're going to like the answer.'

9

Konrad stood for some time outside the front door of Bakar House, heedless of the sleet driving into his face, or the cold seeping into his bones. His hat was long gone, as was his coat — everything. He wore... there was no word for what he wore. A robe, maybe, of materials he had no names for either. The thing hung shapeless around him, puffed about by every breath of wind, so light it might as well have been woven of cobwebs. (Considering its provenance, it could have been). He ought to have perished from the cold by now, so garbed, but the peculiar little spirits Nanda kept company with knew their arts: the cobweb robe kept him warmer than it ought.

Still, he dreamed of the huge, roaring fires he liked to have in his snug study, and in the parlour he'd so often sat in with Nan. He wanted — *needed* — food; his gut informed him he had ingested nothing in some time. (How long? *How long?* The mind shied away from the answer to that question, and especially from the reasons why). He wanted warm water and his own clothes and his own bed.

But were they his own, anymore?

'Are we going in?' said Nanda behind him, mildly enough, but he caught the trace of strain behind the words. Irritation, perhaps, or merely exhaustion.

Yes. He was not the only one who required comforts and care. Nanda had survived an ordeal greater still than his.

He reached forth and — rang the doorbell.

Gorev was not long in answering the summons. The door clanked as bolts drew back — the hour was late, drowned in darkness, poor

Gorev ought to be in bed — and then swung open.

A gasp.

'*Sir*,' said Konrad's long-suffering butler. He looked, Konrad distantly noted, a little askew, for though fully dressed (why wasn't he sleeping?), the perfect order of his grey hair and pristine, dark garments had come somewhat unstuck. 'We thought—' He took in Nanda's presence, and paused. 'We thought,' he said again, 'you weren't...'

Konrad managed a small smile. 'I thought I wasn't, too.'

Gorev stared. The longer he stood staring, and failed to usher Konrad inside, the more Konrad's stomach dropped.

'Can we come in?' he said at length. 'Or— or is it not—'

Gorev visibly shook himself, and pulled the door open wide. 'Apologies, sir. I was only— please, come in. I'll have the fires relit directly, and something sent to the parlour — you'll be wanting baths, and— ah—' His gaze lingered on Konrad's odd garb, and then on Nanda's apple-green gown, filthy from her trek through spirit-lands and Deathlands alike.

'Everything,' Konrad confirmed, stepping inside. He paused a moment in the hall, savouring the various impressions that swamped him. Chief among them: relief, intense and bittersweet. They hadn't yet given his house away. Gratitude, for Gorev's welcome, and Nanda's presence, and the mere fact that he breathed.

Gorev had not yet left. Konrad caught a strange look crossing his face, as he glanced at his employer.

'What is it?' Konrad said patiently.

More than one thing, in all likelihood. One was the fact that Nanda's cool fingers rested securely in his own. He hadn't let go of her since they had left The Shandrigal's Temple, nor she of him. That was unusual enough.

But Gorev had another oddity in mind. 'We had heard that you were...'

'Dead?' supplied Konrad, when his butler seemed unable to produce the word. 'I was, actually.'

Gorev swallowed.

'And I know it has happened before, but this time was different.'

Everything was different. He felt changed all through, mixed up, someone else entirely, since The Shandral had melded his body with his soul, and turned him loose upon Ekamet once more.

No, not entirely. The chill, deep darkness of The Malykt's power: that was not gone. Konrad felt it still, a layer of ice around his heart, a coldness deep within. A dark, harsh power he still had the right to wield, if he wanted to.

But the seed of The Shandrigal's power, laid some time ago, a scant touch scarcely noticed by him *then*, had grown. Half his soul, he knew, was now given into *Her* hands, and he felt that touch deep inside himself. Indescribable, but if The Malykt was a coldness, The Shandrigal was a warmth. If the one was darkness, the other was light.

Simplistic stuff. Konrad snorted at his own incapacity to define either of the Great Spirits' influence over him. Groping blindly at nursery concepts, ignorant as a child…

He'd wandered off into his own head again. Gorev was gone, and he came to himself just in time to see Nanda disappearing into their parlour. He hastened after her, hoping she hadn't tried to speak to him, only to find him unresponsive. What a way to repay her — her — *kindness?* No. That word didn't cover it either.

Konrad abandoned words.

A startled exclamation greeted his entry into the parlour, the chamber not shrouded in darkness as he'd expected but lit up, and a small fire already burning in the grate.

It wasn't Nanda who had spoken.

'Tasha,' he said, overwhelmed with emotion at the sight of her small, dark form bundled up in one of his high-backed chairs. He might never have seen her again, either, and infuriating as she was, she—

Wait. She was the Tasha he'd always known, but not… quite… something else hung about her now, a whisper, a chill breeze—

'*Tasha?*' he repeated. '*Tasha* is the new Malykant?'

'Is that so unlikely?' Tasha snapped, drawing herself up. Her surprise at seeing Konrad was gone; she glared at him now, arms folded. 'Someone had to mind the shop while you were gone. Why not me?'

Konrad groped for words again, and came up empty. 'Um.'

'Thank you, Tasha,' said Nanda softly, folding into a vacant chair with the limp grace of an utterly spent woman. 'I've no doubt you and Alexander have done a fine job.'

'We have, actually,' muttered Tasha. '*Two* corpses, and while we haven't caught the culprit yet we aren't far off. How's that for my first day at work?'

Tasha nattered on, and Konrad's mind slipped away from the flow of words like a wayward river. Tasha was the Malykant. He *was* replaced. The knowledge left him...hollow.

But, no, that was not right either. The Malykt had not withdrawn His power from Konrad; it was still there.

Master? he tried. *Do You still wish me to— hunt for You?*

The Malykt did not reply in words. Konrad instead felt a rush of cold sweep over him, like drowning in ice-water. In the wake of it, he felt his weakened limbs strengthen, felt The Malykt's grip tighten a fraction around his heart.

All right, then.

I will do my best, he promised.

No, wait.

We, he amended, for Tasha wore their Master's mark still. *We will do our best.*

'Can we eat, first?' Konrad said, cutting off Tasha's rambling tale of bone knives and blood. He couldn't focus on the half of it, not with his body turning itself inside out with hunger, and his brain fogged with the need for sleep. Nanda must be in a similar state. 'And sleep? In the morning, we will... um, be at your disposal, Tasha.'

He caught himself at the end there, sensitive to the narrowing of her eyes, the way she'd begun to bristle. He couldn't take this case off her, not when he'd left her and the inspector to handle it without him.

She relaxed a fraction, mollified. 'Wimp,' she said. But she spoke with her own, prickly brand of affection, and Konrad smiled.

The welcoming embrace of his own, dear bed engulfed him soon afterwards, and he lay with that same smile still on his face — for a time. But at the edges of his senses, there was Stev, and Kulu, and Hreejur, their shadows bound to him until the debts he and Nanda owed were paid, and the pacts broken. He could never entirely forget those presences, but they were worth the bearing, when it meant Nanda's life.

Laying one hand against Nanda's warm back, Konrad closed his eyes, and resigned himself to a few nightmares.

'Eyes,' said Nanda the following morning — *late* the following morning, for she and Konrad both had slept like twin corpses laid out side-by-side. Neither had stirred until the serpents, impatient for activity, had twined their shivery selves around a throat apiece, and squeezed.

What a way to wake up.

'I am not sure,' she continued, 'that we're on the right track with those.' She drummed her fingers on the table-top, beside the empty plate which had, shortly before, been piled high with delectables. 'Where did you pick up that little myth, Alex?'

The inspector sat to her right, trying not to stare at either Nanda or Konrad, and succeeding so well he barely lifted his eyes from his own repast.

Konrad sympathised. The tendency of Malykants to die messily over and over again was familiar enough to him, but not so much to Alexander. The total avoidance of Konrad's gaze unnerved him a little, though. Was something wrong with his face? Had The Shandrigal put his soul in backwards?

'Library book,' said the inspector. '*Death Rites and Rituals*; I think that was it.'

'It's a tale I have heard before,' Nanda allowed. 'But *only* as a tale. I was also told that it's nonsense, and if you were to ask the spirit-witches of the Bone Forest enclave they would probably tell you the same.' She looked a little healthier this morning, to Konrad's relief: less white, less drawn, and with some traces of her old life and vigour returning. Konrad wanted to send her back to bed, let her stay there in warmth and comfort and rest until she was well again. But he had no illusions about how well-received that suggestion was likely to be.

'Oh,' said the inspector, looking up at last, and with an expression of such crestfallen disappointment that Konrad's heart, inexplicably, squeezed. He wanted Alexander to be happy, too. *Everyone* should be happy and well; life was fragile and brutal, and if only he could gather up all his precious few loved ones and keep them safe forever, he would.

Well, taking another killer off the streets of Ekamet was one way to do that. Konrad retrieved his wandering thoughts yet again.

'The book seemed reputable,' Alexander was saying with a sigh.

'It was probably written in good faith,' Nanda said. 'But information can become outdated, and stories can sometimes loom larger than they have any right to.'

Tasha was smirking. Konrad decided not to ask why.

'Why take the eyes, then?' Tasha demanded. 'Nobody does something that weird without good reason.'

'Trophy,' said Konrad.

Tasha stared at him.

Konrad cleared his throat. 'Killers sometimes like to take... souvenirs.'

'That's revolting.'

'Get used to it. It's not even the worst example I've seen.'

Tasha's eyes widened. Whether with disgust or unholy glee, Konrad could not tell.

'So,' he said. 'We know that two men have died, stabbed through the heart with knives worked from bone. Both were divested of their eyes. Both were killed in their own homes, after returning from a journey into Marja. Both had travelled there in pursuit of some— unclean thing, which, as far as we know, they did not catch.'

'We only have Timof Vak's letter about that,' said Alexander. 'He might have caught up with the thing after he'd dispatched it, and never got a chance to report as much to the Order. And we have no idea what happened during Rodion Artemo's journey.'

'And we don't know what it was they were chasing, either?' Konrad said.

Alexander looked at Nanda. 'We were hoping to ask Nan about that.'

Nanda met Alexander's gaze, thoughtful, but for the moment she had nothing to add.

'They might have found it, after all,' said Konrad. 'Or at least, got its attention. And it followed *them* home. Did my serpents rule on the manner of those deaths? Were they murdered by another mortal soul?'

No, Master, said Eetapi from somewhere. *We were busy with the small matter of your being dead.*

Right.

'Whatever it was could have been both,' Nanda said.

'Both?' Konrad prompted.

'A mortal soul, bound up with something... other. Unclean, if you like.'

'A possession?'

Nanda shook her head. 'More like a pact. The kind I make are really quite minor, all told. If you were reckless enough, strong enough, desperate, you might make the kind of pact which... well, nobody comes out of those with their soul intact. It's said that such a pact ultimately destroys the soul, leaving nothing to enter the Deathlands after decease.'

'So they're rare,' said Konrad slowly.

'Extremely. They are banned across Marja and Assevan, of course, which is hardly necessary given how difficult it is to *find* a creature who'd bind itself to you, and you to it, in such a way. And few have a powerful enough motive to seek, or accept, such a bargain.'

Konrad watched her face. 'These Warders, of your Order. Are they — you — tasked with watching for such bargains?'

'*Our* Order, Konrad.' That beloved glint of mischief appeared in Nanda's eye, for the first time in many days.

He bowed his head. 'Our Order.'

'We are, among other things,' said Nanda. 'If Timof or Rodion caught a glimpse of any such thing, I can imagine that they might have followed after it. Such bargains are never formed for good purpose.' She looked at the inspector. 'The eyes... you did not have any reason to think they might have been burned, I suppose?'

Alexander nodded. 'We found remnants of burned wood at Mr. Artemo's house, and he kept a coal fire.'

Nanda said nothing more, but her eyes narrowed.

'Nan,' he said. 'What is it?'

'They might have been taken as a trophy,' she said slowly. 'But I begin to suspect that they were taken as... tribute. A pact-price. Harvested and ritually burned, as an offering to the creature with whom the pact was made. Every spirit demands payment.'

Konrad knew that, to his own cost, now. Several of Nanda's pacts now weighed upon his soul, sapping his energy until such time that the agreed price was paid. He felt it with every breath; and these were but minor spirits.

'The bone-knives,' he said. 'Are they part of it, too?'

Nanda shifted in her chair. 'There are... ways and ways, to satisfy such a pact without giving of your own life. All of them despicable, I need hardly add. I have not heard of bone-knives turned to such purpose before, but— Konrad, is it not true that the use of a knife of bone in *your* case creates some kind of — of binding between two souls, the killer and their victim? So that the one may extract its vengeance from the other, until The Malykt decrees that the debt is paid.'

'We prefer the term justice,' said Konrad with a small smile. 'But yes, you are right about that.'

'So, then. Might not our killer have turned this to his own purpose?'

'You mean,' said Alexander softly, 'that these knives might not be made from the bones of a human after all.'

Nanda nodded. 'The bone may have been from something... else, something not human. A creature now dead, but its spirit lingers — and it has pacted with a mortal man. These knives, then, are binding whatever remains of this creature to the souls of Rodion Artemo and poor Timof Vak.'

Konrad shuddered inwardly. He had not forgotten his brief sojourn in the Deathlands, as one of the dead, however much he might dislike to think of it. How much worse might it have been, if he had been bound in slavery to such a creature as Nanda described? If the remnants of his soul were given in pact-price to so evil a thing, to be tormented, slowly drained away?

'I wish it did not sound so plausible a theory,' he said.

'Me too,' said Nanda, and straightened. 'I regret, now, that we did not proceed upon this matter last night, for we must find your killer as soon as possible. He will not stop at two victims.'

'You wouldn't have been much use last night,' Tasha said brutally. 'You could hardly walk in a straight line.'

Nanda conceded this point with a nod. 'I would like to know how it was that either Rodion or Timof sensed this presence in Ekamet, or how they followed it.'

'I would like to know what it was doing in Ekamet in the first place,' said Konrad. 'Or why it has come back.'

Nanda's gaze rested thoughtfully upon him. 'It came back to dispose of the two who hunted it,' she said. 'That, I can imagine it might do.'

'But how did it cross paths with either Artemo or Vak in the first place?' said Konrad. 'Could they sense it across half the city? That seems doubtful, or surely they would have found and disposed of it.'

'If they *could* dispose of it,' said Nanda. 'They may not have understood what they were dealing with.'

Alexander was frowning. 'A fair question, Konrad,' he said. 'If they could not sense such a thing from any great distance, how did they come to its notice?'

'That's obvious,' said Tasha. 'It, or rather *he*, was someone they both knew.'

Konrad blinked, and sat up. 'That's... not a bad thought, Tasha. Someone of their joint acquaintance — someone they'd known, perhaps, before this pact was made— although did not Vak's letter claim he did not know the identity of the person or creature he hunted?'

'It needn't have been a close acquaintance,' said Tasha. 'Anything that would put them in the same building, or make it likely they'd pass in the street? Something like that.'

'But,' said Alexander. 'But they came from utterly different backgrounds, and as far as we've been able to tell, they had nothing in common. Except...'

'Except the Order,' Nanda finished. She looked sick. 'You cannot mean that someone of the *Order* is responsible for this.'

Alexander looked apologetic, but he did not back down. 'Can you think of anything else those two might have shared? We can't. And by we I mean the police. My men have gone through every aspect of their lives, and found no other link between them.'

'No one among the Shandral could *possibly* form such a pact,' Nanda said vehemently. 'Or murder their own fellows — especially like *that*—'

Rarely had Konrad seen Nanda upset at all, let alone so deeply. Anxious to comfort, but unsure how to do so, he took her hand again, and wove her fingers through his own. She was cold, a little. He received no answering look, no real response to his gesture at all, but her fingers did tighten slightly upon his.

'Nan,' he said gently. 'There is no such thing as an incorruptible group. However lofty the purposes of The Shandrigal's Order—'

'Not lofty,' Nanda said coolly. 'That isn't at all the right word.'

'Pure, then. Worthy. It doesn't matter. *Nothing* is wholly immune to — to the weaknesses, the vices and the failures of human nature. Even the Shandral must have their fair share of the fallen.'

Nanda's lips tightened. She said nothing more, but Konrad read in her ice-blue eyes a sick, and deepening, fear. He knew she was going through the members of her Order — *their* Order — in her mind, weighing up all of those that she knew, trying to decide if any of *them* could be the culprit.

'Nanda,' said Alexander, diffidently. He did not relish the task of distressing Nanda, either. 'Nan, were there any others among the Order who had the same sensitivities as Artemo and Vak? Anyone else who could sense a corrupted presence?'

'You would have to ask Katya,' said Nanda slowly. 'But to my knowledge, no. It is not a widespread ability.'

That would explain the recruitment of such different people as Artemo and Vak, and the long membership of the former. The Order had probably been paying him a pension, if not a wage. 'Is it a coincidence,' Konrad said carefully, 'that it is these two who have been murdered?'

'Can't be,' said Tasha. 'Whoever it was knew what he was about. He deliberately removed the only two who could smell him for what he was.'

'Which was foolish,' said Nanda softly. 'For with that act, he betrayed himself.' She closed her eyes, and rested her face in her hands.

'Nan?' said Konrad. 'Are you all right?'

'Course she isn't,' said Tasha. 'She knows who it is. Nobody likes having to accept that their erstwhile friends are monsters.'

'Do you, Nan?' said Konrad.

Nanda sat up again, and lifted her chin. 'I am afraid I might.'

The house they came to some little time later had all the marks of abandonment about it. Situated on the edge of Ekamet, it backed straight onto the city walls; stray, bone-pale branches from the forest beyond reached over the tops of the wall, and grasped uselessly at its roof.

The house was one of a row of three terraced dwellings, all of them veering in the direction of dereliction. The one at the far end was their destination, and that was the worst of the three, with holes in its roof, two of its windows broken and a general air of desolation about it.

'Are you sure this is the right place?' said Tasha, surveying it with a frown. 'It doesn't look like anyone has lived here in years.'

'He always had humble tastes,' said Nanda, and marched on towards the house.

Privately, Konrad agreed with Tasha. Matthias Varis was not there. Probably he had already left Ekamet again, gone back into Marja, as Alexander thought.

But Nanda rapped upon the door anyway, and stood waiting.

Konrad joined her.

When no reply came, she nodded silently at Konrad, and he stretched out a hand to the rusted lock. Its stiff tumblers gave immediately under the cold touch of his fingers, and the door swung ajar with a dull creak.

Nanda swept inside.

'Matthias!' she called. 'Mr. Varis?'

The words echoed off the bare walls of the tiny, cramped hallway. Closed doors led into the house, on either side. Konrad opened the left one: a humble kitchen lay beyond, containing little more than an old-fashioned stove, much begrimed, and a stained table of stripped wood. No one was there.

The room opposite contained a couch, its dark green upholstery fraying away, and chairs, and a low table with a single lamp upon it. That, too, was empty.

But then came Ootapi's voice. *Master. There is a presence. Upstairs.*

Konrad hurried to reach the stairs before Nanda could, or Alexander either. The inspector had insisted upon attending them, though Konrad had done his best to talk him out of it. There could be nothing for him to do; supposing Matthias Varis to be guilty, the next part was Konrad's province. And Tasha's. But for once, Inspector Nuritov had insisted.

Konrad had no wish to see him hurt. He stole up the carpetless stairs, wincing with every creak; stealth was out of the question. Whoever waited above must know they had visitors.

A single door waited at the top of the stairs. Konrad did not bother to pause; he threw it open, and stalked inside.

Their quarry — presumably — lay upon a sweat-stained pallet at the back of the room. A comfortless chamber, Konrad thought distantly; bare of ornament, it bore besides the bed only a cupboard, and a soiled rug of rags across the floor. The fire had gone out long ago, and the room was bone-chillingly cold. It stank, the same way Nanda's bedchamber had, only worse: the layered scents of night-terrors and sickness, probably accumulated over some weeks.

'Matthias,' said Nanda from behind him.

Matthias Varis lay recumbent upon his rumpled and stained sheets. He had Nanda's icy-pale colouring, though his hair was whitened further with age, and his face so pallid with sickness and torment as to appear grey. He stared, hollow-eyed and unmoving, at Konrad, then at Nanda. 'Miss Falenia?' he said dully, his over-bright eyes focusing upon her.

Nanda went to his bedside, heedless of Konrad's attempts to discourage her. The man was likely dangerous; she ought not to get too close. But she stopped only two feet from his bedside, and stood looking down at him with unutterable sadness. 'It *was* you,' she said wearily. 'Wasn't it?'

Matthias Varis did not seem to need to ask what she meant. He said nothing, but Konrad read guilt, resignation and — more surprisingly — remorse in his every feature.

'Why?' said Nanda.

Matthias closed his eyes. 'I did not mean…' he began, his voice faint and faded. His eyes opened again, and now they were sharp, fixed unwaveringly upon Nanda. 'You know how it is,' he said. 'It begins with a simple pact, a small thing. The bargain seems good. You make another, and another.' He paused to draw breath, his hands coiling in the sheets with a shaking grip. 'I… did not know, what manner of thing I had encountered. I made the pact. I knew, almost at once, that I'd made a mistake, but too late, too late.'

Nanda did not move. 'How could you not know?'

Matthias's parched lips curled up in a faint, mirthless smile. 'Young as you are, you must yet know that — not everything is as it seems. The rottenest creatures frequently wear the fairest faces.'

'You were a fool,' said Nanda.

'I was. I have paid dearly for it.'

'So have Rodion Artemo, and Timof Vak.' Nanda's voice was steel, not an ounce of sympathy or understanding in her.

Matthias Varis bowed his head. 'I paid and I paid,' he said. 'It was never enough. And I began to feel… differently. About everything. Things I would once have balked at seemed… simple. I grew frightened. I knew she would always want more of me, more than I had to give. Rodion and Timof…' His face creased in sudden agony. 'They saw me. They knew what I had done. They — would have killed me.'

'You would have deserved it,' said Nanda.

'I know.' Matthias was weakening; the words emerged more strained with every breath, and his chest heaved with the effort of drawing enough air. 'I… regret. If I could undo it—'

'Regret is of no use,' said Nanda, cold as ice. 'And you cannot undo it. Two of our friends among the Shandral are dead, and by *your* hand. What have you to offer, in penance?'

'I have already offered it,' gasped Matthias. 'She is banished. It will cost me my life.'

'Banished?' said Konrad. 'What does that mean?'

'It means the pact is fulfilled,' said Nanda. 'The debt paid, and the creature, whatever she was, is gone back into the spiritlands. Let us hope, forever. Were the lives, organs and souls of Rodion and Timof enough to settle your debt, Matthias?'

'Theirs,' he whispered. 'And mine.'

Nanda turned away from him, and walked to the grimy window. Konrad, after a moment, followed her. Tasha and Alexander stood near the door, uncharacteristically silent, at least in Tasha's case. Alexander watched the proceedings with his customary composure, and Konrad could not guess at the thoughts that passed behind his eyes.

'What do you think?' said Konrad softly.

'Of what?' Nanda said. 'I don't know what your binding-knives will achieve in Matthias's case. The souls of those he killed are already gone. Devoured. And Matthias's will likely receive a similar fate, once he expires.'

Konrad could not help feeling a little chilled by Nanda's coldness. Matthias had committed monstrous crimes, but did not his obvious remorse, the sacrifice he had made in atonement, move her at all?

But that was a spark of fear in her eyes; her rigidity was borne of terror. What had Matthias done, but walk the same road Nanda herself travelled down — only further and farther, all the way into damnation? Did she picture herself in his shoes, on some dark, future day?

'It is not a mistake you could ever make, Nan,' he said quietly.

'You cannot know that. Did Matthias ever imagine himself coming to such an end?'

'You are not him.'

'I know.' She bowed her head, and turned away from the window. 'And I must take care that never changes.' She left the room as she spoke, quietly drawing Alexander away with her. Konrad read the gesture clearly enough. What was left of Matthias was his to finish, his and Tasha's.

Matthias watched his silent approach placidly, all the fear drained out of him. 'You're here to finish me?'

'Yes.'

Matthias nodded. 'I knew the Malykant would come. I've waited for you.'

Konrad looked at Tasha. He didn't need to say anything: she knew what he asked.

She hesitated.

And then, unexpectedly, she withdrew a bundle of cloth from her jacket and gave it into his hands. 'I'll be outside,' she said.

The cloth was plain cotton, unmarked. No blood. Tasha had cleaned the bones of Rodion Artemo and Timof Vak very carefully. She had made her selections sensibly, too, and removed the two stout bones cleanly. He must remember to commend her for it. Already she was making a fine apprentice.

He looked once more at Matthias Varis: a spent, prone husk of a man, reduced to nothing but awaiting his imminent end. Whatever of virtue, strength or worth he had once had was gone. All that remained was useless, sickening regret.

Too many people went to their graves that way, Konrad thought. Like Nanda, he must take care that he did not travel too far down that road.

'Have you anything else to say?' Konrad said. He did not usually give his victims a chance to utter their last words, but something about Varis was different. There was something of dignity about this scene: an acceptance of culpability, that very regret which, useless as it may be, was nonetheless superior to the frantic denials and self-justifications of most of those he'd killed. And the man had done what he could to mend his mistake. Only... too late. Far, far too late.

'Tell her I'm sorry,' said Matthias Varis.

'Who?'

'Miss Falenia. Madam Inshova. All of them.'

10

Bakar House came equipped with one turret, a narrow tower with a domed roof attached to the building's south-west corner. Konrad had always thought it a purposeless absurdity, situated as it was four storeys up, and it was too small to house most of the amenities one might prefer.

Tasha disagreed.

'It's perfect,' she insisted, holding open the turret's white-painted door as though she might, at any moment, slam it in Konrad's face.

'But it's far out of the way of the rest of the house,' Konrad pleaded, stalled on the threshold of said turret as he'd attempted to lure Tasha out of it. 'Even the servants aren't so isolated.'

'I like the height. I'm used to attics, and this is way better.'

'And there's no room for anything, you're lucky you even have a fire in here—'

Tasha laughed. '*I have a fire*. That's already a huge upgrade, even if it's a small one. I've also got a bed, and a closet. What more do I need?'

Konrad just looked at her helplessly. How could he explain? Once upon a time, he had felt as Tasha did. Even scant comforts seemed like princely luxuries to him. Over the years, he had gradually grown accustomed to the superior luxury of Bakar House; though there were still days when he craved the simplicity and isolation of his hut out in the Bones, for the most part he could not imagine living without his study and his big fireplaces, his deep, plush chairs, his cook and his handsome parlour.

In all probability, Tasha would eventually come down from the turret. But if it suited her for the time being, so be it. Konrad raised his hands in defeat, and backed away from the door. 'I'll have a bell fitted,' he said, 'so you can call for service.'

Tasha wrinkled her nose. 'Or I can exercise my own legs, and go down to the kitchen when I want something.'

He grinned, chastened but for some reason amused by it. 'Gorev's going to love having you around.'

'He'll be begging for mercy inside of a week.'

Konrad went slowly downstairs. He'd already given private instructions to his housekeeper — and Gorev — to do something with Tasha's wardrobe. If she was going to be Malykant-in-training, she'd need the right equipment, and he was damned if anyone living in *his* house was going to be left walking around in rags. Well, not rags. Alexander had had her in charge for a while, to some degree; he was no doubt responsible for the few respectable garments Tasha owned. Konrad had a feeling he'd have a battle on his hands about the clothes, though. For some reason, Tasha seemed to prefer her disreputable garb.

Speaking of the inspector. Konrad went down two floors, and peeped into the morning-room situated at the rear of the house. With its big windows, comfortable armchairs, bookcases and elegant dining-table, he hoped it would be acceptable for Alexander's use. He'd declined an invitation to follow Tasha's example, and make his abode at Bakar House; Konrad hadn't been surprised. But he had not objected to the prospect of a room set aside for his own particular use. Mrs. Orista had already done wondrous things with it: dust-free, it had new rugs and cushions, and looked inviting. He'd order the fire to be lit soon, to air and warm the room before the inspector arrived.

He hoped he'd often see Alexander there.

The front door's knocker sounded as he returned to the ground floor, and his heart leapt. This would be Nanda coming back. She hadn't quite agreed to move in entirely, either, but she had consented to spend more of her time there. Now she would be returning with some part of her personal possessions; Konrad had made room for them, ordered a bedchamber to be set aside for her regular use, though he hoped she would generally be sharing his—

He stopped at the foot of the stairs, for Gorev had opened the door upon Diana Valentina. She met Konrad's gaze as she walked in, and wordlessly handed her deep purple coat to his butler.

'Diana,' he said, coolly.

She returned this salutation with about as much warmth. 'I hope this is not an inconvenient time?'

His lips twitched. Where Diana was concerned, there was no such thing as come-back-tomorrow. 'I believe I can spare you a few minutes,' he said.

He didn't take her into the best parlour. That space was sacred, his and Nanda's. He took her instead into the drawing-room, a rather grand and formal chamber he rarely chose to use. It seemed fitting for the head of The Malykt's Order, herself wreathed in a stiff grandeur he found rather offensive. Hadn't they once been on decent terms?

'It's to be a formal visit, then?' he said, taking a seat on one of the uncomfortable hardwood chairs. It had a cushion, but more in theory than in practice. The thing was purely decorative.

Diana sat with no sign of discomfort. 'There were just one or two things we needed to discuss.'

Her tone was cool, even remote, but it occurred to Konrad that Diana had never condescended to wait upon him like this before. If she wanted to see him, typically she summoned him to *her* side. Did it signify a relenting? Konrad waited for her to speak.

She took her time in doing so. He had never seen her hesitant before, either. 'I have heard some part of your recent... experiences,' she said. 'I would be glad to hear about them from you.'

'You mean the malefic, my death, my brief replacement and my unexpected and unwelcome resurrection.'

Diana's mouth tightened at his last words. 'Something like that. Yes.'

So Konrad told her everything, as he saw it. If he lingered rather more upon Nanda's heroism than on his own exploits, well, that was fair. Let her understand how much Nanda had been obliged to pay for her decisions. Let her consider just how far one or two others disagreed with her conclusions.

When he had finished, Diana sat in silent thought for so long, he began to grow uneasy. Was she thinking, or was she... consulting with Someone? He did not sense his Master's presence, nor that of his new Mistress, either. But perhaps she had already had speech with at least one of the Great Spirits that now ruled him. Maybe that was why she was here.

'So you are Shandral, now,' she said at length. Konrad could not tell from her tone how she felt about the development.

'I suppose,' he said, 'I am both. Half one and half the other.'

She looked at him, expressionless. 'I hope you can understand that this leaves me in a difficult position. What am I now to do?'

'With me?' Konrad shrugged. 'Nothing. Forgive me, Diana, but those decisions have been made over your head. There is nothing for you to *do with me* at all.'

'You will continue in your role as the Malykant?'

'As long as the Master wishes for me to do so. When that ceases to be the case, Tasha will replace me for good. And for once, the Order will have a fresh, new Malykant who actually knows what she is doing.'

Diana nodded. 'I cannot disagree with the Master's judgement there.'

'Just the rest of it?'

It was Diana's turn to shrug. 'As I perceive it, your joint allegiance was not of His choosing. He had only to accept it or not, and if He has accepted it, then...' She shrugged again. 'It is not for me to question.'

'But it isn't what you like.'

'I hardly know.' The formality went out of her, all of a sudden. Her erect posture relaxed; her shoulders slumped; she let out a slow sigh, and directed at Konrad a strange, crooked smile. 'It had never occurred to me,' she said. 'I would never have imagined such a duality possible. But I wish I had.'

Konrad raised his brows. 'I do not think you have ever cared much for my well-being.'

'I have cared as much as I felt capable of.'

'You knew, I suppose, that you'd have to order my "retirement" eventually, and were incapable of being a friend to me before that day.' Konrad heard the harshness of his own words, felt the implacability of his expression, and thought better of it. 'I don't know that I would have done any better,' he said, more mildly. 'Probably a lot worse.'

Diana did not quite respond. She looked at him; and finally said, 'The previous Malykant was a... friend.'

Konrad had to think for a moment to recall who she spoke of.

He'd only seen his predecessor the once, and under the circumstances had not had leisure to inspect her closely. He remembered little of her, only her… extreme coldness. She'd been like winter itself, stalking the streets of his city like a freezing wind. 'You were close?' he said.

'For a time, very much so. I had to watch as she… changed.'

Konrad did not need to ask how she'd changed. Had The Malykt taken her warmer impulses, too? Stifled her capacity to feel, made of her a monster? Or had she not needed the same interference as Konrad? Perhaps she had been excellent at her job. Too excellent. It had broken her.

And Diana had been obliged to retire her.

He felt a surge of sympathy for the woman, despite his lingering resentment. What if he had to watch something like that happen to Nanda? How might it affect him? What would he do, afterwards, to ensure that no one had to suffer that way again?

'I think I understand,' he said, more gently. 'And I'm sorry.'

Diana nodded, and rose. 'I am more sorry than I can say, for so many things…' She trailed off, looking sightlessly into the fire. 'But maybe,' she said with a reviving smile, 'maybe, this time, it will be different.'

'Everything will be different, now,' he said. 'And I even think, maybe, everything will be all right.'

Her smile grew. 'Coming from you, that means… rather a lot.'

'Not given to fits of optimism, am I?' he said lightly. He got to his feet, too, and extended his hand. 'I don't ask you to be a friend,' he said. 'But shall we at least no longer be enemies?'

Diana took his hand in a firm grip, and shook it. 'Agreed,' she said. 'Though, Konrad, I was never your enemy.'

It was hours before Nanda returned. Konrad spent half of it lounging before the fire in his beloved study, thinking over everything Diana had said — and everything she had not said. In his urgency to deny the fate everyone had seemed eager to foresee for him — the gradual decline of everything that made him human, his inevitable transformation into an irredeemable monster — he had never allowed himself to think seriously about the prospect. Nor did he enjoy doing so now. He'd been close to becoming that person, he knew; especially while he laboured under The Malykt's stifling of his emotions. He had been better, more efficient at his job under it, but he had also become more and more remote. More ruthless. Less compassionate.

In his heart, he knew Diana had been right to be concerned. And were it not for The Shandrigal's interference, she might have been right to retire him, too.

He did not need any more reasons to bless the advent of Nanda in his life, but he added those to the list anyway.

By the time she finally arrived, he had fled from these dismal reflections — could he be certain such a fate did not still await him, somewhere on the far horizon? — and taken to prowling around the library, picking up books and setting them back on the shelves, hardly noticing what he held in his hands. Then he stalked about the hall, peered into the best parlour, wandered back up to Alexander's morning-room, toyed with and dismissed the idea of bothering Tasha again...

The knocker sounded.

He was out into the hall in a flash, forestalling Gorev's march for the door. He opened it himself, heart hammering with a mixture of anticipation and apprehension. What if it was Nanda?

What if it wasn't?

It was.

'Konrad,' she said, his name emerging slightly muffled. Having dropped some article from the stacks she held in her hands, she'd stooped down to collect it again.

A few more items slipped from her hands, and fell into the snow.

'Help?' she said.

Konrad leaped into action. 'Yes,' he gabbled. 'Sorry, I was just— I'm glad you're here.' He feverishly collected her lost bits and pieces — a memorandum book, a glove, a shoe — and tried, unsuccessfully, to stuff them back into the top of her overflowing case. The clasp was broken, and besides that the bag was far too full.

Konrad saw this as a good sign. The more things she brought to Bakar House with her, the longer she intended to stay...

He conducted her up to the bedchamber he had chosen for her, marvelling at the nervous energy that set his hands to shaking, and interfered with his ability to breathe properly. He thought he hid his agitation quite well, but once he had thrown open the door, shepherded Nanda inside, and retreated to stand meekly by the wall while she inspected the room, he found himself subject to her most amused smile; her dancing eyes gently mocked him. 'Now, when did I become such a gorgon as to have you shaking in your boots?' she said.

'Actually,' he said, with daring frankness, 'You've always terrified me.'

That delighted her. She laughed, and set her overstuffed case down atop the satin brocade bedspread Mrs. Orista had chosen for her. 'Good,' she said firmly. 'That is as it should be.'

Konrad drifted nearer.

Nanda watched his approach with raised brows, and made no move to meet him halfway, or anything else that might seem welcoming. He stopped about two feet away.

'You're wondering whether you're permitted to kiss me,' said Nanda.

Konrad coughed. 'I had been thinking about it, yes.'

Nanda amused herself at his expense a moment longer, with a show of thinking-it-over.

Then she was in his arms, and answering his question in the best way he could possibly wish for.

'Oho,' came Tasha's voice a minute or so later. 'Shenanigans.'

Konrad cursed silently as Nanda withdrew from his embrace. He turned, and subjected his interrupting apprentice to his most terrible stare.

She stood grinning, unabashed. 'Don't mind me.'

'We *do* mind, just a bit,' he said. 'Haven't you got something else to do?'

'Actually,' said Tasha, 'I don't.'

'Actually, you do,' said Nanda, breezing past Konrad. 'I've got an errand for you.'

'Is it daring, dashing and fraught with danger?'

'Yes.'

Tasha blinked. 'Really?'

Nanda nodded once. 'Somewhere up in the Deathlands, there's a lonesome Gatekeeper with a powerful need for distraction. I promised him a visit from the most colourful person I know.'

'And that's me?' Tasha seemed genuinely astonished — and, Konrad suspected, thrilled.

'Do you doubt it?'

Tasha pulled herself together. 'No, ma'am,' she said, with her customary impish grin and a mocking salute. 'When do I leave?'

Nanda cast a sideways glance at Konrad. 'Approximately now would be good.'

ALSO BY CHARLOTTE E. ENGLISH:

THE MALYKANT MYSTERIES:
Death's Detective (Volume 1)
Death's Avenger (Volume 2)
Death's Executioner (Volume 3)

THE DRAYKON SERIES:
Draykon
Lokant
Orlind
Llandry
Evastany

THE LOKANT LIBRARIES:
Seven Dreams

THE DRIFTING ISLE CHRONICLES:
Black Mercury

Printed in Great Britain
by Amazon